ARSTORY

BOOK ONE

THE BEGINNING

BLAZE SEVEN-TEN

You have read history. Now read arstory.

If you have ever wondered, read "Arstory". If you have ever hoped that your life could be better and that you could be happier, read "Arstory". If you have ever wanted more, read "Arstory".

Our story can be wonderful. Let's share a moment and then become unimaginably joyous.

ACKNOWLEDGMENTS

I thank the Great Mystery that is in everything, beyond everything, and surpasses understanding.
I thank the Great Spirits who guide, protect, and provide for me and for all of my loved ones and friends.
I honor Mother Earth for giving us a beautiful home full of love and abundance. I honor the mighty mountains and the hills and the ridges and the valleys, the great deserts and the fertile prairies.
I honor all of the sacred places.
I honor Father Sun for giving us power and energy.
I honor the Spirit of Water for giving us fertility and movement. I honor the great oceans and the lakes and the rivers and the creeks and the mighty underground reservoirs. I honor all of the holy waters.
I honor the Breath of Life, the mystery that is.
I thank all of my brothers and sisters among the plants and the animals, the Great Plant Spirits and the Great Animal Spirits.
I thank all of my ancestors who led me to this place and upon whose wisdom and love I have been protected and sustained.
I especially thank my mother and father.
I thank the mother of my children and my children and my grandchildren for making life precious and for giving me hope.
I thank all of my friends and my love because without you, it wouldn't be so enjoyable.
It is good, because all of you are good.
Thank you.

tenth edition

This is a work of fiction. All characters herein are solely the product of imagination. Any resemblance to persons living or dead or otherwise is purely proof of the Universe's humorous proclivity towards that synchronistic weirdness known as accident.

Thanks to William Douglas Horden for the emblematic cover design and the river to the sea.

ISBN: 0615504949
ISBN-13: 978-0615504940

DEDICATION

TO KIP WHOSE PASSING MADE THIS POSSIBLE

CONTENTS

The Beginning

PART ONE
α

"It is a far, far better thing that I do,

than I have ever done before."

Dickens

ALPHA

CHAPTER 1

THE ACCIDENT

To me in this moment, everything seems alright. In fact, everything seems better than it has been for a long, long time. Maybe even better than I can ever remember my life being before this moment. It seems to be a golden sunny day. I can't tell where the light is coming from though. I don't see the Sun. The pleasant light seems to be coming from everywhere. It is warm, a kind of warmth that I have never known before, a really comfortable warmth that seems to hug me, to comfort me, to cradle me like a mother cradles her new born baby. It is a friendly loving light. Nothing hurts or aches. No concerns or worries nag at me.

I look around and wonder, "What just happened?" Then I look down. My body, I am sure that that is my body, is lying there curled around a tree. Something is wrong with that body, my body, really wrong. Looking closely at my left side, my figure looks like a crumpled piece of cardboard. My left foot seems to be pointing the wrong way. In my confusion I think, "Oh, this is not good."

As I continue to gaze downward, at my body lying there, I slowly drift upwards, backwards away from it. There is a wispy silver cord that is playing out from the center of my abdomen. This rope lengthens as I drift backwards, thirty feet, forty feet, a hundred feet, two hundred feet and this life line is getting thinner as I float away.

Suddenly I realize with a frightened jolt that I am surrounded by darkness, a black as terrible as the deepest, darkest unending night, and this is a night that is full of hunting things. This is a squirming blackness. It isn't the lonely black of a starlit desert night. It is a black that is breathing. I start clawing at the thin silver rope desiring above all of the desires that I have ever known, above all reason to pull myself back down into my battered body which is lying down there by that friendly tree. But as I jerk and pull and strain clinging to this fragile cord with all of my might, I realize that I am caught, as a feather is caught in a current in the ocean and just as that feather is swept away, I am caught against any will of my own, caught against any hope that I can grasp, and I am being swept into infinite eternal darkness.

I peer nervously into the darkness that now surrounds me. Moving about in it are scary things, horrible things, frightening things. These are things that are loathsome. These are things that are slimy, filthy, misshapen, and ugly. These are things that are huge, alien, and lusting with cruelty. These are horrendous nightmarish creatures who without any doubt want to hurt me, use me and abuse me in unimaginably foul ways before horribly murdering and devouring me. One of them notices me and it turns towards me. It grins a grotesque grin. Its leering mouth is full of gleaming white razor sharp pointed teeth. It hungers for my soul. It wants to eat me. It wants to consume my very essence. I whip around to my left to flee from it and stare directly into the leering face of another monster, an even bigger and more terrible fiend. I cling to the silver life line and start jerking and pulling as hard as I can because the darkness is full of demons and they have noticed me and they are coming for me. I know terror. I don't mean that I am frightened. I don't mean that I am scared. I don't mean that I am as a man who has been standing on the edge of a great cliff at the top of the Grand Canyon and who has slipped and is falling over the edge grasping for friends' hands, for bushes, for a rock, for any hope at all. I am not grasping that rope as a man who is only afraid for his life grasps. No, I mean that I know absolute terror, a terror that leaves my mind numb and unthinking. A terror that makes me piss in my pants and scream madly and think of nothing but finding a rock to crawl under and to crawl to the very back underneath that rock and to cover my eyes and to madly scream and scream and to care for nobody and nothing except for myself, pure unthinking unknowing selfish terror.

I look down at my body lying there below me and I love that body more than I have ever loved anything in my life and I never ever want to let go of that body. I want to pull myself into it and out of this terrible darkness with every ounce of will that I can muster. I promise all of the tomorrows that I can or could ever have just for one more moment back down there in that precious body.

As I'm making this promise, I glance back over my shoulder to see if the demons are gaining on me and I look upwards. I look up into the light and I am saved. I see the light and I know anxiety and suffering and pain no more. I care for nothing except the beauty and the peace and the love and the joy and the happiness that streams towards me. As I gaze with adoration at the glowing brightness, I soar into the heavens, into the light.

It is a huge light. It is not at all like the puny little ball of light which we call the noonday Sun. This light fills the horizon, but it doesn't burn me. I love it. I don't know how I know that I love it. I just do. I don't just love it. I absolutely adore it. It is mother, father, children, lover, God, and home. It is security, trust, love, and eternal comfort. It is beauty, joy, wonder, and exciting amazement. It is never ending hope and it is knowing that everything is going to be wonderful beyond my wildest imagination forever and ever. It loves me and it is calling to me. We yearn for each other as lovers who have been separated by war, disease, and poverty for years and are finally being reunited in that promised land that we so desired and promised each other so long ago. As I gaze up at the light, I continue soaring heavenward. Looking down, I am crossing a vast lake of living light. The lake is made of billions of tiny specks of light, all sparkling and dancing and twisting and merging together. Some of them pop into the air, only to fall back into this glowing swirling vast pool. The source of the pool is the beautiful white light that I am gliding towards. The distance between me and the light is immense and is surrounded by the darkest night. As I soar towards the Source, homeward bound, all of my troubles are forgotten, irrelevant.

Suddenly from the great light in the distance, two dazzlingly radiant beings appear. To my human consciousness, they are joyously beautiful. They are of a formless form that includes all possible forms. They are all of the shapes which have ever been, or will ever be, and have never been, and yet are here and now. They are all of the love that I have ever known and they have come to greet me and to welcome me. Seeing them again, I am overwhelmed with happiness. I know them as one knows a lost love. We meet in mid air over the dark shore and dance like fireflies whirling around each other in a midsummer night sky. I begin to remember who I am and where I am and why I am. It is great to be and to know.

Then one of them says to me, "It is time for our decision."

I beg, "Oh please, please, I want to come home. I want to go to the light."

The other one says, "Being human is confusing. I could change everything, but that would change nothing. As long as you think in words as you are doing now, you are caught in time and space, and you and all of creation along with you will continue to go round and round. Truly we are one when we are none. Are you being the light of remembrance, or are we returning into blessed glory?"

"Do I have to succeed?"

"No. The dead only have to die."

They swirl around me, actually merging their light with my light, thrilling me with ecstatic joy. Then more firmly this time, the first one states, "Remember what is to be done," and lovingly asks, "Will you do it so that all of creation may sing in joy and wonder? Remember what it is to be and be, that in being, creation might know itself and vibrate in ecstatic bliss."

Softly I reply, "I am that."

They turn away from me and fly back towards the great light in the distance. I turn and drift back along the dark shore of the vast lake of gleefully dancing radiance and drift toward the inky blackness in the far distance.

The darkness swallows me.

What I remember is pain.

When I move just slightly, I remember a pain that makes me cold, a pain that makes me sweat, a pain that makes the lights

5

come and go, a pain that makes me think that I am going to throw up, a pain that makes me scream; sharp, jagged, real, and intense pain. Everything starts to move away, far away, and it starts to get dark and there's a roaring like water over a gargantuan towering waterfall with a roiling black hurricane rushing toward me. When I look in people's faces, it doesn't matter. Their lips move, but I hear no words. I only see the face of darkness and hear the roar.

Then I realize that I am looking into the face of a concerned young woman in a white dress. Her mouth is moving. She is saying something. What is it?

"Mor", more what? Oh! "Morphine!"

"You have a needle in your left arm, Mr. Parker, Shane, which is attached to that bag full of morphine," she is saying and pointing at the clear liquid in a plastic bag which is hanging above me on a hook at the top of a shiny chrome stand. "You can inject yourself with morphine when you can't take the pain anymore, but the system is rigged to only give you a shot every once in a while, so that you don't overdose and kill yourself. Do you understand? Can you hear me?" she asks. Then demands, "Mr. Parker, please, look at me. Pay attention!"

I am in a hospital. How long have I been here? What happened?

I grab the controls away from her and viciously jab the button. No relief. I desperately jab it again and again and again and again. Finally, life blurs around the edges and darkness returns.

I am in a hospital. I start to think, "Where am I? How did I get here? What is wrong with me?"

It is confusing as most things are in life, but it all starts to come back, to make sense, in the odd way that things always seem to when you think about them, really sit down, and think about them.

I am forty nine years old and divorced with three wonderful grown children. I have had some hard bounces in life, but who hasn't? I could have done some things better, but I didn't. I could have been more careful, but I wasn't. I could have shared more of my time and my love and been more considerate, but I was too busy. I am not complaining. Things are looking up for me. I have a nice house, some money in the bank, and best of all I am in love and marrying the lovely Anna in the spring.

The last thing that I remember is that I was working with my cousin Tyrone and with Mitch and Willy and Davey. We were putting in a new water main up on the top of the mountain overlooking Northwood, Oregon, my hometown. I must be in the only hospital in Northwood, Our Sisters of Mercy Medical Center on the Parkway.

"I can't believe that this is happening to me."

I remember now how this all started. I flash back to yesterday.

It is early in the afternoon and it is starting to rain, the first big rain of the year. It is a light warm rain, but we are working in black mud, the kind of heavy dark dirt that turns to grease and sticks to everything when it gets wet. The fresh new fall green grass is getting wet too and it is getting even slipperier than the mud.

I know and say to the guys, "There is absolutely no use trying to fight the weather and to work in these conditions. One of us is going to get killed. After a good hard night's rain, the slime will be washed away and it will be safer to come back in the morning and go back to work then. So Tyrone, Davey, you guys can go home. We'll start here again when it gets daylight tomorrow."

"Alright, Boss! They need me down at Coyote Jack's," Tyrone shouts with glee and slaps a muddy gloved hand on Davey's back. Davey just stands there grinning.

"Let's go guys," Willy says and they trudge off together through the mud toward the old dented dirty yellow company Chevy Suburban crew carrying truck which they will take down to the bars and to their families.

But I stay here in the rain, I think, "I'm going up onto the top of this ridge and figure out how to get this city water piped over to Mom and Dad's house."

As I drive my new, shiny, metallic blue 4X4 Chevy Avalanche pickup truck with flashy polished chrome mag wheels and big oversized tires up the gravel road I notice how the shoulder of the road drops straight away from the gravel into the canyon far below. It's a beautiful site with the mists swirling in the trees and around the rock bluffs, but it's a little scary too. I remember my sister's only son, Jerry, driving off the road here two years ago, hitting a tree and dying.

I start reflecting, "That was a heck of a sad day. He was so young. It doesn't seem fair that anyone that handsome and that full of life and promise, just home from the Army, and working at his first job, should just suddenly be dead. Oh well, what do I know? God's in charge not me. That's what the preacher says every Sunday. What do I know? I just build things. That's all I know, building things. I just build houses, if I'm lucky, and when I can find a job, and that's getting pretty tough with the banks refusing to give out loans, but I guess that I'll just keep building things till I die. I'll leave that figuring out the complicated matters to the smart guys. Doesn't make any difference to me anyway. I just have to pay the bills and keep Anna happy. I wonder what we're going to do tonight?"

I forgot to ask her this morning. Anna does all of the social planning for us. She knows how to make our lives fun, how to get a good laugh now and then. She adds color, excitement, and love to my hard working life and our community. She is beautiful and likes to be noticed, loved, and appreciated.

When I reach the top of the ridge, I park the pickup in the middle of the road and get out. Nobody ever drives along this road anyway.

"Who cares where I park?" I think, as I wander across the strip of slick green grass along the edge of the road and stand on the edge of the cliff gazing down into the valley far below.

Far away in the distance are the massive sand stone bluffs of Sleepy Ridge in the Coast Range and nearer to the foot of this ridge on which I am standing, the Wanustakila River snakes across Garden Valley. Gazing straight down below my feet I watch the fog snaking through the rocks and the ancient oak trees for awhile.

Then I start arguing with myself, "Oh well, no time for this kind of thing. Enough daydreaming. I want to go home. Anna is waiting for me. I don't want to upset her. Our wedding is only six months away and she is definitely the prettiest, sweetest freckled blond lady in Northwood, well actually in the Universe. Every time that I look into those big, beautiful, blue eyes, framed in that long curly soft blond hair, I just want to bury my head between her breasts and thank her for being so wonderful and for bringing such joy into my life. It is cold and lonely and wet up here. I want to go home."

I grab the GPS surveying gadget from behind the seat and punch in my location. Staring at the glowing green four inch digital screen, I tell myself, "These modern computer instruments are great. They somehow get a signal from satellites flying overhead and tell you just exactly where you are on the earth. They are accurate to within an area the size of a sugar cube. They can't make a mistake. How great is that?"

It is still raining, only a slight drizzle now, but I don't want to walk carrying this thing. Besides it must be at least two football fields from where the pipe line turns and goes south to the water tank and from there back down to the gate to Mom and Dad's house. I decide, "I'll just drive real slow along the road and watch the glowing phosphorescent screen. I'll be done in no time. Besides there's no one up here anyway except me."

I slowly drive along the ridge road, mostly just watching the road, not really thinking about much of anything. I am just doing my job. When I get to the gate, I look down at the screen and it says fifty feet.

"What? That can't be right! I've driven from way up there, down around that little corner past the big rock on the uphill side of the road, and down to here. That has to be at least five hundred feet. What the heck's wrong with this machine? That's not right! Oh well, machines can't make mistakes. I must have done something wrong."

I back, back up the road to where I started. I aggressively punch in my co-ordinates and I slowly start back down the slippery gravel road again. This time I'm watching the GPS more closely. The numbers flash across the screen: 100, 200, 300.

"Three hundred feet, that can't be right either. I'll take the reading backing back up the road from this end. Maybe those satellites can't read that point up by the water pipe line right."

I angrily punch in my position from this end of the road by the gate and I start backing back up the road. This time I am watching the road in my rear view mirror, dividing my attention between the road and the GPS. The numbers start flashing across the screen: 50, 100, 150.

"Something is wrong. I've gone farther than a hundred and fifty feet. Darn it! I want to go home. I don't want to spend all night out here alone and cold doing this. What is wrong with this darn machine? Look at those numbers. They aren't right."

I angrily consider this as I am slowly backing up the deserted gravel road. I slowly veer off the road onto the slick grass between the road and the cliff thinking, "Boy this makes me mad." I'm just staring at that glowing grey green phosphorescent screen when I feel my back driver side wheel drop into a hole. Pow!

"Darn! Now I'm in the ditch," I angrily decide. "No one knows where I am. No one is going to look for me until after dark. I'm stuck in the ditch, in the cold, in the rain. I'm going to have to walk for miles to get help. Darn it! Darn it! Darn it!"

Swoosh! Abruptly the front end of the pickup catapults skyward in a sickening roller coaster ride takeoff.

"My God! The sky," I shout.

I'm looking straight up into a grey sky. I'm lying flat on my back sitting in the seat looking straight up with that sick flying over a hump in the road feeling deep in the pit of my stomach.

"Oh no!" I cry.

Over backwards I go, hood straight over pickup bed. Forty feet down the cliff when the front end strikes the ground, I am slammed into profound darkness, not knocked silly, no stars, no dazed wonderment, no confusion. Bam!! Total, inky, black, infinite, empty void. The world is gone. Life as I have known it is gone, gone forever.

At the exact moment that my Avalanche leaps skyward, the sun pierces the clouds and a beam of light flashes on the front windshield of my soaring pickup truck and just at this moment my father, Travis, comes driving down the road. Travis is eighty years old and has lived a hard life of broken bones and broken hearts and broken dreams. He had been a hard drinking, party going man until Sheriff Robertson decided that he should take anibuse and stop his carousing. To get about now a days, he drinks coffee and rides a lawn mower or drives his pickup truck which is what he is doing right now. He has chosen this exact moment to drive down this lonely road to go out and visit his little great grandson, Eddy, and to talk to Eddy about the good old days, back when Eddy was only one, last year.

As he drives along the ridge road, he sees that flash of light and wonders, "What was that?"

Again the Avalanche leaps into the air knocking branches out of a tree twice as high as a big man can reach. When the back end of the pickup slams down again, I am launched through the back window like a javelin, so fast and hard that I leave the shoes on my feet, on the floor board of the pickup truck. The back window is only twelve inches high. As the Avalanche cart wheels, I shoot straight through that back window with so much velocity that miraculously I am not cut in half as the Avalanche twirls downward like an airplane propeller and I fly through the air for another fifty feet, where I strike a tree. There I lie broken, wrapped around a modest oak tree in the fog and the rain, unconscious and slowly bleeding to death a hundred feet down the cliff.

My left side is shattered. My upper left leg bone is so badly broken that the jagged broken ends are overlapping and spasms are jerking my powerful thigh muscles together. A main blood vessel has been severed by the razor sharp jerking broken bones. I have maybe thirty minutes to bleed out, to live. No one knows where I am. No one will even think to look for me until after dark, and then where will they look anyway? Nobody knows that I am up here.

Travis drives over to the side of the road where he has seen that peculiar beam of light. He stops, gets out, and hobbles over to the edge of the cliff to where he has seen the bright flash. Far below, down the cliff is a new blue pickup truck smashed against a tree, and half way down to the pickup is a body wrapped around the upper side of a tree. Travis is an old school kind of guy. He doesn't have a cell phone and he is alone, alone with his heart pace maker, broken body, wrecked lungs, and cancerous bladder. Over the side he plunges, down to the man by the tree. The man whom he is looking at is his only son, Shane, me. In an unconscious delirium, I beg him to unwrap me from the tree, but Travis can see that if he unwraps me, I will fall on down the cliff. Leaving me there, he climbs back up the hill, drives back to his house, calls 911, gets a blanket, and climbs back down to me

11

where I am singing, "Mary had a little egg, little egg, little egg whose fleece was white as geese, white as geese."

Dad sadly covers me up with the warm blanket from his home. There he sits waiting patiently by me, his dying son, for the emergency crew. Travis who normally finds it difficult to walk from his front door to his pickup has just climbed that horrible cliff twice and is still alive and quietly caring about life and suffering when the emergency crew arrives.

The emergency crew is here almost immediately, because they came up an ungated private access road that runs almost directly down to the hospital and because they are good at their jobs. They stabilize me. Then they strap me to a board and six strong men push and pull my body back up the cliff to the road to the waiting ambulance and rush me to the Our Sisters of Mercy Medical Center, to the hospital emergency room where Dr. Doug Martin is waiting, waiting in the sterile gleaming, cold, ceramic and chrome hospital. The building is new and very expensive. It is six stories high and covers twenty acres including parking lots, outpatient surgical centers, administrative and financial offices, and doctor offices and clinics and special care homes for the elderly. Our Sisters of Mercy is a tax exempt charitable organization owning over 200 hospitals in 13 states. Our Sisters make a lot of money, and they know how to spend it, and they know who to buy to get what they want.

I don't even consciously see the emergency room physician. I don't consciously know that Doctor Doug Martin is there. If I were conscious and could see Doctor Martin's malicious smirk and feel the pain when he grabs my shattered leg and jerks it straight, I would scream and scream and demand a different doctor, because I know Doug Martin, and I know that he hates me, and that he really wants to hurt me, hurt me bad, bad enough to kill me. But my unconscious mind protects me from the pain. I don't consciously know what Martin is doing or saying or writing.

Doctor Martin is a tall, lean, mean man. He rarely smiles. The intense glaring myopic stare is his natural pose whenever I have been around him, which is as little as possible, but he is smiling now. He is smiling like a cruel little boy who has caught a curious friendly little grey squirrel alive in a trap and who has nailed the squirrel to the top of a fence post in the scorching summer noon day sun and who is now enjoying himself as he sits back and watches to see what the suffering squirrel does as it dies. Doctor Doug Martin plans his revenge carefully, a revenge that needs to be crippling, even better, fatal after some long excruciating suffering.

Martin and I are neighbors. We know each other well, too well. I am a builder and I built the neighborhood where he lives and I own much of the land that surrounds this neighborhood.

I have built a lot of homes for doctors. My feeling about doctors is, "In general, they are a cold hearted suspicious bunch. They always think that everybody is trying to cheat them. They don't seem to have any empathy with the people around them and they especially have no sympathy for those of us who work for them. They are cruel and abusive."

The guys joke that doctors must have the hearts' of lizards, the way that they treat us, because they sure treat us like insects. But Dr. Martin stands head and shoulders above most other doctors in his ugly attitude. Martin is a king of the doctor game and he uses his doctor's license like a big sharp meat cleaver on his patients whom he knows are fools. After all, they are paying him and he knows what he is giving them in return for their money.

Doug's mother told him when he was a young man, "Son, when you grow up, you should be a doctor because then people will respect you and you will make a lot of money and you will be loved."

Doug became a doctor. He is the doctor in the emergency room at the local hospital on this afternoon, the only hospital in Northwood, Oregon where Doug and I live. But Doug is not loved. He is a hungry soul. No matter how much money he makes, he cannot stop this gnawing hunger. He is an unhappy man and he shares his unhappiness with everyone around him. He despises his patients, his neighbors, and just about everyone else. He even despises himself most of the time. He believes that everyone wants to take his precious, hard earned money, that everyone wants to use and abuse him and to ruin his life. To Doug, life is a miserable struggle.

"A man has to fight for what he gets and fight hard," he argues.

When people look at Martin, they feel like a chubby little field mouse being eyed by a hungry grey hawk. Martin especially has never liked me and now he positively hates me ever since that Jessica Way Homeowner's Association meeting at Danny Wheeler's house a few months ago.

When we built the community where we all live, we built three different neighborhoods. There was a place for the rich people on the top of the hill, a place for the middle class people on the middle of the hill, and a place for the poor people down at the bottom of the hill. Each neighborhood has a road that serves the group of people who live in these separate communities. According to the Cheyenne County Planning Department, I wasn't supposed to connect these roads together, but I did. I live at the top of the hill at the end of the road. It is three and a half miles from my house to town driving on the rich peoples' road. It is less than a mile if I hook all of the roads together. I like convenience and I like the idea that the police, ambulance, or fire trucks can get to me real quick if I need them. I connected the roads. That is the open sore between me and Dr. Martin. We would not have been friends anyway. At the base of our very being, we diverge on different paths, different points of view, different ways of thinking. The members of the Jessica Way Homeowner's Association are wealthy men and women and as wealthy men and women everywhere, they are not concerned with love and sharing, they are concerned with control and excluding.

Dr. Martin thinks, "What good does it do to live above the ordinary people and not to be able to exclude them from your life? I want them excluded, and I want them to know that they are being excluded, and in that excluding, they will know that I am better than they are. Goddamn it! This story is about me, not about them. I am important, not them."

Doug doesn't want the roads to flow. He wants to control who comes up and down the road which passes by his house. Flowing roads give access to the neighborhood by common people. These are common people who are not stopped from coming up and who are not stopped from becoming part of his community. These are common ordinary people who are not excluded from his important life. These are common people who do not respect Doug in the way that he, Dr. Martin, wants to be respected, in the way that Doug hungers to be respected. Dr. Martin constantly broods, "I have not suffered through years of medical school in poverty, studying cadavers, and memorizing poisonous pharmaceuticals to prescribe to foolish sick people, to relieve their symptoms, and to get all of their money, to end up being a common person. I am a doctor. Doctors should be respected. Doctors should be treated better than everyone else. I should be loved. I have money. I have a doctorate of medicine."

He is cruel and unhappy, and he wants to hurt people, and he especially wants to hurt me.

When I connected the roads, I built gates and placed cement barriers across the roads. I had keys made to open the gates and I gave keys to my friends and keys to some of my neighbors. I am not the only person on the hill who likes convenience and safety though. As fast as I put the gates up, they are torn down, anonymously. The last time I repaired one of the gates, I built a heavy steel gate and set the gate posts in cement. Someone rented a backhoe and tore that gate down within one dark night of its construction. I am done. I don't care anyway. I am in sympathy with the guy who tore the thing down and I am definitely done being the gate police. As far as I am concerned, "Let the people go where they want, when they want, and how they want. Let're flow. I am going dancing and drinking at Coyote Jack's with Tyrone and Anna." That is how I feel.

Every year the homeowners who live on the top of the hill get together and decide how much money we are going to spend on the rich peoples' road, and what kind of projects we would like to do. In the summer meeting this year, after Danny Wheeler stands up and asks, "Is there any new business?"

Dr. Martin stands up and stares belligerently at me across Wheeler's big front room which is full of well dressed, well fed, wealthy homeowners and angrily accuses me, "You have built two roads which connect to Jessica Way and common riff raff are driving up and down our road. The gates have not been repaired and kept closed. Are you going to put in bigger gates and keep them closed?"

I simply reply, "No." I can't see getting in a big discussion with a bully. I know his opinion. He has big shot, out of town lawyers suing me and everyone else he dislikes in Northwood all of the time. I know what he thinks. I just say, "No", and I mean, "No." I know that he not only sues people that he doesn't like, but he also attacks them in sneaky ways.

He is a thorn in my side and a thorn in the community's side. He has even snuck into the water department's yard and chain sawed down the wooden pole that holds up the water tank control device, because he claims that it ruins his view, although it is hardly even visible from his house. The water utility company sent him a letter notifying him that tampering with a community's water supply system is an act of terrorism since 9/11. So, he should knock it off, or else he is going to go to jail. That stopped the Doctor from attacking the water department.

In Doug's world "no" is just the starting point for getting another lawyer and making some more threats and then checking in to see if your opponent has weakened their position. So, what Doug hears me say is, "Maybe, I'll think about it."

Doug ignores my answer, and in a more aggressive tone demands again, "Are you going to put up a stronger gate and keep it locked?"

I calmly reply, "I said No. If you want to discuss this further, let's do it outside." My meaning is perfectly clear to everyone in the room. The room falls deathly silent. Time doesn't slow down. It stops. You can hear sharp gasps from women and men's heavy breathing. I am dead serious and everyone in this room knows it. I am not going to be bullied by Doctor Martin. If the Homeowners want to have a discussion and come up with a plan, then okay, I will go along with their decision, but I am not going to be pushed anywhere by the Doctor.

Doug sits down and shuts up, but he is seething inside. He is furious, but he isn't going outside.

Wheeler quickly says, "Okay, let's move on to the paving and road improvement issue."

Danny gets some complaints from Homeowners about his poor meeting leadership skills demanding that he send an apology letter to Dr. Martin. No one says anything to me.

As far as I was concerned, that is the end of the gate issue between me and Martin, but I am wrong. I will never treat another being other than with kindness and courtesy ever again, even if I am forced to beat them.

CHAPTER 2

THE HOSPITAL

When I come to again, a thin young man is shaking me. "It's time for you to get up", he is ordering.

"Get up? Why? How?" It hurts to breath. To move my lower body, even slightly, sends pain demons roaring into my fevered brain, phantoms so huge, so intense, so dark and mean and awful that all movement, all life has to stop immediately. No doubt. Just stop. Don't move now, now or ever. Any movement no matter how small causes unbearable excruciating sharp jagged pain like a hot knife being thrust deep and hard into my body. I want to scream. I want to cry. I want to beg. But there is no one there, just pain, pain and nothing more. Pain fills my every thought, my whole life. There is nothing but harsh, blinding, pitiless pain. Nothing else matters. Nothing else is real, nothing else except the demanding young man.

He is neither small nor large. He is pale with short sandy colored hair. He is wearing a white hospital uniform and is looking at me as if he is examining a slightly interesting blue green iridescent insect. He smirks, "Come on let's go. Get out of bed." He grabs my ankles and swings my legs out of bed. My feet fall toward the floor, stop, and hang there. I lie with my back tightly pressed against the sweat soaked sticky plastic bed with my legs hanging in the air. I am fighting to remain conscious.

18

"Sit up", the peeved physical therapist shouts. "Quit being such a sissy. You don't hurt. There's nothing wrong with you. Sit up. I can't waste my time on people like you. People who can't take a little pain make me sick. I've got a lot of patients to see before I can leave this hospital. You're just making this hard for both of us."

As he speaks, he whips a white cotton belt around my waist and jerks me up into a sitting position on the edge of the bed. The blood rushes from my face. Hot tears fill my eyes and slide down my cheeks. I turn a pasty yellow grey and like a warm wedge of Jell-O, I slide with my tears downward, down into blessed oblivion.

Another day passes in swampy darkness. No food. No bath. No movement. I just lie here being deathly still to avoid those sharp knife thrusts. Sweat pours from my body and soaks the bed sheets and fills the depression in the plastic hospital bed making a little pool in the depression where I'm lying   A rash and sores start to form on my back. Nobody cares. Nobody touches me. Nobody offers to help, and I am glad.

With morning another therapist, a woman, approaches my hospital room door, plucks my chart from its holder and quickly scans it. "Well Mr. Parker, time for you to get up and walk around," she comments gazing across the room at me. She is all business. There is no way that I am getting up and I am ready to argue, to fight. In desperation, my mind starts darting around like a bat trapped in a farmer's kitchen and being chased by the farmer's wife with a big yellow broom. Whish! Bam! Whish! Bam! Panic. Fear. Desperation.

Fortunately, at that very moment, my friend, Blaire, steps through the door and asks, "Hey dude, que paso?"

"Not too much and nothing good," I answer. "Say Doctor, this is my good friend, Blaire. Could we have a little visit and do this getting up thing later?'

"Oh, sure. I'll come back in a while," she replies.

"Thanks!" I say.

When the therapist has left the room, I ask Blaire, "Can you stay for awhile until that therapist leaves the hospital? She'll try to force me to move and I can't. There's something really busted up inside of me and I can't move. I've been telling everyone, doctors, nurses, friends, relatives, everyone ever since I came to, but no one listens. I've just got to trick her into leaving me alone."

"Sure. No problema, buddy."

Blaire is a tall, tanned, blue eyed outlaw who enters my room like a blaze of sweet springtime sunshine.

We pass the afternoon reminiscing about old adventures. The therapist periodically pokes her head into the room and then moves on up or down the hallway. Finally as the sun slants behind a wing of the hospital, a nurse comes in carrying a tray with mashed potatoes, brown gravy, grey roast beef, a little bowl of un-natural colored canned fruit, and a carton of plain pasteurized, homogenized milk.

Blaire begs off with an, "Alright, better let you eat in peace," and saunters out of the room.

During this peaceful afternoon, my mind has cleared enough to realize that there is something really wrong with my body from my belly down. I try again to explain this to the nurse on duty and to persuade her to help me.

She isn't going for it. She replies, "I'm just a nurse. It says on your chart that you have a broken leg. That's all. I can't help you. If that is what the doctor says, then that is what you have. I have to follow the rules, or else I'll get fired, and I need this job. They don't put up with any back talk, or messing around by nurses or hired help at this hospital. You have to do just what you're told or else. I'm not going to help you. I can't. My job depends on it and my family depends on me to keep this job. Tell a doctor your problems again. Maybe one of them will listen, but don't count on it. Patients and nurses don't know anything. That's what I've been told. If you or I knew anything, then we would be a doctor, right?"

"Yeah, I suppose so. Fair enough, thanks for the advise, but I really do hurt and need help."

Night passes and morning comes again. The prettiest, sweetest physical therapist ever to stroll down the Sisters of Mercy hallway glides into my room. "Good morning Shane! I understand that you've been having a little trouble getting moving. Well don't worry about it. We'll just do this very slowly and gently at your pace. If this takes all morning, then that's all right. That's just what we'll do," she coos sweetly. As she talks, she gently slides her hands under my legs and moves them over to the edge of the bed. Then moving cautiously, like a mother with a new born babe, she cradles and pushes my torso into position, so that she can nudge my legs over the edge of the bed while lifting me up into a sitting position. I gasp with pain, but she gently supports my weight.

She explains, "The object is to get you sitting up in a chair. So, you see that chair in front of us? We're going to stand up and then sit you down in that chair."

"I can't do that," I protest.

"It'll be easy. I'll support you," she assures me.

"Okay," I weakly agree. She is so sweet and persuasive. I really don't want to disappoint her.

She places herself directly in front of me. Puts a belt around my waist for leverage. Then in one swift, graceful, smooth move swings me from the bed to the floor, and into the chair. When my weight settles on my hips, a stabbing pain forces a gasp from me. The room wobbles. I instinctively push upward on the arms of the chair with my upper body strength and hold myself there. The room steadies and I look desperately through a fog at the pretty therapist.

"Good job, Mister Parker," she smiles. "Now, you just sit there for a while. I'm going to go down to the cafeteria and eat lunch. There aren't many of us on staff today. When I get back, we'll put you back in bed," saying this she leaves the room.

As my upper body tires, I settle down into the chair more and more. At first I feel very cold, then I start to sweat. Waves of nausea roll over my body. Patches of blackness start to surround me. Soon there are only patches of light in the darkness, but it doesn't really matter, because the nausea and the pain are the only things that concern me. Where should I throw up? I know that I am going to fall, and I don't want to fall in my own puke.

"Oh, my God!!" exclaims a nurse as she looks in.

Then I pass out. Nothing.

The day swims by in a dark haze of pain and morphine, morphine and pain, pain and morphine, and sticky, stinking sweat, and nausea.

With morning my attending surgeon, Doctor Paul B. Andersen, announces, "Shane, I don't understand. You should be getting well, but you aren't. I'm going to re-examine you."

It is a terrible experience being painfully slid on and off the rolling hospital gurney, off and on, on and off again and again, stripped naked, rolled around, poked and prodded and photographed, and stuck with this needle and then that one. Finally, it is over and I am lying back in the hospital bed in my hospital room.

Dr. Andersen strolls into the room, picks up my chart with the new information on it, looks at the x-rays, and exclaims, "Shit! Shit! Shit!"

These are not the words that I want to hear my doctor say when he looks at my chart.

Andersen announces, "Shane you have a shattered hip, internal organ injuries, and other broken bones. Your initial examination by Dr. Martin missed a lot. In your first surgery to repair the broken leg, I inserted an eighteen inch long half inch thick titanium rod up through the marrow in the center of your left thigh bone, and anchored the rod top and bottom with several three inch long wood type screws which are now embedded in your knee and hip. This apparatus is now in the way for me to repair your broken hip and other bones, and in the way for the procedures that are necessary to reduce the trauma to your organs and soft tissue. The situation is a mess and technically very difficult to fix. I am not sure that I can even do it. I want to consult with some experts at the University hospital in Portland about what to do."

What can I say? I can't even think. I barely know where I am. And when I do know, I give myself another shot of morphine, because it hurts like Hell. I answer, "Do what you gotta do Doc. Please, just stop the pain."

Dr. Andersen briskly leaves the room.

I lie in the hospital bed suffering, listening to the patient in the next bed dying. I lie there, continually running up a bigger and bigger bill to Our Sisters of Mercy, the charitable religious corporation.

The patient in the next bed is an old woman who keeps screaming about pain and mumbling about her dark fears and complaining about not being able to breathe. In the middle of the night she suddenly sits up and screams and screams. Then she starts to sob and begs for help. Everyone ignores her pleas.

The nurses and the woman's weeping red eyed relatives assure me that she is just dying. "That is all there is to it, it will be over in a couple of days," the nurses advise me. "She will die. You should just not let it bother you."

I try to not let it bother me, but I can't. She is the mother of a friend of mine. She is a sweet old lady with sweet little grand children who love her and who come to visit her each day. Even in my confused state, I can see the fear of death in her eyes and in their eyes.

In the afternoon, she makes some sounds like a frightened bird, chokes, gurgles, and dies, shaking and crying alone except for a barely conscious drugged up broken rotting fool, me. It is a pathetic, painful, humiliating awful way for a warm, wonderful grandmother to die.

Dr. Andersen returns to my room, smiles nervously, and begins, "Shane I talked to a lot of doctors whom I respect over the last couple of days and I've thought about your condition and I think that I can fix you. It's risky and I want you to know that. Do you want to go ahead with another surgery?"

"What are my choices?"

"Well, someone has to operate and operate soon or you could die. You might not. I could put you in a body cast and traction for a couple months and you might not end up a cripple."

"What is traction?"

"You'll lie here in this bed, in a cast completely immobilized, with weights on your left leg until the bones heal enough to support your weight."

"That doesn't sound good. What is another option, besides you operating?"

"We could ship you in an ambulance to the University hospital in Portland. The doctors there are more skilled than I am. It would be very expensive and the trip would be bad and I don't know when they could schedule you in. I could check."

"You think that you can do it? Right?"

"Yes."

"Alright. I'll go with you doing the second surgery too. I want to stop this pain. I want to stop it as soon as possible. I can't stand it anymore."

"I'll schedule you for surgery tomorrow morning."

Dr. Andersen hands me a big stack of papers with little tiny print. It is a big legal document absolving the hospital of any blame for anything ever, and if I sign it, I will have to pay whatever the hospital financial staff decides is what they want for my stay and for these operations. Anyway, that is what I think that, that big stack of papers says. I don't, can't, read it all, and I don't know what those words mean anyway. It's not like I can get up and walk down the street to the next hospital and check out surgery deals. I don't see what choice I have. I sign.

Dr. Andersen schedules the surgery and leaves the room again. He talks to the nurses standing by my door on his way out. They come in and stick more needles in my arms and more mysterious fluids start to drip into my body from the clear plastic bags hanging over my head.

Mid-morning on the following day, two nurses are standing by their station just outside my door. Dad is sitting in a chair by the window at the foot of my bed. He is across the room from the nurses. We are all waiting on the countdown to surgery. I start to fade in and out of consciousness. The feeling isn't unpleasant. It is just odd. I'm getting sleepy. I cannot stay awake, even when I try. I am feeling really weak, weaker than a sick cat. I can't seem to breath. Not breathing seems like an odd way to lose consciousness from a drug. I feel weaker and weaker. My body is like lead. Picking up a hand or a foot is becoming a giant effort.

At first I think, "They must have put the anesthetic in one of those bags hanging over me and be dripping a drug into my arm to put me to sleep. They must be putting me to sleep before my surgery. That must be what is happening."

Then something in me says, "No. No, this isn't right. Something is wrong."

But by this time I am too weak to reach up and push the nurse call button. I can't even move my fingers.

With my last gasp, I whisper to my father, "I can't breathe."

Travis who has been dozing, snaps his head up, looks sharply at his unconscious son, me, and shouts, "Nurse! Nurse!"

The nurses rush into my room and see my body slumped in the bed. They quickly grab me under my arms and jerk me into a sitting position. They begin to shake me and to gently slap me while they keep calling to me, "Mr. Parker. Mr. Parker. Can you hear me? Do you see my hand? Mr. Parker. Mr. Parker. Wake up! Wake up!" One nurse simultaneously calls for a doctor.

I feel like I'm drifting in the dark in a row boat with the waves rising and falling, but there must be a storm, because the waves are really starting to throw me around. Maybe I should wake up and check on the boat, or something, but I'm so sleepy and warm and comfortable. Yow! There is something in this boat with me. Something is slapping me. What is that? I wake up looking at two distressed middle aged women in white in a hospital. I just want to sleep. I really can't stay awake.

A small, calm, brown skinned man also in white passes in front of my eyes. It is Doctor Kirpal Singh who is a long ways from his home in Pakistan and making a lot of money being an American doctor. He looks at me and says, "Yes, it is congestive heart failure. Not a problem. Give him Lasix. Stop the IV irrigation. He will be good in two hours. You have just given another patient too much saline solution again." So saying, Dr. Singh leaves the room as casually and as quickly as he had entered.

And He is correct, I am as he says "good" in two hours. The water in my body drains steadily through the catheter stuck up my penis. The surgery is postponed to see if I will recover enough strength to survive an operation. Later, it is decided to go ahead with the operation. Everything has been prepared. The anesthesiologist has traveled over an hour from Oakley, a nearby city. It would be really inconvenient and costly to postpone the procedure. So, I am wheeled into the operating theater.

In the afternoon sunlight, I realize, "I'm alive, and here in the hospital again, or still. It is getting confusing."

The next day Dr. Andersen proudly walks into my room and announces to me, "You are a really lucky man, Shane. You're lucky to be alive. Now, you're also a bionic man. You are better than ever. Better than new. You have a complete set of steel bolts, rods, and screws holding you together, and giving your body extra support."

"Aren't you going to take them out of me some day?" I ask.

"No. Why? Your body doesn't even know that they are there. They improve your health. You are stronger now than before your accident," explains Dr. Andersen.

I do not feel better. And something about leaving those metal screws in me forever doesn't seem right. I don't even like leaving a sliver in my finger, much less leaving an eighteen inch iron rod in my bone marrow, but I can now move without the excruciating knife thrusts. I can sit up and swing my legs over the edge of the bed. I feel stronger too. I still really hurt, but I think, "I am going live. The doctor knows best. This isn't too bad."

Then, the Patient Advocate enters my room, my life. The Patient Advocate is a tall muscular woman of odd angles. She dresses in too warm of dark woolen clothes with a long black skirt and she is wearing shiny black leather shoes. She is accompanied by a very small Mexican woman who carries the PA's brief case. This little brown woman has an uncanny ability to always manage to stand in the bigger woman's shadow. They seem to move as one unit.

The Patient Advocate clears her throat with an annoying, "Harrumph", and says, "Mister Parker I regret to tell you this but your insurance has capped out. You must pay us $3,000 per day for each day that you continue to stay in the hospital plus you must pay in advance for any procedures which are performed on you. If you cannot pay then you must leave the hospital at once. We will accept credit card payment."

"I don't understand. I was injured on the job, in an automobile accident, on my father's property. I pay thousands of dollars each month for insurance. I have workers comp, automobile insurance, job liability insurance, and homeowner's property insurance. How can I not be covered?"

"I don't know. That isn't my business. We have just been informed by your insurance agent, Alice Johnson at FINI, First Insurance Network Incorporated, that there is no more money to care for you. You have to leave."

"Okay. I had credit cards when I was in the wreck. Get them and I'll sign over everything in them. That should give me some time to organize people to pick me up and take me home."

Soon, the Patient Advocate and her little brown assistant return to my room with some paperwork and my credit cards. I sign over to Our Sisters of Mercy all of the money on my credit cards. The Patient Advocate then informs me, "You may use the phone by your bed now to call someone to pick you up at the front door of the hospital. For a fee we will provide a wheel chair to get you from your bed here to the hospital front door in the main lobby."

CHAPTER 3

LOST HOME

I call Anna and ask her to come get me.

She comes immediately and brings Travis with her. They load me into the rented wheel chair and roll me down to the hospital front door to Anna's waiting car.

I am now a useless wooden stick of pain that does not bend very well in the middle or anywhere else really. I am in a cast from my belly to below my left knee. A car door only opens four or five feet. The entering person is supposed to bend over, slide in, and sit down. Neither bending, sliding, nor sitting is going to happen for me. Moving me into a car is not an option. Our learning this is occurring at the front door to the hospital with dozens of people milling around us and not helping. We are annoying drivers who are trying to pickup and drop off their friends and family members. My bloated, stiff, pain wracked body is in their way. They have important places to go and important things to do. My awkwardness and ugly suffering infuriates them. Why should they have to see this kind of thing and why should they have to go around us? Why should they have to be inconvenienced by my suffering?

Bored hospital guards and receptionists watch the scene passively from their stations. They sit and stand leaning against the walls, desks, and counters beneath a huge banner which

28

proclaims in bold letters, "OUR SISTERS OF MERCY HAVE BEEN CHOSEN #1 IN CUSTOMER SERVICE IN THE WEST FOR THE FOURTH YEAR STRAIGHT".

We finally give up. Anna takes the car back out to the parking lot and brings back Travis's full size Chevy Silverado pickup truck. There is room, but the pickup truck is two feet in the air and the seat is two feet still higher. Pretty petite Anna and weak frail octogenarian Travis tip the wheel chair over into the pickup so that I fall face first onto the seat. Then all together each pulling or pushing on a different part of my body, we roll me over and swing my legs up into the truck where I lie gasping like a beached whale.

When we get home, things only get worse. I am really weak and bloated from living on IV drips, pain killers, antibiotics, boxed mashed potatoes, bottled brown gravy, and tinned fruit. We struggle up the driveway and up one terrible step into the house. It isn't a steep driveway and it is only a short step into the house, so we know that we are not going to get me upstairs to a bedroom.

I say, "No problem. Just lay me on the couch in the front room. I'll be alright there." I am beginning to see the end of a lot of things in my life. The lesson that a lack of information and knowledge when combined with a macho will to "tough it out" does not lead to the best solution or even a good solution is forming in my mind.

When I fell off the cliff, I was in pretty good shape. I could sling big iron pipe daylight to dark with the best of men. I didn't climb down from the cab of a big construction tractor. I flung myself through the cab door into the air, using my powerful back and chest muscles, spun in the air, and hit the ground running. Now, lying here, I am weak. I hurt and I can't think very clearly, but I'm hoping that this will all clear up in a few days.

I'm thinking, "Anna can take care of things until then. I'm just going to lay here on the couch and rest and get well. Then I'll go back to work, and everything will be fine, just like it was. I'll just have to work a little harder to make up for the lost time and to pay these big hospital bills."

As soon as we get home, Anna goes in the kitchen and starts preparing a fabulous dinner. The house fills with the wonderful aromas of a fresh pumpkin pie with fresh homemade whipped cream, of chicken broiling in special spices and seasonings, of homemade salad dressing with chopped ginger, mashed garlic, balsamic vinegar, honey, and olive oil. The juicy smells pile one on top of another. While the dinner cooks, Anna showers and dresses and puts on fresh makeup. She prides herself on always looking attractive, but this evening she makes even more of an effort to look beautiful. She tells her daughter, Mattie, to shower and put on clean clothes too and then to come down to the kitchen and set the table. Anna goes into our greenhouse, cuts some pretty pink and yellow and purple flowers, brings them in, and arranges them in a vase on the kitchen table. She puts on some soft romantic country music. Anna wants my homecoming to be special, to be wonderful.

When everything is perfect, she calls, "Dinners ready Honey. Come on in." Mattie and Anna sit down and wait for me with happy proud hearts and expectant joy.

But I can't just jump up anymore. I don't even want to get up. I don't even know if I can get up. I haven't stood up since I fell from that brutal cliff two weeks ago. Nothing any longer works from my belly button down. And if I do feel, what I feel is enough pain to stop me from moving whatever I'm feeling. I can't use crutches because I can't swing my legs or even control my lower body. Dad has bought a stroller with wheels and left it by the couch, but how do I get it to me and then stand up on it? I can just barely reach it by pawing at it with a book which was left for me to read. I finally manage to get the stroller into position beside me, but there is no rope hanging from the ceiling to pull myself up by. I grab on to the low smooth couch arm and pull myself into a sitting position. Then with one hand on the couch arm and the other hand on the stroller arm, I do a kind of vertical chest high push up. This is exhausting. Now I'm standing basically on my arms on the stroller bars. I can't push myself ahead with my legs. They don't work anymore. So, I lean my weight forward and start to move forward, but my feet and legs stay behind. Now I'm in danger of falling forward on my face. I quickly lean back to regain my balance. Next I try throwing my right shoulder and right side forward. I move six inches. Then I throw my left side forward using my left shoulder strength and weight. My left side catches up with my right side. I inch myself across the front room toward the hallway that leads to the kitchen twenty feet away. Time passes very slowly. Nobody comes to check on me. When I reach the doorway between the front room and the hall, the wheels on the stroller jam. Looking down, I see that the wheels are hung up on a dog toy. I throw my weight back and forth, back and forth, lurching left and then right. After several tries, the stroller spins slightly clockwise and shoves past the damned thing. I am totally exhausted. I have been doing full body pushups for five or ten minutes, but I'm not going to give up. They expect me in the kitchen and I'm not going to let them down. If I have to die getting there, I'm still going to get there. I push on down the hall. Now not only am I exhausted, the pain in my lower body is getting massive. As my arms weaken, I'm putting more and more weight on the broken bones. Each lurch sends murderous pains shooting through my body and I shudder and shake. Sweat is starting to soak my already filthy cloths. Finally, after I don't know how long, I stagger to the kitchen doorway exhausted, ashen faced, filthy, and confused by pain and pain pills.

I realize, "I can't take care of myself and things aren't going to be good. I am not going to get better right away. I am not going to be able to feed myself, much less anyone else. I am not going to make it. I am broken and in terrible shape. We are in trouble and I know it."

As I stand at the door looking in, Anna and Mattie are looking at me, and I can see that they know it too. The bread winner, the source of their hope, their future is gone. Their life is gone. I'm ruined. We're ruined. It's all gone.

None of us want to admit this. Neither of them moves. I push forward to the table and throw myself into a chair. I try to eat, but I can't sit up. Even with all of the metal holding me, the bionic man, together, with all of that metal holding me up, the bones are still broken. The internal organs are still smashed. Nothing works anymore. The stomach no longer produces stomach acid. The antibiotics have killed the probiotics in my intestines. My guts are clogged with fecal matter which is festering and rotting, poisoning my blood and poisoning my mind. Hospital food, pain pills, antibiotics, pain, stress, and physical exhaustion have shut my body's vital organs down. Emotionally I'm not there either. I am withdrawn. I am a wreck.

Anna is frightened. This is not good. She depends on me and she is watching me fail. Anna sees herself as cute, someone precious, someone to be enjoyed, someone to be taken care of, but there is no spark left in me. There is nothing there that values her. Nothing that values what she has done. And if she is not valued, then she isn't. At this moment she becomes a hungry soul. She is afraid. She has bet everything that she has or ever had on me. She held nothing back. She has put everything, her whole life into relying on me, and the broken man sitting at the table isn't healing, isn't getting better. He is dying. He is not going to support her and her daughter, but this is all that she has, so she has to hold on.

I see none of this. My world has shrunk. My vision is very narrow. I see that I can't eat this food. I see that I can't sit up. I see that the twenty feet from this kitchen table back to the couch might as well be from the East end of the Sahara Desert to the West end. Crossing that vast expanse is nearly impossible. It is going to take everything that I can imagine and every bit of physical strength that I can throw into the struggle to get from here to there. I lurch up and begin that journey.

I don't say, "Thank you honey, what a wonderful meal."

I don't say, "You really look pretty tonight dear."

I don't ask, "How was your day?"

I don't assure her, "I'm getting better. Things are going to get better."

I am just an unsteadily rising, filthy, wrecked hulk that lurches upright and propels itself smack into the wooden kitchen door frame. Mattie gets up, pushes past me, and goes to her bedroom.

Anna has a very sick feeling in her stomach. She doesn't move to help me. She sits there in her chair at the table unloved, unwanted, unappreciated, alone, and without hope. She wants to cry. The future looks bleak. She wants to escape. How can she escape? She smokes a Lucky cigarette. She drinks a Henrys Light beer. She comes in and turns on the TV. She watches another episode of "Suffering Scene Investigators" and then she watches

"Hopeless Housewives". She drinks another beer and she tries to forget the misery of her life.

The television shows are like jagged sand paper on my nerves. I can't stand the noise, the unhappiness, the violence. There is no peace. I need peace. I need quiet. I can't stand to see another miserable life playing out on the big screen before my eyes, another life full of misery and anxiety and hate and anger and violence. I can't stand another commercial. Commercials, commercials, commercials. Buy this! Do this! Be that! Go here! Go there! I want to scream, "Stop it! Turn that damn thing off!" But I say nothing, this is what we have always done in the evening. I wonder what is wrong with me, but I can't think. I can't reason. After three hours, Anna goes upstairs to her lonely bed where she is unloved, unwanted, and afraid.

I lie downstairs angry, anxious, sweating, unable to stretch out, unable to lie flat, unable to turn over, and then the dog starts barking. The barking goes on and on and on for hour after hour. I want to kill that dog.

Upstairs the future is gone. Anna lies up there in the dark, unhappy, scared. She wants to be loved. She wants to be touched. She wants to be reassured.

She considers, "I was worried about losing him to a floozy, not this."

She starts to dream and the dreams are all nightmares. Horrible, horrible monsters want to hurt her and her children.

In the morning, she can no longer stand to look at me at the wreck lying in the front room on the couch, but she doesn't have time to think about it, because she has to get Mattie ready for school. She has to get the dogs fed. She has to get herself pretty and ready to go to work, to a lousy job that she hates, to a job that doesn't even pay enough to pay for her own small needs, much less to support a family. That job is all that she has now though. She needs that job. She doesn't have time to feed herself, or me, or to see what I need. She just has to get up and get going. So, she does.

I am left in my own filth, alone, only twenty feet from the kitchen. That food might as well be on the top of Mount Kilimanjaro. There is no way for me to get from here to there. I seethe in frustration and anger and pain. The only thing that I can think of to do is to take more pills, more pain pills. I just want to drift away. The oxy-cotton bottle says, "Take one pill every four hours." I take one. Nothing happens. I wait awhile. Still nothing. I take two more. I still hurt. This medicine doesn't seem to do anything. I take another pill. I have to get to the bathroom. The stroller seems to be a really long ways away, but I reach it, and pull and push myself up. I fling myself toward the hallway. Bam!! Smack into a wall.

"A wall", I wonder, "Where did that come from?" I completely missed the doorway. "What was I thinking? Where did that wall come from? How could I miss the door? How has a wall moved? Oh well, who cares where the wall, or the door is anyway? What does it matter? What does anything matter?" So thinking, I fall back onto the couch and go to sleep.

When I come to, I feel worse than ever. This time I take four oxy cottons immediately, and feel better, or really I don't feel anything at all. By afternoon, rather than taking one pill every four hours, I am taking four pills every hour. When Anna comes home, she sees her beautiful lover reduced to a grey, ashen, drooling, unmoving fool. She imagines, "He'll get well. We'll patch things up. It will all be okay."

She makes a light dinner for her and her daughter. She makes a tray with crackers and wedges of apples and cheese with a glass of orange juice and brings it into me. She tries to help me eat something. I nibble on some of it. I am not interested. I don't thank her. I don't even recognize her efforts. I just take it for granted that she should do this for me. I am lost in my own suffering, in my own misery. I don't even see her anymore, except when she turns on the TV and makes me angry, or when I have nothing to eat, or when I push the stroller into some dog's mess while I'm trying to get to the bathroom, or when I wonder why she doesn't stop that damned dog from barking. She is more of a source of annoyance than pleasure to me.

Anna smokes and drinks and watches TV. She goes to bed to more nightmares and loneliness, anxiety, and self-loathing. She is unloved, unwanted, alone, afraid. She drifts into sleep and again the monsters come.

The days pass uncounted, un-noticed, all terrible like the last one.

Then one day, Mattie comes home from school. I yell at her, "You've got to clean up that dog poop! I can't take it anymore."

She angrily yells back, "I'm not cleaning up anymore dog poop. I've already cleaned up a bunch."

"Well there is still a bunch left. I can smell it. It is right here somewhere."

"I don't know where it is. You find it and clean it up."

"I can't. If you won't clean it up, then throw the damn dogs out."

"Okay. Fine."

She grabs Fifi, the Chihuahua, and Fluffy, the poodle, storms through the house and flings them out on to the back porch into the cold winter afternoon. Fifi stands shaking in the cold, nose against the sliding glass door, eyes wide, begging to be let back in. Fifi has never been outside before. She has never been spanked, or told no before. She is not even potty trained.

Mattie storms upstairs to her room with her friend Lucy where they stay watching TV and talking to friends on their cell phones.

When I was in the hospital, one of the doctors who visited me suggested to me that during my recovery I might start feeling a little down and blue. He gave me a prescription for an anti-depressant to help me through those depressed periods. Dad had filled the prescription and set the bottle on the coffee table beside me. This must be the kind of situation that the doctor was talking to me about. I take a handful of the anti-depressants. I am not going to waste my time just taking one like I did with the pain pills. An hour later I am no longer sad about what has happened to me and about the way that I am being treated. I am enraged. People are jerks and I am not going to be treated like this anymore. They are taking advantage of my good nature. Well that is over. I'm fed up. I'm not taking it anymore. I'm just going to tell them. I have never felt the kind of rage in my heart that I feel now.

When Anna comes home from work exhausted and miserable after a terrible day at work where she has been threatened with being fired for being a useless, incompetent, fool, and for being ugly too by her boss, who is actually an ugly, incompetent, useless fool; her daughter storms down the stairs and launches into a tirade about me being a mean awful person.

"He made me throw the dogs out in the rain. They are going to die from pneumonia. Look at poor Fifi," she accuses, pointing at the back door.

The miserable dog can be seen shaking through the back door window.

"What is wrong with you?" Anna cries, confronting me. "You don't have any right to treat my daughter and my animals like that."

"I hate that dog." I yell back. "Can't you potty train it? Can't you make it quit shitting all over the house? And if you're going to let it shit all over the house, then at least clean the shit up. And that barking all night. Why don't you shut it up?" All of this anger about being useless and miserable and not being taken care of in a better way, bubbles up and bursts out.

"I've tried to house break it. I'm trying." Anna explains meekly. "It's hard to train Chihuahuas to go potty outside in the north. They don't like the wet and the cold. And their high strung. Their sensitive. This big old house with all of its noises at night frightens her. They frighten me. I'm trying. I'm doing my best. I can't do everything. "

I explode, "Just get the Hell out! Just leave me alone! Get out of this house and get out of my life!"

Anna sits on the couch opposite me and starts to cry. She doesn't want to go. She has no place to go. She has no support. I am it. But I am disgusting, a wretched, hopeless, futureless mean man. Where can she go? What can she do? No one loves her. No one wants her. She is alone. She is afraid. She cries. She gets up to go, hopeless.

"Get out and stay out," I scream. It's a good thing that I can't get my hands on a gun. If I could I would start shooting.

She puts on her coat, crying and sniffling. She grabs a dog under each arm and with her daughter trailing with arms loaded with clothes they sweep out of my life.

I rage for a few more hours, then as quickly as the anger came, it goes.

I sit there broken hearted and sad wondering, what has just happened? Why did I yell at Anna? I love her. I have always loved her. She is the most precious thing in my life. She is the only thing that makes me happy. We have fun together. We used to have fun together. What is wrong with me? Then I realize, it was the anti-depressants, but it is too late, the damage is done.

I feel terrible and I hurt, hurt really bad, everywhere, even down in my soul. I hurt. I am a miserable mean man. I want to die. And I am hungry and thirsty and dirty and I need to go to the bathroom. But I am alone, completely alone, and I am physically unable to move. But I don't take anymore anti-depressants even though now I am even more depressed.

CHAPTER 4

EVERYTHING FAILS

The next day Travis slowly hobbles into my front room to see how I am doing. I am lying there semi-conscious in my own filth. It is obviously not going to be okay. I am not getting better. I am dying. Travis goes to the local medical supply store and rents a patient's bed, buys a bed pan and returns to me lying on that torturous couch. He then puts a black plastic tarp on the front porch posts to screen the view of the house from the street. Then only through the greatest effort on both of our parts, he gets me on to the front porch, naked, sitting in a plastic chair. There he hoses me off and washes me. He dries me and coaxes me back into the front room and into the new bed. Travis then goes to the local CQ fast food burger joint and buys burgers, fries, cokes, and milkshakes. I learn to use a bed pan and Travis comes and empties it for me. I go to sleep lying flat on my back, stomach full, and sleep in peace.

Every day for two months, we repeat this ritual and Travis also brings chips and candy bars from the local 24 hour convenience store for me to eat when he isn't visiting. Travis doesn't cook. Travis has no idea how to prepare food.

Slowly I get better. Then one day I can move my legs. I start walking on crutches. A while later I only need a cane to get around. But now I weigh nearly three hundred pounds. If my broken body didn't keep me from going upstairs to my bedroom, I couldn't make it anyway. It exhausts me to cross the Shop-mart parking lot, and that is important, because I have to urinate all of the time, sometimes right away. I know that I am going to have to go and see a doctor to find out what is wrong down there from my belly button down sooner or later, but I need money. So, I decide to go see Alice, my friendly insurance agent, to ask about my insurance policies.

On the morning that I decide to visit my insurance company of twenty years and my father's before that for another ten years, First Insurance Network, Inc., I dress and call a taxi which takes me downtown to the FINI office.

I am amazed. The FINI offices have been completely remodeled, actually rebuilt, while I have been recovering. The big metal and glass building is much bigger and shines like a new Ferrari on the show room floor after a really expensive detailing job. The lobby has been completely rebuilt. I am looking into an atrium with beautiful new marble floors and sunlight streaming down from a huge domed skylight overhead. Everything is trimmed in beautiful dark exotic rain forest woods. Brass catches the light and sparkles like gold off the gold on those old buildings in Mexico City when the Conquistadors arrived all of those centuries ago. I ask a smiling, pretty, young receptionist where to find Alice.

"She's on the second floor. Right up those stairs over there, Sir", she answers.

Gazing across the room, I can't believe my eyes. A twenty foot wide gleaming white marble staircase winds gracefully towards the sky.

"Uh, where is the elevator?" I ask.

"Oh, we don't have an elevator, Sir," the receptionist replies.

"You mean that anyone who comes in here and wants to see an agent has to go up those stairs and there is no elevator? Is that right?"

"Well yes, Sir. It's only a little ways."

I thought that there were some kind of handicapped access laws, but I guess that I am wrong, or at least those handicapped laws don't apply to big, powerful corporations.

Shuffling my bulk forward, carefully with my cane, I reach the first step and grab the gleaming brass rail. Going up steps is very tricky for me because nothing in my left side below my belt works anymore. So to move I have to lean on my cane and throw my right leg forward. This works alright on flat ground, but not on stairs. Stairs require me to lean on my cane on my left side and make a precarious hop with my right leg. If I make a mistake, I collapse in a heap on the stairs. I climb the first fifteen steps to where a stair climber who is climbing these stairs, starts around the staircase curve to the right. There I fall too exhausted to get back up. I know that there is no way that I can make it any further up these stairs hopping on my right leg. My only hope is to drag myself around the corner and up to the second floor using my arms, not really crawling, because I can't bend my legs. I pull myself forward shuffle scooting. By this method I reach the second floor, hoist myself out onto the floor and pull myself upright using the wall. A woman sitting behind a desk at the top of the stairs watches me with a shocked look on her face, but says nothing, and doesn't move. I hobble away up the hallway to Alice's office and knock.

"Come in," comes the answer.

I enter.

"Oh, hello Shane. It's so wonderful to see you. You look really good. It's great to see you out and about so soon. You must be really proud of yourself. I know I'm proud of you, to see how well you're doing, and what a great recovery you're making. That was just terrible, that accident. We were all so sorry to hear about it. Terrible. Terrible. My husband, Jim, and I were just discussing how well you're doing at breakfast this morning. You remember my husband, Jim, don't you? Our grandson, Jim the third, just won the state championship in wrestling in the 148 pound class. It was so exciting. I'm really proud of that boy. He's such a good kid, a real success. Get's good grades too, and he's also his class vice-president. Wants to join the Marines like his grandpa did. Keep America free. Oh well, what about you? Bad accident, eh? Time to move on. What can I do for you today?"

"Well, I know, Alice, that I didn't have any health insurance when the accident occurred, because when my wife divorced me and I applied for a new policy I had to take that physical, and I got that higher than normal PSA test result so the health insurance company wouldn't insure me. Then I know that we tried to get health insurance a couple years later from a different company and that company turned us down because they said that if you've been turned down by any insurance company for any reason in the last four and a half years then you are not insurable. I know that you tried to explain to them that being turned down by the first company was a mistake caused by a mistake by a lab technician who reported the PSA reading as 4.5 when it was actually .045, but I know that all of the explaining didn't us do any good. Then I know that you offered to sell me a policy from the state health insurance pool for $1,200 per month about triple the normal rate. Oh, and the $1,200 wasn't tax deductible. So, it would actually cost a couple thousand dollars a month because I would have to pay the state and federal income taxes before I paid you for the insurance premium. There was no way that I could afford that policy. So, we gave up on health insurance. I can't get it. I am un-insurable for health insurance. I know all of that. But at the time of the automobile accident which was on the job site which is on my father's property, I was paying your company thousands of dollars every month for automobile insurance, workers compensation insurance, job site liability insurance, and a homeowner's policy that covered not only my father's house, but his entire ranch. Don't any of those policies cover my injuries?"

"Gee Shane, I'm sorry but they don't. Automobile insurance is meant to cover the vehicle and the costs of anyone that you might hurt or that might be hurt in your vehicle. It covers some of your medical costs but only up to $15,000. Any cost above that you must pay. Of course Workers Compensation insurance only covers employees of the company. You are an owner. Also a company liability policy does not cover the owner of a company. It covers everyone else. The homeowner's policy does cover accidents anywhere on the property, but as the owner's son, you are excluded from coverage under the policy. So, none of your insurance policies cover your accident except for the $15,000 which we have already paid to the Our Sisters of Mercy Medical Foundation. What about new policies? Now that you're up and about you are going to need to get those policies up to date."

"I know, but I'm tired, Alice. I'm going home. I'll work on it later."

Stating this, I drag myself back down those terrible stairs, and out to the parking lot. I need to piss. I feel sick. I am really sick. I feel sick somewhere down deep in my guts, a sickness of the heart, of the soul. I don't know of any medicine for this type of sickness. My brain is locked like a computer with the hoodoo virus. I am alone and I am scared. I am scared and I am sick and I am desperate. Desperate like a tiny, weak, little baby bunny rabbit who is in the bottom of his family's hole, all alone, listening to a big, hungry fox who is digging, digging ever closer. I can almost see all of those sharp glistening white teeth in a deep gruesome red smiling jaw in a face with cold unfeeling eyes, eyes in a beast that only wants to drink my warm blood, a beast that sees me as nothing more than a quick meal on the way to a bigger kill.

I am nothing but an expendable commodity to the FINI corporation. I am an object to be used and abused however it pleasures their management. The goal of the corporate officers of FINI are to make a profit. It doesn't say anything in their minds or in their corporate charter that they should consider the consequences of their behavior on their customers, their employees, the communities in which they operate, or the planet that we share. If it doesn't affect the corporation's profits and it isn't a cost that they have to pay, then it doesn't matter. They don't have to pay for ruined lives or peoples ruined health or ruined planets. That has to be paid for by someone else, by the government. So those things don't matter. FINI doesn't pay taxes. They have good accountants and attorneys. Human and environmental damages aren't a cost in their equation, in their thinking. In fact, paying some of my medical costs would cost the company money. That is a bad thing to FINI's corporate management. That might cost the President of the company his bonus and he expects a big one this year, in the millions.

The CEO thinks, "Gotta keep those costs down and profits up. I really want that new house in Hawaii. My lover just loves Hawaii and Hawaii is a long ways from my wife in New York."

Defeated, I crawl in the cab, and go home to a cold empty house. I worry. I fret. I stew in pain killers and French fries and hamburgers, tacos and pizzas. I can't sleep anymore. All night I am constantly having to get up and go to the bathroom. I am getting more and more exhausted.

In desperation I go to my family doctor, and ask him what I should do. My doctor, Doctor Smith, Elmer Roland Smith III, tells me, "I really can't help you. That is a urinary tract problem. For urinary problems, you need to see a urologist. Go see my friend, Dr. Edward Allen across town in the Professional Building. He will be able to help you. The receptionist out front will give you a referral so that you can get in to see him."

The receptionist hands me a referral slip and a bill and says, "Mr. Parker, you don't have insurance, so we'll need cash right now."

I pay and leave. I call Dr. Allen's office. The woman answering the telephone says that they have an appointment available in three months and asks me if I want it. I say, "Yes." I know why doctors call their customers, patients. You have to be real patient to see a doctor in America.

By the time my appointment with Dr. Allen rolls around, I cannot leave the house without being a few minutes from a public restroom. To get from the suburbs where I live to Dr. Allen's office, first I stop at the rest area on the way downtown. Next, I stop at McQuickie's Restaurant and use their rest room. Then a few minutes later, I rush into the library bathroom and barely make it. Finally I make it to the Professional Building and use the men's bathroom. Why is it called a bathroom? Does anyone ever bathe in there? Then I climb up the stairs to the second floor where Dr. Allen has his offices.

After enduring a painful rectal exam and peeing into a cup, I sit alone on a gleaming stainless steel examining table, studying posters of naked, sliced open men and women showing their bowels to the public. After thirty or forty minutes, Dr. Allen comes back in and says, "You have prostatitis. It's a simple problem. I'm going to put you on an antibiotic. The problem should clear up easily in a couple of weeks. See the receptionist on the way out and she'll give you a prescription."

The receptionist says, "Here's your prescription, Mr. Parker, and here is your bill. Will that be cash or a credit card?"

I pay and leave, but I am happy. I think, "That urologist is a pretty sharp fellow. He didn't spend all of those years in medical school for nothing. He really knows his medicine. I'm going to be better in no time. Things are looking up. Yes siree, up. I'm going to get better and go back to work and everything is going to be alright."

I am wrong. I don't get better. I get worse. Plus, now, I am getting what Dr. Smith calls acid reflux. When I eat, there is this horrible burning pain in my chest that feels like an ape with long fingernails is squeezing on my lungs, while another vicious bastard thumps me just below my throat with a sledge hammer. When it happens I panic. I always think that I am having a heart attack, like it says on TV. Dr. Smith assures me that I'm not going to die. It is just acid reflux and I need to take some more pills for GERD'S disease. I just have GERD's disease? What is that? What kind of disease is GERD's disease? I am getting scared again.

While I am at Dr. Smith's office, Dr. Smith and some technicians do some tests on me and Dr. Smith also informs me that I have high blood pressure, high cholesterol, and that I'm pre-diabetic. Dr. Smith gives me prescriptions to lower my cholesterol and to thin my blood and tells me to buy a machine that I can use to test my fasting blood sugar level every morning. Then he sends me to his receptionist again.

I go to Dr. Smith's receptionist and she hands me a hand full of prescriptions and a bill and asks, "Will that be cash, check, or credit card Mr. Parker?" Again I pay with a credit card. Now, I always pay with a credit card and I leave.

I go back to Dr. Allen and complain that I am not getting any better. Dr. Allen says, "You just need a higher dose of anti-biotics. That will do it." And he sends me out to his receptionist to pay and pick up my new prescription.

But the new drug doesn't do me any more good than the old one did. My health doesn't improve. It is getting worse.

I go back again to Dr. Allen and tell him that the medicine still isn't doing any good. Dr. Allen says, "Well we'll have to use a stronger, better antibiotic." I wonder why he didn't give me the best antibiotic at the beginning of our relationship, I say nothing.

He is the doctor. Dr. Allen sends me out to his receptionist to pay and pick up my new prescription.

The new prescription doesn't work any better than the old prescription. But now I am constipated all of the time. This makes my bathroom stops even more complicated and difficult.

My life is unbearable. I am bloated, sick, depressed, and going broke buying pharmaceutical drugs and going to doctors. I decide to make an appointment with another urologist, one that comes down to Northwood from Portland once a week.

I pick the new doctor out of the yellow pages. I don't know anything about him. I just hope that maybe a big city doctor might know more than Dr. Allen and Dr. Smith, who don't seem to know anything about curing diseases or helping patients. They are just good at selling drugs for the big drug companies at the local big box drug store and collecting their pay. I am right about Doctors Smith and Allen, but I have a lot to learn about big city doctors.

Dr. Jens Jensen is a dapper middle aged gentleman with a firm handshake and a friendly smile, except his eyes don't smile when his mouth curves up. He asks me to urinate into a funnel with a tube running into a machine while a pretty young nurse stands by with a clip board watching. Humiliated, I obediently do as I am told. He is the doctor. The nurse and the doctor passively watch a dial on the side of the pastel yellow machine. It doesn't move much. When I finish, Dr. Jensen declares, "You have a swollen prostrate. Nothing can be done about it except cutting it out."

"Cut it out," I protest. "Isn't there any other solution?"

"No. Sooner or later, it's coming out," he explains smiling. "You'll die if we don't remove your diseased prostrate and the sooner the better, but, for now, I'll give you a prescription for Flomore. That will release a muscle in the bottom of the bladder and it may make things flow better for a while. Come back in four months and we'll check on how you are doing. See my receptionist on the way out."

I pay, pick up my new prescription, and leave.

I go to Shop-mart and pick up my newest prescription. Flomore works. My life improves. I can now even go to the movies and only have to get up once to go to the men's room.

Life is bearable. My hips and left leg still ache, ache real bad somewhere deep down inside. I can't really put my finger on where it hurts, but it hurts bad. I contemplate those long iron screws which are screwed into my knee and hip and that long steel rod that runs up through the middle of my thigh bone. I wonder, "Do I have nerves in there? Does my body not like that metal stuck in me?" I wonder.

I keep taking prescription pain pills. They take the pain to a point where it doesn't completely dominate my life. I still can't cook. I eat breakfast at Donny's, lunch at Orangebee's and dinner at the Taco Well. Sometimes I go to McQuickies or the Dairy King instead. Still, I feel better and the four months pass quickly. Before I know it, it is time for my check up at Dr. Jensen's office.

I enter the examining room, sit in a chair and patiently wait for Dr. Jensen. I only wait ten minutes.

Dr. Jensen enters the room and says, "Hello Shane. Well let's get this over with. Drop your pants and bend over the examining table."

So saying he pulls a long rubber glove on his right hand and starts smearing it with X-Y Jelly. Again, I obediently do as the doctor says. Dr. Jensen shoves a couple fingers into my rear end and gropes around. Then he gropes around some more. This is different. Dr. Allen always just stuck a long bony finger in a long painful ways, felt around, and pulled it out. This hurts. Dr. Jensen pulls his hand out.

"Shane pull your pants up," he tells me. "I'm going to send you to a friend of mine. He is in Portland. I know that it is a long drive from here, but he is the best at what he does. I don't like what I felt up there. I believe that you have cancer. We won't know for sure though until we do some further testing. We should do that just to be safe don't you think?"

"Cancer! Hell yes we should do something to be safe," my mind screams.

I say, "Definitely. Where's the office? When do I go?"

"My receptionist will get an appointment for you and give you directions," saying this, Dr. Jensen leaves the room.

My head spins. "I have cancer? I am going to die? Oh, no."

I am really scared now. "Is this the end, death? Is it here? No. No, it can't be."

I have always worked hard, and had a nice house and a nice car and a pretty lover. I have always been wealthy and felt respected. That is who I am, but now I'm alone and I don't have much and what little I have left is quickly being eaten up by more medical bills. I don't know who or what I am anymore. Well, actually I feel like I'm nothing at all. What I am is unhappy, lost, and dying miserably. Even my soul hurts.

I'm dying with no hope or faith left in the doctors and the health care system which I think of now as a sickness system. I call the Sisters of Mercy the Un-merciful Medical Foundation after their finance department broke me.

I guess, "I am going to have to try something different. What do I have to lose?"

CHAPTER 5

GABRIEL

I pray, "God, if I could just have five more years with health and vitality, I'll trade all of the rest of my life away. I would rather have five more good years, than thirty years of this misery."

I look in the yellow pages of the local phone directory. There are hundreds of types of doctors, but they are really all the same. They went to the same schools as the men and women who have poisoned and hurt and cheated me. They have the same capital letters after their names, the same MD's. I want an alternative, something different.

My mother tells me that she has a friend, who has a friend, who went to an acupuncturist and the acupuncturist really helped her friend's friend.

She asks, "Why don't you go to an acupuncturist? What can it hurt? I mean, if this acupuncturist knowledge is all Voodoo, worst case, you're just out a few dollars. Look at it as entertainment. And if it does a little good, then that is a bonus. Right?"

I consider, "Acupuncture. That is where they stick needles in your body. I don't like that idea. Needles hurt. I know that for sure. I hate having a dentist stick those long dripping needles in the tender gums in the back corner of my jaw. And I really don't like it when nurses stick a needle in my arm to draw blood, especially when they miss and keep jabbing and poking and digging around. Needles really hurt. I don't like them, but acupuncture is an alternative. It is a downright weird alternative. I don't know anyone who has ever gone to an acupuncturist. Sounds mysterious, maybe even a little creepy, but maybe, just maybe, a little magical too, and I need some magic in my life. I really need something to change. Magic would be a good thing."

After many phone calls and much searching, Mom and I finally find a telephone number for Gabriel Rinpoche, an acupuncturist over on the Parkway. I call the number and a friendly male voice answers the telephone immediately.

I tentatively inquire, "Do you have any openings for new clients?"

The voice warmly answers, "Yes, I do. When would you like to come in?"

I'm stunned by the question. I mean. I get to choose? What to say? I reply, "Uh, how about tomorrow?"

"Fine what time?"

"In the afternoon?"

"Yes, I have time. Come in tomorrow afternoon at 2 o'clock. And your name is?"

"Shane. Shane Parker."

"Excellent. I will see you tomorrow afternoon Shane."

"All right. I'll be there. I'll see you tomorrow at 2 o'clock." I hang up the telephone completely flabbergasted. I say to my mother, "That is definitely an alternative way of being a doctor."

She asks, "No wait? You get in tomorrow?"

I shrug, "Yes."

"Well that certainly is different," she agrees. "This could be the beginning of something good for the both of us. I certainly hope that it is," she concludes our conversation in that sincere way that mothers hope for good things for their children.

The next day I park in a small parking lot on a hillside overlooking the city and waddle over to the front door of a friendly looking cottage and walk in through a green front door. There is a hammered brass eye which looks ancient nailed on the door frame above the door. Gabriel is sitting there in a small room behind an antique carved oak desk surrounded by what looks like the Amazon jungle. There are wooden drums with eagle or turkey feathers on them behind him under the plants and gourd rattles with interesting geometric designs burnt and painted on them lying on top of the drums. On Gabriel's left there is a big ancient wooden cabinet which looks like it has a thousand little drawers with little brass handles. The cabinet looks as if it has been used in many castles and palaces over many centuries and some of those palaces must have burnt down around that cabinet. At least that is how it seems to me. On his right there is a big ornately carved oriental book case full of books. Opposite Gabriel and the high backed wooden chair with dragons carved on it which he is sitting in is a smaller plain wooden high backed chair which I sit in. There is a smaller bookcase to my left. I glance at some of the titles: "Healing with Form, Energy, and Light" by Tenzin Wangyal Rinpoche, "The Teachings of Don Juan" by Carlos Castaneda, "Chinese Herbs" by Ron Teeguarden, "Moby Dick" by Herman Melville. "Sound interesting," I consider. In the corners of the room to my right and left are large white porcelain vases with the most exquisitely beautiful lacquer Chinese paintings of mountains and streams that I have ever seen. My eyes wander along the walls where diplomas and licenses hang: a degree in physics from the University of Arizona, a license from the state of Oregon to practice acupuncture, a degree from a school in New Mexico in Chinese medicine, a diploma in Ayurvedic medicine from a school in New Delhi, India. There are more documents that look like degrees but they are printed in weird foreign scripts. One has the English words Lhasa, Tibet on it and another has Shao Lin, China as the only recognizable words. Hanging to the right of Gabriel is a sketch of John Lennon, signed "Our Mother sends you love and luck, John". Under the portrait are words that I recognize from a Beatles song:

"I am the walrus

I am he as you are he as you are me and we are all together.

See how they run like pigs from a gun, see how they fly.

I'm crying."

My eyes finally rest on the man himself. I cannot tell his race or age. He has golden skin and long black wavy hair. He has a long, noble nose and large round eyes. His eyes sparkle. They actually flash with light. It's hard to tell their color. They are dark brown, I think. It's hard to tell. They might be black. When I look into those eyes I kind of fall in and have to pull back. He is smiling. I can't look him in the eyes for long without feeling dizzy and disoriented. He is wearing some kind of white cotton peasant shirt. At first glance, he seems small and wiry, but when he stands up, he is taller than I am, moves with the grace of a leopard and when he shakes my hand, I realize that he is really powerful, really strong. It is all very confusing. I really do start to feel dizzy, maybe even a little nauseous, like that feeling of motion sickness coming on.

"It is indeed a wonderful pleasure to meet you Shane," he says. "I look forward to serving you. I know that we are going to have a wonderful and fruitful journey together. Large things start with small beginnings."

He starts to talk. I feel as if I have just accidentally stumbled into the "Sermon on the Mount" as it is happening and I have just met Jesus Christ. I am watching Gabriel speak and hearing the most amazing things. All of life makes perfect sense and I know for absolute certain that God loves me personally and everything is going to be good, really good. But what is most intriguing to me is that when I look at Gabriel closely, I see that he is as interested to hear what his voice is saying as I am. There are tears in his eyes and it is breaking his heart to hear what his voice is saying. It is all as new to him as it is to me. It is Divine Being coming through his mouth and he is letting it shine. He isn't intellectually delivering a speech from his mind, from his memory. I don't know where Gabriel is. The essence that is him is watching the body of Gabriel and is hearing what that body is saying and is as amazed and as emotionally moved as I am. It is an incredible thing to see and to realize that I am in the presence of the Divine, but so is the body that is shining the light aware too of what is being said as Divine, apart from itself, and tears are streaming down Gabriel's face too. Never have I ever imagined that anything of this nature is even possible. I am delighted. I can't understand or remember exactly what is being said, but I sure feel good for the first time in a long time.

The next thing that I know, I am standing on the steps outside of Gabriel's office looking at an appointment card for tomorrow in my right hand. Gabriel, that is an odd name. I wonder where he is from. He certainly doesn't seem to be from around here. He is not like anyone that I know. There is something special about him.

The next day I enter Gabriel's magical little office. Gabriel smiles, stands, shakes my hand, and warmly greets me saying, "Come in. Sit down. It's nice to see you again Shane."

Before he can say more, I cut him off asking, "How much is this going to cost?"

Gabriel responds, "In China the patient used to come to the doctor every month, or even every day sometimes. The patient was not a patient. He was not a person who patiently sits in a little room patiently waiting to see a doctor for a magical potion, a pill, a cure, or to have an offending something hacked or burnt out. He was a friend and guest of the doctors. The doctor patiently paid close attention to his friends' health and nurtured them emotionally, spiritually, and physically. He made sure that they didn't get sick. In return the doctor's friends supported him financially, spiritually, and emotionally. If a doctor's friend got sick, then that meant that the doctor had failed his friend. It was then the doctor's obligation to get his friend well again. Until the sick person was returned to health, the sick person didn't pay the doctor. He only paid the doctor when he was healthy and happy. This was a health system. In this country you have a sickness system. You don't go to the doctor until you are sick. Then you want a magic pill to make you well. You make yourself sick with your life style choices. In this country, you dig your grave with your teeth. Then you want a doctor to get you out of the grave before you can be covered up. The cost of this treatment will be your idea of yourself."

"What?" I exclaim. I stare at him, but he is just calmly looking back at me. He is serious.

"What are you talking about?" I ask. "I meant, what is the cost in dollars? Your services aren't tax deductible and insurance won't pay. What is this going to cost in money, in cash?" I repeat. I'm serious too.

He smiles and asks, "How much will you pay," as if we are discussing yesterday's weather

"Forty dollars," I say.

I'm thinking that forty is a ridiculous number. I have paid those doctors and druggists thousands of dollars to get me well and they have actually made me worse.

"I agree," he agrees. "The price is forty dollars."

"Great!" I respond. This is going to be a bargain I'm thinking. I tell him, "First can you stick a needle in me and stop this terrible pain that I have in my lower back?"

He doesn't move. He just continues looking at me and says, "Maybe, but first let's talk about life. What is life? What is death? Can you tell a dead man from a live man? What is missing from the dead man that is still in the living man? Western science takes a dead body and hacks it up and labels and defines the parts of the dead body. That kind of misses the point, don't you think? You and I are concerned about what makes a man shout, 'Whooee!!! I feel good'. We are only concerned about what causes pain and death when health has departed."

He continues with excitement in his voice, leaning slightly forward towards me, "Sir Isaac Newton got famous for sitting under an apple tree and getting hit on the head by an apple. He described gravity and gave us a mathematical system that explained how things fall. Don't you think that a more important question is: How did that apple get up there? By what force did little bits of energy unite and ascend, overpowering great forces and coalesce into a living beautiful delicious red apple? Let's explain levity. Let's explore the origin and meaning of life. Let's be vibrantly healthy, happy, beautiful, loving beings of shining pure light. Why settle for reducing the pain in your back?"

Shocked, I answer, "Uh, I don't have any idea what you are talking about," and I mean it. Doctors don't say things like that. I don't know any people who talk like that. My minister hasn't ever even said things like that. I think that we might be getting into blasphemy here. Certainly none of my science teachers ever mentioned any of these concepts. I am pretty certain that my teachers, doctors, pastors, and most of the human race would call Gabriel a fool for talking like this. Still he seems sincere and it is only going to cost forty dollars to go on and see where he goes with this. So I decide to go a little further by asking, "Where would we even start with a wild and crazy conversation like that?"

He smiles like the Cheshire Cat in Alice and Wonderland and leans back in his chair like a mountain climber who has just summitted a great Himalayan peak without using oxygen.

"Well, there are many places that we could start. We could start on the cosmic level, or we could start on the energetic level, or we could start on the material level. Let's start with a truth that crosses all levels. Life begets life and death begets death. Know the difference between life and death and see what causes life and what causes death."

"But first thank you for being here. I am excited to be here sharing with you because just by being here you have proven to me that you are a person who cares about your health, about your friends, about your neighbors, and about the world that we all share. And what I have learned is that caring is the most important thing that we can do. I am going to share part of my life journey with you, the part that began with caring about my personal health."

"When I entered my 50's, I was obese, sick, and dying. My relationships were a mess. I thought the four food groups were: fast food, frozen food, coffee, and whatever that is in the tin foil in the back of the fridg. The problem with fast food is that when it gets to the stomach, it parks and the fat gets off and applies for citizenship. My body and my life were a mess. I knew that I had to make a change."

"What I am going to tell you is what is working for me now. For you it may be something quite different. Our relationship with our food is very personal. I am going to share with you the information which has most influenced my decisions. I have journeyed from the Standard American Diet, the SAD diet, through vegetarianism, then veganism, and on to raw veganism and green juicing and into being a breatharian and finally an immortalist. I didn't make this journey in a straight line. When I decided that I had to make a change I started studying health related issues. Most of the literature agreed that we should cut red meat out of our diets. So I ate more chicken and fish, but then I started craving red meat. So I ate some burgers. Then I didn't feel very well. So I didn't eat anymore burgers. Instead I ate some pepperoni pizzas. Then I didn't feel very well. So I quit eating pork. I learned to listen to my body. Slowly I quit eating flesh altogether. My mind started to clear and I became aware of the spiritual reasons for not eating flesh. My life started to change. I began on a voyage of discovery that included not only my physical body, but my emotions, and my spiritual connections. I started that transition through being a vegetarian, a vegan, and then a raw vegan unintentionally. As my diet changed, my attitude changed and I saw possibilities which I hadn't previously even contemplated. I met breatharians and immortalists and started practicing their techniques. I have learned that when I get somewhere that that isn't the end of the journey. I haven't succeeded and arrived. Here is just where I am at now. This is just a phase that I am passing through on my way to a more vibrant life full of happiness. We all share this journey and are at different places on this path with different answers to life's questions. Some paths lead to better health and happiness than others. I am sharing with you what has worked best for me. I have also done many of the alternative healing protocols and the standard American medical practices on my way to health, happiness, and a long life. So if you are interested, later we can discuss the differences between all of these systems and my thoughts on each one."

"You have heard it said that you are what you eat, but has anyone told you that you are what you think, see, hear, touch, sniff, and dream. Everything is connected. Everything that we do counts towards whether we are sick or healthy. The things which cause us to be sick are deficiencies, poisons, and toxic relationships."

"Let's begin our discussion about life and death by looking at plants because in this world life begins with plants. Green is the most wonderful color on this planet. What do plants need to create the miracle of life? They need air, water, earth, and sunlight and heat. With these elements, they create proteins, carbohydrates, fats, enzymes, vitamins, and phyto-nutrients. They create life. The intelligence of plants is astounding. The smartest man or woman on Earth cannot replicate what the simplest blade of grass out on the lawn can do. Our lives are dependent on plants and we have no idea how they do what they do. We do know that if you eat a spinach leaf from the garden or an avocado from the orchard it will be absolutely loaded with enzymes, phyto-nutrients, minerals, vitamins, proteins, carbohydrates, and fats. The blood of the spinach plant is only one molecule different from the blood in our bodies, magnesium rather than iron. However plants do it, animals cannot live without eating plants or else eating other animals which have eaten plants. When we are eating plants to get all of those vital nutrients, green is a good color, but our plates should look like a vibrant rainbow. The more vibrant the plants colors are, the more packed they are with lively nutrition. Each color provides us with a different set of nutrients and we need them all."

"It is also known that if you heat any of your food over 118 degrees, the enzymes are all destroyed and most of the vitamins and phyto-nutrients are ruined and most of the minerals have been leached away. Also whatever has been cooked is dead. A cooked seed will not sprout and grow. Its liveliness is gone. A wild animal such as a mountain gorilla doesn't cook its food. The gorilla just wanders around in a garden breaking off pieces of plants and eating them. Something that might interest you is that mountain gorillas in the wild don't get heart disease, cancer, or diabetes. It appears that the difference between the sicknesses of modern humans and the health of wild mountain gorillas is that the wild animals are getting a more vibrant form of nutrition in a form which is free of modern industrial poisons. You are thinking that mountain gorillas aren't people and that maybe people are different from gorillas somehow and that difference is the reason that people are getting cancer, heart disease, and diabetes. I think that you would agree that people who live in America are similar to people living in Japan. Several researchers have noticed that Japanese born in the first half of the twentieth century didn't get breast cancer or prostate cancer while Americans of the same generation got both of those diseases at high rates. At first the researchers thought that the Japanese were somehow physically different than Americans. But as they studied the two groups of people, a new fact appeared. Japanese who moved to America and started living the American lifestyle started getting the same diseases at the same rate as Americans. It is the lifestyle that causes cancer, heart disease, and diabetes. Finally the China

Study ended the debate for those people who are interested in the truth. A whole plant based diet leads to health. Variations from this way of eating lead to sickness."

"Let's go back to the gorilla. How is the gorilla's diet different than the typical American's diet? How is a slice of white bread different nutritionally from a fresh salad straight out of the jungle? The difference is that there are many things which are in a wild wheat seed which have been destroyed in its domestication and its processing into bread. So the person who is eating the white bread is getting a bunch of calories without the nutrition that was in the seed. Plus the bread eater is also getting a bunch of toxic chemicals which were added in the processing of the wheat berry into bread. These substances were added to protect the plant from insects and other weeds and then to preserve the bread and to enhance its texture and flavor. Eating white flour is the nutrional equivalent of eating paper mache without the paper. Meanwhile the gorilla, who is quietly eating his wild seeds along with the plants that they grew on, is getting all of the power packed nutrition in the wild seeds plus the nutrition in the plants that they grew on and he is getting no added toxins. Plus by eating a variety of the plants which were also standing beside the seed plants, he is getting many more lively nutritious substances too. This is the live nutrition which if the seed would have fallen on the ground would have created another living plant."

"Ideally everyone should eat like mountain gorillas and be as strong and healthy as a gorilla, but some people don't. Some people like to eat potato chips and chocolate pie with whipped cream and hot dogs and barbequed baby back ribs, and they like to eat them more than they like to eat salads. Those peoples' diets are deficient in enzymes, probiotics, vitamins, minerals, and phyto-nutrients and high in fibreless empty calories."

"If these people were to drink the juice, the blood, of the plants direct, they would be getting all of those missing nutrients that they are failing to get, but they do the opposite. They pay someone to process out all of that juice along with all of those vital nutrients and then they eat what is left after it has been mixed with a cocktail of poisonous chemicals. Usually they further cook this mixture at a very high heat often in chemically altered toxic fats, or even worse now a days they pay someone to feed the plants to animals and then they eat the animals getting even further from the nutrition that their bodies so earnestly need and adding even more dangerous substances."

"As a consequence, they begin to suffer from numerous health issues such as cancer, heart disease, diabetes, and nervous disorders. After someone has started living this way it is very difficult to change. A short term quick solution is to start supplementing. It would be better to eat right and exercise, but because it is difficult for a person living this lifestyle to change right away, the next best thing is to start supplementing with enzymes, probiotics, minerals, anti-oxidants, vitamins, and high value super nutritious super foods. I keep saying these words: enzymes, vitamins, probiotics, and minerals. What are they and why do you need them and what are some good sources for them? Americans know something about proteins, carbohydrates, and fats, but seldom hear about enzymes, probiotics, and minerals; and yet they are an essential part of life. Enzymes are intelligent organic compounds that begin and organize every chemical reaction in your body. That means that they are absolutely necessary for you to build your body, digest your food and for you to see, feel, and move about. Enzymes need minerals, clean air and water, and sunlight along with carbohydrates, proteins, and fats to do their job of building you and keeping you healthy and happy."

"There is another key set of players in this drama that you and I are calling your body. Did you know that you have more viruses, funguses, bacteria, and parasites on and in your body than you have cells and that you are dependent on some of these organisms for your health. These micro-organisms help you digest your food, create some of your vitamins, and protect you. Others of these critters as you are aware are working against you. What they are doing is going to kill you and take your body back to the soil for the plants to use again. When you take antibiotics, you kill the good bacteria along with the bad. Biotic means life. Antibiotic means against life. For some reason after you take antibiotics, the harmful little life forms get started in your body again before the helpful ones get going again. The result is damaged gastro-intestinal and immune systems. This results in constipation, gas, bloating, indigestion, inflammation, flu like symptoms, and over time to chronic pain. Now is always a good time to add some probiotics, some fermented foods, to our lives, but after taking antibiotics it is especially important to take some pro life forces, some probiotics. People used to eat fermented foods such as pickles, sauerkraut, relishes, kimchee, yogurt, cheese, beer, and vinegar and get plenty of probiotics, but in the modern world, these foods are pasteurized. The good helpful life forms that are helping your enzymes to keep you healthy are killed in the pasteurization process along with the destructive ones. Anything that has an expiration date that is two years from now isn't food."

"You know that minerals are necessary for healthy bones and teeth, but did you know that they are also necessary to regulate your heart beat and for you to have feelings and emotions. We constantly need billions of things which are used in billions of chemical reactions which are started and controlled by the catalysts which we call enzymes. The enzymes and minerals in your body are in a very delicate balance and all kinds of things can disturb that balance. Your body's blood pH is around 7.35. If that pH changes just a few hundredths of a point, you will go into a coma and possibly die. This is such a small amount that it isn't even measurable with the pH paper that people buy to test their swimming pool and hot tub water. Every time that you eat processed foods, meat or dairy, or drink a soda your body has to quickly find an alkaline buffer to neutralize the acidity of what you have just consumed or else you are going to be dead soon. That gives new meaning to eating a balanced diet, doesn't it? So if you absolutely insist on eating macaroni and cheese with a big slice of meatloaf with ketchup, then eat a big salad first. Vegetables and fruits tend to be alkaline. If you don't eat a big salad, then your body is going to go after your mineral reserves and after those are depleted, it will to start dissolving your bones to neutralize those acids that you just ate. Another way that a mineral deficiency can become fatal quickly is to have a potassium or magnesium deficiency. These minerals along with sodium and calcium are used by the body to regulate your heart beat. A little this way or that way of any of them and you may experience a heart arrhythmia which can be fatal."

"Another way that you can get out of balance is that you can be poisoned by a toxic chemical that disturbs a body process. All of those things which kill weeds, bugs, and funguses affect you too. If it will kill a weed, it will kill a human. If it will kill a bug, it will kill you. If it is a preservative and stops mold from growing, it affects you. You are a life form just like all other life forms. So when a chemical is affecting other life forms, it is affecting you and everyone and everything that you know. Pesticides, fungicides, herbicides, larvicides, preservatives, radiation and toxic chemicals of any type hurt everyone. Just because someone isn't dead or doesn't appear to be dying doesn't mean that they are as vibrantly healthy as they could be. If those chemicals are present, then your body is struggling with them and they are causing chronic illnesses and pain. This struggle against toxic chemicals includes pharmaceutical drugs too. Pharmaceuticals are poisons. Look at the side effects listed in the packaging when you pick up a prescription."

"Earlier I said that our thoughts affect our health. Now let's discuss how they do it. Negative thoughts and physical stress can have the same affect on our health as toxic substances. Worrying and anger cause your body pH to become acidic. Remember that if your blood becomes acidic, you die. Your body isn't going to allow that, but what it has to do to protect your life when acid is constantly being dumped into it requires great effort and takes resources away from areas where they are badly needed. The result is chronic inflammation, pain, and sickness. Our thoughts matter. Working or playing too hard or an automobile accident will also acidify your body in the same way as anger or worry. Now throw in a nutritional deficiency and some poisons, and you have a recipe for disaster."

"We want a recipe for health and happiness. This recipe begins with good friends, sunshine, clean water and air, and tiny little angstrom sized mineral particles. If you needed iron, it wouldn't do you any good to eat a handful of iron shotgun pellets. To be absorbable the minerals have to be in a form which your body can use. That basically means that the minerals should have come up through the roots of a plant. Plants have the knowledge to know which minerals in what form are useable by their bodies and if it's good for their bodies, it's good for yours. Your body also needs enzymes and vitamins and proteins and carbohydrates and fats. Plants create these from sunshine, water, air, and minerals. So you need to eat raw plants and to be happy. If you don't eat enough raw plants then you need to supplement. In America the big corporate farmlands are so poisoned and depleted of minerals that you need to do both, eat raw whole plants and take supplements. Another way to get the vibrant nutrition that you need is to buy your food at local markets from local farmers who you know are people with integrity. You could also get your food from Community Supported Agricultural groups. So, that is what I want you to do and to be happy."

"You are to begin eating only raw, vegan, organic foods. This way of life will not only give you a whole new healthy body, it will also make you more perceptive and aware, raise your consciousness, and fill your soul with delight in God's grace."

"Wait. Stop right there," I demand. "Are you saying that I have to quit eating meat?"

"Humans are not supposed to eat flesh, but if you want to continue eating flesh, and can eat it raw, then alright, go ahead and eat it. There are a lot of good health and spiritual reasons not to eat flesh. First of all flesh products are full of pesticides, herbicides, hormones, parasites, bacteria, and viruses. Second, they are loaded with unhealthy fats and contain no fiber. Third they are protein dense and can throw your body over to the acid side causing all kinds of chronic pain and degenerative diseases. I could go on and on, and we have not even discussed the emotional and spiritual aspects of flesh eating, but I won't. Stop eating flesh though and your mind will clear, and you will quickly understand the dangers of a flesh eating addiction. You believe that you are eating to live, but actually you have been dying to eat."

"Gabriel," I protest, "You are lecturing me. I don't like being lectured. Leave me alone. I just came here for some medicine. I don't want to be told what to do by some evangelical know-it-all health food guy. Are you going to give me a treatment or not?" I am angry, almost shouting in his face.

He answers me pleasantly, reasonably, "Shane, I want you to take charge of your life. Remember, life comes from life. Death comes from death. Try to eat more live, raw, organic fruits, vegetables, nuts, and seeds and everything will become clear to you in a while. Your health will improve and your mind will clear."

"Eating your food raw will not only improve your health, it will also improve the Earth's health. We have not even discussed the damage that food cooking does to our planet, our home. More energy is used to cook food, than is used to fuel cars and trucks and planes. Global warming could be solved today, right now, if everyone quit cooking their meals. A time of abundance with no one going hungry and everyone having plenty of fresh clean water could be here now, if everyone quit cooking and eating flesh. Think about how many pounds of corn and wheat and fresh produce that it takes to feed a cow to get a couple pounds of hamburger. Then realize that a dozen people could live comfortably for days on that produce. And think about the water that is used and polluted in the operation of the cow, pig, and chicken factory feed lots. The amount of pollution flowing from feed lots is huge and as toxic as, if not more toxic than, what comes out of our cities. The answer to everything is right here, right now, and we are it. Live large. Be grand. Be beautiful. I love you very much and I just want you to be the happy vibrant soul that you are. Start juicing vegetables and live."

While Gabriel is talking, I start feeling woozy, kind of like being sea sick. I can't concentrate. My head feels like it is going to explode. I hate to throw up. I'll do anything to put that moment off. I quickly stand up and say, "Goodbye Gabriel." I stagger outside for some fresh air and get in my pickup and leave.

But when I get home, that throwing up moment is here, and here again, and here again, and here again. I have the worst flu of my life. Gunk is pouring out of me top, bottom, and everywhere in between. I have the flu and a cold. I have a runny nose. I am throwing up. I have diarrhea. Two weeks go by. My oldest daughter, Ashley, tries to bring me some vegetable soup, but I won't even let her in the house.

"Leave it on the porch", I tell her through the door. "I have something terrible and I don't want you to get it."

Finally, I call Gabriel. "I'm dying. I have a terrible flu," I tell him.

"Congratulations," he responds, "I will be right over."

"Congratulations! What do you mean, congratulations? I'm sick. I might be dying."

"Yes, I know. Isn't it wonderful? You are healing. You are getting well. You are becoming a Super Hero. You are changing molecule by molecule. Out with the old. In with the new."

"Quit talking crazy and just get over here and give me something, a magic potion, a silver bullet that will make me well. I want some real medicine."

When he enters my home, I am sitting in a recliner trying to eat a bowl of soup. He says, "There is nothing wrong with you. You are having a healing crises. Your body is full of toxins from the from the drugs that you have taken, from the food that you eat, from the air that you breathe, from the clothes that you wear, from the water that you drink, and from the toxic emotions that you experience. Your immune system is overloaded. Your energy body is weak. I changed your energy. You are resonating at a different frequency now. So you are excreting all of the poisons which you have accumulated in your lifetime. The throwing up, the diarrhea, the mucous, the sweating, the frequent urinating are all good. They are symptoms that you are healing. You shouldn't want to stop them. Gather all of those ugly, putrefying, stinking, unwanted, poisonous things that are coming out of you in a bucket. Then look at them and think about the fact that a little while ago they were all inside of you. Better out than in. Get it all out."

"That is crazy. I have a virus. I have germs. I have the flu. I am sick. I need medicine. I need an antibiotic."

Gabriel casually takes the bowl out of my hands along with the spoon and eats the rest of the soup. "Now, I want you to notice that I won't, don't get sick. If your germ theory is correct then I have most definitely by eating with your spoon been exposed to this terrible disease that you imagine that you have, a disease that nobody can resist. Correct? And there is no hope for me. I am doomed to get the flu and your cold. Isn't that what you believe? You say that you need an anti-biotic. Remember that biotic means life? So you are telling me that you want to solve your problem by eating something that is anti-life. Does that make sense to you?"

I stare at the idiot thinking, "What kind of fool comes over to a person's house, a person that has a potentially deadly illness and licks the sick person's spoon. Is this so called healer suicidal or worse yet dangerously insane?"

He continues talking, "Your problem is that you believe that the mind is in the body, but really the body is in the mind. All illness is mental illness first, then physical illness. Even Louis Pasteur on his death bed recanted the germ theory and admitted that germs are nothing, the bio-terrain is everything. We swim in a sea of germs. They are everywhere, in us, on us, and all around us all of the time. Why do some people get sick and others in the same situation not get sick? Strengthen the bio-terrain, the immune system, and never worry about germs ever again. Think right and fear nothing. You are not sick. You are healing. People in America constantly believe that they have a cold or the flu, but they are actually poisoned and their body is trying to get rid of the poison. The more poison that you ingest, the more cold and flu symptoms that you experience. When you suppress the symptoms by stopping the mucous from running or by stopping the diarrhea or vomiting, you are just prolonging and worsening your illness. The dis-ease will just pop up somewhere else in the body and be much more serious when it re-emerges, because the so called medicine has added to the bodies toxic overload. For example, if you take antibiotics during this discomfort you will destroy the friendly bacteria in your digestive system. Then your digestive system will be damaged. Bad bacteria will proliferate and secrete toxins into you which will make you even sicker. Now on top of the flu and the cold, you will suffer gas, constipation, irritable bowel syndrome, and acid reflux. We are terra forming you. We are building a new terrain for you. You are becoming a new world."

"Shane, there is something that I want you to do for me. Vitamins and minerals are gateway drugs. They can be the gateway to Heaven. Everything that you put in your mouth, your eyes, your ears, or your nose affects your consciousness, your being, your experience of life. You can be a heroin junkie or you can be a hamburger and French fries junkie. A hamburger and French fries junkie lives in a hamburger and French fries world.

Like a fish swimming in the ocean, who never sees the water, the hamburger junkie never clearly sees or understands the world in which he is living. His world is just the way that it is, that it was, that it has always been, and that it will always be. There is no 'other' way. It is not possible for the fish to even see that another way is possible. To the fish, walking on land and breathing air is not even thinkable or even imaginable. Well, I want you to quit being a bottom dwelling, scum sucking fish and to become a lovely bird and to soar in the heavens. Imagine that!"

"The place for you to start this journey is at the Supplement Store on Garden Valley Boulevard. I want you to go there and to visit my good friend, the beautiful Lilith."

So saying, Gabriel leaves me sitting alone with an empty spoon and bowl in my hands, stunned.

CHAPTER 6

LILITH

I painfully shower and dress, and I slowly drive over to the Supplement Store, driving in a dense mental fog. My eye sight has been getting worse and worse. It is hard to even drive in the dark anymore. The Supplement Store is in a cozy little stone building which sits back away from the street in a quiet, peaceful part of town. I enter the store looking and feeling like Eeyore from "Winnie the Pooh".

I am thinking, "Nothing can help me. I feel awful. Why am I here? I should just go home and take a nap." My shoulders slump. My head droops towards my chest. My whole body sags downward, as if gravity is about to overcome my whole being and pull me downward, down, back into the earth.

A tall dark attractive Italian looking woman glides over to me. She radiates concern and a heartwarming sympathy. I don't care. I hardly notice her. I try to think, but the effort is tiring. She asks, "Can I help you find something?"

I wonder, "Find something? Find what? What am I looking for? What am I doing here? I don't even want to be here. I don't want to talk. I want to lie down somewhere and go to sleep for a long, long time, maybe forever. I don't feel good. I hurt. I'm tired and nothing is ever going to get better. Never. Never. Never. Ever."

I say, "I don't know."

She looks at me carefully, thoroughly. She feels my pain and suffering and confusion. It hurts her. She hurts all over, but especially in her stomach, she hurts for me. She wants so much to grab me by the shoulders and to shake me and to cry out, "Stop it! Wake up! Wake up! Stop! It doesn't have to be this way. I can help. You can be better. Better in only a short time. You just have to hear me and change your life a little bit."

She feels like she is a woman standing on a street who is watching a building on fire. The building is burning and she knows that there is a man who is sleeping in there in that building. She wants to dash up to this building and start screaming, "Fire! Fire! Fire! Your building is on fire. Wake up! Please, Wake up. Wake up now. You are about to die. Do something, anything. Get up! Oh please wake up."

She says, "Hello, my name is Lilith. Won't you come sit with me over here?" and she points to a couple of overstuffed arm chairs.

I look up and see the store for the first time. I think, "This ain't no Right-Aid."

There are aisles with mysterious elixirs, bottles and boxes and bags and a glass fronted refrigerator, but a third of the store is an area with big friendly looking chairs, small tables covered with literature and books, and soft music is playing with water running and birds singing somewhere.

"This is kind of interesting, kind of different," I ponder. I look at Lilith for the first time. A vision of ancient Greece drifts across my mind. I think of the oracle at Delphi greeting the sick and confused at her temple.

I wonder, "What did that oracle do?" I can't remember the story. "Didn't she talk to God or something like that and then solve all of the problems that the people brought to her?"

I think, "This is kind of a weird thought for a good Southern Baptist boy like me."

Nevertheless, I take the hand that she offers and follow her into the temple of supplements and cross over into a more mysterious life than I could ever have imagined before now.

We sit and talk and the afternoon pleasantly drifts away. Again, like when I was talking to Gabriel, it is like being in a dream and waking up. We are having a great conversation, but as soon as the words are gone, I can't remember what we are discussing.

Then she says, "Shane, I want you to start taking a liquid, bio-available multi-vitamin with minerals, some high quality enzymes and probiotics and eating some super foods, such as blue green algae from Klamath Lake and raw cacao and maca."

While she is talking, she is walking around the store picking up bottles, boxes, and bags with me sheepishly following along behind. She gathers up what looks like more pills and potions than I can carry much less swallow.

My mind starts to focus for the first time in a long time. I ask, "What are these things? How do I take them? How much do I take? What are they good for? What will happen to me if I take them."

I am considering, "I don't like pills. I can't stand to swallow one little one. This stuff could be poison. Didn't I read in Readers Review, or somewhere that doctors say that you don't need vitamins? Wasn't there something in The Fox News Report about supplements being dangerous, like causing cancer, or something? Maybe I shouldn't do this."

I say, "How much is all of this going to cost?"

"It is $112," she replies, "You can pay now or later."

"What, what do you mean?" I snap.

"I mean you are investing right here, right now in the most precious possession you have, or will ever have in this life, your health. You have cancer and you are dying. How much have you already paid your cancer doctor and how much have you paid all of those hospitals and drug stores and food stores and those retail outlets to poison you and to ruin your health? Remember, we are all One. I love you. Someday there will be another way, but for today you must trust me, and you must do this. If you will not do this for yourself, do it for me. Reach down below your fear factor and grab onto the grace of God. Do it now."

We stand staring into each other's eyes, into each other's souls, and I decide, "Yeah, I'll do it." And I do.

At first, I don't notice anything different, except that I notice that I am noticing. I haven't noticed anything for a long time except how awful and tired that I feel. Now, I am thinking about being healthy, strong, and attractive. I am thinking about having some fun. For so long, I have only thought about mortgages, bank loans, credit card bills, the war, terrorists, and the wrecked economy, about being fat and ugly and unemployed, about not being liked by any of the people or animals or anything else around me, and about not liking any of them, not much anyway, either.

I think, "This could work. There is an alternative. There is hope."

CHAPTER 7

THE METHODS OF HEALING

I start going to see Gabriel almost every day. He does energy healing techniques and acupuncture treatments on me on Mondays. We do neuro-feedback, meditation, yoga, and chi gong on Wednesdays. On Fridays, he electronically stimulates the area around my broken bones with one machine and then with another device he bathes my body in different energy frequencies using a plasma tube hooked to a frequency modulator. In between these sessions, he teaches and counsels me. For my edification and enjoyment at home he gives me books to read, movies to watch, and music to listen to.

And during all of this time, I keep visiting Lilith at the Supplement Store. Always I am taking vitamins, minerals, enzymes, and probiotics; and eating super foods such as: blue green algae, maca, raw cacao, goji berries, powdered concentrated Siberian ginseng, cordyceps, bee pollen, and royal jelly. Lilith and I are becoming good friends.

I can't believe how fast that I'm healing. I am losing weight and getting stronger every day. Everything that we do is interesting and makes me feel stronger and happier.

The energy treatments are really helpful. I get up on a massage table and lie down. Gabriel's office is very quiet and peaceful. Soft music is playing. We talk for a bit.

Gabriel tells me, "Relax. Breathe deep. Breathe down into your belly. Now close your eyes. Visualize your favorite place to relax, a garden, a mountain lake or stream, a high desert hot spring, a peaceful meadow full of yellow flowers."

He stands on my left side down by my feet. He is holding both hands over me about six inches above my body, palms facing downwards towards me. His eyes are closed. He is in deep meditation. He begins to slowly move up my body. I know that he is moving because I can feel his hands. They are radiating heat or something like heat. I can feel him.

When he reaches a broken bone or torn muscle, he pauses for maybe five minutes, just radiating energy into the hurt. As the bones and muscles heal, he moves his concentration on to the damaged organs and then to wherever I have aches and pains. The bones heal. The prostrate shrinks and starts working again and all of my organs get better and my aches and pains go away.

The more he radiates, the better, the more peaceful and happy that I feel. I don't understand what he is doing, but I know that I am getting better and better all of the time. I don't need an x-ray or a blood test or a cat scan to know. I feel it. I feel better. When I hurt, I know that something is wrong, and then everything is wrong. I start dwelling on my pain and on my misery. Then I begin thinking about how unlucky I am. Then I think about how depressed I am over the government and over my relationships with my family. Everything is a problem. But when I am healthy like when I was a teenager, I didn't worry about any of those things. I was too busy thinking about my next adventure. I was on the move. Well that is how I know that I am getting better. I am on the move. I can feel it. I feel better. In just a few short months my health and life have completely changed for the better.

I buy a bicycle and start bicycling over to Gabriel's. He brews tea for me at his office and makes bags of tea for me to make at home. He makes teas with as many as twenty five ingredients for me from the mysterious cabinet of many drawers. The teas include the roots and leaves and bark of plants. They include mushrooms, nuts and berries and seeds and leaves and roots. There are three types of herbs. The highest level which are known as the royal herbs, are adaptogenic. There aren't many of these herbs, but tonics from them work magic in the body. If the thyroid is over active, then taking an adaptogenic herb will relax the thyroid. If the thyroid is under active, then taking the same herb will stimulate the thyroid. Ginseng, cordyceps, and reishi mushrooms are examples of these tonic herbs. The second group of herbs either stimulate or relax a condition, but won't do both. These herbs are like supplements which help, but don't hurt a person. The practioner needs to know which of these herbs to give to his patient for each condition. The third group of herbs is known as medicine or the poisons. These herbs are like pharmaceutical drugs. There are a lot of herbs in this group and they are used for example to kill parasites. Gabriel gives me tonics full of the royal herbs which he says increase my vital essence.

We sit and talk and talk. We talk about Jesus and Buddha. We talk about the Tao, about physics, and about the science of the mind. We talk about ancient cultures and the environment. We talk about art and literature and music. We talk about men and women and relationships. We talk about food, what it is, where it comes from, what is done to it, and what it does to us.

We go for walks. He buys me a camera. Through using the camera, I start to see details. I stop and carefully look at everything around me. At first, I'm looking for pictures, but then this new way of looking becomes my way of seeing the world around me. I am no longer going from one place to another just to get from point A to point B. I am seeing everything between here and there, between point A and point B. I am seeing that everything is interesting, fascinating, mysterious, wonderful, and beautiful. I am seeing the texture in the thousands of other lives that surround our lives. I am seeing the colors, the changing patterns in the thousands of other plants and animals and birds and bugs and fish with whom we are sharing this adventure, this life.

I visit friends and loved ones and spend hours laughing, joking, and talking with them. I reconnect with old friends and associates. I watch the sun rise and I watch the sun set. I walk in the moonlight. I go to the high mountains and gather glass bottles full of crystal clear living mountain spring water. I take the bottles home and enjoy drinking the fresh, clean spring water. Spring turns to summer.

I eat only raw vegetables, fruits, grains, nuts, and seeds. I drink lots of green juices. I fast and begin to internally cleanse my body. I give myself colonics. I take herbs to cleanse my liver, blood, and kidneys. I do a gall bladder flush.

Gabriel teaches me how to make raw vegetables into delicious dishes: soups, appetizers, classic entrees and burgers, cakes, pies, cookies and parfaits, crackers, sprouts and fermented cheeses and drinks. He teaches me how to make delicious sauces and wonderful smoothies. He shows me how to get all kinds of pleasing textures and colors with different combinations of fruits and vegetables and nuts and seeds. He teaches me how to make raw cacao into raw chocolate, fudge and brownies.

He teaches me how to use my mind and body. He introduces me to the ancient techniques for meditating. He shows me how to do yoga and chi gong postures. We exercise our bodies and our minds constantly.

He wires my head to a neuro-feedback machine and leads me through lessons which teach me how to get from an agitated state of mind to deep relaxation or to deep concentration whichever I intend. He tapes bare electrical wires to my scalp, hooks these wires to an electrical gadget that has a screen like a television set and a printer. As I think different thoughts and feel different emotions, different wave patterns run across the television screen and the printer prints a record of these patterns. Gabriel knows my state of mind by the shape of the waves. There is a bell hooked into the system. He has me watch my thoughts and emotions, or enter a state where I have no thoughts or emotions. When I achieve my goal, the bell rings. Doing this type of exercise hour after hour, I learn to control my states of consciousness under various circumstances with various goals.

He speeds up my meditation practice by putting headphones on my head with the sound of rain playing in each ear at different frequencies. This forces my brain to rewire itself. The right side of the brain is creative. The left side is logical. Normally a person is right brain or left brain dominant. This exercise forces the two hemispheres of the brain to work together in a more coordinated fashion which makes a creative person more rational and a logical person more creative.

He has me journal my dreams and imagine alien worlds and other dimensions. He asks me to imagine what I would be like if my parents would have taken me to Africa and raised me as a Zulu from birth. What would this Zulu me be like now? What part of me wouldn't have changed?

He has me journey into my past and remember everyone whom I have ever known. He has me give back any energy which I have taken and take back any energy which has been taken from me. I forgive everyone who has wronged me and I forgive myself for all of the mistakes which I feel that I have made and I ask everyone whom I have wronged for their forgiveness. I retrieve the lost pieces of my soul and become whole as a child again.

He sticks little acupuncture needles in me and this procedure, those little needles, have radical consequences on my health and well being. I start to think about those big metal wood screws in my body and about that big iron rod up the middle of the thigh bone in my left leg. If those little acupuncture needles can change my life, what are those pounds of steel doing to me? Is what they are doing good or bad? My leg and hips hurt. I think that what those metal screws and that metal rod are doing is bad and that I need that metal to go, to leave my body. Summer changes to fall.

I call the office of the surgeon who put the steel in me and get an appointment for next week. I enter the big shiny new modern spotless waiting room, fill out a stack of papers on a clip board, and sit down to wait. I read 'Architectural Review' and 'Hunters' Field and Creek' and 'Gentleman's Monthly'.

Finally a nurse calls, "Mr. Parker, please follow me."

I enter a big nice examining room and climb up on the examination table.

The nurse says, "The doctor will be with you soon," and leaves.

A short time later Dr. Anderson enters the room and greets me with a friendly, "Ah, my lucky bionic man. How are you?"

"I am really doing excellent," I respond. "Dr. Anderson, I'm wondering, can't you just take this metal out of my body?"

"Well yes," he responds. "It is just screwed into your bones. We can just unscrew the screws and pull the rod out, but if we do that the bones could buckle and break. You are better off with that support in you. I recommend that you leave them in. You are better off, stronger with them in than out. We very seldom can take that support out without catastrophic results for the patient."

"What would I have to do to get you to take them out?"

"You would have to prove to me on your x-rays that the bones are strong enough to stay together and to hold you up."

I am ecstatic that Dr. Anderson is open minded enough to consider my request. Over the next few months, he takes three sets of x-rays and finally agrees to do the operation.

Pointing at the third set of x-rays, he informs me, "I can't believe how fast these bones are healing and how strong the area where the fractures were, are now. Your bones are actually stronger than when they were broken. They are thicker in the broken areas than they were before the breaks."

But he warns me, "When the screws and the rod are taken out, the bones are like etched glass. They can shatter or break at any time if they are stressed. You have to be especially careful until the places where the screws and rods were, fill in."

Thirty days later after removing all of the metal from my body, he looks at my new x-rays and exclaims, "I can't believe it. Not only have your bones filled in, they seem to be stronger than an ordinary bone. This is incredible."

"Dr. Anderson, thank you so much for saving my leg and my life, and thank you for being open minded enough to take the metal out of my body. I am so happy to be alive and walking without any pain."

"You're welcome Shane. Good luck and be careful."

I leave Dr. Anderson's office a happy man.

I am thinking, "I think that I'll go to Alaska and see the bears and I think that I'll go to South America and climb mountains and I think that I will start skiing."

And I start right in on doing it all.

CHAPTER 8

ALASKA

I buy airline tickets to Alaska, but it is still winter. Throughout the summer and fall, Lilith and I have been collecting fruits and vegetables from her father's orchards and garden and going to farmers' markets and buying fresh produce to juice and make into fresh sauces and dishes. We have been hiking in the woods collecting mushrooms: chanterelles, king boletus, morels, and puffballs. I decide to ask her to go skiing with me for a few days during the holidays. Lilith is so charming and she has a wonderful sense of humor and she is so interesting that time just flies by when I am with her. I really like her.

I go down to the Supplement Store and walk in. Lilith is alone behind the counter. She smiles when I come in and meets me and gives me a hug.

Encouraged, I ask, "Lilith would you like to go skiing up at the Snow Forever Lodge?"

She doesn't even pause to think. "I'm not a skier Shane. Skiing involves snow and getting cold. I would be more of a ski lodge person, but I don't have the right outfit and I'm busy with family matters anyway. Call me when you get back and we'll do dinner at Alex's and check out a movie and go see Bill and Leonor. How does that sound?"

I am disappointed, but I can see that I am trying to impose my guy trip on her and I feel good even though she said 'no', because we have a date when I return.

"Okay. That sounds good. I'll come see you next week when I get back. It was nice seeing you. By the way, you look great. Tell Diana hi for me."

I walk out and I go skiing.

I head for the mountains very early the next morning. The top of the snow on the road melted yesterday and during the night it has refrozen forming a clear glassy ice cap a few inches thick over the road, over the mountains, over everything. Then sometime after midnight a blizzard blew up and covered the ice with four to six inches of snow.

It is like driving on an invisible ice skating rink. A rink in which you have to keep your speed up to keep traction propelling you forward. I am driving a two wheel drive pickup with not much weight in the back over the back tires. This is dicey. I am worried. When my attention drifts, the pickup drifts. The rear end of the pickup tries to become the front end. I am gripping the steering wheel with both hands, drilling the road ahead with an intense stare, jaws clamped, willing the pickup to stay moving straight ahead, but I'm sleepy. It is still dark and I was up most of the night packing my skiing and camping equipment.

I blink my eyes, shake my head, slap my face, and glance into the trees on the left side of the road. The back end of the pickup breaks free with that sickening roller coaster plunge feeling, picking up speed as it comes around. I'm awake. I'm awake! I fling the steering wheel left. The back end whips back in the other direction. I fling the steering wheel to the right. Foot off the gas pedal, right left, left right, whirling around, waiting for the blue metal projectile in which I find myself to come to a stop, hoping with each sickening whip not to smash into that snow bank on my left or to rocket over the edge of that cliff on my right.

When the pickup stops spinning, I get out, look up and down the deserted snow covered highway, rub my forehead and temples, wait for my heart to quit pounding, and thank God that I survived again. This is the third time that this has happened. Then I climb back in, spin the tires, and start up that lonely snow covered highway again.

When I reach the mountain, there is no mountain. There is a blizzard. I can't see the mountain. Sitting here at the base of the mountain, I can look at where the mountain should be and I can sometimes see some of the mountain come and go, but snow is always blasting through the air. I stall for half an hour. I meditate for another hour, but neither the weather nor my courage improves.

There is nothing to do but go up on that mountain or go home, and I'm not going home. I climb out, pull on my snow gear, grab my skis and poles and shoulder my way into the blizzard and onto the ski lift.

When I get off at mid-mountain, the wind is howling. The ferocious wind blows me around like a sailboat on the sea. Visibility is only thirty or forty feet. The snow is half way up to my knees with the consistency of wet cement. Every time that I get up any speed and initiate a turn, the snow trips me and flings me down the mountain.

Suddenly, as I'm blindly skiing forward, I catapult over an unseen ledge, sail a dozen feet and leaning too far forward catch both skies in the snow and pitch forward planting face and chest in an ice encrusted lower ledge, then rocket down the face of the cliff leaving pieces of skiing equipment and clothing strewn across the mountainside. Lying there bleeding from gashes on my forehead and under my left eye, I think that I am having a heart attack. I can't breathe and my chest really hurts, aches. After a couple of minutes lying there clutching my chest, I realize that I'm not going to die. I've just cracked a rib or something like that. The pain is awful and it is still hard to breathe even if I am going to live. Looking back up the mountain at my skis, poles, goggles, gloves, hat, and mask scattered around on the snow, I know why they call crashing a garage sale. It's hard to gather everything and put it back on when you're buried up to the waist in snow and ice on the side of a cliff.

When I get back down to the bottom of the mountain, there is no way that my mind can reason with my body and convince it to go back up on that mountain. There is only one thing to do. Drugs. Drugs are the only way that I am going back up on that mountain.

I go over to the Pinnacle Coffee Shop at the Snow Forever Ski Lodge and order a large mocha with a quadruple shot of coffee and a chocolate chip cookie. Thirty minutes later, I am strong, I am smart, I am a great skier, and I can do this.

Back up the mountain I go. At mid-mountain I get off the ski lift to make a mid-mountain cross over. It is grey. The sky is grey. The ground is grey and everything in between the sky and the ground is grey. I can't see my feet. I can't tell up from down. I don't know whether I'm moving or stopped.

I decide that I must be stopped and I stop in my mind. Unfortunately, my body is going ten or twenty miles per hour. When my mind stops, my body trips and starts rolling around on the hard, frozen, grey ground.

I think, "Oh, I thought the ground was over there, but it is over here."

I get up, brush myself off, and peer about. Off a few feet away, I can see a green trail marker. I realize that it is useless trying to move using my eyes. My eyes are treacherous and they are deceiving me. Not only can they not get a bearing on my whereabouts, or tell me up from down, but every time that they see anything, what they tell me is, "Watch out! Look out for that snow drift. It is going to trip you and throw you over that ledge. Don't go over there. You can't get down there. That's impossible!" My eyes are worse than useless. They are paralyzing me with fear. There is no way to depend on my eyes.

The only way to get around is to move by feelings, feeling my way around by reaching out with my feelings, to completely ignore that snow drift, that drop off, or that rut, or the fact that I can't see any of those things, or anything else, and just intend to move in the direction which I want to go with grace and beauty, and to just flow ahead knowing that anything other than my feelings deceive me. I just need to flow ahead with my feelings with perfect movements despite whatever I'm finding in the terrain, whatever I'm finding on this life path.

As soon as I change my attitude, the obstacles all disappear and what I am doing up here on this mountain all becomes fun. As I glide ahead being guided by my feelings, the sky opens up and I can see a whole path of green trail markers ahead of me. I just float through this white space, not only the white snow covered ground, but the white sky and white everywhere in between out to the edge of a cliff which I recognize.

I can see down the face of the cliff. There is no contrast. I can't really see where my feet are, or if there are any rocks or bumps, but I can see down. I jump over the face gliding, turning, flowing ever downward.

Suddenly the Sun comes out and there is contrast. I can see. I can really see, but it doesn't matter because I am no longer moving by eyesight. I am moving with my feelings and it is all good.

I start to ski like a fourteen year old boy on the first day of Christmas vacation who is showing his buddies that he is made of courage, strength, grace, and beauty. As soon as my attitude changes, as soon as my intentions change, the weather changes and the snow which had previously been an obstacle is now fun and challenging and it is all good and the day is beautiful.

I slide out onto the next drop and drop straight down. The past is gone. The future hasn't arrived. The sky is blue, happy blue, bright blue. I push my left foot. Push hard. Push harder! Yes! Yes! Yes! The razor edge of the fluorescent red Atomic ski catches. The Sun sparkles on the peaks of the Three Angels and slides across Broken Top. The wind drives tiny icicles into my cheeks. From here the white snow covered cliffs drop into the dark pine forests far away on the shoulders of Mount Snow.

The drop is on! Swivel my hips. Shift my weight to the right foot. Rocket over that blind edge. Drop forty feet. Heart in throat. Eyes bulging toward that landing spot. Wait! What landing spot? Where? Swoosh! Swivel! Left blade in the icy white cliff face. Stick it in. Push it in. Drive it in. Lean on that razor, lean hard, lean now. Slide fifty feet in a graceful curve to the right. Swivel on the right foot and plunge straight down.

This is it! This is the moment! This is life, life and maybe death. Bounce! Crunch left. Burst between two dark ancient firs. Slide right. Straighten left. Whoa! That is a lot of snow, for a long ways straight down. Whack! Ohhhh. Was a lot of snow that went by really fast, really really fast. Grab an edge, skid left throwing snow like a snow plow into the forest, swooshing to a stop, and gaze out at the Three Angels. God loves a skier. What other purpose could life have been created for?

I joyfully ski out the rest of the day and then go down to the mighty boisterous Koskimo River where it bursts through an ancient black basalt lava flow. I climb out onto a rock rising above the river rapids between waterfalls and sit down, put the "meditate like a Zen monk' CD in my little CD player, put the headphones on, push play, and there in the midst of the rushing river begin to meditate as the Sun sets over the foaming waterfalls.

All of the little drops of water spirits who have gathered together as this mighty River Spirit carry me away with them in their joyous, lustful rush to the sea, the Cosmic Sea, the All. And as I fly with Spirit, I ask, "Now that we are One, what are we going to do?"

I seem to hear the Spirit respond, "Enjoy ourselves. Enjoy everything. We are going to have fun. We are not going to do anything, or be anything. We are going to enjoy everything. We are not doing anything. We are being everything and enjoying being."

"Okay", I say. "It is my intention to be joyful and happy, living in abundance and beauty."

"Well quit intending! Be joyful, happy, and living in abundance and beauty right now."

"Got it. Get it. See it. Stop doing it. Be it."

"Yes. Be it now. Not do it now."

"I am not doing something so that I will be happy. I am happy. That is enough. That's hard."

"That's easy."

And it is. I have the best time ever sitting there in the middle of the Koskimo River meditating with the River Spirit.

I ski the mountains and hang out downtown with Lilith through the winter. When spring comes I fly to Alaska.

In Alaska, I stand knee deep in the lush green grass of the Katmai Forest and gaze out over the open prairie towards the river a mile away and watch small groups of grizzly bears graze like buffalo. Huge, hairy, brown animals whom I have been told all of my life are ferocious man eaters, are peacefully grazing on tall green grass. Grizzly bears eat grass just like cows and berries and flowers, and bushes most of the year. They don't eat people.

Who knew? Not me. I didn't know that. Here where no hunting is allowed, as I wander amongst them, I realize that they don't consider me as either food or as a dangerous enemy. They treat me like the lone wolves which occasionally wander through the bush country which surrounds us.

As I climb a steep twelve foot high brown dirt river bank climbing up from the grass lands by the river into the low brush, a small 800 pound cute roly poly golden female grizzly runs out of the brush to my right, then slows as she crosses the grass, and starts to graze, oblivious to my presence. I turn and start climbing up the trail again and suddenly come face to face with a 1400 pound monster grizzly. His head is as big as my chest and from here only a few feet away, I can see that his face is covered in ugly black scars earned in many brutal, bloody fights.

"Fights with what, with whom?" I wonder.

I am staring right into his big wide open brown eyes. He is staring into my no doubt wide open blue eyes.

My heart leaps. Time slows. Now is now and nothing else matters. I see the same surprise that I am feeling in his intensely staring big brown eyes, in his frozen stance. Kill or be killed or --- ? What to do?

A moment ago he was chasing that beautiful lady with nothing but lust on his mind and now here is this possibly dangerous white ape right in front of him.

"What to do? What to do?"

All of those bear etiquette lessons flash through my mind. "Don't run. Don't make direct eye contact. Don't surprise a bear. Don't get between a bear and what it wants or loves. Don't. Don't. Don't."

Too late. I stand paralyzed, looking away into the bushes, away from the bear, not thinking, just waiting.

The giant brown hulk with teeth an inch and a half long casually steps off the trail to my left and walks around me without even looking at me and joins the lady of his desires on the grasslands below. He lies down and stretches out on his belly, legs pushed out in front and behind him and admires the lady who casually munches on the grass nearby.

I walk to a nearby log and sit down. I wipe my forehead and think, "The world is way more strange and wonderful and safe than I have ever imagined."

I photograph them cavorting in the green grass in the great Alaskan wilderness.

In this spirit of joy and wonder at a world which I have never ever even imagined, I fly to Chile in southern South America and start climbing through the Andes.

I hike the Circuito Grande and climb the Towers of Payne. I am carrying a fifty pound back pack through miles of steep treacherous mountains eight hours a day. Thirty five pounds is a full load for a man. I am carrying not only my camping and climbing gear, but I am also carrying my traveling clothes and supplies and my lap top computer and my photography equipment. I am carrying all of this, over fifty pounds and running joyously through every day.

For me language has become such a weak form of communication. The wild essence of creation, of being alive which I am experiencing is just so grand, so awesome. If I were to take our whole language, put it in a shot gun shell, load it in a 12 gauge shot gun and blast it into my forehead, into my mind, our whole language, every word would only be a very a minuscule BB, that held only the tiniest fraction of what is, or could be, or has been, or isn't, or can't be, or has never been. I wouldn't even notice.

As I stand out here in the wilds of the Southern Andes, my soul fills and expands, soaring like a giant, colorful hot air balloon. As I gaze out over the vast plains at the massive mountains with their jutting rock spires so steep that even snow doesn't cling to them, as the clouds skitter across grey glacier fed lakes, my voice fails my soaring heart. I stand in the awesome silence listening as the wind whispers, murmurs, mumbles, shouts, and sometimes roars loud enough to knock me on the ground and roll me around, and that is a very serious matter when the narrow foot path which I am standing on clings to a cliff that plunges a thousand feet straight down into a huge, deep, freezing cold lake with rushing treacherous currents. These Antarctic ice sheet lakes are not the placid calm lakes of California or Michigan. As I gaze downward from my rocky perch, I can see giant swirling whirlpools and trees rushing by.

And as I wander, in between conversations with the wind, I have discussions with babbling brooks, rushing river torrents, and roaring cataracts. This landscape has attitude, personality. Sometimes it is unbearably cute. Sometimes it is brutal, but always it bewitches, surprises, and amazes.

There is no direction that I can look but that I stare in awe and wonder: forests of both small and mighty twisted lenga trees like evergreen oak trees with small leaves, acres of colorful flowers, flocks of bizarre birds, big fuzzy fluorescent orange bumble bees against yellow dandelions, and always the mighty soaring massive peaks. It is just hard to believe that this is the same planet, the same world that we normally inhabit daily. It is just so much more wonderful, so magical, so awesome.

It is like a slap in the face saying, "Wake up! Be amazed! Be here now in this moment. Enjoy life. To be alive here now is a wonderful gift. Enjoy it."

Then I see the ice field. Nothing else matters. It stands as tall as the mountains and it isn't all jaggedy and up and down. It is a massive sheet of white that eats mountains. It is the skyline. Mountains that seemed huge only minutes ago now are being devoured by an ocean of ice at least 5000 feet tall and I don't even know where the bottom of that mighty sea lies. The ice field dominates everything. Bits of once mighty mountains stick out of it. The icy surface is ragged and torn with bright fluorescent blue crevasses as it flows toward me across the flat green plains. This is how it must have been during the ice ages.

The ice field never stays the same. One moment it is calm, clear, bathed in a bright, hot sun. Then fog flits across it and rises forming a cloud. Wind gusts away from the frigid cold flinging rain and snow ahead of it, but not before flashing a beautiful rainbow that coats the jagged peaks like a gaudy aurora borealis. Then the searing sun comes back only to be blotted out by rushing dark grey clouds. Nothing is static. Nothing stays the same, but it is all wonderful.

As I look at all of this beauty and wonder, I think of Oregon. And I think, "I have come 3,000 miles to this wonderful place which reminds me of the rivers and mountains of Oregon. I am going home. I live in a wonderful place."

CHAPTER 9

OPENING THE COFFIN

Returning home, I decide to go see Gabriel again.

I pick up a phone and call him greeting him with a friendly, "Hi Gabriel, I have had the most amazing and beautiful experiences. We must get together and share."

"It's good to hear your voice Shane," he answers. "Yes, we really must get together again right away. Can you come over at tea time today?"

"Absolutely. I'll be there. Bye," and I hang up the telephone.

In the afternoon, I drive over to Gabriel's tiny warm and mysterious office. He greets me at the door with a welcoming hug.

I blurt out, "I am so happy to see you. I'm always thrilled to see you."

We enter his office. He has green tea and dehydrated flax crackers laid out a black lacquer tray which is painted with a colorful Chinese mountain scene lying on his desk. We take our accustomed chairs. He pours a cup of tea for each of us in blue and white porcelain cups with dragons flying around on the sides of them.

I say to him, "You know Gabriel, I'm feeling so differently. There is so much that I don't understand. Eating differently has really improved my physical strength and appearance and changed the way that I think, that I view my life and my friends. Shoot! I even feel different about the whole planet. After I went through that healing crises where you did that bio-terrain altering thing and changed my frequencies, something really shifted in me. I just don't think or want the same things anymore. I don't enjoy watching TV or reading the news anymore. I like to spend my time hiking in the wilderness and reading books about mysterious places and wonderful men and women and their amazing ideas. I have lots of new friends and there are all kinds of expos and conferences that I am going to attend."

"I want to get started on some new ventures. I want to live life differently. I'm starting to wonder about things, things that didn't used to interest me, such as, what is the importance of dreaming to me, as Shane Parker? What are dreams? Where should I start?"

He pauses beaming at me as if I am the returning prodigal son, then says, "Shane, I can't explain with words how to get from here to where we are going. I cannot describe the nature of the infinite with the words and thoughts of the finite. I cannot measure the eternal with the temporal tools. I cannot describe the absolute from the relative. We can only experience a knowing of the absolute of the infinite. That knowing is not within your memory of this experience yet."

The clock downtown begins to toll the time in that annoying modern synthetic bell chiming, "Biing, biing, biing."

"Gabriel, when you talk like that, I remember that most of the time, I am scared and confused. I don't know what to do. What should I do? And tell to me in plain English. Don't frighten me or confuse me."

Concern floats across his face. He takes a sip of tea.

"Shane, you are like a beautiful ship which is caught in a mighty storm, lost in an unexplored, unknown sea. You are being driven onto a cruel rocky shore. Suffering and death are certain. But at the last moment a miraculous wind catches you up and you soar over the deadly cliffs of peril and you land in a calm cove beyond the dark and threatening headland. That wind, that unimaginably powerful and loving wind is unexplainable, but here you are, still alive, safely floating in a wondrous new place. I am explaining that leap. We are making that leap, but that leap is not explainable with your current understanding. You are left wondering, a loving hurricane force wind? What? How? Where did it come from? Why? How does one explain the unexperienced to the someone who is inexperienced? How does one get the unexperiencer to experience the unexperienced? If the situation is way outside of one's experience, how can one understand what is happening? How can one even imagine it? How does one imagine the unimaginable? Why would anyone ever leave the known for the unknown, the safe and secure for an uncertain future? The unimaginable is not within your experience. So, I am providing a pathway for you to follow. I am giving you a way to experience knowing the All."

"Stop! Gabriel, please just stop. You are confusing and frightening me. I have changed my mind. What was I thinking? Leave me alone. I don't have time for this. I have to get a real job and get serious about my life. I don't want to end up living under a bridge somewhere or even worse insane and suicidal. I have important things to do. I know up from down, but when you talk, I start getting confused and upset and I'm not sure what is up and what is down anymore. I can't waste any more of my time on weird confusing stupid mumbo jumbo. Besides, I'm tired. When I get some time and money, I'll come back and we can continue this philosophical discussion, but I don't think that any of this is of any use to me now. I don't really want to change."

I stand up and put my teacup down.

Gabriel stands up and puts a hand on my forearm.

"Shane, please wait. Will you give me just another moment of your time before you leave? It saddens me to hurt and confuse you. I truly care about you and want you to be safe, enlightened, and happy. Please forgive any opinions which I have that offend you and just share with me what you don't understand or what you disagree with. My thoughts are only my opinions and I could be completely misguided and I will be eternally grateful if you can correct any misconceptions or misunderstandings that I labor under. Every word which you speak is precious to me. Before you go, allow me to answer your question about dreams. This is not what dreams really are, but for you, you might as well think of them as fantasies, so that you don't get confused by your intentions. Your intentions are important, but we don't want to get your intentions and the Multiverses' intentions confused. I know that this is confusing to even say, because your intentions and this Universe's intentions are the same thing, but it's hard for you to understand this because sometimes you intend things to happen and they don't happen as you think that you intended them to happen and then your confusion makes it seem to you that your intentions and the Universe's intentions run counter to each other. Then you are disappointed and depressed. You believe that you have no control over events and no importance to anyone or anything. You are in a random cruel Universe in which everything is happening to you. You come to the conclusion that you are unimportant, that you can't make things happen. You start to believe that things just happen to you. You believe that God isn't on your side and that He is punishing you. Or the opposite happens, you intend something to happen and it happens just as you intended, then you are off on a bunch of new power dramas. You think of yourself as incredibly powerful and the center of everything important. You become lost acting out dramas of self-importance."

"I don't want you to get lost in either of these scenarios. The second alternative is closer to the truth. Life is not something that happens to you. You are something that happens to life and what happens matters. It's hard to communicate with you in a big picture sense to help you see the nature of, I was going to say, what's happening, but actually there is nothing happening. Our situation is hard to explain within a syntax, a language that you will understand. Here is the thing. If you think of dreams as being real, something more than just fantasies of your imagination, if you believe that they are occurring in actual places with purpose and meaning, then you will start indulging in dream psycho dramas. In other words, you will start trying to influence dream reality and then you will start trying to use dream reality to influence waking reality. That is the nature of your human personality, your ego, of who you imagine that you are. It isn't that dreams are or aren't real and that they can or cannot be influenced and that if they are or aren't influenced that this may or may not influence the waking world. It's just that all of that is another dead end. There are a lot of ways in which you can pass

89

your time here in this place. There are a lot of ways in which you can satisfy your perceived needs in this here and now. There are a lot of ways in which you can answer the questions of who you are, and why you are, and what is happening, and what you should do. But here time has a use, a purpose, and you are continuously using up time. During this conversation time is passing. More time just passed. You used that time to be confused and fearful when you could have used it to be happy and in wonder or you could have used it to do a thousand thousand other things and to be a thousand thousand other ways. But when I said dead end, I meant to emphasize the word dead. We must carefully consider what we are doing. Everything which we know and love, is passing away as we speak, getting nearer and nearer to their death."

I am sitting in a wooden chair across from Gabriel. He is sitting behind his desk in his high backed dragon throne chair. As he speaks, I am watching him, but in the corner of the ceiling above him on his right side, there is a spider web. The web is shaking and vibrating. A fly has flown into it and is stuck. The fly is violently struggling to free itself. It pushes with its legs and swivels its head shaking the web. Then it buzzes its wings vibrating the web. The more that the fly struggles, the more desperate its situation becomes and the more certain its death is.

I look back at Gabriel. He is saying, "So, although there is no time, there is time, and you need to be ---. No, you don't need to be anything. Let me say this differently. Everything that you can be, or do, is just being or doing that thing. And being and doing takes up all of your time. You don't have unlimited time in that body. So, the Divine Wind hasn't let you succeed, you haven't let yourself succeed, or else you wouldn't do what it is the Wind's intention that you do with that body. If you were to succeed in playing a particular role such as a lawyer, fireman, or politician, you would think of yourself as that person, a fireman in the sixth brigade, the President of the United States, an important man with big responsibilities. You would not seek any understanding outside of your perceived and understood role. Why would you? You would already believe that you know who and what you are. The Wind's intention, your intention, is that you stop being and doing, and start seeing and enjoying. The Divine Wind does the being and doing. All that you have to do is to stop your being and doing and to allow it to do the being and doing. I know that it is really hard for you to have trust, and to cease being and doing, because it would appear that you are giving up all control when you do that, and that nothing is going to get done, and that bad things are going to happen if you don't get things done. Bills aren't going to get paid. After all, where are you going to get food, clothes, and shelter, and how is your family going to get taken care of, if you don't take charge and act? One can go on and on and on spinning off these dramas. Think about it for a minute. That is what's happening. Let's not go there. Let's go somewhere else."

"You keep getting more and more information, more and more knowledge. Any piece of this knowledge is astounding to you and it is astounding to the people around you. It keeps opening doors to possibilities and options that no one thought were possible and this knowledge makes people's lives more interesting and better. Wait, rather, this knowledge could make peoples' lives better. Knowledge doesn't necessarily improve lives. Improvement depends on the response of the people to the information, but that doesn't stop the information from being fascinating or powerful. Let's say that you discover a new theory. For example, for a long time it would appear that many people thought that the world was flat and then someone showed them that the world is round. The world understanding is now more, oh, I was going to say is more in tune with what is real, but that is not really true. It is just more in tune with the new understanding, and the new understanding seems to create a new life that is better, that is more in tune with what is real. Then people go off for a thousand years, or for two thousand years, or for ten thousand years on a round earth theory and their lives are enriched and made more interesting and entertaining. But the round earth theory is just another theory that is no more real, well maybe it is more realistic than the flat earth theory, but neither theory really has much to do with what is really happening here. Of course, there is no here. I am trying ----. We are trapped in our dialogue because the language that we are communicating in is limited to what people believe and this limits our thoughts. We are limited even by communicating in a language. Language itself is a strange small box. We are restricted in our comprehension of each other and of our situation by the communication techniques which we are using."

"Anyway, my point is, a new theory just creates a new drama. In a world of change, each idea is relative and subject to change. So, here a fact is only relatively true. It may be true today, but tomorrow, who knows. You have to give up on all of the dramas, the dreams, and the theories. You have to let them go. That may seem to you, and to everyone around you, that you are really a failure, but what you are gaining is your freedom to see."

"Each action is an invitation to participate in a drama and each drama is a wonderful joyous experience. It could be an experience of terrible suffering, but none the less, it is a drama of experiencing the Divine Myself, yourself, creation. What we are talking about here is standing at the center of creation and seeing and of being the drama and not being the drama. It is just the drama. It is just a play. Stand at the center of the stage. Stand at the center and be not, to be all"

I am watching the fly bounce up and down on the web. I wonder what I am going to do for dinner tonight? What is Gabriel saying? His theories bore me. He sure talks a lot about nothing important. That blue symbol on his shirt changes shape as he breathes. It kind of does a kaleidoscope thing. I wish that he would talk louder. I can't seem to hear what he is saying.

"You have to learn the art of being actively passive, passively active. You have been taught that you have to actively take charge. You have been told that you need to think about things and that you need to get things done. You believe that if you don't do it, it is not going to get done. And now lately, you have learned about intentions, that you need to intend it for it to happen, that your intentions make it happen. Everyone is watching the movie, 'The Top Secret' which teaches that to get something to happen, you must focus your intention on getting that thing to happen. While it is true that your intentions and your attitude and your desires are important on this level, it is time for you to move beyond that understanding."

What is he saying? This is ridiculous. I am not going to let this New Age acupuncturist push me around.

"Gabriel, I'm not sure what you mean by, I have to move beyond my intentions, beyond my desires. What are we, if we are not our intentions and our desires?"

He leans into me, locks eyes, and nearly gleefully shouts, "Yes, precisely, that is the point! What are you if you have no intentions or desires? And, secondly, what would happen to you and to your loved ones, if you had no intentions or desires? That is exactly the point that we are trying to get to, to make that step. That is where we want to move to next. So you need to step up to that state of consciousness and to do that. Let's do that! That's where we're at."

Damn. He's got me interested. I look up at the weakening efforts of the fly and ask, "Alright, how? What's the technique for getting to this joyful state of being? Am I going to use William Horden's stop thought technique? This is a pretty frightening thing to me. You know, I've got credit card bills. I've got problems. I've got people relying on me. I have to be realistic. I just can't see how to do what you're suggesting. What's the? How? Yeah, how, what? How does one do no desires, no intentions, and yet exist, live? And not create tremendous harm? I'm just not getting this. There are some subtleties here that I am missing."

Quickly standing, he glides around the desk and is suddenly beside me in one fluid action.

"Yes, that's the whole point. You are missing the whole point. That's the point. That's the subtlety. You are now going off into indulging in another drama, another anxiety, another fear. You've just taken this whole thing and spun it off into another drama."

He raises both hands palms towards me and demands, "Stop it!"

"Okay," I lean back and agree, "that is fine while I am sitting here in your office. I can imagine ceasing all action. But how does one do all that while being active? How is there no action, action? In other words, when tomorrow comes, it would seem like I have to act. I am under a compulsion to act. I know that I have to act. And yet how do I not act, act? I mean, that's it. I was going to try to define that aim. But how do I, how do I pay the bills? Of course, you are saying that, that is just another drama, and that, that drama is taken care of. And now I am worrying about another drama that is underneath that drama, but the drama that is underneath that drama is another non-drama too. This is getting very confusing. But, look, let's just focus on active non-action."

He sits back onto the edge of his desk, smiles, clasps his hands together chest high as if he is praying, leans his head slightly forward, closes his eyes momentarily, then opens them, looks at me and says with complete certainty, "There is no credit card debt. What you have done is create an energy deficit."

I rock back away from him. He is mad. He is hallucinating. I am shocked. "No credit card debt? I have the bills to prove that I'm in debt. What in the world is an energy deficit? How do I create, or how do I be an energy asset, an energy surplus?" I ask.

Smiling as if he is playing black jack and he just told the dealer to hit him while standing on sixteen and he just drew a five, he answers, "With love and joy. Get out there and be generous and be giving and loving."

This doesn't seem like much of an answer to me. It seems a bit obscure. Generous to whom? Generous with what? What should I do share my bills around? Then the idea hits me like a shark coming up fast out of deep water.

I jump up and shout, "No way! That is how I got into this trouble to begin with. That is the role of the deluded spendthrift, the out of touch with reality fool. I don't know about this energy deficit thing, but I do know that, acting like that, is going to max out the credit cards and get me in deep, deep trouble."

"That is a perfect example of what we are talking about," Gabriel snorts as he leans into me. "You have just spun off into fear and anxiety. You have just contracted. You have sucked back in. You are sucking energy. You are creating an energy deficit by your current action. You just did it. Perfect example. Stop it. Be the opposite, expand. Expand! Create an energy surplus. Right now, create a loving and generous thought, a loving and generous action."

"Man, I can't." I fall back in my chair and look up past Gabriel at the fly now tightly caught in the web. "I'm scared. I'm boxed in. I'm afraid of failure."

"Yes, I know. That is why this is the perfect opportunity, the perfect moment. Transcend! Transcend now! Break the bonds! See!"

"I just don't understand. If I don't go make this money, and if I don't pay those bills, how are they going to get paid?"

"Well, your problem is more basic than you're seeing because there are no bills. You are just off again into one of those worlds and dramas. That is what we are trying to help you understand."

"What am I, Shane Parker, responsible for? What am I in charge of doing?" I ask, tired and hopeless.

"You are responsible for ----, well, nothing really. What you are to do is to perceive and to enjoy. As far as those words responsible and in charge of, you aren't even responsible for your next breath. You aren't even aware of it and yet you get it. So, enjoy it. Focus on your breathing. Who is responsible for your next breath? Who is in charge of your next breath? If you don't get your next breath, how are you going to feel? If you don't get the next five breaths, how are you going to feel? And then if you get the sixth one, how are you going to feel? Now just work that out through water, food, friends, a place to live, and credit card bills. Think about it."

"Energy is the substance of creation. If you want to move to a better understanding than you have, then you have to focus on ----, well, you don't have to focus on anything, but it might be more pleasant for you when you understand energy, more than if you were to understand time and space. Energy and mind, consciousness, that is what shapes time and space. Time and space is the illusion. So are mind and energy, but mind and energy are a more basic underlying power than time and space. They are a more basic psycho-drama, if you will. Because you are so confused by time and space, it would be better if you thought about energy and mind, and see how they influence time and space, or rather how they create time and space."

To me that sounds loony. This is like walking through walls weirdness. But rather than saying, "Gabriel, you're a loon."

I resignedly say, "Well, I don't see how that is going to help me pay the credit card bills."

"I know," he says as if he really does know and sadly knows much more too. "That is the point. You are looking at credit card bills. You are not looking at energy deficits. So you are not going to get the credit card bills paid because you do not see what credit card bills actually are. That's what I'm trying to help you see. You need to look at your problems differently. You need to look at them on the energetic level."

Suddenly it all clicks into place.

"I think that I get it," I say. "You can be a master of breathing like those Hindu yogis by not mastering it at all. Those beings who have mastered the art of breathing, those beings whom we can call master breathers, what they know and do, is to allow themselves to breathe. All that the master breather is doing is joyously allowing himself to breathe. As for the next breath, he can control the next breath. He can study the next breath. He can do breathing in a multitude of ways and he can perceive breathing in a multitude of ways and all of those things are good things to do, so that he can understand more about breathing, more about living, but in the end, all that he does is take the next breath, accept the next breath. The master breather doesn't even think about any of that. He is a master. It is just the next breath. All that he can do is breathe and enjoy it. And that is the same with any activity. All that you can do is accept it and enjoy it. You actively do it. You passively accept doing it. And you perceptively enjoy doing it. Although you are the doer, you are not the master in the sense of being the creator and the controller, but at the same time the doer, the creator, and the master are all one, just not the same."

"Okay, so, how do I put this into practice. I mean obviously we don't put anything into practice. You know what I mean."

"No, I don't know what you mean. Don't worry about those credit cards."

"Okay."

"You've got other dramas. Move on. Enjoy. Envision a new world, a world in which you want to live. Do not look at that which troubles you. Look at that which excites you and calls you to happiness. Then a beautiful life will magically be. Magic is done like this: conceptualize, visualize, ritualize, realize."

I am dazed and confused, but hopeful and something seems to make sense, but I can't quite remember what that something is. I am going to think more about this breathing business.

I stand up and hug Gabriel. He hugs me back. I step back and we touch fists.

"Thanks Gabriel."

"It's all good Shane. All hipikats flow in the cool. Absolute zero. Absolute zero man."

CHAPTER 10

MAGICAL MYSTERY TOUR

I leave Gabriel's office wondering, "What should I do? Where should I go?"

I am thinking, "I need to get out in nature. I need to get some space and some peace around me."

My head is whirling with this new world view, these questions. I get in a pickup truck and head for the high desert. I see everything differently now. I think differently now. I feel differently now. Strange words, strange ideas drift across my awareness. Where do they come from?

In the evening of the first day, I stand on the rim of deep, mysterious Crater Lake and watch a golden sun sink into an orange glowing horizon. Then a few hours later the silver moon rises over the black shadow rim rocks casting a sparkling white trail which dances on waves across the fathoms of deep black, black waters. It is sublime.

In the morning, on a raw cacao cloud, I drift downward with the Beatles' "Magical Mystery Tour" blasting me across the Klamath Lake of blue green algae bliss fame and on through Chiloquin, Indian Country, Squaw Flats, Kia Ma Ya, drifting further along the bright yellow orange fall colors cloaked Sprague River.

There are those lyrics again. "I am he as you are he as you are me, and we are all together."

Chubby little chipmunks, gentle brown eyed doe, sharp beaked hawk seeking, seeking.

Oh, no! It's hunting season. Word has come down from the Serpent King's authorities. Blessed are those who slaughter the deer, the bear, the cougar, all of those beings who do not respect the barbed wire fence. Wild eyed killer white apes are everywhere looking behind every tree, every bush, everywhere, roaming about in big pickup trucks and little four wheeler ATV's. In the distance whump, whump, boom, then frenzied chattering by the nearby killer apes. Time to move further into the wilderness beyond electricity, beyond noisy machines, beyond roads. Peace. Where is peace?

Up. Up. Up into the snow amongst the great sugar pines with the flickers flashing their florescent orange wings as they fly in their peculiar bouncing flight from tree to tree. At night I sit alone watching the fire as the Weezils and Kafeedlers, and the Lumpidos and the Cadeedleehops dance on the snow in the shadows around the fire.

Onward out of the trees to where the sage brush plains stretch from horizon to horizon. Finally a sign from God or the American Government Forest Service: "Unload and dismantle firearms before proceeding". I am in Heaven. A hundred pronghorn antelope nervously dance across a sage brush covered ridge to the west. Their rumps flashing white with every hop.

Now I stop, strip naked and baptize my body in a holy hot spring before making the final desert ascent. I climb out of the hot spring clean and hot. I dress warm, but prepare to travel fast and light. I eat a hand full of raw cacao beans and a hand full of goji berries. I start to climb through the lava rocks, dry brown grass, sage brush, and snow. I cross the first ridge and look to the next with its rocky cliffs and juniper ridge line. The peak is always like a mirage leading higher and higher, ridge upon ridge. Finally through the great canyons, a vast high mountain valley begins to appear on the other side of these mountains. I am near the peak.

Then, what is that on the furtherest ridge to the west? A man? No, it is bigger than a man. It is a strange ominous foreboding figure standing there on the peak all alone. Who or what can it be? Always watching it, I climb higher and higher. It never moves. Is it watching me?

After crossing the next ravine and trekking along the jagged black basalt cliffs, through the snow drifts in the mountain top whistling winds, there it is, ancient phallus, Paleolithic sky hook, an old, old lichen covered cylinder of rocks three feet wide stacked at least ten feet high, high over my head, higher than I can reach. Who built this monument? Why did they build it? How did they build it, here where a body can go no higher? From here one must travel on wings of vision. I fall to the ground at the base of this monolith in lotus and launch into the eleven dimensions of interstellar space.

Later, darkness is descending in the valley and to be caught up here in the dark would be harsh. I sadly leave the mountain top and the ancient ones.

Up at dawn, I head south across the desert. Herds of mule deer and antelope stare with curiosity as I pass. Hour after hour I push south across the desolate high desert mesas, then thrillingly plunge through desert swamps hoping that there is a bottom somewhere in these murky waters, then onward across giant dry Paleolithic lakes where ancient peoples lived at the base of the black cliffs where creeks flowed into the ancestral lakes. On and on, hour after hour after hour. No one as far as I can see in any direction. Finally late in the afternoon, after descending a boulder strewn draw there at the head of a dry lake that stretches as a grassland to the horizon to the east is a deserted old cattle ranch house with out buildings and a collapsing water tower, windows broken, gate open. Deserted, silent, lonely, grey and lost in another time, in another place. Haunted, I hurry on. Still it is another hour of steady moving down the dry shores of Guano Lake before I see pavement. Eight hours of steady driving without seeing another human or human artifacts other than this road, a road that is really just a trail, hours of bashing across boulder strewn benches and sliding down water washed ravines, more creek bed than road bed. For company I have earth spirits, falcons and large desert hawks, deer and antelope, and the lone wary coyote big as a wolf there and then not there. A lot of open country. I am exhausted. I was worried at times that I could have gone wrong somewhere, gotten lost out there, but it is all good, and as always I turned the right way at each turn. Once in doubt, I stopped and scouted the tracks in different directions, checked in with the gut, and then moved ahead, and here I am at the pavement with just enough gas to get to Longview, fifty miles to the west. Yahoo!!!

In the morning standing again on the east rim of Crater Lake as the sun rises lighting the vermilion cliffs which reflect purples and pinks into the deep blue waters, I realize why I now wander alone in the wild places. In the wilderness, alone, one gains a deep sense of the sacred. One wanders in the wild places to know the Holy Earth. One wanders Mother Earth's breast to be a holy man full of wonder and full of the joy of being, to be astounded by every sunrise.

Now I descend back into the valley, back to Northwood, my home. I have a wedding to attend.

CHAPTER 11

THE VISION

After the wonderful wedding at the Hilltop Vineyard in Garden Valley, early the next morning, I go to Gabriel's to share my new found vision with him.

We are sitting comfortably in his office drinking Chinese red ginseng and ho shu wu tea with a heaping teaspoon full of five to one Siberian ginseng concentrate, a genuinely powerful and stimulating elixir. Gabriel and the plants lean into our conversation.

I begin, "My concept is to create a better way of living by speaking a truth so great that it is immediately recognizable by all beings, a truth that is so wonderful that everyone knows in their heart that their life is going to only get better and better when they act in accordance with this truth.

"I see a new world being born. The ritual is living the new truth. And because multitudes of people accept and be that truth, suddenly there is a tear in the shared idea of what is happening. It looks like a tear in a movie screen. It breaks the illusion momentarily. Belief is suspended. For a moment, the tear is a black gash. Then light streams through and it is magical light. It is a creative wave of blazing living light. Wherever it shines, grass grows, flowers bloom, trees begin to tower, birds appear, animals wander, variety, happiness, and beauty burst forth; and the poisoned battered landscape recedes. The Darkness is not destroyed. It retreats to the high places where it broods and waits. All of life honors and respects the dark side, but stays on the bright, creative, joyous side of being. Balance is restored."

"This vision is very important. Energy flows where attention goes. So, we need a complete vision to focus our attention, a vision that lets everyone know where we are going and one that assures everyone that when we get there, it is going to be the best place ever to be. We will be more happy, secure, loved, and respected than we have ever even imagined that we could ever be. Once everyone sees the vision and everyone commits their heart to it, then all of the energy needed to make it happen flows into it, and it is. But first we need a vision, a complete, all encompassing, believable vision. We need a vision which is a rune, a mantra that we can sing into being. So here we go."

"We are not going to live in a world controlled by a centralized top down bureaucracy with all of the wealth and power in the hands of a few. The new world is going to flow in a decentralized system of prosperous crafts people who live in a clean, beautiful, peaceful environment which is full of trusting, loving, healthy plants and animals and people. All of whom are coexisting in a joyful dance of creative well being and happiness with mutual respect and love."

"I am envisioning the new world now. I see a world of harmony, cooperation, love, peace, beauty, diversity, incredible diversity: cultural, artistic, species, plants, animals, humans, clothing, behavior. It's a world in which it is okay to be different. In fact being unique in a positive, humorous way is not only accepted, it's expected and rewarded. People recognize that by exploring different avenues of being our life experience is enriched and that is what life is meant to be, a rich joyous happening. Life is about exploring different expressions of creation and reflecting those experiences back to the Creator. Each life is unique, diverse, and beautiful."

"What can I say? It's the exact opposite of a totalitarian army where everybody is in the same drab uniform, marching with one master's mind, a master who sees himself as separate from the rest of creation and superior to everyone and everything else with a God given mandate for complete dominion over all other beings and things. This new world of the vision is a community of individuals who are united by the awareness that what happens to one, happens to everyone. Everyone shares a realization that everything is alive, everything is spirit, and everything is connected. What you do to another, you do to yourself. This means that anything that you do to anything, anywhere, anytime, you do to yourself. This realization creates a community of persons who are expressing their joy and creativity and love for each other in a creative cornucopia and this is not only a community of humans who have become fairies and elves, but it is also a community of deer and raccoons and asparagus and roses and trees, oaks, figs, vines and rocks. It is also a community of mountains and rivers."

"Yes. I see it clearly now. The rivers are bubbling and singing and rushing through mountains which are filled with joyous beings who are all singing and smiling and creating all of this wealth that is just pouring out of their happiness and joy and these riches are being consumed by everything around them and all of this wonder and mystery is then creating more wealth and joy, spiraling to ever higher levels of ecstasy and abundance. Looking at this scene is like gazing at the most incredible moving tapestry of colors and activities ever created. Everything and everyone is having the absolute best time ever. The whole picture radiates joy and happiness in the most incredible ways. I am looking at it, at the diversity and unique colors and beings, but what I am also noticing is that the whole thing is sparkling, emanating, vibrating. It is buzzing, humming with joy and happiness and prosperity and life, incredibly beautiful life. It is the most luscious garden imaginable. Everything in it is pressing to express its joy and uniqueness. There is fruit and lusciousness abounding everywhere and it's clean."

"This place is really clean. The air is clean. The water is clean. You can see into the water. You can look twenty feet straight down into the water and see pebbles and see that the water is running. The water is crystal magic, liquid magic! It is alive and singing. I am thinking back to the sluggish old water on the Earth that we know. It is sick. It has lost its life force. Not only is it full of garbage. It isn't lively. This water in the vision is alive.

This water talks to you. You can hear it. It is like listening to the wind in the trees in the vision. Unlike the wind on the old Earth, in this new wind you can hear the trees singing and talking to each other. This is the way that water is meant to be. In fact, now that I am looking around in this vision, everything is singing and dancing. It's not moving at our human pace, but it is alive. There is a vibrancy to the landscape. It is alive and enjoying being with the beings that are moving more quickly. You can see that the mountains are thinking that the quick beings are frivolous."

"The mountains are saying, 'Look at them. Aren't they amusing? See the show. Look at the trees grow up the hill over there and recede over here and look at the colorful little village over there. How amusing."

"The mountains are crystal intelligence. They are alive. I don't know what they are but they are alive. There is no doubt about it. It's a very deep, very ancient, and very patient form of being, but it's definitely conscious and alive. Mountains of patient wisdom, what can I say? Everything is alive and connected."

"I realize that the old landscape which we live in now seems almost drugged. Maybe it is drugged. Maybe all of the chemicals, poisons, and toxins and all of the mean, greedy, violent thoughts that have been and are being poured on it actually make it sick and dying. Yes, it is sick and dying. These giant mountains and vast oceans that are our home are dying. The planet is dying. Its alive and you can make it sick and sad. It can be an ugly dirty show. It is an ugly dirty show."

"In the vision the mountains are lamenting, 'How long do we have to sit here and watch this? How long will it take to clean up this mess?"

The clouds outside of Gabriel's office part and a sun beam shines through the high window behind Gabriel. The sun shines through the crystals standing on the window sill casting dancing rainbows along the walls. I shake my head and clear the mournful mountains from my mind.

"Oh well, that is not the way it is going to be. Happy and clean, that is the way that I see it, happy and clean." I continue, "The ideal which I envision is a tribal community, a very large tribe. A community of all ages, races, and species living together in a pastoral setting where everybody is happy and healthy. There doesn't seem to be many things like cars, or trucks, or electronic stuff like TV's , neon lights, or signs in the vision. People seem to be walking around talking to each other and visiting and gardening. One doesn't see any police, or army types walking around. People are dressed in colorful clothes that mimic the paradise like nature of their surroundings. There are no freeways or big airports. There is technology, but one doesn't see much of it. The energy source is not oil based. People are telepathic and they are able to move their awareness, their bodies, and objects such as produce about by some means which are not visible to me. There are a type of anti-gravity hovercraft machine which they seem to enjoy using in various ways. These devices float and zip about wherever the operator wills pulling or carrying whatever they please. It would appear that people are mostly vegetarian. One doesn't see any feedlots or that type of farming operation. The churches are different. They don't teach doctrine. They are sharing/caring centers. There are mystery based spiritual centers where ceremonies are performed and people share their vision of life and its meaning and possibilities. The houses are wooden, rock, and some kind of turf or wattle. They are brown and very natural looking with some gingerbread and painted trim and decorations. They remind me of a combination of Swiss chalet and Hobbit burrow. They are clean with wood accents but mostly tile interiors. They are warm in the winter and cool in the summer. There are lights and hot and cold running water and modern types of appliances like refrigerators and dish washers."

"Life is good, very good."

Gabriel has been listening intently to me nodding in agreement.

"I like your vision Shane," he says. "It is a beautiful utopian vision, but how do we get from here to there? In the here and now we are dealing with real humans with real problems. Some of these people are pretty unpleasant. How are the governments and the schools going to operate? How are the governments and the schools and the businesses going to evolve from one way of operating to another?"

I contemplate his question for a moment as I take another sip of tea and a bite from a piece of a dried fruit rollup. The tea is starting to kick in. I am feeling great.

"Well, let's use your example of food to explore this process. Food is key to the vision," I reply. "Why do we eat? What is food? The obvious answer would seem to be that food is what we need to live. Asking that question is like asking why do we breathe? Because, if we don't, then we die, right? Maybe not!"

"What is going on Here? What we seem to be doing when we eat or breathe is taking in a form of energy that is needed to maintain our physical body. When I look at the menu at the MacDairyKing, I now realize that most of what I would take in if I eat the food on that menu is not benefiting me as much as I hoped. I realize that what we are calling food is not energizing, is not consciousness building, and is not what we should be taking into our beings to energize us, to make us happier, healthier, more beautiful people."

Gabriel is sitting behind his desk with his hands held together in front of him chest high forming the steeple in a prayer mudra. He is slowly nodding yes in agreement and smiling.

I continue, "You have convinced me that food, air, and water are the most basic ways in which we are interrelating to this World. It is with food, air, and water that the vision must begin. I believe that it is when we separate ourselves from something called food, something that must suffer and die so that we can live, that we kill the new vision and maintain the old paradigm. We become the subject, the center of the story, and the food becomes just an object in the story. The food is only important in that it serves the pleasure of the subject of the story, the eater. Well in the vision, we are all subjects. There are no more objects. There are just standing room only subjects. Everybody treats everybody else as they want to be treated themselves. Every cow is an infinitely important being of light and beauty. Every deer is a friend to be cherished, adored, and loved. Every pig is a manifestation of the Divine capable of shining a complete understanding of everything that is, and that is not, into our being and of blessing us with total bliss and joy. It is unthinkable that we should tear anyone out of their home, take them away from their loved ones, chop them into pieces, fry them in hot oil, and then devour them. What are we doing? Is there not a better way to be? Is there not a way to connect directly to the creative energy that manifests these beings and get our energy pure from the source? Where did this whole idea of 'food' come from? Where did his whole idea come from that we are beings who must consume each other to live?"

"Good question, Shane. You must have given it a lot of thought if you are asking the question. What is the answer?"

"I don't know, but certainly, there is a better way to live than the one that is represented by that menu at MacDairyKing's. That menu doesn't give life. It gives death. We can certainly come up with a better vision of life than the one that we are currently living, a much better one. We need a definition of food. We need to understand what we are doing when we are eating. We need to understand life and our connection to life before we can talk about how to live. Discussions about money, working, governing, distributing, and housing will fall into place with a new understanding of eating and breathing and being, with a new understanding of who and what we are. We need to recognize that our lives are all interconnected, and that the misery or happiness that we create in others, we create in our own lives. Do you have any ideas on how to start this process?" I ask.

Gabriel vigorously responds, "Great! Sure. Yes, I do. You have already danced around the solution. Institutions mimic the hearts of the people. As the awareness and feelings of the people are, so their institutions will be. Your world is based on the corporation. Corporations' only purpose is to make a profit. They are the ultimate soulless predator. They care about their product, customers, employees, communities, and the planet only in so far as these affect their profits. Corporations view themselves as separate and in competition with all other beings. This is the opposite of a being who sees that we are all one and everything is connected. When we see everything as alive and valuable to our personal well being, we are reluctant to pour toxic chemicals into a river or the ocean or others' food. We are reluctant to bomb communities and take their resources. We are reluctant to use, abuse, and enslave others. We are reluctant to destroy other cultures and entire eco-systems. The answer is simple. Change your hearts.   Realize that everything is alive, that everything has spirit and is precious, and that everything is vitally connected to your personal well being.   When you act with this awareness and understanding, you can only create happiness and prosperity.   You will create institutions based on caring and sharing, joy and beauty.   These new institutions will replace the old institutions which are based on separation and exploitation.   Love will replace fear.   Change the hearts of the people and you change your world.   Would you like some company on your discovery trip?" he asks.

I stutter, "What trip?"

He answers, "The one you are planning to take to meet all of the beautiful beings with whom you are going to share this wonderful life, develop this vision, answer these questions.   I have decided to close my practice and to go with you."

"Well of course I want you to come," I say, but silently in my heart I know that until he says this I didn't really intend to go on any vision quest for 'The Word'.   I am not ready to put my vision into action.   I was just up on my soap box ranting like people do.   Now, I am trapped between my professions and intentions and his bold action.

I stammer, "I don't really want to go right now, today.   I have things that I really need to get done before I can go.   I have important things to do, things that I can't put off.   Also, I'm short on money.   I can't do it now, maybe later, if everything works out."

"Our time has come," he proclaims.   "It will be great fun," he says with force and jumps up and starts for the door.   "Come on. Let's go."

I timidly follow asking, "Where shall we start?   What shall we do?"

"We flow with the flow.   We don't start or do anything.   We learn synchronicity," he answers.

"Synchronicity?" I ask looking down at the floor, at my feet.

He pauses at the door and turns towards me, stopping me in mid-stumble, and answers, "Yes, synchronicity.   Up until this moment, we have been living in His story, history.   Now we are living Our story, arstory.   In arstory, we are all One, all God, and God loves us, and we love each other as God, and God has prepared only the absolute best possible world for us to enjoy and to share this joy with the All. So, because we are not wiser or richer than the All, it would be best to let the All take care of all of that starting and doing. The trick is to catch the correct train at the train station and of course this is a train station in a foreign land with the schedule printed in a foreign language and there are really a lot of trains coming and going really quickly. But of course this is a train station in a most wondrous land, and being as we are rich with infinite wealth, and everything is absolutely taken care of, we really cannot go wrong. Right?"

"I don't have any idea what you are talking about," I answer wide eyed, mouth open, "and that 'can't go wrong' thing leaves me with a queasy feeling in the pit of my stomach. Could you give me a clue about the difference between arstory and history and how this synchronicity fits into the flow?"

He turns and walks through the door with me following and catching up. Outside, he stops and turns towards me. I stumble again and stop facing him.

Gabriel looks me directly in the eyes and carefully answers, "You fail to understand my intent and purpose. So I'm going to have you go and talk to your real estate buddy and business associate Johnny Jones so that you might understand who I am and what I am and who you are and what you are, so that you can understand why we're doing what we are doing. More depends on this understanding than you can imagine. I am trying to heal not just your body, but your soul, and in that healing is the healing of your people and the healing of this planet. You all share the same problems, suffer the same anguish, feel the same fears and insecurities, know the same defeats and guilt. You cannot see this in your own life. Look at the lives around you. Look at the lives of your friends. Look at the lives of your relatives. Look at the lives of those whom you don't even like. Look at the lives of your enemies. Look at yourself and watch as you repeat the same mistakes, the same behaviors over and over again. Even when the truth is revealed to you, you still make the same mistakes again and again. Look. Watch. Be aware."

"I hear you Gabriel, but I cannot bring myself to really believe you. I cannot believe in the miraculous in my day to day life. I just don't see it. I realize that my existence is miraculous, is a miracle moment to moment, and yet I have a really hard time turning the reins controlling my life over to the Divine. I don't trust unseen forces which are beyond my understanding and control. Miracles don't happen anymore and there aren't any angels to help us. Science has shown us that that is all foolishness. We believe in scientific facts. Science is what explains our lives to us. Evolution explains who we are and how we got here. That is all that there is to it. Nothing more. Period."

"Alright Shane. I have to do some things before we go. Why don't you go meet your friend Johnny for breakfast, like you do all of the time and talk these matters over with him."

So saying, he leaves me standing alone outside of his office which is just a short distance from Alice's Restaurant where Johnny and I meet in the morning.

CHAPTER 12

JOHNNY

I drive on over to Alice's Restaurant which is located in a friendly little white cinder block building in the industrial part of town over on Mill Creek Boulevard. I park, wander in, grab a wooden kitchen table chair and pull it up under one of those vinyl topped chrome tables sitting over by the front window and sit down with Johnny, who is already sitting there chatting with Joanne, the friendly chubby blond waitress who always waits on us.

It is a Friday morning in the fall. It is the day before deer hunting season. I look at Johnny and point at the platter of food in front of him and say, "Johnny, you gotta quit eating flesh and eat more fresh fruits and vegetables and get some exercise. Look in the mirror, man, that stuff there is going to kill you."

We are sitting right next to the big plate glass windows where you can watch the loaded log trucks rumble by. I am looking at Johnny's big overstuffed frame as he shovels another piece of bacon in his mouth. Joanne has just put an extra large American sized plate covered with hash browns smothered in greasy brown gravy, surrounded by eggs over easy and golden brown toast dripping with butter or something that looks like butter and six pieces of bacon in front of him. It is the same breakfast that he eats every morning and washes down with a 44 ounce soda pop and tops off with a big black cup of coffee with cream and sugar. Sometimes he trades the toast for a stack of pancakes with a big lump of melted margarine on top. He then smothers the stack with imitation maple syrup.

Johnny is my friend. He is a big man with a big heart and every year he is getting bigger. All six feet plus of him leans across the table towards me smiling from under his baseball cap which he always wears along with a plaid loggers shirt, heavy construction boots, and a letterman's jacket, and says, "Breakfast is the most important meal of the day. You need to start out your day with a good breakfast."

Johnny is my friend and I want him to live. For his fiftieth birthday, his doctor has just given him a special gift which he shares with me, "You might be onto something though, I went to Doc Smith's yesterday and the doc told me that I have heart disease and that I'm diabetic." As he speaks he points another piece of bacon at me. Then he emphasizes this declaration by jabbing that slice of bacon in his mouth and quickly following it with a heaping forkful of hash browns and gravy.

As he talks, he pulls a white paper bag off of the seat next to him and pours little yellow plastic bottles out onto the table. "See these," he declares. "I've got pills to reduce my cholesterol. I've got pills to thin my blood. I've got pills to control my blood sugar. I've got pills to reduce my anxiety. Shoot, I've got pills that I don't even know what they are supposed to do. I've got the best medicine that insurance money can buy. And the doc says if I don't take'em, and do what he says, I'm going to die, and die soon."

"What you gotta do is lose some weight," I reply, "and quit eating all of that food which is full of fat and cholesterol and God only knows what else. Just start eating more raw, organic fruits and vegetables, get some exercise, and you'll be okay. Especially quit eating red meats."

"You're crazy," he counters. "Nobody wants to hear that I eat better than you self-righteous sermon. What makes you carrot crunching rabbit food eaters so holy? Come on you're not being any fun. I can kick your ass any day of the week and twice on Sunday, Bozo."

I'm not really a rabbit food eater and he knows it. He is joking, making a point and he is right. Gabriel is having an effect on me. I am changing. I don't eat the same, or think the same anymore, and the more that I change my eating habits, the more that I see things differently. And the more that I think differently, the more that I eat differently. I have quit watching TV and drinking and fighting and I have started going for long walks in the woods and on the high desert. Old friends are falling away like leaves from a big white oak tree in a fall wind storm.

I tell Johnny, "I'm just saying that I care. I've started studying Gabriel's ideas and I believe that it is important that we, you and I, change our ways. Now your doc is saying so too. Let's do it. Let's do it together."

"Ah, I don't want to change my ways. I mean what can happen if I don't?" He asks. "Granma lived on marshmallows and soda pop and she lived to be 99."

He pushes his chair back away from the table, hoists himself up with his arms, smiles, puts a twenty dollar bill on the table, and says, "I'm going to go make some money," and walks out.

That is how we leave Alice's Restaurant and go to work.

Johnny is a deer slayer. Every year since he was a teenager he has killed not one deer, but several deer every fall. He also kills anything else that moves, grey digger squirrels, grouse, and rabbits. Whatever crosses his path when he has a gun, he will blast. He'll shoot squirrels in the head just to see which way their eyes pop out.

But this year his heart isn't in the whole hunting thing. We have been discussing this hunting and killing thing and animal feed lots, meat factories, and stuff like that, a lot. We have been discussing heart disease, cancer, and diabetes too. He is thinking, "I should quit eating so much meat and lose some weight. I should add a salad to my lunch and dinner. I should eat some fruit for breakfast. Something is really wrong with my life, with the way that I'm living. I don't really much enjoy hunting and killing anymore anyway. In fact, I'm kind of unhappy in general, period."

By the time that he arrives home that evening he has decided, "I'm not going hunting this year."

He pulls up in his Jeep Cherokee to his front door and walks into his house. His wife Marilyn greets him with, "Johnny, you know tomorrow is the first day of hunting season. I feel a big buck up on Mount Scott just waiting for us to get up there and get'em. You got the gun sighted in and ready to go?"

Johnny doesn't like to argue with Marilyn. He doesn't even like to disagree with her. He doesn't like to argue with anyone, but he really doesn't like to argue with his wife of thirty years. Marilyn does like to argue, and to fight, and she takes her fights seriously. She is mean and she hurts people who disagree with her. And Johnny knows that his wife has a lot of ways to hurt him. He answers, "Yup, ready to go."

The next morning, they are up at 3 AM. They get going early, way before daylight, just like they have done every other hunting season opening day for decades. As the black night starts to fade into purples and then into greens, and you can start to see off into the woods and the brush, Johnny and Marilyn are creeping along a narrow mountain logging road in their Jeep. Suddenly Marilyn whispers sharply into Johnny's ear, "Stop! I think I see something in the bushes down there." She is pointing over the side of the road into the brush in an old logging clear cut unit. The fog is blowing up out of the canyon through the timber but you can still see down into the unit pretty good.

Johnny stops. Carefully opens the car door and quietly gets out. He leaves the door open, so as not to scare anything when he slams it. Looking over the hood of the Jeep about a hundred yards away, he can see a big buck with a big rack of horns on its head with at least four points sticking up one each side. This trophy buck is standing half hidden behind a bush. The deer is standing as unmoving as a statue. The buck thinks, hopes, that he is hidden from the humans up on the road. He is wrong. Johnny uses the hood of the truck as a gun rest, takes careful aim right behind the deer's front legs, and carefully, slowly squeezes the trigger.

Bam! The deer leaps in the air, ribs smashed, lungs filling with blood. At that same instant another buck which was lying down beside it's cousin behind a nearby log jumps to its feet and makes a dash for his dear life. Seeing the second buck leap up, Johnny reacts with cat like quickness, smoothly puts the cross hairs on him, and blasts that boy into deer heaven. The first buck has only run a few steps and dropped down, blood pouring from its mouth, tongue hanging out.

Standing there looking down the mountain at the dead or dying deer. One is still kicking and trying to get up. Johnny starts thinking again.

He thinks, "They're dead. A moment ago they were living and had lovers and children and were part of a family of deer and I just killed them. This is how their story ends. Now I have to go down there and finish their lives. I have to grab them by their heads and cut their throats ear to ear and bleed them out. Then I have to gut them and haul them back up here and take them home and butcher them. And what got into me? Why did I kill that second guy? One dead deer would have been plenty of meat for us. What was I thinking?"

Meanwhile Marilyn is jumping up and down excitedly clapping her hands and shouting, "Good shooting! Great Shooting! Good job! Wow, you killed two big bucks. That other one just popped up and bam you dropped him like a piece of wood. Go get'em Johnny."

So, Johnny does go get them. After much effort, he gets the two bodies home, butchered, and in the freezer. He has two complete bucks in there, eight packs of back straps.

CHAPTER 13

COREY AND THE FORKED HORN

He hasn't even eaten a bite of any of the flesh of those deer when he comes home from work a couple of weeks later and smells an awful stench in the house. He starts looking all over the house for the cause of this wretched odor. Finally he traces the smell to the utility room, to their eighteen year old tom cat, a seal point, short hair Siamese cat, whom they call Corey, who is lying on the freezer top in his bed with a heat lamp on him. Johnny goes over to Corey and he can see that Corey is looking pretty frail.

He starts petting on Corey and Corey starts coming up to his strokes. And as Johnny pets him he says, "Oh, Buddy, you're not well." But still Corey's coming up to Johnny's strokes and Johnny says to Corey, "You're only a rack of bones. You only weigh three or four pounds. Oh my God, the flies have laid eggs on you."

And Johnny decides, "Oh Bud, you have to be put down. You're suffering. I have to do something for you." Johnny takes Corey on his bed out into the yard and places him on the lawn in the back yard and continues to pet the cat.

The cat is coming up to his strokes as if to say, "Yeah Dad. It's good to see you. Haven't seen you for a while. Your petting feels pretty good. I like it. You got me out here in the sun. We're feeling better. It's just you and me, Dad."

Johnny can see that friendly enjoyment on Corey's face and Johnny has a confrontation with the committee in his mind and the committee decides that Corey should be shot dead, right here, right now.

Johnny reasons, "Well, I shouldn't use the 22 mag. That would be a little messy. I probably should just use this here little 22 pocket pistol. I'll pop him in the back of the head and take him to the pet cemetery and bury him with the rest of our critters."

This is a kind of heart hurting event for Johnny because Corey and Johnny are close. Corey is one of Johnny's personal pets. But Johnny has made the decision to kill Corey.

So he gets behind him and starts petting him. Corey stands up to the petting. Johnny has him standing upright in the sun.

Then Pop! Johnny shoots him in the back of the head with his little 22 pocket pistol. Corey's legs buckle and he collapses, rolling onto his side, shuddering, blood oozing from a hole in the back of his head, eyes frantically rolling around.

Johnny goes in the house and puts the pistol back in the sock drawer.

When he comes back out to the yard, he gasps "Oh my God." There is Corey alive. Johnny's bullet didn't kill him. That hot chunk of lead didn't blow a big enough hole through Corey's brain to be fatal. Here Corey is standing on his back legs on his tip toes, kind of dancing around in a circle, with his head hanging off to one side. He looks at Johnny kind of like, "Hey, Dad. What did you do that for? You were just petting me. You and me are friends. What's going on?"

Johnny cries, "Oh my God, this is horrible." He rushes back into the house for the pistol. When he gets back out, Corey is down to his last kick and he dies.

Tears in his eyes, lips trembling, Johnny wraps Corey up in Corey's blanket and buries him in the family pet cemetery with a very formal religious ceremony, praying to God that Corey will get to Heaven, and doing all of those good things that people do for their beloved pets. That's the same way that he buries all of his pets.

But when Johnny gets the cat buried and he goes in the house and he walks back by the freezer, he goes, "Johnny, smell that smell. Oh my God, what's that smell? It wasn't Corey."

He pops the freezer lid open and here's two complete bucks just floating like dead meat in a swimming pool, stinking in that freezer. Foul fumes are coiling around the glaring hot heat lamp. That heat lamp has broken the seal on the freezer. His wife, Marilyn, had been putting that heat lamp on Corey to make him feel better.

"What was I thinkin'?" Johnny screams in complete lonely stupid self-hating misery.

So Johnny ends up taking all of that stinking rotten wild deer flesh back out to the woods and feeding it to the cooty mongers. Those killings just created misery all around.

After he has gotten Corey buried and he has gotten rid of the rotten flesh, a few days later his wife's hunting blood comes up, and she tells Johnny, "You need to get out there and kill another buck. When you're up cutting wood today, kill us something."

Johnny replies, "Woman my heart just isn't really in it. I don't have the heart to do it anymore. I've crossed the line here somewhere. I kind of know the laws of nature and one thing is for sure, we could hunt for the next two years from the crack of daylight opening day till sunset on the final day and it's not going to happen for us. We have crossed over the line here and now we have a debt to nature to pay."

"Oh Johnny, just take the gun with you," she begs him. "You don't have to shoot anything, but just in case you change your mind, take it. If you change your mind, then you would wish that you had it. You don't have to use it. Just take it."

Johnny has been an avid hunter. He has killed a lot of deer. He is beginning to feel that he has killed maybe way more than he should have, but that is just kind of the way it is in Northwood. All of the guys kill as many deer as they can get away with killing, legal or illegal. Johnny has a fabulous German Borishnakar 30-06 with hand twisted rifling that will shoot a hole right through a quarter at a hundred yards every time. He ain't no Annie Oakley, but he's pretty close.

So, Johnny takes the gun and goes up into the woods to a logging landing with some logging debris on it which he intends to cut up into firewood.

The first thing that he does when he gets to the landing is step out, walk around the Jeep, and starts to take a leak. Up out of the canyon stomps this nice big butter ball forked horn buck. He even has a pretty good sized rack for a forked horn, a young deer with only two points on his horns on each side of his head. Well a committee of two in Johnny's mind goes to work. The guy on the right shoulder says, "Scare that buck away. You don't want to kill him."

That is what Johnny tries to do. Johnny yells, "Heyah! Shoo! Get on! Get on out of here!"

Well the strangest thing happens. The deer doesn't shoo away. He isn't even afraid of Johnny. On the contrary, he just steps back, gets those big old loving brown cow eyes on him, and looks at Johnny as if to say, "So what? You think that you can scare me away by yelling and waving your arms? I'm not going. I'm your buddy. I'm your friend. I like you. Let's play."

The deer is giving Johnny that big beautiful doe eyes look and the deer is leaning over to one side and turning his head this way and then that way and then he is leaning over to the other side and turning his head one way and then the other. Then the deer gets down on his knees and pushes his front legs out straight in front of him and leans his head down onto his outstretched legs just like he's down on his knees praying. Then he looks up at Johnny with those big friendly brown eyes.

Johnny is yelling, "Heyah! Shoo! Get on out of here! I don't want to kill you buck get on out of here! Go on!"

Johnny can't scare the deer away. The next thing you know Johnny's thinking, "I wonder if this guy would just let me rack one up and let me put a round in the old 06?"

The confrontation starts up again between the two guys on Johnny's shoulders and the next thing you know Johnny's standing over there on the passenger side of the Jeep with the rifle and he racks one up, right into that 30-06, just as loud as he can do it and follows it up with a, "Heyah! Get on out of here boy!"

The buck just doe eyes Johnny some more. The two of them, Johnny and the buck, are just standing there looking at each other. It seems to Johnny as if the buck is saying, "Come on you're not scaring me. We're friends. We're buddies."

But Johnny's starting to think, "He's sure a nice fat buck. Someone could sure use him, someone could use that meat."

One more time, Johnny shouts, "Heyah! Shoo! Get on out of here!"

Johnny can't scare the buck off and he has lost the confrontation with himself. He has reached the low ebb in his life. He decides to kill the beautiful buck for someone else to eat. He aims the gun at the deer. The buck is only twenty feet away, smiling at Johnny going, "Hey, we're buddies. We're friends."

KABAMMM! Whump, that awful sound of lead crashing through flesh, blowing a hole the size of a quarter going in and a fist coming out, blood muscle and nerves tearing in every direction, shock, disbelief!! Over the deer goes shuddering and kicking. Johnny gets in the passenger side of his Jeep. Puts the rifle away. Whips his hunting knife out, goes around to the driver's seat and sits down waiting for the guy to quit jerking and kicking, to die. Johnny is not really feeling good about what he has just done. He doesn't know the reason. He has killed many, many deer. He has killed thousands of times

He gets out of the Jeep and walks around to the back of the rig, looks at the deer and gasps, "Oh my God." He hasn't killed the buck. He blew that round right through the deer's neck, right alongside his neck bone. Usually Johnny cuts their neck bone off and pole axes them just like you chopped their heads off and they are just instantly dead. That is not what happens this time. When Johnny walks around the corner of the rig, here is this buck standing up, dancing on his tip toes on his back legs, about seven feet erect. His head is hanging off to one side because Johnny has blown the muscles away on the other side. He is looking at Johnny with those lovely brown eyes. Johnny can see the fear of death in his face. The eyes are saying, "Wow man. What did you go and do that for? Me and you were friends. We were buddies. I was trying to be your friend." Blood is pouring down the fellows shoulder.

Johnny is going, "Oh my God! Oh my God."

And the deer is dancing around in a circle on his tip toes with his head hung over to one side.

Johnny is still going, "Oh my God! Oh my God!" as he runs back to the Jeep and grabs the 06, slams another shell in it and races back around the corner of the Jeep just in time to see this boy hit the dirt and tumble over the edge of the landing and fall down into the bottom of the canyon.

Johnny has to climb all the way down into the bottom of the canyon, cut the deer's throat and bleed him out. Cutting someone's throat and watching in their eyes all of their hopes and desires and possibilities pour out in the dirt onto the bottom of your feet is not the way that Johnny wants to have fun anymore.

After the deer's life is gone, Johnny slices his belly open and pulls his guts out, puts a stick through holes that he has ripped in the fellows legs, and carries the dead carcass back up to the Jeep. He takes the body home, hangs it in the garage for two days, then skins it out, cuts and saws what is left of that fellow into pieces, wraps the flesh in packages, and puts the meat in the freezer.

Sitting in Alice's Restaurant one morning after Johnny tells me about all of this, he starts talking a lot about praying to Jesus, and about getting his life straightened out. We start talking about treating our neighbors the way that we want to be treated, but we still haven't quite got the lesson about treating our neighbors, all of our neighbors good yet, but we're thinking. We are looking at the options. We are talking life over.

Right then is when I start to understand synchronicity, or rather this is when I really start to think about the strange coincidences that fill my life, Johnny's life, our lives, our stories. I believe that Carl Jung coined the phrase while working with the physicist Wolfgang Pauli. Jung used the word synchronicity to cover the situations where events that seem to be causally unrelated are conjoined in such a way that they coincide in a meaningful way. Nonsense begins to make sense.

Most of us live our lives as if we are trains rolling down a railroad track. We know who we are and we know what we are to do because we have been told who we are and we have learned what we do. Things happen, but they seem random, accidental, un-directed, acausal. We just do what we are told and what we have learned seems to work for us. We don't change much once we've gotten on the track. At least that is how I was until that pickup truck wreck. I was going to say accident, but I have stopped believing in accidents.

Paying attention to synchronicity throws our train off of the tracks, but unlike a real train, when our personality train is derailed, it keeps moving, rapidly moving, charging cross country, across an unknown unrecognizable wilderness, a strange new terrain where we expect to crash at any minute, but inexplicably, we don't.

If events which seem to have no causal relationship coincide meaningfully and this happens not once but over and over, what do these events have in common? What is going on here? How did events decide to coincide? How does one even frame this question?

The weak part of my thinking about all of this is the word meaningful. Meaning is purely subjective to the experiencer who is experiencing the experience. But, of course, I am the experiencer. Meaning is what my personality is about, what I am about, what Shane is about. I care about me and that is the only ground which I have to stand on for sure. I can tell you what is meaningful to me. I know what I care about. I don't have to justify what I say that I care about. If I say so, I do. I know what has meaning to me. Now I can see synchronicity underlying the fabric of Johnny's life and when I see it in his life, his story, I see it in mine too. I am beginning to see synchronicity everywhere all of the time.

Johnny's life is spinning out of control. He needs to do something different. I need to do something different. We all need to do something different.

CHAPTER 14

SAM FERN

A few days later, as we are eating at Alice's Restaurant, I point out to Johnny, "Not only does your doc want you to change your ways and not only do I want you to quit eating flesh and eat more fruits and vegetables, now the Universe is telling you to make some changes in your life."

He grunts non-commitally and we drop it. He leaves Alice's and goes to work.

The next morning when I enter Alice's and start walking towards the window table where Johnny is sitting, I notice something strange. Johnny is sitting there silently drinking coffee, eating nothing.

"You're dieting?" I ask sarcastically.

"No. I am not dieting. I am hurting. I am suffering," he replies angrily.

"Why? How?" I am surprised.

"You know that I have started eating differently," he answers. "I used to eat all of the time. I had snacks in the car and snacks at the office and snacks at home on the kitchen counter. I used to like chocolate fudge ice cream, orange sherbert and vanilla ice cream bars, and classic potato chips, but lately I have changed to nuts, seeds, and dried fruits from Happy Days, the local health food store. I kept a half gallon jar in my Jeep filled with almonds, walnuts, Brazil nuts, cashews, sunflower seeds, and shoot, seeds that I don't even know their names, but some of those seeds were hard, real hard. There were also raisins, goji berries, cranberries, and other dried fruits mixed in with the nuts. You can have that whole jar of nuts and seeds and dried fruits. I won't be needing anything hard to eat for awhile."

"Yesterday I forgot that nut jar at home. So on my way home after work yesterday afternoon, I was feeling real hungry. I started searching around in my rig as I drove along and I spied down between the seats the bright red color of a pack of something to eat. I reached down there and picked it up. It was a pack of jerky. I had bought it months before and lost it down there between the seats and I had completely forgotten about it. I like jerky but I had kind of gotten off of eating it. But I was hungry. I hadn't eaten anything since breakfast. I hadn't eaten lunch. I had just worked straight through the day. I was real hungry and I thought, 'a piece of that, jerky would be really good right now.' I picked up a piece and took a bite of it, pepper and garlic. I was chewing away on it when I heard this snap."

"I went, 'Hey what's that?'"

"I had split the back top cusped clear through the root, the complete back of the tooth, which made it unsaveable. What a deal. I was in really bad pain. Luckily my dentist took me right in. It was a real nasty extraction. My dentist broke the tooth off a couple times. Then he had to slit my gums with a scalpel and go in there and buzz that tooth in two with a dental saw and tear the tooth out in pieces.

"I thought, 'I can't believe that I grabbed up that jerky and stuffed it in my face like that. It's just an ongoing saga. Why didn't I stick with nuts and fruit? Why did I go back to dried meat? When am I going to learn?"

When Johnny finishes his story, I don't answer. I'm thinking. He's thinking.

We are thinking things over a little more. Old stories, old memories are starting to come up in our minds, in our consciousness. Strange things are starting to happen to us, and we know it.

"Say, Shane, you ever hear the story of Sam Fern, the last of the Molala Indians?" He asks.

"No. No, I've never heard of Sam Fern," I answer.

"Well, Sam Fern isn't his real name. That's just the name he died with. Sam Fern was the last chief of the Molala Indians, and he had a pretty tough go of it in the final analysis. He never did find a woman to marry and he was finally brought to the point where he realized that he was the very last living one of his tribe, of his kind. In Protobaskan Indian culture it is taboo to marry a woman from another tribe unless you capture her as a slave, buy her, or win her in a gambling debt. You couldn't just go over there and ask her to marry you. That wouldn't happen. And for Sam those other options weren't going to happen either. So he ended up being a sole survivor, the last one of his kind, of his tribe, of his nation. He was living in Molala, as we know it today. Back then it was Molala Territory.

"He had another reason that he wasn't feeling good about himself too. He was working for the big railroad company. The railroad had come to town and he is now cutting white oak railroad ties for the railroad. Well, that kind of was a problem for him because in the Molala Indian culture the white oak is a brother to the Indian. It is the only thing in the plant realm, in that side of nature, that they felt that they could absolutely relate to. They could talk to a great white oak tree. And now he is killing them. He is out cutting them down and chopping them up. In Indian culture, that would be like going out and murdering your brother. To cut down a great white oak tree and to slab it up into railroad ties was like killing a friend, butchering him up, and selling the little packages of meat to a Korean corporation in Newport Bay for money. The Protobaskans felt that they could communicate with the great white oak by reaching high up on the tree and meditating. Even now, they say that people who are in the know, and have the way, can put their hand on a great white oak and feel something come back from the tree to you. So, Sam was really down over the tree killing, too.

"Plus, he had Indian agents trying to buy the land, Molala, from him, because he was the last surviving Molala Indian. So the territory, the entire territory, was his, and he had Indian agents trying to buy it from him for gold. Well, somewhere in the line of events, he broke down. He must have needed money. He'd gotten far enough into the white man's ways that he knew that he could do a lot with this gold. He knew that the gold, like killing the great white oak, was taboo to his culture. He knew that selling the land is not something that he should be doing either, but in his low ebb, and as the final surviving being of his kind, his tribe, with no one to bring the council together, and with no one of his people to talk to, and with not another living soul from his people to discuss these matters with, he fell.

"He had a white friend who would pick him up on an old buck board. They would go to work together and they would come home drunk together. Then his friend and he would drink more whiskey into the darkness. He had developed a taste for lum, which is whiskey in Chinook jargon, to make the pain from the loneliness and from cutting the great white oak go away.

"Well, the Indian agents kept on dogging him. Finally they showed up with an absolute wheelbarrow load of US gold eagles, bagged gold eagles, and Sam agreed. But the Indian agents couldn't make this deal because they have a white man's contract and a white man's contract takes two names, a first name and a last name. They asked him, 'Who are you?"

"And he tried to tell them that he was a child of the Earth.

"He said, 'My mother is Yohilahee, the Earth, and my father is Tamminus, the Great Spirit in the sky. I am one with nature. I am part of everyone and part of everything that you see, the trees, the leaves, the grass.''

"And he pointed to a fern and said, 'I am one with this. I am part of this.''

"And the Indian agent said, 'Fern, huh? That sounds like a good last name. Fern, so be it, Fern.''

"And then in trying to come up with a first name, the Indian agent turned to the other agent and asked, 'What's he look like to you, a Tom, a Dick, a Harry, a what?''

"Uhhh, he looks like a Sam to me," the other agent replied.

"So be it then! He's Sam Fern."

"And the Indian agents named him Sam Fern. He was really a Kuhmiama, a child of the Earth. His mother was Yohilahee, the earth, and his father was the Great Spirit in the great blue sky, Tamminus. He was a brother to all living things and a friend of all of the spirits.

"All of the Indians wore turquoise jewelry back then that so they could hold it up to the sky and remember their Father, the Great Spirit in the sky. I don't care if they came from Mexico, or up around Washington, they would all be wearing blue jewelry.

"So, the Indian agents ended up naming him Sam Fern, the last of the Molala Indians. We don't know his real Chinook Indian jargon name. We only know that he was a Kuhmiama, a child of the Earth. That was what he was trying to explain to the Indian agents, the white men, when they named him Sam Fern. So, when the land was taken from the last Kuhmiama, the last child of the Earth lost his real name, and he became Sam Fern in exchange for a wheelbarrow full of gold.

"Crazy thing of it is, is that just as soon as he sold the land, he got sicker. He went up to the top of the hill behind his home, to the Indian cemetery, and spent days up there crying, because he had crossed the taboos of the tribe, and now he was also drinking lum all of the time, a lot of lum. He got his friend from work to just drop by his house with fifths of whiskey on a regular basis, no more going to work. Finally, he had his friend bring some whiskey over and they filled their pockets with as many of those US gold eagles as they could. Then they went walking down by Molala Creek and skipped US gold eagles across the creek like you would skip a stone into evermore. He felt so badly about what he had done that he threw the gold away. He skipped it away on the creek like you would skip a stone. After that he may have felt a little better, but doing the deal, led to his demise.

"He also had a large following of children that knew he was wealthy with gold. He would take a couple of gold coins when he would take a run down to the Golden tavern by stagecoach from Molala and he would throw a gold coin in the dirt when he got on the stage in Molala and he would throw another gold coin in the dirt when he got off in Golden. He was like a pied piper. Of course, this was like winning the lottery to the children. A US gold eagle back then was a lot of money to anyone, much less to a kid. So, he had a fabulous following, but he ended up passing away lonely and hurt, because he had crossed the taboos of the tribe, the taboos of life.

"Because he didn't maintain his integrity in his older age and stay with his commitment to the tribe, he died miserable. When he crossed those lines, the torment, and the agony of what he had done could not be resolved in the Indian cemetery in days of tears and whiskey. Couldn't do it. He had screwed up. He destroyed nature and allowed the land to be turned into private property to be bought and sold by the strongest man for his personal pleasure and exploitation.

"Well, Shane, I'm starting to feel like Sam Fern."

"I know what you mean, buddy. I definitely am seeing the connections," I reply and ask, "What are we going to do?"

"I don't know, Chief. I been praying to Jesus a lot," he answers. He puts a ten dollar bill on the table, gets up, and adds, "Something has to change and change for the better. I am going to work. See you later," and he leaves. No breakfast.

CHAPTER 15

MY REALIZATION

It's Thursday, my day to have tea with Gabriel. I go over to his place. We are sitting in his office laughing and joking. He is telling me Nasrudin, the holy fool, stories.

Nasrudin and his buddies, the Professor and the Doctor are drinking coffee at the local coffee house when the conversation gets serious.

The Professor asks the Doctor, "What would you like people to say when they look down at you in your coffin?"

The Doctor thinks about it for a moment and then answers, "I would like for people to say that I was a good man. I was a real benefit to the community. I healed many sick people and contributed generously to the Library and to the University and to our Church. I want them to say that they will miss me because I was a good man."

The Doctor then turns to the Professor and asks him, "What would you like people to say over your coffin?"

The Professor deeply contemplates the question and replies, "I would like them to say that generations of this community have benefitted from the wisdom and skills which I have taught. This is a much better community than it would have been if not for my hard work, dedication, and generosity. I will be greatly missed and remembered as a great man."

"Yes," the Doctor agrees, "that is the way that it should be."

Then he turns to Nasrudin and asks him, "What about you Nasrudin? What would you like to have people say about you as they gaze into your coffin?"

Nasrudin doesn't even think about the question.

He says, "I want them to look into my coffin and gasp, 'Omigod, he moved. He's alive."

It takes me a beat to get it, then laughing, I agree, "That's a good one Gabriel. That's really good. I'll match it with my realization."

I tell him about what is happening with Johnny and say, "Johnny says that he is praying to Jesus. He should be listening to Jesus too, especially that advice about loving your neighbor as yourself, you know the golden rule and all of that wisdom. And I don't mean that golden rule that says, 'He who has the gold makes the rules', either."

"After all of what has happened to Johnny and me, I now see our personal story cycles repeating themselves and spiraling into more serious and bigger dramas with each turn of events. I see that there is something big happening here and we are constantly given the opportunity to do something different, something wonderful, something amazing; but usually we don't. And there are all of these weird coincidences happening. I understand synchronicity now. Things just show up when you need them. But you have to see them. To be able to understand them, or to use them, you have to be able to see them. That is synchronicity, seeing those fortuitous coincidences, knowing that they are coming, then grabbing them as they go by just for the sheer joy and delight and wonder of the ride.

"But most of us miss those fortunate moments and our story seems terribly sad a great deal of the time. Our story is the story of the buffalo, or worse the work horse who after a lifetime of misery and drudgery ends his days horribly at the dog food factory. Our story is the story of the losing grade school soccer team, the extra in the play, the victim, the jilted lover. History is the story of the predator, the great victor, the winner, the King, and in the end there can only be one winner, him, whoever he is. Sometimes we get to taste triumph for a while, or at least hope to get to taste triumph, but mostly we are beasts of burden who grow tired and weary and sick in a confusing world that makes us anxious and scared, clinging to our loved ones and a few possessions. We seem like drowning children all alone hanging on to a life preserver on a treacherous, cold, deep sea which is full of sharks and other unknown but cold slimy heartless ferocious beasts."

"This is his story and we don't even know who he is. We are like the buffalo in the hunter and the buffalo story. He is the hunter. He is the subject of the story. The buffalo, us, we are just an object in his, the hunter's story. The buffalo is just an extra, a prop in the buffalo hunter's story. It really isn't important what happens to one buffalo or another. The buffalo is nothing more than food or hide or fun or a trophy. He is not the father of these children that the hunter is killing. He is not the lover of that mother over there. He has no story. He is un-important. The hunter can do anything that he wants to the buffalo because the buffalo has no importance other than as an object in the hunter's story."

"This attitude of winner/loser, food/eaten, them/us, causes everything to go wrong in our lives as soon as we accept it as the truth. And that is the conceptual basis of history. To them we are just objects in their story, in history. There is always a bigger fish in the pool and it is always his, the bigger fish's story, and we, the little fish, are used and abused any way that the history owner chooses. From the beginning of history, we have been harnessed to build the cities, dig the gold, pull the plows, clean the manor house, and wash the dishes."

"But there is another way to tell this story. There is another way to be. In this other way to tell the story, we are all subjects. There are layers and layers of subjects and objects in history and it is only by recognizing that all is subject, no objects, and that we are all one, that we can break the addiction to self, and the suffering, and history. We can still self, but we have to recognize that all selves have their own story and that their story, each story, is unique, beautiful, and precious. We must honor and respect and enjoy each other's beingness. This new story is a story where there are still buffalo roaming free. This new story is a story where there is no war, no hunger, no hatred and anger, no paved rotting cities, no destroyed jungles, no dirty air, no dirty water. There are no winners and losers. There are just beings enjoying being."

"This new story is our story. All of us get a story. In this new world, all of us get to be important. There is no hunter and hunted. There is no hunting at all. There is no eater and eaten. There is no soccer team captain who is the winning champion and no crushed loser. There is no species that is so unimportant that it can just go extinct. There are no monkeys and rats in cages that are so unimportant that anyone can do anything that they want to them to see if toxic chemicals are toxic or not. There is no more of that. There are no objects. Everything is subject. It is our story. All of those monkeys in the cages are set free. They are us. We are them. We won't even have that attitude of separation from other beings that allows us to treat each other as nothing of any importance."

"Our story is about things as they are. It is the story that is. It is the story of what we are. This is arstory, our story. Arstory is completely different than history. Understanding arstory changes everything. His story is a story about him, where he is the center and the subject of the story. And whenever "the" story isn't the way that he wants it to be, he changes it. His story, history, is not only a glorification of him, it is also a justification for what he does. So, he changes it whenever he wants to, so that it glorifies him, and it justifies him in what he has done, and in what he is doing to all beings, and to all of the Earth. History has nothing to do with the truth, with how things really are. He rewrites the arstory, the things that are, our story, to make it history, his story. He writes it to be like he wants things to be, so that he and his actions are justified and glorified and our story is unimportant and we are nothing but fodder for his grist mill. This is the remembering of our story, the story of things that are, of arstory, of our story."

"What do you think?"

He rocks back in his chair, making a pyramid with his hands which he pulls against his chest, then rocks towards me spreading his hands as he glides forward, ending the movement by slapping his hands palms down onto his desk top. I lean back and sip my tea.

"I like it, but let's go further," Gabriel replies enthusiastically. "You're describing arstory so that it is like history only in your arstory, so far, there are no winners or losers. It's an inclusive deal, including him, the master of history, but for me that's not really a big enough story. That's just making a new story, an our story with us not being losers. That's a good story, but it's like an anti-war movement in which the anti-war activists fight a valiant and victorious battle for peace. In fighting, the anti-war people have become what they originally opposed. You are proposing an anti-history movement. It's not really that much of a different story. It's just flipping it to a different winner, a different type of winner, a different type of winning. It is not taking our story far enough. Let's go further. Let's transcend story, not just history coming to an end, and our story starting, but go beyond story. Let's go to the end of the story. No more story. No more his. No more ours. I'm thinking bigger than yours and mine. I am thinking transcendental eternal moments. All beings and all not beings going beyond story, going beyond comprehension and imagination. Let's move beyond duality. Let's move into total, well beyond total, and beyond oneness. Come on if we're going to do it, let's go beyond going beyond. Yeah! What do you say to that? Let's live a story where everybody is subject, every thing, every non-thing, and we all cross into total eternal ecstatic bliss. Come on, you know that we are God. We can do it. Right? All stories are happening somewhere, sometime. Speak this story into being. Let's hear the word. Sing the vibration to me that I might resonate that essence. Let me hear you say that word. What is that word? Let me hear it. Just for the fun of it. What the heck? Let's do it."

And I do it. I stand up and I say the word, "Yes."

Gabriel beams. Tears stream down his cheeks. He jumps up, comes around his desk and grabs my arms in his hands and admires me as if I were his new born son. I am slightly embarrassed, but very happy.

He says, "Go home and pack your back pack, we leave immediately for the desert to fast. Fasting is feasting. Prepare to feast on Divine Presence."

CHAPTER 16

THE DIVINE CONNECTION

We go to our separate homes, get our gear, and join up in the parking lot at Gabriel's office. But by the time that we meet again, I have had time to think, time to worry, and I'm having second thoughts, third thoughts, maybe even some fourth thoughts. I am especially worried about fasting. I don't understand fasting. I'm reluctant to do it for a long period of time, and I still don't want to leave my home. When Gabriel arrives, instead of piling everything into the pickup and joyously blasting out of town towards the desert with a light heart and a song on my lips, I start an argument.

I belligerently confront him, "Gabriel, I want to know something. I want to get some things clear. What is this Divine Presence stuff? How do I make a connection with Divine Presence? How do I even figure out what you are talking about? I mean, what are you talking about? I've got money problems and fasting for a long time in the desert seems dangerous."

"Shane, I understand," he says soothingly. "I don't want you to fear anything. You're on the right track with feasting on lots of fresh vegetable juices and eating fruit. Don't worry about money. Remember Jesus and how he went into the desert and fasted for forty days and forty nights. That is where you need to be going. What I mean by this is that you need to be moving in that direction, towards fasting. Keep juicing and eating fruit. Lighten up the amount of this heavy world that you are absorbing. Keep lightening your load."

My teeth clamp shut. My lips open wide and pull back. My eyes widen. I step back as if I've been slapped. I can't stop myself. What he is saying is hurting me somewhere that I didn't even know that I have nerves. I don't want to give up anything.

"Yes, I know, I saw that thought cross your mind when I said to lighten your load and I meant for you to lighten your load physically. Sell your possessions: house, pool table, motor cycle, scrap iron, whatever. Keep lightening your load, but that's not what I'm talking about."

I'm confused by what he is saying. He's insane. Disconnect from everything! Disconnect from life! I take another step back away from him, from his words.

"What I'm talking about is ---, yes, I saw that thought too. I have the ability to read your mind, to see your thoughts. I am more than you realize. I felt you think the word disconnect, but I don't mean to disconnect. What I am suggesting is really a different direction than you are thinking. I mean to connect, to reconnect. Your connection to Divine Presence is dirty. It's, uh, what? Obscured, constricted. It's actually, I'm looking for a word, hazed over. It's, uh, sealed off, covered, plugged, clogged, buried. What I'm saying is, it's as if you have to dig for your connection. Uncover it. There are layers of dramas, personalities, and bad eating habits over your spiritual connection, and if you lighten your load, keep clearing those things away, you'll understand."

"Think of your connection as a window and that there's a bunch of dirt on the glass. If you keep rubbing that glass and cleaning that window, pretty soon you can see through it. Once you can see through it and light shines in, you can find the latch and open the window and let the light pour in, but right now, you can't even see the light. Well, you can see the light. You are not in total darkness, but it's pretty dark here. It's as if you are in a cave and it is totally dark as it is in the Oregon caves when you are inside the caverns in the darkness, but when you are near enough to the entrance that a little light is getting in. Your situation now is like that. You have the ability to move closer to the light or to move further from the light. The glass window analogy, a glass window at the mouth of a cave, is the best picture that I can give you of your life."

"By purifying yourself, you are moving closer to the light. You move closer to the light in your eating habits by lightening your load. Food wise, that means, eat less. You should not even be eating. You should open the window and let the energy in directly, but because you don't know where the latch is, and because you don't know how to open the window, you can't open it. You don't even know how to clean enough of the dirt off from the window so that you can see well enough to look for the latch. You certainly don't know how to open the window to let the energy in to your being directly."

"You have to get as close as you can to the beings that know how to get their energy from the source. And the beings that know how to do that are the plant beings. That is why I told you to talk to the plants, to learn their language, and that is what you did when you communicated with that redwood tree in Northern California. The tree told you about the dark spot at the base of your being and your inability to go deep. It told you about your inability to connect to the true energy source, to the Divine. You were able to make the connection with the tree and you heard what the tree said."

I flashback to my trip to California. I am driving on a lonely, winding mountain road going to go to the Living Light Institute to study how to prepare delicious raw vegetable dishes.

It is a beautiful fall day and I am passing through the majestic redwood forest of northern coastal California. The trees tower above me, but it isn't just that they are big, really big, there is something more to them, something greater than just their size. In fact maybe I see them as physically large because their emotional, spiritual, and energetic presence completely overwhelms me. I want to wade through the lush rain forest jungle that grows in their shade and touch their bark, hug one of them to my breast.

I park in a road wayside and start wading through the waist high ferns, pushing aside great tangles of green bushes and shrubs, and climbing over rough logs as tall as suburban houses. After a short time of this struggling, I feel sleepy. A beautiful, mighty, towering redwood tree ahead of me to my left, an easy short walk through some friendly ferns seems to beckon to me to come over to it. Walking around this huge ancient tawny tree, I realize that the folds in its bark are so big that I can sit down on the ground and back into one of these folds and be completely sheltered from the wind and the rain that falls every once in a while. The ground is deeply covered in soft green moss. I feel warm, safe, and comfortable here in the arms of the tree.

As I'm falling asleep, I think that I hear the tree say, "My name is Xolocoyotescatl."

I seem to hear a voice say something strange like that. I am not sure whether it is saying that Xolocoyotescatl is my name or the tree's name. It is speaking an odd language full of unfamiliar long words that I can't pronounce or remember. I ask, "What?"

I hear again a long un-pronounceable word. I'm disturbed, agitated. I want to get up, go somewhere, do something, but I'm asleep.

Then the voice says quite clearly, "Little One stop moving. Lay still. Relax. Watch. Your consciousness is jerking around in circles on the surface of a vast ocean. Your body is bouncing about here and there and back again without ever going anywhere. That is why you are not able to connect to the Divine, to the true energy source. The darkness between you and the Source is like a wall between you and an unlimited supply of food, of energy, but you cannot get past or even see through that wall of darkness. So you are forced to eat the scraps of creation, of light, of energy, of food that you find on this side of the wall of darkness. I want you to see the darkness at the base of your being and to understand your predicament. Stop Moving. Stay still. Stay in the moment. Hold on to my awareness, my understanding. Open your mind. Now sit quietly on the Earth. Let your energy roots go down deep and untie the knot of un-remembering that you now see as a dark spot which is choking your energy body."

As the voice speaks, I visualize what it is describing.

I know that I am in the presence of a being who has stood unmoving in this exact spot for hundreds and hundreds of years, a great universal presence. I try to imagine what that is like, to imagine what this tree has been doing and thinking standing here down through the ages. My mind staggers. The vistas open and they are huge, but I can't understand. I cannot imagine standing in one place, never moving day after day, month after month, year after year, century after century. How will I live if I don't move? What importance will I have? I know only this little place on this side of the blackness.

"You are less important than you imagine," the tree says to me in response to my thoughts. "Who would miss the mightiest of God's mean men? If you died today, what difference would it make who noticed? If a dragonfly becomes enlightened, who knows, who cares?"

That thought disturbs me. I ask, "So I can just walk away from everything that I'm doing? I don't have to participate. It doesn't matter what I do or say or think or imagine?"

"Imagine!" It booms. "Now you have hit on something that has consequences in an inconsequential way. Stay still and listen to me. I want you to see life from a natural perspective, rather than from the perspective of humans, human dramas and human ideas. I want you to see life from the point of view of butterflies and grasses and dragonflies and hawks and animals and sage bushes and redwood trees. I want you to experience life as a meadow, as a forest, as a mountain. I want you to experience freedom, freedom from cares, freedom from woes, freedom from suffering, freedom from thinking. I want you to penetrate the dark spot at the base of your being which separates you from Creation. I want you to sink into the bosom of eternity. I want you to start following the natural rhythm, the rhythms of the Sun and the Earth and all of the Great Spirits that surround you, the plants and the animals. I want you to connect with the rhythm that sustains our being. I want you to perceive and feel moments when you perceive and feel the moment and each and everything that has presented itself for your enjoyment in this moment. Let this awareness burst the bonds of time and enter the ecstasy of eternal joy and being and bliss."

I lie there happily as the Sun sets. Night comes. Dampness and frost settle on me. I lie there shivering and afraid in the cold, in the dark. A long, long time passes. Finally the Sun comes again and light and warmth return and with them joy and life return. I experience the joy brought by the rising of the Sun and the joy of the return of heat and of light and of life, the joy of receiving another day full of possibilities, another day full of wonders, another day full of hope and happiness.

The tree says, "Now you know the return of the Sun in a place with water and air and life. Now you know the darkness and the cold and the slowing and the ceasing of life. Now you know suffering and the will to survive until the Sun returns again. You know about curling up alone in the darkness and holding on to the spark of life until the Sun can return."

"Thank you for this gift of understanding Holy One," I reply. "I understand now carrying the gift of life from the Sun through the night and waiting for the Sun to come again, just as I carry the water in my flesh until I can drink again, and just as I hold the breath of life until I can breathe again. This is a precious balance but when it works, it is wonderful. When it doesn't, lying here in the dark shivering in the cold, the joy goes away. The long wait, the surviving begins. So life is a combination of Sun, Water, Earth, and Air? What is the spark? Holy One how can I greet the Sun and continue this joyful dance of life without harming anyone or anything else?"

"Child of the Universe be still and open your heart to Divine love. Eat the Sunlight. Drink the Water. Breathe the Air. Absorb the Earth. The tree continues, "I know that this is hard for you. All of humanity is full of suffering and drama. People are constantly moving about seeing themselves in these self-important emotional serial events. Stand still, watch, and free yourself from this ocean of imaginings which is the human life, the human drama, a drama that essentially never goes anywhere. These dramas are movements like the tide coming in and going out, coming in and going out. Imagine seeing life from inside of the mind of a dragonfly. The dragonfly sees its life as infinitely important and busy, full of friends and enemies, and important things to do. Now look at the life of that same dragonfly from your human perspective. You see an unthinking, unfeeling insect eating, breeding, and dying, unimportant. You don't look at a dragonfly as if it has an emotional life and an emotional investment in its being. Now look at humans from my point of view. I have been watching you for over eight hundred years.

What else do you human's do besides eat, breed, and die? The rest is just drama and internal dialogues. You are a dragonfly. Be a redwood. Stay still. See the darkness which cuts off the Divine light from you. Step through that veil and bathe in the light of Creation."

My unimportance is beginning to sink in. Although it is humiliating, it is also liberating. I am a dragonfly in a meadow. No more. No less. I am a dragonfly full of inner dialogue and personal drama. I am a dragonfly who flits about here and there preening.

I cannot sit still one minute longer. I stand and hug the tree, hugging only one little piece of this great being. Tears are coming down my cheeks, but I must move. I say, "Thank you Holy One." And I walk away.

The tree calls from behind me, "If you sit in the council of men all of your days, then you are taken up with the concerns of men, but if you sit in the council of the Uncreated Eternal One, then you are taken up with the concerns of God and you become godly. Go into the wilderness and fast and meditate. Remember my name is -----," but I forget as soon as I hear.

Gabriel loudly clears his throat. I snap back to the parking lot in Northwood.

Gabriel is saying, "Now I'm trying to deepen your understanding. You're looking now and you're seeing that you're not connected and that there's a dark spot covering your connection with God. Well here's how to start working on that dark spot. Make the connection with the plants. Drinking plant juice, the blood of plants, is your connection to the live plant force, intelligence, and understanding. Anything that you do that kills that plant energy before you imbibe it will destroy the connection, the information, the understanding. Living water has this connection, this information also. Drink water gushing from the ground in high mountain springs. Do you understand what I am saying?"

"I think so," I reply timidly.

What he is saying does seem to make sense on some level. It is a level deeper, more real than science, than physics, than chemistry, biology, psychology, mathematics, anthropology, and sociology. He seems to be speaking to a pre-conscious mind that knows great secrets that my conscious mind doesn't know, a mind that I wasn't aware of a moment ago. I am not sure what he is saying but he is pulling me back towards him with my curiosity, with my heart, with his heart. I want to know more. I sit down on a rock wall next to where he is standing.

Gabriel is proclaiming, "The plants are energetically connected more directly to Divine being than animals, fish, or insects. Water is the blood of Divine being and breath is the soul. Plants can convert pure energy, pure essence, into life in this world. They are divine beings. The connection of that huge, beautiful ancient redwood tree whom you were communicating with is very profound . Remember when it was telling you to stop moving, to cease your moving, and just to be, and to accept. That was a truly divine lesson and a profound moment for you. You couldn't stay in it but you're going to look back at that moment in your life some day and remember what happened to you there wrapped in the tree's folds at the base of that huge ancient tree in that lush rain forest and you will realize that as an important moment."

My mind drifts back again to the mist dripping from ferns under giant redwoods in Northern California. Here in Gabriel's parking lot I am gazing at thousands of pink blossoms on a cherry tree just to the left of Gabriel who is explaining, "What I'm getting at is that you are imbibing that consciousness when you are taking in the plants' blood. The blood is the distilled essence of that knowledge. The knowledge is encoded in the blood. Your body decodes the information as it enters your being. Blood, juice is the divine connection. It is the divine sacrifice of those beings, the beings that give that connection to this world. So when you imbibe that sacrifice, when you drink that divine juice, you are making a connection with Divinity. Your connection is going deep. But if you take that blood and cook it, you have destroyed the connection, the information, and you will remain in the darkness. If you heat up one of your music CD's on the stove and then try to play it, it doesn't play very well does it? That is what heat does to your food."

"Fire is not a step up towards greater happiness, towards greater beingness. Fire is a trick. Fire entraps you. When you humans were given fire by the Angel of Darkness, you looked at the fire, and you were captured by fire. For a hundred thousand years you have lived in the shadow of the Angel of Darkness and for the last ten thousand years you have lived under the dominion of the Serpents, that great shape shifting race of evil tricksters who gave you monotheism and paternalism, savage wars and degraded slavery, kings and misery, ghost daggers and devil dances. You looked at the fire and you looked away from the Divine. To see the Divine you have to look away from fire. When it starts to snow, does a squirrel go in the house and sit by the fire? No. It still has the Divine connection to keep it warm. But I want you to look at what is possible, rather than to look at what you are not seeing."

I jump off the wall, startled out of my daydream and face Gabriel, "Wait! What did you just say? Fire is a trick? Someone is tricking me? Are there any other tricks?"

"Yes, agriculture. Fire and agriculture. You are both, you and the captured plants, whatever you want to call them, the domesticated plants, you are both enslaved in the same way."

"What? Who enslaved us, Gabriel? What is an Angel of Darkness? Who are the Serpents?"

"I don't want to go into that. It's not important. The important thing is that you are enslaving yourself. You do not have to be a slave. Your enslavement is of your own doing. You have the power to be enslaved or not to be enslaved."

A terrible irrational fear suddenly grips my heart. I feel a cold breeze.

My mind tells me, "This is crazy talk."

But I still irrationally jerk around searching for my captor, for my master. Master? What master? Where did that thought come from? Am I going insane? Doubt and weird thoughts cloud my mind. I see ancient ziggurat palaces in the desert flowing with lovely hanging gardens, guarded by statues of winged lions with eagle's heads collapse and burn in the darkest night while the screaming terrified people are butchered by evil men and half men in an orgy of power drunken madness.

The cold wind picks up. Leaves begin to move about in the parking lot. Petals blow like pink snow around us.

As I gaze in horror upon my ghastly visions I hear a voice, more in my mind than through my ears, and it states with magisterial authority, "I have power over you and you cannot defeat me. I've got that credit card debt over your head and you can't escape. It's not true what that pathetic old fool, Gabriel, is saying. If he is the Angel of Light, command him to restore you to the Garden of Paradise."

Gabriel, suddenly steps around behind me and whacks me on my back quite hard and loudly proclaims, "Don't worry about it. Quit thinking about it. Focus! Focus. You are the master. That's right! It is on your left. Don't look over there. Fire, agriculture, credit cards, those are way, way up in the darkness, that dark knot in you. You have got to get way below that. You have to go way further below that before you can understand what a redwood tree is talking about. You have got to get way below that before you can connect with the Divine energy source. But when you can, you can take what you're given, the energy, directly, so you will not need to ask for the holy sacrifice of the blood of the plant beings. But because you can't go through the darkness to the light right now, now you can only have the blood and the flesh, the live flesh, of the plants. That is as close as you can get to the Divine truth for now. You have to start moving towards fasting, true fasting, and I don't mean fasting in the sense of denying yourself anything. Fasting is feasting on the light, on true energy, on the direct connection. Do you see that?"

A visualization flashes across my consciousness of beings of pure white light in a garden of Eden. I am feeling better, more stable, less shaky.

"You are a divine being of light and that is something completely different than being a human and that is something completely different than what you think you are and that is something completely different than your perception and your definition of yourself now. Your perception of yourself right now is that you eat food to live. You are eating it and if you don't eat food, you won't live. That is true on this level but that's not what you are and that's not how you are supposed to get your energy. In fact you are not supposed to get your energy. You are energy. You are divine light. You are divine beings. You are the source of

Divine presence here and now, the source of life and light and energy, and that is why you have become a human. You have been captured and enslaved and you are being cultivated, eaten, and sucked dry."

"Whoa! I didn't see that coming." I screech stepping back away from Gabriel towards the wall. I want to get my back against the wall. I crouch down and lean against the wall. I want to get back away from that icy wind. My body starts to shake uncontrollably. I suddenly remember, and I start to turn slowly to my left toward my tormentor. I turn in the manner that you would turn in if you were about to look in a coffin at a vampire with a stake driven through its heart, a vampire that you hope is dead, but that you know isn't, isn't dead at all. The wooden stake should have been carved from an ancient white oak tree but it was carved from a second growth pine tree from a commercial tree farm. That modern commercial pine shaft has no power, no magic, no Divine connection. Bad mistakes have been made. I know it. I am scared.

Gabriel steps forward, grips my right arm with his left hand and pulls me to my feet. The cherry blossoms swirl around us in a cyclone. I am gasping for air and can't straighten up. He is pulling me forward but darkness is starting to surround us, even under our feet. There is a hole opening in front of us. It is like looking down into a big bottomless well and the hole is growing.

"Yeah, that kind of slipped out of there didn't it? Let the cat out of the bag, but let's just not go there on that one," Gabriel says calmly. "Let's just go right. Don't look left! Have courage. Keep listening. I know. I know. I know. Hang on. Hang on. Stay! Focus! You can make it. You can get back. Don't look down. Let's just. Let's just stay. Stay steady. Focus. Meditate. Whatever you've got to do, do it. Just get a grip. Here, let's just focus on where we're going and on what we've got to do. You've got to remember: live plant blood and raw fruit flesh will pick you up, will clean your connection, will make it better, and then you need to work towards fasting. Remember, fasting is feasting. Fasting is feasting. You are not denying yourself anything when you fast. What you are doing is feasting on divine light and love as you are meant to be doing. That is what you are. You are divine light and love. You are the most creative powerful force of all created beings and what you are doing when you are getting pure is cleaning off the window enough to let light in and to see the light. You haven't got the window open yet, so you cannot breathe the light. What did I say, 'breathe the light'? The analogy breaks down because you can see the light. What happens when you open the window is you can eat the light. How do I explain that? You don't understand eating. Eating is something you do because ----. I don't think I can get that through to you. If I can get that through to you, you will have a moment of enlightenment. You eat because you can't remember. And now eating is the only way that you can get tiny little bits of essence, of being that barely keep you alive."

"It is horrible the way you do it, the way that you are forced to do it. Oh, the cruelty, and then the way that you force other beings to ---. Oh, the suffering. It's so disgusting. We just aren't there. You can't see what food is. How it's not food. You've got to ----. Let's just stop and work on this for a minute. Just get beyond food and you will see that food is not helping you. Food is blinding and enslaving you, just like fire. You cannot eat food. You are the divine essence of food. You are the creative force behind food. You are being food but let's not go there. Let's stop right here. We are close enough. We just have to take a few minutes and work on that."

I am panicking. My heart is racing. My breathing is shallow. I keep telling myself, "This is stupid. This is irrational. What am I worrying about? There is nothing here to frighten me. I am standing in a parking lot in the sunshine, in a small town in Oregon. I am perfectly safe. There are only Gabriel and me here in this parking lot. What is happening?"

I am hanging on to Gabriel now with both hands. My self-assuring chatter doesn't do any good. My anxiety is getting worse and worse and worse. My chest is starting to burn. I am gulping air. Nothing around us looks like I know that it should. The only thing that I can think to do is the double count to nine on the in and out breath meditation technique. I focus on my erratic breathing and draw a breath deep down into my belly and I count, "One" on the in breath.

As I exhale, I count, "One".

On the next in breath I count, "Two".

On the exhale, I count, "Two".

I continue counting like this to nine. Then I start over with, "One".

As I count, I start to worry, "What is Gabriel talking about? What is going on? How did that hole appear in the parking lot? What just happened? Who is eating whom? Why doesn't anything ever work for me? Should I go skiing? Twenty three. Twenty three? Damn! I was supposed to start over at nine."

"One".

Breath out, "Two".

Breath in, "Three".

Breath out, "Three".

I do this count to nine and back to one, twice more. I am calm and stable. I am focused and here in the moment with Gabriel. I let go of him.

Gabriel is looking directly into my eyes and saying, "Eating is actually a cruel hoax, a trick. Actually every time that you eat, you participate in an addictive ritual that separates you from your divine nature and you take great joy in doing it but it is a destructive behavior. Eating doesn't sustain you. It kills you and destroys you. Stopping eating actually allows you to feast on the divine. It allows you to go back, to be, to go forward, go back, whatever. Fasting allows you to be the divine creative being of light that you are and to get your beingness directly. Fasting allows you to be your whole bright beingness. Every time that you eat, you take away from your beingness for the gratification of a blind, destructive desire. Eating is a trick, just as fire and agriculture are tricks. Stop eating and start feasting on the divine. Feast on the light. Be the light."

"It is critical that you understand that fasting is feasting. It is important that you understand that when you quit eating what you call food and when you start feasting on what you are going to get when you are fasting that you will be full of a greater joy than you can ever remember. Fasting is feasting. It is not denying yourself anything. Quitting eating is not a denial of anything. Eating is a destructive addiction like consuming heroin. When you quit taking heroin into your body, you do not die. Except for a short period of suffering, you do not get worse. You get better. And what you are calling food is like heroin. When you quit doing it and when you know how to get your nourishment direct, you do not die. You actually get better. There is a better source of being than food and when you fast, you will connect with that other source of being and that other source of being is far more nutritious, more powerful, and more satisfying than food . Food is not a source of being. Food is a source of addiction and enslavement. You do not need food. You've got to stop eating food and break the food addiction. Fasting is feasting. Fasting is feasting is the key concept to the salvation of the human race. It is the key that will free all of you from your bondage, your addiction, and your enslavement."

"Gabriel, I am afraid this is really confusing me. This sounds not only impossible, but crazy. And whatever just happened was creepy. I'm okay now, but let's just keep it simple. What am I going to live on while I am fasting? You say that I'm going to feast on Divine light, Divine energy? Is that a form of sustenance that I can live on?"

"That's the source of life as you understand it. That's the source of everything. That's the source and you are not a separate light being as you are envisioning it. You are envisioning yourself spiritually as something separate like a luminous egg, but that's not really how it is. You are actually a consciousness within the One divine light. You are actually a Divine light yourself and that's why you have been captured and are being eaten. You are Divine light, Divine energy, Divine being."

"Stop! Don't even go there. I just want to know, what are we going to be fasting on, I mean feasting on when I'm fasting feasting? What am I going to eat?"

"Divine being. You are a divine being. You are Divine being, not a divine being . You are Divine being. You are the Source of being. So you will be. It is kind of beyond your concept of being right now because your concept is that you are eating to maintain your being. You believe that if you quit eating you will quit being. Whereas what I am explaining, what is true, is almost the opposite. You already are being and when you are eating, you are actually diminishing your being. The act of eating is actually blinding you and destroying your beingness. You have the whole concept upside down. So it confuses you when I tell you that when you fast, you'll feast. You are thinking that when you eat something that you are getting something from that which you have eaten that will make you be something, but you already are something and you are diminishing your being by what you are doing when you eat. Did you get that?"

I am stunned. I stutter, "I don't know, that's --------? That doesn't make sense. It's not scientific. It reminds me of Jesus turning the stones to loaves of bread and multiplying the fish. But that fish and bread thing doesn't make sense either. I mean that it doesn't make sense scientifically speaking. I think that I'm going to have a fit. My body feels weird, all tingly. I have to sit down for a moment. I need to focus."

"No you need to do the opposite of focus. You need to let go. You need to relax. You need to accept grace. Quit being, doing, focusing. Relax, relax, relax. Accept. Be."

He hits me on the back with a flat palm again and in a loud authoritative voice proclaims, "If you eat a Schmuck's classic potato chip, it won't kill you in the sense that you are thinking of dying because you are already dead. If you weren't already dead, you wouldn't eat a Schmuck's classic potato chip. So, by eating the potato chip, or smoking a cigarette, or doing a line of heroin, it isn't going to kill you. You are already dead or else you wouldn't do it. All you are going to do is continue to be dead and to be more dead. You are going to be less alive. Liveliness is a continuum, a spectrum of being for humans. It's what you leave out, not what you put in that matters. If you leave out eating the potato chip, you are more alive. The more that you leave out, what you call food, the more alive you will be. The more that you eat, the more dead you will be. Eating is an addiction, a self-destructive behavior that accumulates. Eating is not like taking a gun and pointing it at your head and pulling the trigger. It's like shooting heroin. The first shot is incredibly pleasurable and seems to be enlightening. It seduces you. It's the same with a bite of Schmuck's potato chips. The first bite is delicious. It opens a whole new realm of pleasure and it seduces you. Did you ever see that advertisement where the food scientist in the white lab coat gives the guy a new type of potato chip and dares the guy to eat it saying, 'Bet you can't eat just one.' That food scientist knew what he as saying. You can't eat just one. So you eat a potato chip and being a food eater becomes your life. But eating actually becomes your death. It's a little hard to see that in the case of a potato chip. It's easier to see it in the case of heroin. This is true of all of the things which we call foods, even plant juices. Although juices are closer to the light, you are still eating. You are still thinking that you need to eat to connect to the Source. You are still not remembering that you are the Source. You are still in an aberrant behavior that blinds you and confuses you."

"Do you remember the analogy of the window? Remember that you are trying to clean the window so that you can see the light, the Divine light. Then you are going to open the window and let the Divine light into your being and be the Divine light."

His words don't seem to have the same meaning that I thought that those words had. It's like saying that the reason that my clothes are wrinkled is because I have an iron deficiency.

I am trying to listen and to feel my breath on the tip of my nose. I am feeling different, better. The whack on my back has refocused my attention but I'm still frightened, upset, struggling.

I simply answer, "I'm still confused."

"Well maybe you can understand food better by looking at this all another way. Let's look at the other kinds of things that you do that darken the window, that separate you, and that take you out of the present."

"You indulge in dramas around good memories or bad memories. First you indulge in the memory and then you start to get into a fantasy about a new something that you are going to do that is going to be good or bad. It can be both ways, but let's imagine a good memory. You remember making raw cacao fudge with Lilith.

I flashback to a morning last summer. Lilith is calling. It is 9:30 Sunday morning.

"I did like that book that we were reading said," she informs me.

"What book? What did you do," I ask confused.

"I got up a little later than usual this morning. I was feeling lazy and a little tired. I was lying about reading and the book advised me to add two tablespoons full of raw cacao to my morning smoothie. So, I did. I got out a bag of raw chocolate nibs and a measuring tablespoon. I carefully scooped out a spoonful of nibs and scraped the extra nibs from the full spoon with a knife, making it a perfect tablespoonful and added it to my smoothie. Then I did that again, adding a total of two tablespoonfuls to my morning drink. Then I drank the mixture while I continued reading. I feel wonderful. I have done my laundry, cleaned the house, and balanced my checkbook. I need a friend. I want to do something. I have a little jar of something called cacao fudge from work. Let's make our own raw cacao fudge."

"Sure," I answer. "Let's make the best fudge ever. Come on over."

"Be there shortly," she says and hangs up.

I have acquired all of the right gadgets to prepare delicious raw dishes. I have a powerful, double gear juicer that will juice lawn clippings if I want to, and sometimes I do juice some interesting wild plants with amazing effects on my body and mind. I have a big strong food processor and a great blender. I have a dehydrator and a thing for making raw zucchini into noodles. I have a coffee and spice grinder and a citrus juicer. I have handfuls of big knives and little knives, spoons, and cutting boards. I may not own much anymore, but I do have the things to prepare good, nutritious, whole foods. My pantry and spice shelves are well stocked and my refrigerator is full of produce.

Lilith is suddenly here. She is tall and thin and beautiful. She is almost as tall as I am. She is maybe five feet nine or ten inches. She is always dressed in nice attractive outfits. She is graceful and reserved in her movements and in her thoughts. She is cautious, but open minded.

She raps on the sliding glass door to my front room/dining area. It is also my front door. She doesn't need to knock but she always does. I am sitting at my dining table reading "The Life and Teachings of the Masters of the Far East". We are looking at each other.

I smile and wave and say, "Come in."

She slides the door open and asks, "Did you know that cacao is one of the secrets of the vibrant native economy that existed on this continent when the Spanish arrived?" She doesn't wait for an answer. "The cacao bean was the Aztec unit of money, one bean, one dollar. Because the bean was their money, they had no usury or hoarding in their culture. If you hoarded your money, it rotted. So money had to be spent soon after you earned it. As a result, Mexico in the 1400's had the world's richest, most vibrant economy. They had more libraries, bigger cleaner streets, and better utilities than anywhere else in the world. The cacao bean will do the same thing for us. If we consume it, we will have a vibrant life too, but it has to be eaten raw. It can't be cooked. So, I have an idea."

She hands me a little jar with a label that announces that what is in the jar is raw chocolate fudge. She opens the lid, hands the jar to me and commands me to, "Try it."

I get out a little spoon and eat a spoonful of the brown mixture.

"It is pretty good," I say, "but it is a little bitter and it has a kind of grainy dry texture that dries out my mouth."

"Exactly!" She cries. "I can do better. I want my fudge to be creamy smooth and sweet, but I don't want it to make me gain weight. I want my fudge to be delicious, but I also want it to help me lose weight. I have decided that our recipe should be: one cup of raw cacao beans, one cup of raw organic honey from the Amazon, one cup of organic extra virgin coconut oil, blended together into a smooth concoction. Then a cup of raw cashew flour added to the mixture to give the fudge a thicker consistency. Then a cup of mixed almonds and macadamia nuts lightly chopped and stirred in along with a cup of goji berries. I could add maca, Siberian ginseng, and blue green algae for a real boost, but for this dish we're going for flavor. So, we are also going to add four vanilla beans and a spoonful of cinnamon."

"What about losing weight?" I ask. "That sounds pretty rich."

"Lots of people don't know it, but all fats aren't the same. Coconut oil is a medium chain saturated fat. The more that you eat, the more weight that you will lose. Farmers learned that way back in the 30's when they tried to fatten cattle on coconut oil. The more coconut oil that they fed their cows, the slimmer the cows became. The vegetable oil association put out that fat scare propaganda demonizing coconut oil just to get people to use the newly developed polyunsaturated hydrogenated vegetable oils rather than the old saturated fat coconut oil. And we fell for their "information campaign" just like we fell for the old pyramid of foods posters which were put out by the Dairy Association. And although raw chocolate is one of the best super foods, full of anti-oxidants and vitamins and minerals, it is also a mood enhancer that gets you going burning calories, burning off that fat."

"Win, win," I say, "but the proof is in the taste."

I start blending a cup of cashews down into cashew flour in the food processor. Lilith smashes raw cacao beans in an old yellow, hand held, lemon juice squeezer. She uses it just like a nut cracker, cracking a half dozen cacao beans at a time. She cracks the cacao beans, drops them onto a plate, squishes them around, and then steps outside and blows across the plate, blowing the cacao bean shells away from the chocolate and out into the yard. She comes back in and puts the cacao nibs, the broken pieces of chocolate, in my coffee grinder along with the vanilla beans and the cinnamon and grinds the mixture down into a fine powder.

I put the cup of coconut oil and the cup of honey on the stove and heat them up until they are liquid enough to stir, but not hot enough to burn my finger which means that they are about one hundred and four degrees and certainly not over one hundred and eighteen degrees. All of the enzymes, vitamins, and phytonutrients are all still whole and living.

Lilith pours the cacao powder mixture into the food processor. I pour the sauce pan of coconut oil and honey into the food processor and punch the power switch.

Lilith is carefully watching me. She laughs, "You are like a bull in the kitchen."

"I just like to get things done," I respond. "If something is in the way or slowing down production, I don't like it. I just push it out of the way. I hope that I am not offending you."

"No. You're all guy," she says. "I'm alright with that. I'm just noticing."

We watch the chocolate blend for a minute. Then we take off the lid, take spoons and taste the mixture.

Lilith looks at me with sparkling eyes and says, "That's delicious," and carefully licks her spoon.

I agree, "Yes it is."

I pour the cashew flour back into the processor and continue blending the chocolate, coconut oil, honey, and the vanilla beans and cinnamon. The mixture starts getting pretty firm, firm enough to burn up a less powerful machine.

Lilith takes out a big wooden spoon and spoons the mixture out of the food processor bowl and into a big mixing bowl. I pour the chopped nuts and goji berries into the bowl on top of the chocolate. Lilith stirs everything together.

This time we take out big spoonfuls and eat them.

"I've never had anything like this before," Lilith says. "I really like it."

"I really like it too," I echo as I eat another heaping spoonful.

We spread the whole concoction in a big baking dish and smooth it and put it in the refrigerator to let it set up.

"I can't wait until it's done," Lilith says.

"Me neither," I agree and I really mean it too. I add, "That chocolate is really good."

"This raw lifestyle is awesome," Lilith says with the deep conviction of an evangelical preacher at a revival. "The best way to improve your health and invigorate your life is to add more raw fruits and vegetables to your diet."

"Yeah," I agree, "but eating all of those greens would be hard without your dynamite sauces and dressings."

"I know," she replies and asks, "what's your favorite dressing?"

Without even thinking about my choices, I say, "the creamy Thai one, the one that is: two thirds of a cup of Bragg liquid aminos soya sauce, two thirds of a cup of lime juice, two thirds of a cup of maple syrup, and a cup of hemp oil, and then some spices like garlic, jalapenos, cilantro, parsley, basil, you know, whatever you have in the kitchen. That's delicious and I really liked it the time that you added baby Thai coconut milk and meat and I like the way that you make it creamy by adding in a cup of cashews."

She concurs, "That's my favorite too."

I start dreaming about all of the wonderful dishes we make and are going to prepare and all of the wonderful things that we are going to do. I am in full blown fantasyland.

Gabriel snaps his fingers. Hello. Now you are imagining what you are going to do when you see Lilith again and about how what you are going to do is going to be a good experience. Again you are dirtying the window, losing your presence in the here and now."

"It may be easier to see that you are dirtying the window, confusing yourself, if you look at this in the unhappy direction in the continuum of liveliness, if you look at this in the sense of bad memories, memories in which you lost money or memories in which you hurt someone's feelings or they hurt your feelings, memories that send you into a dark place."

When he says "bad memories", I am reminded of my divorce. I see my ex crying and screaming and yelling at me, "You never change. You never change. I've tried over and over and over and I'm sick of it. I'm sick of you. I'm leaving."

I am devastated. I promise, "I'll change. I will change."

She weeps, "You say that every time but you never change. You don't hear me. You don't see me."

She goes up to her bedroom and I can hear her sobbing and sobbing and I know that she is right. I have completely failed as a husband, as a father, as a lover, and as a friend. I always intend to change while she is yelling at me and crying, but somehow after a while I just lose interest in pleasing her, in changing, and go back to my old ways until she is crying again. My lungs won't suck air. I have a feeling something really bad is happening this time and that it is going to get worse, way worse. I'm sick, sick of me, sick of life. I'm trapped. Badness is everywhere. I don't know what to do. Everywhere that I look is a dead end, a bad dead end. I start thinking about all of the awful things that have been done to me, the awful things that I have done. Scene after scene flash through my mind.

In my misery, I realize that Gabriel is talking to me. I come back to the present. He is saying, "It's easier to see that bad memories take you away from the light, from the present, cause separation, make the window smudged up, put layers of non-beingness between you and beingness. By looking at bad memories, you can see how your past has created a crust, a cement layer between you and the light, between you and what is happening here, now. So all of this history and drama and doing is

155

as damaging as eating. It doesn't mean that you won't be and do any more after the window is opened. The exact opposite is true. You will be and do much more. It just means that the type of being and doing that you have been being and doing is causing trouble, problems, and disconnection. You should change if you wish to be vibrantly healthy, happy, and living in abundance with other loving, joyous beings."

"What you are to be doing is cleaning the window and opening it and connecting with the Divine light, or rather remembering that you are the Divine light. You are to begin fasting immediately."

"Are you ready to let go and begin a long fast?"

CHAPTER 17

LETTING GO

I hop back up on the rock wall, put my hands flat on the cool stones, gaze down at the solid pavement, nervously sway my feet back and forth, and quietly say, as if I'm begging, "I don't know, Gabriel. I'm still thinking about this 'letting go thing'. I don't want to sell my property. I need to have some place to come back to. There are some things that I don't want to let go of. And I don't see how I'm going to pay for doing all of this. And I'm not sure about this eating Divine Presence thing. As I understand it, Divine consciousness, or consciousness of Divine Presence, in other words feeling Divine love, is greater than poverty, loneliness, and even bad health. I guess there are people who are quadriplegics, who are ecstatically happy, because they know God. This awareness, this consciousness must be something very powerful, but how does someone tap into that Divine Presence, become aware of Divine love, or become loved by divinity, by God? I mean theoretically we are all loved by God right now, right?"

"Divine love absolutely destroys a human."

My head snaps up. My jaw drops. My feet stop moving. We lock eyes.

"What do you mean? I don't get any food or shelter or anything?"

"No, those are your human needs. You don't need those anymore."

"Well ,where will I live?"

"Everywhere. Nowhere."

"What will I eat?"

"Manna."

"What is that?"

"Divine Presence."

"Divine Presence? I still don't understand this."

"No, I know, but you asked the question and that is the answer."

"So everything is lost?"

"Yes, everything is lost, or nothing is lost since there is no thing. Again you are thinking in human terms, and in human understanding, everything is lost."

I can't believe what I'm hearing, or at least I don't want to believe what Gabriel is saying.

"So, what is gained?" I ask.

"Everything is gained."

"Ooooh boy. Okay, I understand that I am to leave my home. Where is this everywhere that I am to live? Where am I going? Everything is gone. I'm giving up my home, my possessions, and I'm leaving. Where do I go?"

"Well, first get rid of them."

"Well, I sure don't like that answer. It kind of puts everything up in air in a frightening place, kind of no way back."

"Yes, from a human point of view I suppose that it does. That just definitely shows a lack of faith on your part, eh?" he says and laughs heartily as if he has just told an old joke that everyone gets. Then he rocks back on his heels, puts his hands in his pockets, and smiles shyly at me.

"Indeed it does," I agree smiling back.

"Give your furniture to your daughter. Sell whatever you have for whatever you can get."

"Where am I going to live?"

"Don't worry about it."

"That's what you said about the debt, and I'm kind of worried."

"Yeah, I know but that is your answer in human terms."

"Forget about what you are doing. Move on. Now! That means physically, spiritually, mentally, and emotionally, move on. Let go. Drop human concerns. Quit stewing and fretting. Do it. Do it today. Everything has to go, every thing. Let go."

"Ohhhh ! I don't want to."

"Doesn't matter what you want. You do understand that it is all lost anyway? You never could hold on to it. You can't hold on to it. So why hold on to it? I know that you understand that intellectually but grind it around a bit. Then let go. You have no choice anyway. In the end, and all humans come to an end, you have to let go. So, why not let go now, at a beginning rather than when your life is done, and you are passing over to me? Do it now in the midst of your life. Meet me now and we'll do grand things. We'll have fun. We'll have great fun, more fun than you can imagine."

"Oh, oh, oh. I don't want to."

"You don't have a choice. Look at Johnny. Johnny's story and your story are the same story, same story different words. If you won't let go, you will be forced to let go. You might as well just do it now, consciously, with awareness and perception, and step out of the human dilemma, the human world. Step across the line of consciousness and awareness. Let go. Think about the Johnny story and let go. Become angelic. Be divine."

"Do you see the flaw in the old Shane story? You don't win the Mega-Riches lottery to win, you lose the Mega-Riches lottery to win. Do you see where the doorway out is? You have to let it all go. That's the way out. That's the way in."

"That means to let go of your worries too. You're thinking, 'what am I going to eat? Where am I going to live? What is the difference between a saint and a hobo?' You have to let your worries go too. That's the difference between a hobo and a saint. A hobo is worried about things: food, power, money, possessions. He doesn't have them, but he wants them. He needs them. A saint doesn't need them and he doesn't want them. The saint knows that that's all taken care of."

"So let the worries go first. That's number one. As long as you are worrying, you haven't let go. Even if you have nothing, even if you are a hobo, and you're penniless without a friend in the world, you really are in poverty and friendless when you're still worrying about things. So you gotta let the worries go before you let the things go."

"The mind has to go too. The ego has to go. The worries have to go. Let them all go. You have to let them go anyway. You are going to die. You can go a piece at a time as you and Johnny are doing now, but you are going to go, one way or another. So, go now, all at once, and its only now, so do it now, and do it complete. Not just let the possessions go, or the, what, the money go, or the hopes go, everything goes, that means the worries go too. That means the philosophies, the theories, the worries, everything goes. What good are any of them? What comfort are they to you on your death bed? Think about it! You're dead! You're a dying man. As you are lying there in your last moment, what comfort, as you are about to step across, are you going to get from anything? Let it all go now. Die now. Step across now while you are alive and be alive for the first time ever. Be the first living human in a long, long time. It's time do it. Anyway the point is, the worries gotta go. Now that I have told you that you have to let go of everything, that includes worrying, thoughts, philosophies, any of those dramas that you can come up with, let them go. They aren't going to do you any good."

"Don't worry about what you're trying to do or what you are going to do. Just make yourself available. Agree to go."

I hop down from the rock wall. "Okay. I'm available. I agree to go."

"Yah Hey. Wah Hey."

"How do I sell my things?"

"Don't worry about it. They're sold. It's taken care of. "

"Huh? So, what am I doing?"

"Nothing you are making yourself available. Remember?"

"Whoa. I don't think I quite got that."

"Yeah I know. We'll work on it."

"So, all that I'm supposed to do is to enjoy the rest of the day and to pay attention to what comes up, what the Universe presents for me, Just flow in what Divine Presence is presenting."

"Yeah, you can look at it that way. Just be aware and accept what's happening. Just be a hollow bamboo and let the light shine through.   That's a wonderful image from that Tommy Anton song."

"I feel better already. Of course there is a trust factor problem here, and I know that I'm going to fall back into worrying, but your argument about death is pretty convincing. Your picture of Johnny and me is pretty convincing too, and there is no comfort anywhere else. That is pretty convincing also. I don't like it, but I see your point. Okay, I'll just enjoy right now. I don't know what else we're going to do. I mean, we could do a lot between now and forever. I'm going to just enjoy your offer and presence. I'm just going to do that. It's nice to be here with you. Whatever we are doing here, if there is a here. I'm just going to enjoy."

CHAPTER 18

THE ATTRACTION

Laughing, I turn to go, then pause wondering, "What was that you said about losing the lottery to win the lottery? I've been using the 'power of attraction' to win the lottery. What is wrong with that?"

"If you win the Mega-Riches lottery, then you have lost the Great Universal lottery. If you would win everything, if you would win your soul, then you must lose everything. You must lose the Mega-Riches lottery and then you have everything. You have your freedom. You have your time. You have your knowing. You get to be."

"You are better than a lottery winner. You are more than that. You are all things. You are all possibilities. Why settle for a small sparkling gem when you can be all sparkling gems? "

"Ask yourself, who is the attractor? What is going on? What is the attractor doing? Don't go attract things. Think about what is being the attraction. Don't get lost in the attracting. Understand your basic nature, your beingness, and who you are. And awaken! Wake up! See that you are the source and that you are being deceived. And don't be dazzled by a few small trinkets and a little trick of creating trinkets."

"Be careful when you start manifesting things. It isn't so obvious when you manifest a couch, because having a chair to sit in seems pretty basic, but now, let's say that you manifest a great house on a hill, a beautiful, beautiful house full of wonderful furniture and lovely art and nice convenient appliances and a great view and a few nice pets to live with you and a lover. Now the question is do you possess the house or does the house possess you? Think!"

"Now, you have to start looking at the meaning of fear, the meaning of security, the meaning of anxiety, because now, you have to start worrying about losing your nice new big house, the house that you love so much. So the question of security arises in your consciousness and it is at that point that fear works on possessing your being and you become manipulatable. You become enslaved. You worry about losing your house. You have just created a trinket that is now controlling your being and you are no longer being the source in creation. Your creation is being you and your fear makes other beings that would use you and abuse you, capable of using and abusing you. So if you are to use the law of attraction, beware of what you are attracting. And be aware that you are the great attractor. You are the great attraction. You are the great show. You are the great mystery and you are not alone. So be aware and consider the consequences of attracting things and then shine with the greatest joy, happiness and vibrancy, and all of the beauty and greatness and all of the possibilities that are possibly possible. Lose attracting and be attractive."

He laughs joyfully and exclaims, "Yeah! Shine on. Shine on you beautiful, beautiful diamond."

"Yes! You are absolutely correct," I exclaim. "I see it now. I will cut up all of my credit cards and I will accept the grace that I am given as enough and I will no longer rob the future with the present and be caught in a vicious cycle where I have lost the present by attracting a bunch of things into my presence and lost my future and my ability to be. I will slice up every credit card now, today."

"Yes! Yes Shane Parker, those of you who have little are blessed because in your poverty of things of material wealth, you can hear my voice and you are not afraid because you have little to lose, whereas the rich have much to lose and they think that they are wealthy, but all of their days will be lost protecting and hoarding their wealth. So they will die in great poverty of the soul and great misery of the spirit and sickness and suffering of the body, and go into the darkness clinging to their lost bodies and lost things. Whereas those of you who have little in the way of material wealth have the possibility of eternal happiness and wealth and joy because you can let go of the trinkets and be the source of all wonder and being and knowing. So blessed are the poor and the meek and cursed are the rich and the powerful and the arrogant and the knowers that believe that they know, when they know not."

"The law of attraction is a trick, a deceit of this time. You are in danger of losing your soul, if you are seduced by a law of attraction which attracts things. You are lost in the trinkets that you attract. Don't go there. Turn the opposite direction and look back at the attractor, and ask, 'Who is doing the attracting? What is the attraction? What is the attractor?' Those are the questions. That is what to look at and then realize that you are the source. Then contemplate the source. Look at the source. Don't turn back around and look at those objects that you are attracting. Look at the Source. Go back to the Source. Be the Source. Remember that you are the Source. And then if you want to turn around and create pretty sparkling little gems, that is okay. Go ahead, but see them for what they are, and recognize their value, which is nothing, because you have an infinite mountain of little gems. If you want to have gems, and do gems, and be gems, and enjoy gems, and whatever, go ahead, but don't trade your essence for a gem and believe that it is the only gem in the pile. Look back at the Source from which you are being, and remember, and be that, and realize that you are not attracting anything. You are creating everything."

"You are the Source. Do not fear anything. Speak the truth. The darkness has no power over you. Fear not. There is no fear."

CHAPTER 19

THE SOURCE

I am excited. Gabriel has rallied my spirit. I am ready to go.

"Gabriel, that is fascinating. So, what is the source of this dream, and by this dream I mean, this waking life? Where does this all arise from? What is the exact point that this all comes into being? Where is that moment that is before this be's? Where is that happening? What is that happening? What isn't that happening? What is, isn't? Where does the moment come where isn't, is? Where are all of those other moments, the ones that are dreams and fantasies, and that are isn'ts that aren't? Where is isn't where isn't is? The Source. Only that. What is the source? And I mean by what is the source, I mean what is it? What is the essence? Where is it? What is I AM? If I am the source, then why am I not creating anything, except misery?"

I'm agitated, sincere, leaning into Gabriel. My arms are waving about, stabbing words, pointing at Gabriel.

He leans back, smiling, rubs his chin with his left hand as if contemplating something important, all the while looking directly at me, and says, "Ahhh. That is a good question. Now we are getting down to it finally, yeah!"

He places his right hand on my left shoulder and gently pulls me clockwise to my right saying, "Okay, turn around. Turn around and look back at the source. Look at that split second upon which everything is coming into being. Where was everything a moment ago, before everything here that you are experiencing is here? Where is that? Now keep looking! Look back! Quick!"

He laughs wildly as he spins me faster and faster.

I experience an odd vertigo looking at the parking lot. It is like watching a cartoon show where the pictures aren't being changed fast enough to make a smooth motion picture. There are dark moments between each movement, each picture, but the movie is always there. I spin round and round like a ballerina. The world is always there, everywhere. I spin faster and faster, but nothing changes except my equilibrium. I stop spinning and wobble about.

"You can't look back quick enough, can you? It is always there. Where is it? What's happening? Where is that moment before this moment? Wherein is everything arising that you are experiencing and perceiving now? Where was that in the then? Where is then? Where is the second before this second? You have to see it. You have to answer that question."

I lean over and grab my knees. "Wow! That's hard to do."

From behind me he grabs my left shoulder with his left hand. He jerks me into standing up and then pushes me forward with his right hand between my shoulder blades, or at least it seems as if he pushes me forward because my body doesn't actually move. He is still holding me steady with his left hand, but my awareness seems to fall forward into darkness. I am looking down, down into darkness a long, long ways. Somehow though, I know that in this darkness is the light, the Source. Who in their right mind though would go further in there? How could anyone ever find their way back to here from in there? There is big, really big, and there is so much there, so much power in the Source that I might decide to merge with it and be all, but not be me anymore. I am in a place where I can simultaneously see life, ordinary life, going on in the present, going on as usual, but I am outside of this ordinary time and space in a great darkness with a great light. I am somehow in ordinary reality and in a non-ordinary reality at the same time.

"Yes," answers Gabriel, "that is hard to do. In your ordinary day to day life you have been experiencing things as if they always have been in existence. Within this context you are used to thinking about what you want. You are used to visualizing yourself as being a type of lens that is focusing new things which you desire into being and into your possession. You're used to seeing yourself as a focal point for the source of creation in which you are focusing the resources that you believe are surrounding you and creating and bringing the things which you desire to you. Look over there at what you have been thinking of as your life. Now turn around and look at that which you are focusing, that source of energy with which you are creating an image and then forcing that image into being using that source. Turn around and look at the source. Look right down into it and see from whence your ordinary consensual life is arising. Now don't stand between it and the future. Go down into it and muck around in its beingness. What is that great brightness? See the source of your life before it is being. Don't stand up here between Source and life and be as Source's unformed pure energy. Form it. Get down and see what the nature of pure unformed energy is. What is that? How in the world are you being separate from it and looking down into it? Go down and merge with it."

I am now standing in this darkness, like the darkness of outer space, like the darkness of the void and I am looking down into a vast white light, but I can turn around and look at Gabriel's parking lot too, at cars and trees and a city.

"Well this could be my last teaching. I mean if I go down in there will I even be?" I ask.

He is standing beside me in the void and quietly answers, "Blessed are you who have gazed upon me for you will see the face of God and it will be your salvation. You are saved."

"Holy Shit! That's powerful!" I exclaim. Then realizing what I just said, I apologize, "Oh gosh, I guess I shouldn't have said that. How about gosh that's powerful?" I laugh nervously, surprised. "You kind of caught me off guard there. I'll have to watch my language."

"Okay, here we go," he says ignoring my surprise. "Let's go down there."

"Alright, I'm going to place myself, place my consciousness, my awareness at the moment that creates this moment," I agree. "That's where I'm going, right before now."

I am confused. I am not sure of what to do next. How does one move about in this space between the life that I've known and the source of that life? How does one fly from here to there? What should I do? I am not frightened. I just cannot understand what to do.

"To see the Source, be the Source," Gabriel cryptically prompts me.

"Okay, I'll try to remember a moment ago."

"You can't get to the Source by remembering. If you are remembering, you are already separate. The show is happening. It has already happened. That won't work."

"Okay, how do I go back?"

"You can't go back. That is not how you get there. You are not understanding what the Source is. You are not ----. Okay, look at it this way. I know that this is a paradox but you have to go forward to get back. You have to look into the future to get back to the past. Don't carry the past into the future. Carry the future forward into the past and make it a future that you want to live and a past that you want to have experienced."

Go into the future to get to the past? Paradox indeed. I can't think that thought. The only way that I know to get beyond the mind is to meditate. I suggest, "Maybe I'll meditate."

"No, you can't meditate. That won't work either."

"Okay, you say everything is streaming into being."

"Yes, it is streaming into being."

"Where is the stream that is streaming coming from?"

"Go to the front end of the stream to go back in time and space. To get to the moment before, you have to go ahead into the stream of beingness to the end."

As he is talking, I am scanning the parking lot quickly looking from one object to another trying to see something pop into existence. "Damn! Every time that I look at something, or hold it in my mind, like that truck over there, it is already there. I can't see how to go to the moment when it wasn't there, or before it was there, or uhhh, because there is no before. I can't. I have to step outside of time too ----. Oh, time is the stream that it's all flowing in. I have to leave out time."

"Stick with that! Stick with it! If you can get that, everything else will be irrelevant. Keep on it!"

"Ohhh, I can't get there. I have to lose the I too. The I is part of the time stream, isn't it? I have to lose the I. Let's see ----. Oooh boy! Umphhh! Time. I. I'll go there as you. I'm going to drop me, I, Parker. I'm going to go there as pure Godness. I'm going to have to step over there into Yourness to get there."

"Okay. Drop Parker. You're right. You've got to leave him. You've got to leave that. So do it. You're doing alright. Stop trying to understand! Any understanding already is. For example, if you try to understand by using an astrological chart or a statistical formula and looking at the numbers and trying to understand what is going to happen and understand what has happened, you are looking at your understanding of what is and your understanding of what is going to be. Too late! Stop it! Stop understanding. You cannot look at things that are to get to before they were. Keep looking at the source but you cannot get to the source by understanding the source. You can't understand. Understanding is another trinket. That won't work either."

"Oh man, I would like to give up, but I'm going to be attacked. I am going to suffer, to die."

"Yes. You are going to be attacked if you don't succeed. It is absolutely imperative to your happiness that you succeed. If you do not succeed, you are going to be very unhappy. So you need to succeed."

"Ohhhh, I hate this. I can't do it. But I don't want to be unhappy. You really hurt me when you said that."

"Yes, I meant to. It's a fact. If you want to be happy, you have to succeed at this. You are a being that is dying. You are running out of time. And those moments of time can be pretty miserable if you don't succeed."

"Okay! Okay! Okay! So my ability to create has been taken away from me so that I might be the creator?"

"No. You were the creator. Now you are the substance of the creation."

"What is that?"

"You are not looking forward now. You are not looking back. You are looking at the substance which is before there is substance."

"What is that?"

"The wise ones exist outside of existence."

"Ahhhrghh. My mind is just starting to crack! I wish that I were smarter."

"This isn't an intelligence test. You cannot think your way there. That won't work either."

"Well, how do I get there then? I can't meditate to there. I can't think to there. I can't go to there. I can't look to there. Can you push me or direct me or point me in the right way? I need some help here. How? Where? What? I'm lost. Give me a hint. Help me out. Push me over to somewhere where I can get a new perspective on this."

"This includes the dream realities."

"They are doing the same thing aren't they? This includes realms of being that I don't even have memories of, but that exist, and I exist in them somewhere, some place, some time."

"I remember, I tried this, this going back to the beginning in a dream once. I was having a conversation in a dream. I was trying to figure out how to get back to the moment that was before that moment. I was confused and I was trying to go back in the dream to an earlier part of the dream, but I didn't know that I was dreaming. I was talking to my mother."

She said, "Your father has been down talking to the bears again."

I was surprised. I didn't remember my father ever talking to any bears. I asked, "What bears?"

You know. "There's three of them," she answered. "There's that grey one and there's that black one."

I couldn't grasp what she was saying. I mean, talk to bears. How? When? Where? I asked, "Where? Where does he talk to the bears?"

"After you cross the creek, you know. Down by where that rock machine is, whatever it is, that you guys threw away."

I went, "What rock machine? What creek?"

She said, "That white thing down in the blackberry bushes."

"What is it Dad?" I asked.

He said, "I don't know. It's just one of those things you know ----------. Those things that you and Fred and Pat and those guys Casey, Casey Gardener used for mining."

"And then I realized that I thought we were talking about coming up to the house, the house on the hill where my parents live in the waking world. Then I realized, no way, I'm trying to go back in time and the beginning that I'm trying to go back to isn't even a time that even exists in the waking world. I am dreaming. This is a dream. But it's so real. I can't tell the difference even after I realize that I am in an alternate universe, a dream world. That's ----. My mind stopped and I woke up."

"Yes, you can go back any way, any place, any time. You can go back in a dreaming world too if you want to, if that helps you. You can try to put the two different realities together the same way that you are using the Johnny and the Shane stories together to understand synchronicity and arstory. You can take a dream reality and a waking reality and put them side by side and trace them back. You can ask yourself the same question. Where do dreams come from? Where are dream worlds before you dream them? If that helps you."

"It doesn't. For me, they just are. All being is. All worlds are. They just are. I can't dig in behind areness or in under areness."

"Try," he encourages.

"Wait, how about this?" I ask. "Let's look at dying and at being born. What does dying mean? Dying? Dying? Dying?" I suggest, " Let me explain my idea of dying to you and see if that helps. Dying is the end of areness. I can search for the beginning in the end. Death is at least the end of this point of view, my isness in the here. It is something that I'm considering unpleasant, and something that is driving me to solve this problem. But what is dying? Maybe I should consider dying not as something bad but as an opportunity. Maybe that is a point of view, another point of view that would help me understand where areness comes from. I could think of dying as a birth."

"The world, worlds, certainly seem to be able to exist independent of my beingness. My awareness and consciousness doesn't seem to bring the entire world into being. It's the old question: If a tree falls in the woods and no one is there to hear it fall, does it make at sound? I believe that I only manifest a little piece of awareness of something much bigger. Is that true? I mean, if I die the world goes on? Right? Of course. I'm not sure what dying means. It would certainly seem to me that death is when my consciousness departs this space and time and other beings are no longer aware of my being. What does that mean? I need some help."

"It doesn't matter how you look at it. You started looking at death on an individual basis but, as you now are, you can look at it on a generic All basis too . You then are just asking the Big Bang question. Where does the All come into being? Where does it go when it goes out of being? When did the All come into being? Where does the All come from? You have just come to the famous Steven Hawkings' 'turtles all the way down' conundrum. You know, the one where Hawkings starts "A Brief History of Time" with the story of a well-known scientist giving a public lecture on astronomy. The scientist describes how the earth orbits around the Sun and how the Sun, in turn, orbits around the center of a vast collection of stars called our galaxy.

At the end of the lecture, a little old lady at the back of the room gets up and says, "What you have told us is rubbish. The world is really a flat plate supported on the back of a giant tortoise."

The scientist gives a superior smile before replying, "What is the tortoise standing on?"

"You're very clever, young man, very clever," says the old lady. "But it's turtles all the way down!"

"The question is still the same. What is that last turtle standing on? Where is the moment before it is this moment? Whether it's the moment before the moment of this conversation or it's the moment a billion, trillion years ago. Where is it or where is it not before it is and where is it going/coming from not to is?"

"Stop it Gabriel. I can't understand. I'm feeling woozy, disoriented, spacey. I'm not going to make it today. I just can't do it. I have got to go back over everything, over letting go, and then over the law of attraction, and then turn slowly from the trinkets through the focusing lens that is the intentions, the consciousness that is Shane, and look back at the source and go into the before that is, and I can't seem to do that right now. Let's come back to that question of, where is before this all is, later. This weird talk makes me nervous and frightens me."

CHAPTER 20

FEAR

"Gabriel, you mentioned fear and anxiety, when we were discussing possessing things and the 'law of attraction'. I am confused, anxious, and fearful now."

As I focus on my fear, the window to Source closes. We are now simply two men standing in a parking lot in a country town having a conversation. Fear changes everything. Fear closes my possibilities and shrinks my world to one which my mind imagines that it can handle. I feel that I can grasp the things which I fear.

I continue questioning Gabriel, "I would like to discuss fear. I have a question about fear. To me there seems to be some person or persons in my life who are always using a fear factor technique on me and my fellow humans where they directly or indirectly coerce us into doing what they want. They push and deceive us into doing their dirty work. They first create a fear in us and then they offer a solution and the solution is that we do what they wanted us to do in the first place. We wouldn't do what they wanted, if we were directly told to do it, because their solution always requires us to give away more of our time, freedom, energy, and happiness."

"The way that this technique works seems to be that on the public level, everything is fine. Suddenly there is a crisis, terrorists, banking collapse, tainted food, or something. Then a solution is offered for our own safety. The solution is always more laws and regulations that take away more of our opportunities and freedoms in exchange for safety and security. We are constantly being herded into a smaller pen. On the personal level, they create a fear of failure and starvation and suffering, and then offer a job, a position which takes complete control of most of our personal creative energy in a task that we would quit if we weren't afraid of what would happen if we lost our ability to 'make a living'. We are constantly kept anxious and fearful by news which is only half true and that doesn't touch our lives personally most of the time anyway."

"That's what I think. But that is a question, not a statement of fact. I am just guessing, venting my feelings. I don't have any idea who the 'they' in my scenario even are. Am I being paranoid? Is what I said true or is any part of it true and how can I protect myself and my loved ones if it is true? Maybe you could give me some guidance about how fear works, about how fear affects each of us. I know that it affects me a lot. I know that it affects me all of the time. I couldn't even start to make a list of all the things that I'm afraid of. My fear drives me and stops me from enjoying myself, from taking the time to be with you. I'm afraid that if I do anything except what I am doing, what I've learned to do, except the job that I've got, that I'm going to end up out in the cold and the wet, starving, and that the best solution is to go to work for someone in his story so that he'll take care of me because I serve him. I am afraid that if I change, if I switch sides, that if I work over in our story, well play over in our story because no part of our story if I'm dreaming it, is ever work, then that story, our story will have a bad ending. That is what I'm afraid of. I'm scared. So what do you say?"

"I don't think that there is anything that I can add to that."

"Well then how about some assurances. How do I deal with fear?"

"Your fear is, so let it go. What is there that you are fearing? In order for fear to work, you have to be afraid of losing something. Fear comes from attachment. Fear is a construct of the self, the ego. You are just protecting it, the self, the Parker. With your fear, you are protecting an illusion that is actually

175

causing your suffering. What can we do to make you see? Pick a fear."

"Okay, uhhh, I'm thinking. Fear of ----. It's hard not to pick one that isn't mundane. Okay, fear of not paying the credit card bills."

"Okay, fear of not paying the credit card bills. Let's walk around in that. If you don't pay the credit card bills, what's going to happen? Your creditors are going to put liens against your wages and take most of the money that you earn. And that still won't be enough. So they'll foreclose and take anything that you own that they can seize. And then what is the use of making wages, if they are all lost anyway? So you'll quit working and then you won't own anything, and then you will have to go bankrupt. So then you will have a loss of reputation. I guess that is the only thing that you have really lost because you didn't have many of those other possessions left to begin with. So I guess that is really what we are talking about here. You think that you have lost your future. You've lost your integrity. So, it is really an attack on your sense of self and your sense of being able to build that self up at some future time and your belief that a built up self is going to get you some future reward. So what we are talking about is a self and a self's future, right? In that jobless future which becomes a jobless present, you are still breathing and eating and sleeping somewhere, and now you actually have a bunch of free time to do with as you want. Does that make sense to you?"

"Yeah, I guess. I'm as you say going to have to walk around in that a bit and go back and rethink what you said. But yes, I'm following you. That's definitely what I'm worried about, that I'm not going to have a future, or that at least it is going to be a pretty dismal, bleak, unhappy future, if I don't get things done."

"So let's imagine that there is no future self. There is only now because haven't you traded your happiness now for happiness in the future with a glorified future self?"

"Uhhhh. Yes. I guess so."

"So, what happens if you never get to that future with that glorified self? You are being manipulated and beaten with a fear of losing a future glorified self that never comes into being while being trapped forever in a diminished now. So, how about just trading that possible glorified self that you are afraid of losing for a happy, wonderful, beautiful, present now that involves whatever you've got now, and are doing now, and not being afraid?"

"Well, I see what you are saying but it is pretty hard to actually do. I find it pretty hard to let go of that fear of losing my future."

"Yes, and that eternal future is the sharp stick that is being shoved into your guts and twisted, and that is what makes you so easy to manipulate, and what makes you blind to what is happening now."

"So, let go of the self, and let go of that idea of the future, and let go of the fear, and be, here, now, and then you will be in an are story, a story about what is, with us, in our story, now, arstory."

"I see what you are saying intellectually but I'm still afraid. It's like trying to convince me that it is okay to run across a road in front of a firing machine gun by convincing me that I can make it without being harmed. From your point of view, you may know that I can make it, because you know things that I don't know. You have knowledge that the machine gun is going to jam when I jump up. But from my point of view, I don't know that the machine gun is going to jam and that when I jump up that I'm not going to get shot. Developing faith and trust in synchronicity and in the love of the universe is baby steps, one step at time. It's hard to do. But, okay," I continue, "let's look at fear again because fear is really what is driving me. No doubt about it. Fear is a problem for me. It is fear that is holding me back. If you could walk me past fear, if you could just walk me around in fear a little more, I guess, so that I could get more of an understanding of what it is and some way to constructively cope, hope, deal, to get beyond it, that would be really, really helpful, because that seems to really be the center, my stumbling block. Shoot, it's not a stumbling block. It is a big brick wall. It is a gigantic cliff. It is a prison in which we are held. I am held. I can't speak for anyone else. I know that it is a prison that holds my heart, soul, and body. I could definitely use some more teaching and advice about fear. It exhausts me just to talk about fear, much less to deal with it."

"Well, you pretty well hit it on head. Fear is what's being used to control you but it isn't really fear that you have to fear. The basis, the root of the problem is ignorance. If you remembered what you are, if you understood your capabilities, then this would all seem absurd. It is because you don't remember, because you have been blinded, because you can't see, and because you don't know, that you are unable to act, to act without fear. And because you cannot act without fear, you are easily manipulated."

"You are like deer in the forest who are afraid of hunters because they have guns when you, the deer, have nuclear bombs and powerful lasers. You have lasers in your eyes. All you have to do is look at a hunter and he will evaporate, but you have forgotten that you have laser eyes, so you cower and hide. You are in an absurd drama generation after generation after generation and you are so far down the road from your ancient home that you don't even have the myth any more of the powerful ancestor deer with laser eyes who lived in paradise. The memory is just lost to you, completely lost to your consciousness. That is the situation here. If you could remember, you could turn on the laser and evaporate the monster and be free. That is why he has history. It is so that you don't have your story, because in your story, you would simply remember and laser him."

"Do you see the importance of knowledge and of remembering? When you remember, you won't have any fear. So the problem isn't fear. There isn't anything to fear. There isn't any fear. Fear is completely an illusion, a creation, and you have accepted it, and you are deluded by it, and that is why you have to meditate. You have step outside of the history thought form and then you will start to see and to remember. You will then know that, that which you are holding near and dear, is neither near nor dear, but is actually a mask with no eye holes placed over your eyes that blinds you to what is, to our story, and holds you captive in his story, history."

"You hold on to this tiny, tiny, tiny, little gem, a tiny, tiny, tiny little sparkling little diamond. You hold on to a really pretty little diamond when you could have a mountain of diamonds, but you don't believe that is possible, and you can't even see the mountain, and if you could see it and those of you who can see a little piece of it, you are afraid that if you put down this little diamond, this little itty bitty one, and reach for the big mountain of diamonds, multi colored diamonds, much more pretty diamonds, that you will fall short and won't make it to the mountain and you'll lose even the little diamond that you have now. Well that is why you are lost. That is what fear is and that is what the lack of knowledge is and that is what the human life is."

"Wake up! See the mountain of wealth that is your birthright and boldly drop the little bitty self and be divinely One with your Creator and live in total knowing bliss and wonder and efficacy."

"Fear nothing for you are God, godly. You are godly. I don't mean that you are everything, but you are. This is a holographic Universe. You are an itty bitty tiny teeny weeny speck, but you are an itty bitty tiny teeny weeny speck of God, and that makes you a powerful speck. It is like every cell in your body is an itty bitty teeny tiny little cell but to you all of those cells are precious and you don't want any of those cells turning into cancer. You don't even want any of those cells dying. You want everyone of those cells to be healthy, happy, and living fully. Well that is how you and God are. You are an itty bitty tiny teeny little speck in God but you are a part of God. You are of God nature and just as you want every part of your body to be healthy, God wants you to be healthy, and not to be toxic, cancerous, growing weird, doing weird stuff. God wants you to be strong enough to resist viruses and bacteria and not to be sucked on by parasites and eaten by yeast. God wants to give you the nutrition, the strength, and the knowledge to be able to resist those parasites and viruses and if you were to understand your Godly nature and your strength, then why would you ever fear an itty bitty tiny virus or bacteria, even if it were bubonic plague or something really bad like cholera? It can't catch you. You ain't getting it. Don't worry about it. Are you starting to understand fear?"

"Yeah. Yeah. I really am. Let me think about that holographic God thing. That idea really gives me courage, and to think of all those credit card companies as nothing but viruses and parasites attacking me and that I have an infinitely strong immune system is like, wow, hmmm, and I get that thing about the little bitty gem and that mountain of gems too. I really do have a problem defending something that is pretty pathetic. I see that too. You are absolutely right, I've got so little but I'm hanging on to that little that I have with all of my might and trying to get another few pieces knowing all the time that I can't get them. Hmmm, but I didn't know that if I let go of this little piece that I have, that I will get a mountain."

"Yeah, well, it's not a perfect analogy because the little gem that you are letting go of is your I, so your I cannot really get to the mountain and the credit card companies are God too. The analogy breaks down right there and it is a little hard for me to think of another way to say this because the fear, the little gem is your I and so it's your I that you are giving up and what you are not seeing is that the mountain of gems is what are you getting exchange for your I. I can see that I need to give you another explanation but I'm not sure that I can get this through to you yet. This is where you need to understand the holographic God, that all is One. You need to actually know this not just understand it intellectually. You need to comprehend what this all means in the big picture sense. You don't seem to have that yet."

"That is where you have been made blind. You've lost your connection to the All, and you have lost your understanding of the All, and you have lost your memory of the All. That's where the sickness as you would call it, is. That's where the tool, the weapon, that is being used on you is creating the fear. That is exactly the point where it works on you. The weapon is not like a gun that you are being shot with. It's more like a whip or a shock collar around the neck. It is not like a knife that you fear that you are going to be stabbed with. It's more like a bullwhip. You are getting beat with it and it hurts. It wouldn't do any good to stab you or to shoot you and to make you die. It's not like you are actually bleeding to death. It's more like you are being beaten and then beaten again and again, back in this case, into harness, and back into work."

"So, you have to, well actually you don't have to do anything, I'm lost for words, struggling around in English here. I'm trying to get to you the glory and the power and the wealth that is yours. If you could just get out of the pasture for a day and wander on the wide open prairies and in the mountains, then you would never be tempted to go back into the pasture. But we have to go wander in the wilderness first for you to see this. Well maybe not the wilderness. Wilderness has negative, fearful connotations for you.

We have to go wander in paradise. If you could wander in paradise for awhile, who would wander in paradise and then want to go back and live in a prison? But because you know nothing but prison, it's difficult to describe paradise to you and to make you believe in its actuality. You are a race of souls raised in captivity and slavery and you know nothing else but that, and you believe that there is nothing else but that, and you fear losing even that, because that little bit is all that you think there is, and you think that you could even lose that at any moment. It is an astounding trick that is being pulled on you. That whip is so puny and small and yet so effective. The not seeing, the lack of vision, and then the cruel snap of the whip is all that fills your consciousness and awareness and leaves you fat for the harness and the slaughter."

"So you have to look at the fear. You have to look at that whip, but you have to see the bigger picture. You have to see that you are a two thousand pound Brahma bull with nine foot long sharp horns who is standing on the prairie with nobody else around, except this one yahoo, and all he's got is a chunk of leather to whack you with. You have the power of life and death over him. He's got no horse. He's got nowhere to run. He only weighs one hundred and fifty pounds. He's got no gun. He's got nothing, just that little tiny whip and he's got you and the whole herd cowed and tricked. You see that? And he is you and you are he."

"Well I see the image. But I also see that what you are saying is absolutely correct. He has the whole herd cowed with that whip. I can't look past that whip. The fear really does eat at me. I really am afraid of him and it."

"That's why you have to look around. That's why I'm saying to forget the fear part and to look at the knowledge part of it. Take an inventory, but take an inventory outside of the history that you have learned, and see another possible story. This story that you could be living isn't the story of the bullyboy. This could be the story of the mighty thundering herd that ran over the bullyboy and lived happily ever after free on the prairie. I know that these are just words and in the harsh light of day when you are looking your tormentor in the face, you lose your nerve, but remember ---. What can I say to you that would give you courage?"

"Meditate. Stop the mind. Stop the committee up there in your head from constantly chattering gossip and self-puffing nonsense. Stop the story, history, all stories, and try to see the story that is, the story that could be. Don't try to see it, just let it be. And see that it is an immense story of immense possibilities. Just see that, and when you see that, then if you want to fear something, there are a lot bigger things to fear. Let's just look in that direction and then you'll see that there is really nothing to fear because this isn't really about losing or getting. This is about being and enjoying or not enjoying. It's up to you. I mean obviously you've chosen not to enjoy right now. That is why you are here now, but it is up to you. You get to choose. You have the power to do, or not to do, whatever or not whatever. Meditate and let the knowing expand. Meditating is important. Your dream is the world. The greater the dream, the greater your wealth. The dream is your support. We are about to do great things, greater things than have ever been done before. A new world is being born, a world of great beauty, wonder, joy, and happiness. Are you ready?"

"Yes. Yes I am!"

Much to my relief, Gabriel says, "Let's postpone our trip to the desert."

"Shane, you are doing really well now with your diet but I want you to lose some weight and get more spiritual. Eating right isn't the end of the trip. I want you to watch the movie, 'the Secret', and read Ernest Holmes' book 'The Science of Mind', and work through 'A Course in Miracles'. Read David Wolfe, Gabriel Cousens, and Viktoras Kulvinskas. Read Don Miguel Ruiz's 'The Four Agreements', and Esther and Jerry Hicks, 'The Teachings of Abraham'. As Wolfe is fond of saying, 'Readers are leaders'. Read Gregg Braden's 'The Divine Matrix' and Michael Talbot's 'The Holographic Universe'. Practice using William Horden's 'Toltec I Ching'. Enjoy a copy of 'Life and Death in the Hotel Bardo'."

"I want you to consider why some people are happy and why some people are sad. I want you to consider why some people suffer and why some people don't. I want you to consider why bad things happens to some people and why some people live charmed existences and seem to have incredibly good luck. Think of Donald Duck. He is always in these incredible dramas. He can never seem to get ahead. Meanwhile his Uncle Scrooge and his cousin Gladstone Gander are incredibly lucky. Gladstone can't even consider that something unlucky would ever happen to him. That isn't even a thought that can enter his consciousness and Gladstone has nothing but incredibly good luck. Scrooge McDuck's wealth is legendary. What makes Donald's life different from his Uncle Scrooge's life and different from his cousin's life?"

"What causes bad things to happen in our lives? What causes suffering, adversity, and sickness? What should we do to turn those situations of suffering into great moments of joy and ecstatic enjoyment of being?"

I read them all. This New Age thinking seems simple enough. You just think positive good thoughts and good things happen to you. If you want something you visualize it and that attracts the thing to you. Simple. Easy. No problem.

PART TWO
π

"Be the change that you wish to see."

Gandhi

DON'T TAKE IT PERSONAL

CHAPTER 21

THE POWER COMPANY

Life is good. The future looks bright. Everything is beautiful and full of hope. All I have to do is think positive thoughts and good things will happen to me, to the people I love, and to the community that I live in. It's simple. I am just going to think the best, most loving thoughts that I can think. I make a wish list and put a copy of it in my wallet so that I can be reminded about what I want all of the time. I make another copy of my wish list and post it right next to my computer screen. All of those wise peoples' positive advice is great. Let go and let the good times roll through me.

My health is great. In fact I am 20 years younger but my financial problems haven't improved. In fact they are getting worse, a lot worse, reaching critical mass, reaching apocalyptic melt down level. At least that is what I think. I am having a hard time maintaining a positive attitude, thinking good thoughts and believing that good things are going to happen in the face of the facts. At least that is how I see it.

I go to the Supplement Store and ask Lilith, "What shall I do about my money problems?"

She says, "We need to write letters to the Universe about what you want and say positive affirmations."

So, we do. I win the Mega-Riches Lottery. I win three dollars.

I say, "Lilith, I need $300,000, not $3."

She says, "I'll keep writing. I'll get my friends to write. The effect multiplies the more people that you get to focus their intent on a particular thing happening and we'll be more specific about what we want."

I call Johnny. He is my real estate agent. I say, "Johnny I want to sell. I'll sell everything. I'll sell anything."

He hesitates and starts explaining, "Well, the market is really bad. The banks aren't lending any money. There is no money in circulation. If you want to sell anything, you will have to sell at foreclosure prices. That's about thirty to fifty cents on the dollar, and you'll be lucky to find a buyer even at those prices."

I waver, "Let me think about it."

Then Johnny calls back and says, "Hey Shane that guy, Blaine Goodman, who bought the last lot that you developed before you fell from the cliff wants electrical power."

"Hey, I am too busy to get involved with trivial issues like that", I tell him. "I am having fun. I've got more important things to do than get involved in putting in electrical power to Goodman's place. There isn't any problem. Everything is ready. It's easy. Just tell him to get a green tag approval from the County Building Department for an electrical power hookup and then call up Sunset Power Company and the Power Company will send out a representative who will give him a contract and he can sign it and get electric power. It's simple."

Well that is how it was two years ago. Today Sunset Power Company is owned by new owners. It has changed ownership twice in the last two years. First, our local Power Company was taken over by a foreign mega-corporation which squeezed everything that they could out of the company and their customers, us, and then the foreign mega-corporation sold our electricity company to an American gazillionaire whose best known quote is, "I make money, not friends".

This is the company which I had built the electrical infrastructure for to hookup the power to the house being built by Blaine Goodman. This is the company which had designed, inspected, and approved the electrical system which I had installed. And this is the power company which had quoted a price of $25,000 to hook up this new system to Goodman's new dream home. And that is what I have set aside to pay this bill, not $26,000, not $30,000, but exactly $25,000.

A few weeks later Goodman calls me on the phone and says, "Sunset Power Company wants half a million dollars to hook up my new house."

My heart stops. I get that sick feeling you get in your stomach when things go terribly wrong, hopelessly wrong. I need to sit down. Fantasies of running to somewhere safe like Tahiti and hiding flash through my mind, but it's too late to escape. I have that sick feeling, that very sick feeling.

"What, half a million dollars to hook up a house, one house?" I ask incredulously. "They want $500,000 to hook up electricity to one single family home? Is that what you said?"

"Yes", Goodman responds. "They say that they have to hook up a new three phase commercial line to my house so that the lights won't flicker when the heat pump comes on."

"Wait a minute. I have hooked up over a hundred houses on three separate single phase electrical trunk lines in this area over the last thirty years and no one has ever said that their lights flicker when their heat pump comes on. What is going on?"

"I don't know," Blaine says. "That is just what they are saying. The Power Company is demanding that I pay them $500,000 before they will hook up electricity to my house."

Blaine isn't angry at me. He is just confused and upset like I am.

"Well, I don't have half a million dollars. I can't get half a million dollars. There isn't half a million dollars in cash left in this town," I state flatly. "What are we going to do?"

Blaine suggests, "I'll check with the manager of the Power Company and see what he has to say, to see if he can't do something different."

I am worried. All of Gabriel's empowerment, I am the Source, talks are forgotten. I am caught in the jaws of life, real life. Reality 101 has my complete attention. I immediately revert to my old ways of thinking.

A month passes.

Then one day the manager of the Sunset Power Company, Justin Lee, calls me on the phone. "Hi, is this Shane Parker?"

"Yes. Yes it is," I answer.

"This is Justin Lee from Sunset Power Company. I have good news for you Mr. Parker. I have a new proposal for you on getting electrical power to the Blaine Goodman property."

Relief floods through my whole body, I exclaim, "Great. There is no way that we can afford the other proposal."

"Well how much did you expect to pay?" Lee casually asks.

"We budgeted $25,000."

"That isn't going to work, but we have reduced the price to $80,000. We can come from another direction, from the freeway straight up the hill direct. You will have to build another underground infrastructure and access roads, but you will only have to pay us $80,000. "

I am in shock. "Why don't you just do what we agreed to do and put the power in the way we agreed to do it."

"Mr. Parker, do you have anything in writing saying that Sunset Power will do that?"

"No, as you well know. Sunset Power Company never will put anything in writing. Your company has never put anything in writing in the thirty years that I have been dealing with it. Sunset Power Company has always refused to put anything in writing until a homeowner has their meter green tagged and calls for power."

"Well if you don't have anything in writing, then I'm afraid that we don't have an agreement and you are going to do what I am saying."

"What do you mean we don't have an agreement? You designed the system. You inspected the installation of the system and you approved the system. I installed the system. You told me what the hook up was going to cost. Isn't that an agreement? Don't you have any integrity. Don't you honor your word?"

"It is going to have to be our way or Goodman doesn't get electricity."

"You are a lying, low life bastard," I shout in the phone and hang up.

I have never ever called another person a blasphemous swear word in anger before in this life time. I don't talk like that. I am in shock. I fall into a chair. What Justin Lee is demanding besides the $80,000 is that I destroy a strip of government protected wet lands and build a road through an endangered salmon habitat area. The State of Oregon isn't going to allow it even if I had $80,000 to give to Sunset Power Company and if I had another $200,000 with which to build the power line infrastructure. It is impossible, and yet Lee is demanding that I do it and I have a contractual agreement with Goodman that requires me to do it, but I can't do it. I can only see one hope. When I fell from the cliff, I was developing two developments and the one that Goodman is in is the East Parker Ridge Subdivision. I was also building a West Parker Ridge Subdivision which I had sold to a Portland builder for $1,500,000. Since my accident the economy of America has crashed and there isn't any money for house buying, so my Portland buyer has failed and cannot pay me for the development, a development which is now worth pennies on the dollar, if it can even be sold. However, selling that development even for pennies is my only hope.

While I ponder my dilemma, Chicago United Bank repossesses my pickup truck and the South Wanustakila Bank repossesses and sells my house. I am homeless and rideless.

What is going on? A couple years ago the banks were willing to lend money to people to build houses. Developers and builders could get a credit line with which we could build roads and houses. Then we could sell the houses, pay the credit line, and then start again. Now there are no more credit lines. And the Power Company wants half a million dollars to hook up a new house to the electric power grid. What is happening? I am thinking all of these positive good thoughts one day and the next day the whole world goes bad. So much for the power of positive thinking. If I am the source of anything, it seems to be misery and suffering. How in the world does one be abundant and empowered in the real world?

Oh well, what can I do? I can't pay the Sunset Power Company. I can't sell anything. I can't find a job. I couldn't finance a job even if I could find one. The Power Company has a monopoly. I can't not get electricity for Goodman's house. I am under a contractual obligation to Goodman and I have to perform by supplying him with electricity to his new home.

Maybe I can get an alternative electricity source. Larry Church, another builder who lives in a house which he built in my East Parker Ridge Subdivision has solar power hooked up to his house.

I call him, "Larry can I get solar power to generate enough electricity to run a house?"

"Well I don't know Shane. I made a lot of mistakes when I put in this solar system here at my house. You can really get taken putting in a solar system. There's a lot of bad information out there about solar. There's a lot of cons going on around solar and alternative life styles. I got a guy in Portland though who really knows his this subject. He is really an expert. Call him. His name is Rick Edwards and his number is 666-212-3434."

I call Rick. "Rick, I got a big problem. I need to get electricity to a house but the power company wants half a million dollars to hook it up. I can pay some serious money for a solar system if it will power a house as the only power source."

"Well you got a real problem there Shane. Solar power can't be used as a standalone electricity source to power houses."

What if I put in natural gas too? Will solar work then."

"Not really."

"I'm willing to spend $50,000 on a system. I'm willing to put in a lot of panels, a lot of batteries. Can't you make an alternative power system that will work for that kind of money?"

"There's two problems Shane. Number one ...."

Wait, I interrupt, "We get at least half of it back in tax credits anyway, right?"

"Well that's problem number one. The problem with the tax credits is that you don't get them unless you are hooked up to the electricity power company. You have to be hooked up to Sunset Power Company even though the purpose of the solar power is to generate power to replace the utility company electricity. If you aren't hooked up to the Power Company, the Power Company that you don't need anymore when you have solar power, you don't get any tax credits. You still have to pay for the hook up even though you aren't going to use it. And second, the answer to your big question is no. Solar power won't work standing alone, no matter how much money you spend."

I thank Rick and hang up the telephone with a heavy heart.

I am cornered. There is no standalone alternative power source and Sunset Power Company is a monopoly. The only thing to do is fight these guys through the Oregon State Public Utility Commission. The PUC is the state regulatory agency which is supposed to regulate monopolies and stop consumer abuse and fraud by monopoly utility companies. So I file a complaint. I throw everything that I have and am into this fight trying to change this situation, trying to solve this problem.

The Public Utility Commission sends out an investigator, Jerry Noddington, and he investigates the case.

Noddington decides, "There is nothing that the PUC can do for you. $500,000 to hook up a house does seem high, but regulations put in place by your state legislators support the Power Company's position. You are going to have to take your case before an Administrative Law judge and examine the tariff system."

Incredulously I ask, "Tariff system? What is a tariff system?"

"Oh don't worry Shane. May I call you Shane? The PUC is a consumer friendly system. You can fill out the paper work yourself. You don't even need an attorney."

What other choices do I have? I fill out the paperwork and I file it.

Sunset Power has lawyers on staff in Portland. Their lawyers immediately file for dismissal. The PUC is not as consumer friendly as Jerry claims. I am forced to hire attorneys from Harris, Smith, and Douglas at $400 per hour to fight the Power Company's attorneys. Now I am going to be spending $30,000 on attorneys, and if I win, I am still going to have to spend the $25,000 on getting power to Goodman's house that I was going to spend anyway. And if I lose, I am going to have to come up with the $30,000 for lawyers on top of the $280,000 to $500,000 that Lee is demanding. None of which I have or can come up with.

Good news arrives. Johnny calls, "Shane, I sold your West Parker Ridge Subdivision for $200,000."

"Great! We are saved."

To sell a lot, you have to have water and electricity to the lot and a way to dispose of sewage from any new house. Lee approves the electric power to these lots in this subdivision from the single phase line which is already on the property. The County issues septic system approvals for the houses.

I apply to the Wanustakila Water Association for a water meter for a water line hook up to the first lot that the new buyer, Christian McGee wants to build on.

When I fell from the cliff, I had just finished installing 9,000 feet of six inch ductile iron water pipe, a 225,000 gallon ceramic coated stainless steel water tank and a pumping station to get water to this subdivision. Since then, I have nearly died and spent another $100,000 on medical bills. I did all of this to get water into this subdivision for a total cost of $475,000.

Like the Sunset Power Company, the Wanustakila Water Association has a new manager. When I apply for a water meter for a water hook up, the new manager, Buddy Loveless informs me, "You cannot use that six inch ductile iron line that you installed into that subdivision. It has too much pressure in the line. You must extend an old eight inch ductile iron line from a mile away down at the bottom of the hill up the newly paved road to your West Parker Ridge Subdivision. We estimate the cost to you will be $500,000."

"A half a million dollars!" I shout. "The whole subdivision isn't worth half that much."

The more that I fight and struggle, the worse the situation gets. I argue with Buddy "Why would I have put that water line, water tank, and pumping station into this subdivision if you weren't going to give me water? Plus your company required a complete set of engineered drawings and your employees inspected and approved the complete installation. Why didn't anyone notice or say anything about this water pressure thing before now?"

"I don't know," he angrily responds. "It doesn't matter. We aren't giving you water. The pressure is wrong. If you want to, you can hire an engineer and study the problem and give us a copy of the study"

I hire an engineer, Fred Davis. Fred studies the problem and submits a report which shows that the best way to solve this pressure problem in the West Parker Ridge Subdivision is to at the first valve cluster put in a pressure reducer on one line and run it down to the houses at the bottom of the hill and then to run another line without a pressure reducer to the houses higher on the hill. This is a simple inexpensive solution.

Loveless replies, "No. The only thing for you to do is to extend a new 8 inch ductile iron pipe from the old existing line a mile away at a cost of half a million dollars. That is what I said that I wanted and that is what we want done. You cannot have water from the 6 inch pipe that you extended into the subdivision, period. End of discussion."

After eight months of study. That is the decision that the Wanustakila Water Association board of directors comes to, too.

Meanwhile the court case before the Administrative Law judge for the Public Utility Commission on the Sunset Power Company case is quickly coming to trial. That will be the end of that option for better or worse. Bankruptcy and ruin are rapidly approaching.

Goodman asks, "Why don't we make one more attempt to settle this with the power company?"

I have been studying the "Course in Miracles", doing the Sedona method, and reading the rest of the books that Gabriel has given me.

Gabriel advises me, "Shane you should treat everyone including people who are attacking you with trust, love, and respect. You should also do what you can to help them. Don't attack when attacked. If you want to go for a walk and you get a cramp in your leg, you don't get angry at your leg and attack your leg with a sharp knife and yell at it and try to intimidate it, do you? You don't try to stop the leg from cramping by frightening and hurting the leg, do you? You don't take the cramp in your leg personal, do you? You love your leg. You care for your leg. You try to help your leg get healthy and well and not have cramps. Well don't take these attacks personal. Treat these people who you see as attacking you as you would treat your own leg when you are having a leg cramp. They have their own agendas and issues and problems, you need to help them. They need your help.

You are their salvation. They are yours. Get well together. Stay well together."

So with this understanding when Goodman says, "Let's give it one more try. Let's not attack them in court yet. Let's see if we can resolve this."

I say, "Alright."

I don't feel like this is a good idea. I want to mutilate the bastards, but my options all look like lose, lose, lose, even if I win. I need to change my way of thinking, my way of doing things, my way of living. This "turn the other cheek" thing seems stupid, counter-intuitive. Still I decide that I am going to try it. There is a lot at stake here but I am going to try it.

I tell Blaine, "Set up a meeting between me and Lee."

Goodman calls Justin and Justin says, "Good idea. Let's meet on site Wednesday at 1:00 and I'll bring my design engineer and we can discuss the new option."

On Wednesday at 1:00 o'clock, standing by the open door of my father's old pickup at the end of a gravel road in the sunshine, I feel a lot of apprehension and tension as I am watching Justin walking toward me. In my mind, I am replaying our previous conversation in which I called him a lying bastard and hung up on him.

But I send him as much friendliness and love as I can, smile and say, "Hi, Justin. It is good to see you."

This is our first face to face meeting. He is a tall, wiry, casually dressed nice looking, intense, dark Eastern European looking man. To my surprise and great relief, he responds likewise, "Hi Shane. It is good to see you too."

We both smile and shake hands. He introduces me to his design engineer, Lawrence O'Neil, who looks like a friendly bear. Lawrence smiles and shyly shakes my hand.

We start to walk the route that the new electric line would follow in Sunset Power's $80,000 option. The terrain is very steep, rugged, oak tree covered, and difficult to put an electric line through. Justin is having some doubt.

I say, "We can't put it here anyway, because there is a wetland at the bottom of this hill and the State Department of

Lands won't allow us to go across the wetland with an electric line trench."

Genuinely surprised, Justin replies, "Oh, I didn't know that."

We walk back to the road that passes in front of Goodman's property. Justin looks down the dirt road to our right, to the north, away from Goodman's house to where the dirt track disappears down the hill into the trees. He announces, "We'll have to come up this road then."

I say, "This road ends a quarter mile down the hill because the Oregon Department of Environmental Quality has issued a stop work order because muddy water running down the ditch alongside the road could possibly get into the Wanustakila River and the river is a spawning ground for endangered salmon. So no one is allowed to build a road or any infrastructure in this area."

Surprised again, Justin says, "Oh, I didn't know that. If I would have known that, I wouldn't have demanded that you do this." This is the area where the $500,000 option would go.

We walk back up Goodman's driveway to where the old electricity vaults are and to where the old electricity line is coming along the ridge top into the subdivision. Justin points down the hill and says, "Then we can come up this draw with a new line."

He is pointing away from Goodman's house to the south towards a new drainage system which we haven't discussed yet. We are half a mile back up the hill south of Goodman's property. We are standing on a high hogback shaped ridge and looking down a creek which runs down the ridge which we are standing on towards the valley below. This creek runs east and passes far to the south of the Goodman site. What he is saying seems reasonable if you are not experienced with Department of Environmental Quality regulations. I am.

I respond, "We can, but you are going down a stream which runs into the Wanustakila River, so we can't get any mud in that creek either."

Justin knows that it would be very difficult to build an electrical infrastructure and not get any sediment into that creek.

Carefully contemplating this new information, he says, "Well, I guess that option is out too. We'll have to use this old line here but you won't be able to put anymore houses on this line."

Immediately I agree, "That sounds like a good alternative to me. I would like to be able to build but given the problems with the Oregon Department of Environmental Quality and with the Oregon Department of Lands with the wetlands issue, I really can't see how we can keep building anyway."

"Okay if you will sign an agreement saying that you won't build anymore houses on this hillside, then we will go with the old system," Justin offers.

I nod in agreement.

The problem is completely turned around after a year of vicious fighting. When it finally came into my being that I shouldn't fight with the Sunset Power Company anymore than I would harm my own arms or legs if they offended me, the problem is instantly solved.

Justin continues, "If you will agree not to build anymore houses and drop your court case, I will agree to put the power in under the old system and for about the same price that was previously estimated."

In my mind I'm thinking, "Wait. If I drop my court case now, first, before he signs an agreement, what's to stop him from coming back on me and demanding that I put in the $500,000 system and now that I have ruined my court case and I can't re-file it or appeal, and I'm completely out of luck, my position will be totally, irredeemably desperate."

I ask, "Why don't we sign an agreement and then I'll drop the law suit."

Justin counters, "No. You drop the law suit. Then I'll sign an agreement and install the power in line with the old understanding."

This puts me in quite a bit of jeopardy. Relying on the teachings, I cast all of that old idea of the best defense is a good offense out of my mind and I look Justin in the eyes and I state, "Okay, I am choosing to trust you. I will drop the law suit immediately and sign a no build agreement."

Justin says, "Good."

We smile at each other and shake hands and part friends.

And I do what I agree to do. All of the time I worry about this risky way of living. My lawyers all advise me against this line of action. They advise me that we can win in court and what I am doing is risky and foolish.

They want to know, "Where's your protection? What's your back up plan? Why should we trust a manager and company that has attacked and abused you over and over for eight months? Where is the evidence that they have changed their ways?"

But I keep my agreement with Justin anyway and Justin does what he says he will do.

I am astounded!

I have to change my ways, change my ways at a heart level. I have been talking about changing and thinking about changing but that is only on an intellectual level. On the gut level, I haven't really changed much. When I am having fun and things are easy, I do things the new way, but when things get tough, when I am tested, I fall back on my old ways. My core beliefs are back there in my old ways at some deep level. Those old values are what I still believe at some deep level of which I am not aware. When pushed, I just act that old way. I have to change. Those old ways aren't working for me anymore.

I sure didn't see this coming.

CHAPTER 22

EVERY DAY AS THE LAST

Meanwhile all negotiation, all attempts to reason with the Wanustakila Water Association and with its' directors, and with its' engineers all fail. There is no hope of getting water from the Wanustakila Water Association to Christian, the buyer. It is half a million dollars for a hookup. It is half a million dollars to get water to a piece of property worth $200,000. It doesn't make any sense. Plus I already owe $100,000 for paving and other bills on this piece of property. So, if I went ahead with Loveless's idea, I would have $100,000 with which to pay a $500,000 water bill. I would be even further in debt.

I am thinking, "I should sue the Wanustakila Water Association just like I did the Sunset Power Company and force them into negotiating. I should try some other tactic where I can force them into hooking up a water source for me. I need to attack them and force them to give me a water hook up. Maybe I could find a place where their water line crosses on to my property and cut the water line, stopping water service to their customers. They are being completely stupid and unreasonable. I really don't like those guys."

But then I think, "That is not what Christ taught. That is not what the Buddha taught. That is not what the 'Course in Miracles' teaches. Am I smarter and wiser than Christ or Buddha?"

In my final conversation with Loveless, I smile, thank him for his time and walk out of his office and down onto a cold rainy street. I drive home depressed in a grey downpour.

I call Johnny and I say, "Johnny we are not going to get water from the Wanustakila Water Association. I am not going to fight with them. We are going to have to drill or to develop springs. That is all there is to it. You are going to have to tell Christian that public water is not available."

In my mind, I am thinking, "The sale is lost. It is gone. There is no hope. If there is no public water source, then there is no sale. However, I am to recognize that the guys at the Wanustakila Water Association have their own problems and I need to help them and be supportive and not cause them misery, suffering, and anxiety."

Johnny calls Christian and tells him the Water Association's decision.

Christian responds, "Great. I didn't want Wanustakila Water Association water anyway. It is full of chlorine, fluoride, heavy metals, and toxins. I've heard that they put so much chlorine in their water that it isn't even safe to swim in much less to drink. I would much rather have a nice private clean well or a spring. Plus then the water is free."

I am in shock. I have been fighting, attacking and counter attacking for public water for eight months. I have spent $475,000 adding 9,000 feet of six inch ductile iron water pipe to the Wanustakila Water Association system and adding a 225,000 gallon water tank and installing a new pumping station and I nearly died. After all of that, I end up getting no water from them. I quit attacking them and a wonderful solution appears immediately. Who wants poisoned public water anymore? People who know, don't want that stuff anymore, and Christian is a water treatment engineer. If we can develop a good private source of good clean water, that is way more valuable, and Christian recognizes that. The Water Company and the Power Company problems which have kept me depressed, eating wrong, gaining weight, and unable to pay the bills for a year are solved overnight just by changing my attitude and looking at the people whom I see as my enemies as good reasonable friends who are just trying to help me, and all of the sudden the world is full of love, friends, and abundance.

The following Thursday, while I am over at Gabriel's drinking tea, I tell all of this to Gabriel and he says, "Advances in your life, your health, and your wealth are based upon your relationship with Self. As your relationship with Self improves, other parts of your life improve."

Gabriel is always saying things like this. I have no idea what he is talking about. He confuses me. I want to understand though, so I ask, "Self? What are you calling Self? What does self have to do with the Wanustakila Water Association and the Sunset Power Company? I want to know how to get good things to happen in my life and how to get the bad things to stop. How does one change the bad life experiences of 'The Bad Secret' into the good experiences of 'The Good Secret'?"

"Through love, trust, courage, and integrity."

"Good words, Gabriel, but what do they mean?"

"They mean that everything is taken care of. It is not something that you have to worry about. Life is not about worry. Life is about joy."

"Okay, but that is not our experience as humans. We don't feel secure or experience abundance. We experience separation, lack, and loneliness and insecurity."

"Those are your feelings. Those are your emotions. Those are your perceptions, but that is not your experience. If you experienced that, then you wouldn't be existing. You wouldn't get your next breath. You wouldn't get any water to drink. You wouldn't get any food to eat. You wouldn't have any friends to share your day with, to talk to."

"Okay, you're right, but that doesn't solve my problems or lessen my suffering. True, I'm not starving and I have some friends to share good times with, but I also have a lot of problems. What about the problems?"

"What about them? Which problem is making you suffer?"

"My inability to make a living, to pay the bills, to support my family in the way that they want to be supported."

"That is an interesting point of view, your inability to 'make a living'. You're responsible for making your living?"

"Well, yes. That is what we have to do. That is what a job is for, making a living."

"You don't make a living. You get a living. Living has already been given to you. You are living a living."

"What does that mean? I don't seem to be making a living or getting a living, or living a living. I seem to be failing to make a living. I am making a suffering situation, a separation, fearful, insecure, painful situation. I want out. What can I do? What can I do right now this minute to change my circumstances, my situation from insecurity, fear, lack, loneliness, and self loathing into one of super abundance, joy, and happiness?"

"Accept super abundance, joy, and happiness."

"Okay. I accept them. Where is my pay check?"

"You say that you accept them, but in your heart you don't believe. In your heart you're like Peter in the boat with Jesus on the sea when Jesus gets out of the boat and walks on the water and beckons Peter to come out and join him for a walk. Peter steps out and at first the water holds him up. Then he looks around and realizes that he is standing on water and he sinks. You want to believe me, and you kind of do, and so you can take the first step but when you look around at the world that you know, that you think that you know, the world that you have experienced, you lose your faith and fall back into your old belief system which is based in insecurity, separation, and lack. Then you sink."

"Yes. I know that. How do I overcome my fears, my belief that there isn't enough, that I don't have what I need? I don't think that I have what I need. That is a knowing to me. I know that I don't have what I need."

"And for you here now that is right. Your knowing is causing you to not have what you need. You need to change that knowing to knowing that you have what you need. In fact you do have what you need. You can't not have what you need."

"Well I certainly seem to not have what I need. Where is the $100,000 that I need to pay my bills?"

"Quit talking about your bills and your need for $100,000. Quit focusing on what you see as problems. Quit looking backwards. Imagine you are standing on a high mountain top looking into the west into the darkness of night that has fallen and you are complaining because it is dark when all that you have to do is turn around and look towards the east where the morning is dawning and walk away from the darkness into the light. You are looking towards the dark and living in the dark. All that you have to do is turn around and look towards the light, towards the morning, and you'll be in the light. You would have to be pretty tall for this analogy to work, but you get the idea. Imagine that you are standing at a place where you can either look into the darkness or you can look into the light and all that you have to do is look one way or the other. All that you have to do is change your viewpoint, change your opinion, change your attitude, and by doing that, you will change your experience and your reality."

"I hear that over and over and over and I don't see a change even when I have a positive attitude."

"That is because you don't ever really have a positive attitude. You say that you do, but you don't. You are like the student fire walker who says that he can walk on fire, but he doubts. In fact, he knows that he can't walk on fire. So, when he steps out onto the burning coals, he gets burnt. Other people in his fire walking class say that they can walk on hot burning coals, know that they can walk on hot burning coals, and they do walk on hot burning coals without any harm to themselves. Check it out on YouTube."

"Yeah, I know that you're right about that. So with all of these teachings, how do I get them from just being words, words which I want to be true, to where I experience them as real? In other words, how do I get from being insecure, feeling threatened, endangered, and being in fear, to experiencing unlimited abundance, total fearless freedom and ecstatic joy?"

"That does seem to be a problem for you doesn't it?"

"Yes, that is a super problem for me. I have to really get going and work hard and be clever."

"Well, those are all good things to do, to be, but you are kind of missing the point."

"Well that is what I mean. What is the point? What's your point? What should I do, if it isn't get going, work hard, and be clever? What is it? I mean I'm ready. Let's do it right now."

"Okay. Here's what you do. Nothing. Realize that it is already done. Relax. Have the best day ever. Spend time with your friends, with your family. Take a walk in the woods. Tell the trees that you love them. Greet the sun. Spread your arms to the wind and tell the spirits how much you enjoy their friendship."

"But the bills, all of those requests for payment, for gratitude, they aren't going to get paid."

"Yes they are. They are already paid."

"That's crazy. No one has told the people who want their money that they have been paid. No one has done some Jedi trick and waved their hands over the eyes of the people that I owe money to and said, 'You do not need that money. You have already been paid.' Nobody has done that and they don't perceive that they have been paid."

"Your thinking like this is why they haven't been paid. That's why you are living in lack. That is why you are not getting done what you feel that you should get done. If this is your experience, then this is your reality. If you want a different experience, to experience a different reality, then think a different way."

"I can think a different way. That is easy. I can think that I can walk on water, but when I step out on to the river, I sink."

"Yes, you need to know a different way."

"I need to know a different way?"

"Yes, you need to know a different way."

"What? How do I do that? I'm confused."

"Yes, you are confused."

"This conversation isn't going anywhere. We are just going in circles. You are not helping me break out, break through. I need help. I need to wake up. I need to see. I need to understand. I -----. Help me. Please. Please. Help me to experience what you are saying, rather than to experience what I am saying. How do I get from the experience of bill collectors and people who disapprove of my behavior to one of abundance and love? How? What should I do today? How should I act?"

"You should make the most of the day. What would you do today if you were going to die tomorrow?"

"What would I do today if I were going to die tomorrow?"

"Yes, what would you do if you were going to die tomorrow? What would you do? Tell me."

"I would go see everyone that I know and tell them that I love them, that I really do love them and that I am going to miss them.

I want them to be very clear on that, that I love them and I that I don't want anything, any of those fights that we have going, I don't want any of those to be between us. Those fights aren't important. I just want them to know that they are really important to me and that they are really precious to me and that I really do love them and enjoy them, no matter what dramas we have or have had between us."

"What about the bills?"

"Well, I wouldn't worry about the bills. Who cares? I am going to be dead. Nothing is going to happen to me today and I am not going to be here tomorrow. Why should I worry about them? They are done. They are forgotten."

"Is it going to take all day to express your love for everyone, to straighten out all of your relationships? Are you going to have time for anything else?"

"Actually, I don't think that I'm going to get that done because I've got some people that I'm not really going to be comfortable with talking to. I don't think that I'm going to be able to get that all straightened out in a day."

"Hmmm. What are you going to do about those people then? Are you just going to leave them and go into eternity with them hating you, or at least not liking you?"

"I don't feel comfortable with that but I don't know what else I can do in twelve hours, twenty four if I don't sleep or eat. I see your point though. Those relationships are more important than those bills. Those bills though are relationships too and I certainly would like to resolve them too. I've got some bigger unresolved situations. Uhhh, I guess they are bills too. They are not pieces of paper demanding money. They are psychological bills, emotional bills. But I don't have the exchange to satisfy them either. What am I going to do if I am going to die tomorrow? Well I am certainly not going to work and I am not going to waste time doing things that I do not enjoy. I am not going to worry about my resources. I am not going to worry about having enough for tomorrow. I am going to spend everything today. Whoa! That is a liberating thought. That is a pretty frightening thought. What if I don't die tomorrow? Then I won't have anything for the day after tomorrow."

"Ahhh. Now we are at the crux of your problem. You're needs are taken care of today. What you are really afraid of is that your needs are not going to be taken care of tomorrow. So you spend all day today worrying about tomorrow and not taking care of what is really important today. You do what you do in order to get the resources to get through tomorrow. What if tomorrow never comes? You have wasted today. What is more important today or preparing for tomorrow, especially a tomorrow if it doesn't come?"

"Okay. Okay. Okay. But my whole belief system, my whole way of being is based on my belief that tomorrow is going to come and if I worry about it and prepare for it, then it will be better than if I don't worry about it and prepare for it."

"So you are going to spend all of your todays preparing for a tomorrow, so that when tomorrow becomes today, you will have a better today than you are having today, or would have if you didn't worry about that tomorrow today. Is that what you are telling me? You are going to ruin all of your todays for a better tomorrow that never becomes today?"

"I don't really see it that way. I mean tomorrow is becoming today, and if I don't prepare for tomorrow then tomorrow when it gets to be today, it will be a bad today. It will be a day without what I need. If I quit my job and have the best day ever which of course I will have if I quit my job and go spend all of my money and go see all of my friends and tell them how much I love them and pay for every party and have a good time, but when tomorrow comes I won't have any money to pay the rent or buy food."

"How do you know that? Have you tried it?"

"Well, no."

"Are you sure that you are creating wealth through your efforts? Are you sure that you are making a better tomorrow by sacrificing today's happiness to tomorrow's happiness?"

"That is what I believe. I am definitely afraid to do something different. I can't imagine that the resources would just appear tomorrow, magically, to take care of my needs tomorrow, if I quit working today and did everything to set everything square and make everything good today."

"We are at the fulcrum here. We are at the tipping point. We are at the moment where a choice needs to be made. We are at a turning point in the road. We are at a fork in the road."

"So, you are saying that I should live like there is going to be no tomorrow."

"I am saying that you should live as though there is going to be no next minute. Create everything that you would enjoy to create in this minute, this minute. Enjoy this minute. Enjoy this second. Enjoy it absolutely to its fullest. That is your only reason for being. Everything else is taken care of. You live in super abundance. Your only task is to be and to enjoy. And that is not a task. That is a joy. So, you have no task."

"That, I think, is the hardest thing that I have ever heard. Okay let me try it. So I am to live every day as if it is the last day of my life."

"Yes actually you have to live it as if it isn't the first day either."

"What? There is not a first day? What does that mean?"

"It means that you were never born, that you will never die."

"Don't get all esoteric on me. It is not helpful."

"I just want to clear up some confusion for you."

"Okay, but it has to be something adaptable, something that I can use right now to get me out of suffering, loneliness, and insecurity."

"Absolutely. Why else would we be sharing?"

"Okay. I just don't understand. I was never born? I certainly am sitting here talking to you. What is your point? What are you trying to say?"

"I am saying that what is going on here isn't what you think is going on. What is going on isn't what you perceive is going on. You're not understanding clearly. I am just trying to clarify your understanding."

"And that is going to help me how?"

"That is going to change everything. Everything that you are experiencing is based upon your understanding and your attitude."

"I am all for anything that will improve my situation, but aren't we wasting time if we only have today. Shouldn't we be out doing something? Getting it all done? Having as much fun as we can? Acting kind of like Calvin and Hobbes in those manic cartoons when they realize that today is the last day of summer vacation?"

"That is why I bring up the never being born thing. You kind of have to take the time factor out of existence. Otherwise there is going to be a fear factor and you are going to have to rush around and get things done. You are going to have to spend all of your money and have all of your fun before you run out of time, but that is kind of like the ultimate fear of things to run out of. If you are insecure because you don't have enough money, then you are also insecure because you don't have enough time. If you are out of time, then a lot of things get clear, but let us be clear on that there isn't any time. That is why I bring up the being born thing. I know that it complicates things a little, but I have to get it out there."

"Well it isn't helping. It is confusing me."

"I've got an idea. Why don't you go see Johnny and talk this matter over with him. If you sit down and talk this through, you will see that there is a pattern and that there is a solution which will get you to the good times. And you will see that for you to get to the good times, Johnny has to get to the good times too. We all have to go together."

"Synchronicity is the clue that points out that there is an underlying structure and purpose to everything. Synchronicity is the proof that we aren't accidents and that something wonderful is happening here, now. Synchronicity is the witness that there is order and purpose in this riotous jungle of events which when strung together we call our lives, and synchronicity is the evidence that there is meaning in these events and seeming accidents."

"To judge these events, we need a guide post, something that I will call success. And if we are to talk about success, we will need to have a definition of success which we agree upon. I am saying that success is being joyously happy and vibrantly healthy in a world full of abundance, beauty, and peace; based on the understanding that everything is alive, that everything is intimately connected to the well being of everything else, and that everything is sacred. I will call the opposite of success, suffering. Because everything is connected, when someone causes suffering for someone else, they bring suffering into everyone's lives including their own. And because people are far more than you think that you are, you need to expand your understanding of the causes of happiness and suffering so that you may be vibrantly alive and joyously happy."

"Keeping all of this in mind, listen to Johnny from a cosmic point of view, enlarge your perspective, widen your knowing. Then answers and solutions will become apparent. Ask him to describe his life from the perspective that he found himself in that time that he fell asleep in the front seat of that 67 Camaro going over the top of Black Top Hill, the time that he shot out of his body and out into outer space. Tell him to tell you the Black Top Hill story and then from that peak point of view to tell you what is happening to him now."

"I didn't know that you knew Johnny."

"I know much more than you think that I know."

"Okay, whatever. I don't know what you are talking about, but I'll give it a try. It's good to have a plan."

He smiles, embraces me, and says, "Stay high and stay cool. Remember, where one goes, we all go."

He walks away.

I get in the old blue Chevy pickup that I'm borrowing to get anywhere and drive to my home in the country, playing old rock and roll hits on the radio loud, smiling through a sunny afternoon.

CHAPTER 23

BLACK TOP HILL

The next day early I call Johnny.

Johnny says, "Boy Buddy, you aren't going to believe what is happening to me."

Johnny sounds like there are dark black clouds hanging over his head with thunder rolling and lightening flashing and cold wet rain is pouring down his back soaking him and he didn't expect this terrible storm and he didn't bring a hat or coat.

He says, "Meet me at Elmo's. I gotta talk to you."

I get in old Blue and drive down to Elmo's, get out and walk through the wooden cottage style door. There's Johnny sitting in the first booth. He doesn't even get up. He hardly looks at me. He looks bad. He looks sick. He's lost a lot of weight. He looks like he hurts. He is in pain. His skin is white, grey white, and it sags. The break in his eyes rusts his being.

The waitress comes up to us. "Hey you boys want anything?"

I begin the great struggle of the addict when presented with the object of his addiction. One of my major desires is chocolate cake. Chocolate cake combines three of my biggest cravings: white flour, sugar, and fat. When I am asked, "Would you like a piece of cake?" What should I do? Should I righteously state, "No. I don't eat cake. Cake is bad for you." If I act like that, I am insulting and angering my hostess and I will go away angry and desiring a piece of cake. I will go for hours thinking about how much I want a piece of cake. Or should I say, "Yes please," and eat the cake meanwhile feeling guilty and cursing myself for being a weakling and a fool? Or should I say, "That would be lovely," and eat the cake knowing that it is the last piece of chocolate cake that I will ever eat and savoring every bite with all of my being because I do not ever intend to eat cake ever again. I believe that argument causing self-righteousness and deep remorse and guilt are more destructive to my well being and my hostesses well being than a piece of cake.

I do not intend to insult myself or my host, the Universe, or to live in guilt and denial. If I am at Elmo's, I am celebrating. I say, "Yeah, I'll have a piece of chocolate cake. Your chocolate cake is great."

She agrees.

Johnny says, "I'll have coffee. Black."

The waitress asks him, "That's all?"

He firmly states, "That's all."

She gives in, "Okay. Coffee, black, and chocolate cake," and walks away.

I tell Johnny, "Man, this is Elmo's. People come here to celebrate. People come here, you know, to have some sugar, to have some spice."

"I don't want any sugar. I don't want any spice. I can't afford any and I don't feel like celebrating," he replies sourly.

"Whoa, okay," I back off.

"I'd die, but I don't think that really solves anything," he adds glumly.

"What? What are you talking about? What's been going on? Say, Chief, did something strange happen to you one time when you fell asleep in a 67 Camaro going over Black Top Hill?"

"Yes, that was a long time ago. Why do you ask?"

"Well, just tell me the story. What happened?"

"I'd been working on the weekend and I was riding home with my friend Terry Anderson in his 67 Camaro. This Camaro he had been out racing with the night before and he had dump plugs on that Camaro and he had opened those dump plugs up, but he had never got them closed back up. So here we are coming home from work, we're all tired out. I'm slumping in the passenger seat in the Camaro. We are starting up Black Top Hill and all of the sudden I recognize this vibration from this wide open racing exhaust. These headers start doing this reverb sound and I immediately recognize that sound as part of the process to astral project from an experience that I had before when I was a teenager.

"In that experience, me and a couple of my buddies are at my place in Neptune. The Beatles are over in India. The Beatles are getting into all of these wisdom teachings with the Indian gurus. We are intrigued by what the Beatles are doing over there in India. That guru information really kind of intrigues us. What they are doing is learning how to astral project.

"Well this Indian guru comes on this special television program which we are watching and says, 'Let's just get you out of your body to start with the simplest way that I know how. The room in your house that you are going to remember what it looks like more than any other room is your bathroom. So you can concentrate on what your bathroom looks like, mainly because your bathroom has some different colors, or different distinctive tiles, or obviously there is a very recognizable shape to the toilet and sink, and your bathroom is a small space where you have spent a lot of time just looking around. Your mind will be able to visualize it. Just lay down somewhere and concentrate on being in your bathroom.'

"So my buddies and I lie down and start doing what this guru on TV says to do. There are three of us. We are all just lying around in the living room, concentrating on being in my bathroom. Well, I don't know whether my buddies are thinking about being in their bathroom or my bathroom. They must have been thinking about being in their bathroom, but I had the memory of my folk's bathroom. That bathroom is this really deep maroon red with sea foam green tile about four feet high on the wall. It is a very distinct bathroom. You could not forget the tile. Anyway, I am lying down on the floor with stereo speakers on each side of my head, one on each ear. I am listening to some Beatles rock and roll really cranked up and all of a sudden listening to that music I get this really weird sensation that I am not hearing the music on the right side of me. I am not hearing the music on the left side of me. Somehow, I am hearing the music right in the center of me.

"It is like the music is in my brain and it kind of makes me a little bit nauseous at first. So I decide to get up. When I get up, I just about walk into a wall. When I stand up, I do not have any equilibrium. Whatever those vibrations are that are going through my body from that music affect my ability to move. I get over to a sectional that we have there and lie down. I'm just recovering from this little nauseous affect of this music being right in my third eye. The sound is just right there in the middle of me and no left or right.

"I am lying on the couch and I am recovering from this experience, I am not really thinking about it. All of the sudden I am reviewing our bathroom. For some reason as I lie there, I am thinking about the bathroom, the colors of the bathroom. To tell you the truth, I am not actually thinking about astrally projecting. I am just thinking about what the guru said and I am just replaying what the guru has said about the bathroom and when I replay him saying bathroom, I'm seeing my bathroom.

"The next thing that I know I kind of wake up and I'm kind of confused. I'm really confused. 'Where am I? Geez, how did I get here?'

"I am standing right in front of the toilet in the bathroom.

"I think, 'God. What is going on? You didn't get up and walk into the bathroom. You don't even have your pants unzipped. You're not even using the bathroom.'

"I'm looking straight at the head, wondering, 'What the heck?'

"The door isn't shut. The door is open a little bit. So I back up a step and look through the open crack of the door into the living room, down the hallway kitty corner into the living room and I can see somebody's feet lying on the sectional where I was lying.

"I'm going, 'Well geez, I didn't hear any of my friends come back in. I thought that my friends left. Omigod. What's going on? One of my friends must have come back in and laid down on the sectional.'

"So I walk over and position myself in front of the sink and the mirror. I'm standing there looking in the sink, looking in the mirror and I go, 'Whoa Bud! What's not right here?'

"Then I realize, 'Omigod! There's no me in the mirror.'

"I'm looking in the mirror and I'm seeing the wall behind me. No Johnny at all. I think, 'Omigod! I have done it.'

"That spooks me. It spooks me bad. I am standing in front of this mirror and there is no me and I realize that, that body on the couch, is me.

"Bam! Man I slam back into that body on the couch hard, hard enough to have a heart attack. Heart thundering, gasping for breath, I come to and I say 'Bud you did it. You did what that guru said and somehow that vibration from that music had something to do with it."

Our waitress suddenly appears and sets Johnny's coffee and my chocolate cake on our table. She says, "If you boys need anything else just wave."

"Thanks. The cake looks delicious," I reply and I really mean it. I want that cake. As she walks away, I stare at Johnny and exclaim, "Not in the mirror!" and ask, "What does that mean? What happened on Black Top Hill?"

Johnny continues his story, "It's all connected. So when I hear that Camaro racing exhaust reverb going waaaa, waaaa, waaaa while going over Black Top, I think to myself, 'Whoa, that's that sequence to astral project.'

"I'm just lying there resting in the Camaro on the passenger side as we're heading up Black Top Hill. I decide that I will just go into launch sequence and see if I can't just go out of body coming up Black Top Hill. Well, sure enough, I use that vibration from those headers and I come right out of my body, right inside the Camaro. We're going up Black Top at about sixty miles an hour.

"I intended to astral project out of my body, to go right through the window and out into space. But just as soon as I come out of my body, before I can go through the windshield, I look on the left hand side of the highway and there is a line of fire, shsssp, a line of fire about five feet tall, just a line, and out of that line dives a Samoyon husky, the most beautiful Samoyon husky that you ever have seen in your life and I immediately think to myself,

'Omigod! Terry doesn't see that husky. I gotta get my body to talk to him and let him know that we are going to smash into that beautiful animal.'

"So from outside of my body I command my body to tell him, 'Look out for the Husky!'

"Terry just looks over at me and kind of smiles and says, 'Right on.'

"That is all he says or does, 'Right on.'

"And that Husky when it hits the shoulder of the road, and I mean the beautifulest biggest white Samoyon Husky that you ever saw, heads on a compass heading directly north. He puts his nose down on the shoulder and leaps to the center of the highway. He hits square in the middle of the center lane. The highway is three lanes. From the center lane, he leaps to the right shoulder of the road. When he leaves the outside shoulder, he leaps over a fence. At the apex of the leap over that fence, he explodes into a sunburst and is gone.

"I fall back going, 'Omigod! Omigod! Omigod!'

"I am shocked. The sunburst knocks me over. I am in my little out of body nucleus hanging out between my friend Terry and my body in the center of this Camaro going up Black Top Hill at sixty miles an hour and suddenly I am lying behind the passenger seat on the back floor board.

"That is where I'm at and I'm asking, 'What am I doing back here?'

"I can look up around the passenger seat and see myself sitting there. I say to myself, 'Bud, you gotta get out of here. You gotta launch.'

"So at that point I just launch right out through the windshield. And here I am, the Camaro is coming up Black Top Hill, and I am just going to cruise right up into space.

"Suddenly I'm scared. 'What is going on? What is going on?'

"All of this grey material is whisking by. I am in this tunnel of grey. I can't see anything.

"Wow!! What is happening?' I'm wondering.

"All of a sudden there is this open spot. Then everything goes grey again. Then it opens up again. I realize, 'Bud, you have done it. You are astrally projecting straight up through the clouds. You are in the clouds now. You are going to break out of the clouds.'

"And sure enough, I break out of the clouds and I am in space and I can see the earth below me and I freak, 'Oh God! What about my body?'

"I think, 'Oh Bud, let's not mess up things. Go check on your body. Shoot a probe down there.'

"I don't know where I come up with this idea, maybe from Star Trek or something? Shoot a probe back down? Sure enough though, the moment that I think it, I shoot a probe which is just like saying, 'You stay here on course and we'll send part of your little brain back down there on a string and we're going to look over how your body is doing and meanwhile whatever it is that you have here will maintain itself.'

"Boom. I am back down there on Black Top Hill. I'm up in the air and I see the 67 Camaro down below and it's getting bigger and closer. I come right back down to about a hundred feet above the Camaro. I decide that if I'm going to look into that car then I had better make that roof disappear. So I just cut away a little area of that roof. This hole is shaped kind of like an amoeba, no specific right angles or anything, kind of a ziggy zaggy little pattern. Looking through this hole, there my body is. The roof has become invisible and I'm gazing through this pretty good sized window right through the roof, right at my body in the passenger seat. Everything is cool.

"Right on!' I think. I'm satisfied.

"Ziiiiip! Right back up I go. My awareness which I had left back in space is still climbing vertically going straight up. Earth is now down to about soft ball size below me. I am still going straight up. Then I am worried about that body down there again.

"I decide, 'Bud you had better check that body again. See it one more time. Make sure that that body is still there.'

"Boom! I shoot a probe down to the body and open up the roof. There I am. My body is cool. There is no problem. Boom! I go back up to my astrally projected form but when I come back up to my astrally projected central core from this probe, it shocks me, because now I am going horizontally through space. I am thinking, 'This is really different.'

"If you are looking into space standing on the ground on earth, space might as well be a flat picture laid out on your ceiling, but Buddy when you get up there and you go into that horizontal travel mode instead of that vertical travel mode, then all of a sudden space has all kinds of dimension. It is not like looking at a flat picture anymore. You can see depth and I can't believe it.

"Suddenly I go, 'Anti gravity shields, force field.' I'm protecting my body just like I'm the commander of a star ship and I'm on the bridge looking out over everything. Way out there I'm seeing whole galaxies getting sucked into this huge black hole and there's these massive gas flumes with hundreds of galaxies in them. I'm traveling through this black space corridor with these massive gas flumes and galaxies on my left and dead ahead of me, I don't know how many hundreds of light years out in front me, is a black hole. It is a funnel and there is a galaxy in the funnel, a whole complete galaxy getting sucked into this black hole.

"I think, 'Bud, let's alter course.'

"I alter course. I turn away from the black hole and I say, 'Let's shoot a probe into the black hole.'

"I shoot a probe right down into the black hole. I probably close the distance as much as a nine power scope. I suck it up about nine times. Bring it real close. Look it over real good and go, 'Bud, this is real spooky.'

"I go back to my central core and alter course again, further away from the black hole. I increase the power to the anti-gravity shields. I don't want to get sucked into any gravity situation going into that black hole. I am kind of admiring all of these amazing things. I am just flowing through space. I have no ideas.

"Then, all of the sudden, I see something grey, a little grey hole in space.

"I go, 'Bud, that has got to be a worm hole.'

"I don't know where these ideas are coming from.

"Everything else is black. The gases are fiery orange. They are big, huge gas flumes the size of a thousand galaxies. I am looking beyond the black hole. I am looking I don't know how many light years that I am looking out into space. It is not like looking at a photograph. When you are there, you can go right in and go around that object that you are looking at, and there is depth and dimension, and you don't know how many tens of thousands of light years you are looking out into space.

"I shoot a probe off to my left as I'm traveling into space at the bottom and kind of just to the outside of this huge gas flume at this grey hole. It looks just like a little cave in space.

"I say, 'Shoot a probe down there,' and I shoot a probe down there.

"I am right up close to this grey hole. All of a sudden, bam!!! A pair of willow leaf eyes appear in the hole. The iris is black. The rest of the willow leaf is red. That pair of eye balls blink. When they open again, there are two sets of eye balls. I'm going, 'Whoa. What is going on here?'

"When those two sets of eyeballs blink again, there are four sets of eyeballs.

"I'm going, 'They're doubling. Every blink, they are doubling.'

"When they go from eight to sixteen sets of eyeballs in that worm hole, I scream, 'Back to the ship. Bring the probe home.'

"I cut off the probe and zoom back to the central core where I am at. I look at the black hole. I look at the worm hole. I think of a pea shaped earth way behind me and I go, 'Bud, we are out of here.'

"And man do I hit my body lying in that 67 Camaro hard."

"Whoa Johnny, that's an amazing story. I don't know what to say. Do you think that that really happened and that you were really in space, or were you dreaming?"

"Oh I was there alright, but that terrifying experience has kept me from doing astral traveling again. I have a terrible fear of what those red eyeballs were in that worm hole. The whole experience is in character up until the worm hole and those eyes and I am left going, 'How the hell can you be clear up there in space, find a worm hole and there be these sixteen guys in this thing with these big red eyeballs?"

"That part is a real mystery to me and it is spooky, but I can say one thing clearly, every one of us can travel through space, every single one of us. What has to be conquered is the fear of doing it. What has to be conquered is the absolute fear of somebody cutting you off from coming back to your body, to your living safe body. That worries me. All of the sudden some cosmic event happens and you are in this astral projected body in space, alone, no way home forever."

"But we could even be more magical than we imagine because I absolutely protected myself from all of those things with ideas from Star Trek. Protection just comes automatically. It was just like I was on the helm of a craft in complete control, until the red eyes appear in the worm hole. I was able to realize that I needed to correct my course away from the black hole. I even recognized that piece of space because I know the correlation from the black hole to the gas flume. I could recognize that big gas flume. The gas flumes in space are just incredible. They add some cosmic beauty to space and there are galaxies right in them. They are very intriguing."

Johnny is almost shouting now and he is wildly waving his arms and making his points by stabbing a long finger in my direction. He is excited. He has completely changed since we met a few minutes ago. He rushes on words tumbling from him, "I realize that the human brain is capable of doing some really incredible maneuvers and I have experienced some incredible adventures. Where to go with it from here is a real interesting thing but the fact of the matter is, if we had a picture, such as a picture of the lunar surface of a specific location with specific features, we could use that photograph to astral project to that location on the moon. That I feel real confident of. There is a lot of power in a photograph. I don't know what it is but there is something intriguing, powerful about a photograph. I could astral project right to where a person is standing in a photograph, if I could conquer my fears. If you can do it on earth, if you had a photograph of another planet, you could do it on another planet. Obviously I know that you can interstellar travel. I have done it, gone way out there. I don't know how far, but a long, long ways. This was my final out of body experience. This one kind of spooked me."

"The one thing that I have realized from my little experiences is, Shane, we are each individual full blown star people. We do not need a space ship to travel in space. It is absolutely not necessary. We have just totally, totally underestimated our abilities. Like you say about how magic and powerful we are. Somehow these bastards have subdued us."

"Well said. Well said Johnny," I agree.

CHAPTER 24

THE FIGHT

"Say Johnny, I hate to bring this up, but with that cosmic frame of mind, tell me what's been going on in your life. I know that you got into a fight with a neighbor at the fence behind your house and nearly went to prison. What's the story on that? You get where I'm coming from?"

"Not really. I kind of stay away from that incident."

"Exactly!" I exclaim. "You have to tell that story."

"Well there is a lot of blank in that story," he answers evasively. He seems to be shrinking right in front of me. His energy is plunging downward. I can feel it. He is now just sitting there with his arms hung down by his sides. He is staring down into his coffee cup.

"Doesn't matter. Just tell it like you think it is," I prod.

"You want to do that now?" He asks as if some other time, any other time would be a better time.

"Go for it," I say. "Let me add something though. You get through this and you conquer your fear and everything changes. This is the moment right here where everything changes."

"All right Buddy," he agrees.

"Your fear now is the same fear as going into that picture," I point out. "See your emotions and what's happening to you as that same fear. They are the same deal. Gotta go in there, but we are going through."

He begins, "Okay this is a long running gun battle between my wife and me on one side and our neighbor on the other side. It was really more between my wife and my neighbor by a long ways. The fighting would go on while I wasn't at home. He would do his thing. He enjoyed bullying and harassing my wife, Marilyn. Our neighbor's name is Frank, Frank Kobalski. Kobalski is a little over six feet tall and around three hundred pounds. He is a big barrel chested son of a gun, a road building contractor. He wears a plaid wool shirt, Carhardt pants, big boots, and a lumber supply yard baseball cap. He drives a red one ton Ford pickup truck with dualies and a pickup bed full of tools and big chunks of rusty metal.

"Our house is a little 1954 ranch rambler. It was originally just a two bedroom, one bath house. It is just a little cottage sitting under a grove of poplar trees, with a shop, a garage, and a chicken coop. It sits on just a half acre lot at the end of Willow Street on the edge of town next to similar houses on similar half acre lots, except for Kobalski's place.

"Kobalski's place is a big ranch on the hill behind our house. The driveway to his place goes along our north fence line. Originally he lived in a single wide trailer a few hundred feet up the hill on the east behind our house. Then he built a big new house up on top of the hill above us and converted the old single wide into a rental.

"By zoning rules, there can only be one residence on Kobalski's ranch. He was supposed to tear down the single wide when he built his new house, but he didn't. Instead he starts renting it out to a gang of party hard young men. The extra traffic and the party noise late at night starts wearing on Marilyn.

"I don't want to turn Kobalski in to the police, to the County Planning Department, but Marilyn insists, 'You are a Realtor. You know the building rules. What are you going to let him do?'

"She is mad. She is fighting dust in the house and doped up teenagers at night. And she knows that I know that Kobalski is breaking the law.

"I say, 'I don't want to rock the boat with the guy. Eventually it's an old trailer, it's going to fall apart. Let's make sure that we know for sure that it's an illegal rental because it can be turned into a storage building or a guest house.'

"That gives me a little reprieve and we let it go for another month or so.

"Then one evening Marilyn says, 'It's a rental Johnny. Kobalski is renting that trailer out to those guys. You need to stop him from doing that. You need to go down and file a complaint at the County Planning Department.'

"She really gives me the hot seat.

"So the next day, I go down to the Planning Department. I pull a number and sit down in a plastic chair and wait my turn. Finally a short, chubby guy who looks as gelatinous as the wrinkle free polyester clothes that he is wearing, calls my number.

"I step up to the brown synthetic wood chest high counter with the grey vinyl top and inform the amorphous clerk behind the counter, 'I want to let you know that I know that Frank Kobalski has some form of contract with you that when he built his new house on Willow Street, he was supposed to move the old single wide trailer off of that property. He hasn't moved it. I want to let you know that he is using that trailer as a rental house.'

"Well we need to have you sign a complaint to that effect before we can do anything', the clerk states.

"I don't want to sign a complaint. This guy's m.o. is that he is a bully. He has been bullying and harassing my wife and if I file a complaint that is signed by me and he knows that I am the one that filed the complaint against him, he is going to come after me, after my property. He is going to get aggressive with us and give us a bad time. He will do something. That is his m.o.. He'll come after my wife. You need to do something about this violation of your rules. Something that doesn't involve my name.'

"Mr. Jones', the snooty, obnoxious, self-righteous clerk declares, 'If you want us to do something about your complaint, we need to have it official, and we need to have it signed by you, otherwise we're not going to do anything.'

"But you have a contract with Kobalski to remove the trailer house when his new house is finished. You don't need me. I am just letting you know that he is not following the guidelines of your agreement, and I am making you aware of that, and I don't want to sign anything.'

"You seem a little slow, Mr. Jones. Let me say this so that you will understand. Sign the complaint or else we won't do anything. We are the government. Do you understand?'

"I sign the complaint.

"The Planning Department forces Kobalski to tear down the mobile home. Kobalski is not happy. He is mad, real mad. He is looking for pay back.

"When the grass in our front yard is real high, I mow the lawn with the flapper up. Otherwise the lawn mower just won't mow the grass. This isn't a nice neat little lawn. This is pasture that I am mowing. This is hay grass that I am mowing. So, to make it work, sometimes some of the lawn clippings will get sprayed out onto the road in front of our house. This happens while I am mowing this time, some lawn clippings spray out onto the road. After mowing, I go in the house.

"Frank rides down the hill from his house and up our driveway to our house on a four wheeler motor cycle, gets off, and walks up to our porch. I hear him coming and go out to talk to him.

"Frank says, 'I want you to go out and sweep the lawn clippings off of the street because those lawn clippings are affecting my ability to get to my property. My tires are spinning out on your lawn clippings.'

"This is pure bull. These are a few pieces of grass spread out on a flat gravel road which is being driven over by a one ton, four wheel drive contractor's pickup truck in the summer time on a sunny day.

"As you know though Shane, this is not my fight. I am talking to the guy saying, 'Well Frank, let's look at the problem and see what can be done to make the road safe for you.'

"I step off the porch to talk to Frank.

"Boy, that Marilyn comes right around me and lights right into Kobalski, 'That is just the biggest bunch of bullshit that I have ever heard. You son-of-a-bitch. Get the Hell off of my property.'

"She is on him. He backs up to his four wheeler.

"She absolutely loses it. She picks up a piece of firewood and flings it at his four wheeler with spit, hatred, and red hair flying.

Then she starts picking up big pieces of oak firewood, one piece after another and flinging them at him. He gets back on the four wheeler and is sitting there glaring at her. There is murder in his heart. She picks up a big round piece of firewood and starts beating on the handle bars of the four wheeler.

"She's screaming, 'Get your ass off of my property,' over and over and over, throwing her skinny wiry body in the air and then slamming down hard on the bike handle bars with each blow.

"He lets off the brakes on the four wheeler motorcycle and starts backing down the driveway. She is chucking wood at him, hitting the four wheeler. She is still shaking and screaming, "Get the hell out of here you no good worthless son-of-a-bitch and don't you ever come back here ever again you ugly potato headed asshole.'

"Frank goes up to his house, gets a sprayer, comes back down to our house, and from his property sprays all around the fence line of our backyard with a heavy dose of some real toxic herbicide or some other kind of real poisonous stuff mixed with diesel fuel.

"Everything along the fence is dead immediately, a real ugly wasteland. The over spray kills all of Marilyn's wisteria and climbing decorative vines and most of her plants along our back fence and all along the fence between us and Kobalski's driveway. It kills most of our koi in our fish pond and sends me to the emergency room at the hospital gasping for air. The only plants left along the north and east fence lines that we share with Kobalski are some bamboo along the north fence between our yard and Kobalski's driveway.

"Marilyn loves that bamboo. When we bought our place on Willow Street, there was one sprig of bamboo out there in that yard and because our septic system is out there in that part of the yard, I wanted to kill that bamboo, but Marilyn is a nature friend and she put up a scrap. She won and the bamboo stayed.

"Then this little bamboo plant grew up into a big patch of bamboo and Marilyn loves this bamboo. It shelters her from the neighbors, the dust, and the road noise and gives her a little private sanctuary off the back porch in between the bamboo and Kobalski's driveway.

"I come home a few days later and Frank and Marilyn are fighting and arguing because Frank has been in there trimming some of that bamboo. I come around the corner behind Marilyn just in time to see him stick his doubled up fist in Marilyn's face and tell her, 'This is war. I'll have you in jail before the night is over.'

"I'm going, "What? What?'

"He turns and goes back up to his place.

"I get in my rig and go right up to his house and talk to him. I say, 'I do not like what I just saw down there. I am having a real hard time between the correlation of you needing to trim some bamboo off of the fence and of you sticking your fist in my wife's face and saying 'This is war.' I don't get the correlation at all, and I don't ever want to see that again.'

"It is kind of a one way conversation I just meet him face to face and tell him what I think of the situation and tell him that his current bullying behavior is not acceptable to me and has to stop now. He doesn't say much and I leave.

"But Frank and Marilyn keep having their problems between them while I am working. Then he decides that he will take a weed eater to Marilyn's new wisteria vines on the fence and square them up. That sends Marilyn right into a tirade. She puts a sign on the back side of the house facing Kobalski's house that says 'angel's garden and asshole' with an arrow pointing up the hill toward Kobalski's.

"This goes on for about five months. Then one Saturday I have to write an offer at work and then I go meet my brother at Elmo's because he has picked up our Mom at Cascade Village and we are taking her out for a little luncheon thing for her 85th birthday.

"Things are just wrapping up at the birthday celebration when I get a phone call from Marilyn. She says, 'Hey, Frank is out there plugging our ditch. It's flooding our house. You need to get home right away and straighten this situation out.'

"That ditch runs across the back of our lot. It catches all of the water coming down the hill behind our house and diverts that runoff water into a ditch running alongside the road on Kobalski's side of the fence like these two ditches have been doing for at least fifty years. When it rains, a stream of water eighteen inches wide and a foot deep runs through this ditch. Any water that gets out of that ditch flows right into our house and makes a real mess. Plugging the ditch is important. A plugged ditch is an emergency, a big emergency."

"So I cut the party short. I was going over to Epitome Jewelers to buy Marilyn a special little Christmas gift after the birthday party with my Mom. But I decide to cut that short, cut the birthday party short, and I head for home. I get to the house. I park my rig in the car port.

"I am running through my head, 'Gee Marilyn, I asked you not to confront him on the fence. This is a civil matter for the courts.'

"I was ready for this fight to go to civil court. I don't want to go up to the fence, but I think that I should get some pictures for proof of what is going on for a civil suit.

"I can hear Frank and Marilyn screaming at each other out back.

"I go in the house and get my digital camera. I have real estate photos on the camera so I have to very quickly eliminate three of the ones that I don't need so that I'll have room on the camera for some new pictures.

"I go back outside. They are still screaming at each other. I pick up a shovel that is leaning against the plum tree by the back door. Marilyn and I have an understanding that if I come out to the ditch, I am to bring a shovel to clean the ditch with.

"If I don't bring a shovel, Marilyn always gives me trouble, 'Why would you come to the ditch without a shovel? What are you doing out here? You don't have a shovel. Gee, go get a shovel. Help out,' she always demands.

'She is always on me for that. So, I grab a shovel. I am just going out to the fence trying to support her. I go out there, stick the shovel in the ground, hold up the camera and take my three pictures of Kobalski over by the ditch on the other side of the fence, standing by his four wheeler motorcycle with a trailer behind it full of digging tools. Frank is smiling and making obscene threatening gestures at Marilyn. The ditch is plugged with a dirt dam with a big rock in the ditch. Water is flowing over flooding into our back yard.

"Kobalski is badgering Marilyn, he is going, 'Chirp, chirp, chirp. That is all you can ever do. That is all you will ever be able to do Marilyn. Just, chirp, chirp, chirp.'

"I turn around to talk to Marilyn and, 'My God', Marilyn can't catch her breath. She can't talk. She is absolutely splattered from head to toe with mud. She is dressed in nice white clothes which she has dressed up in to go to the Christmas light show.

"I wonder, 'What has this guy done to Marilyn?'

"We are standing way back from the fence, twenty or thirty feet. I hand Marilyn the camera, pick up the shovel which I had stuck in the ground, and head for the plugged up ditch. I have no intention of even talking to Kobalski. I just want to see what has happened and clear the ditch. Marilyn can't talk. She can't tell me anything. She is shaking and gasping like a fish on land. Frank has obviously done something terrible to Marilyn.

"He is still bullying her going, 'Chirp, chirp, chirp.'

"I quietly walk up to the fence. I start digging some of the dirt out of the ditch on our side of the fence. Frank has dammed up the ditch right at the fence so that the dirt is spilling over on both sides of the fence. I am cleaning out the ditch and listening to him bullying Marilyn. I am looking down into the water and the mud.

"All of the sudden I realize that this bastard had to have dumped that big potato sack sized rock, that eighty pound boulder into the bottom of the ditch while Marilyn was down in it trying to clean it out.

"I want to talk to him about that. But right about then things get kind of crazy. I'll explain it this way. When a great white shark realizes that he is in a fight, his eyes glaze over with white film, a lens that goes over his eyes. That is what happens to me. Just as I realize what that bullying bastard has done, he simultaneously screams at me at the top of his lungs, 'Johnny you're trespassing. I am going to kill your ass.' And he lunges across the fence and grabs me by the back of the neck. Great white shark, Bud.

"I now know that he has assaulted my wife. How do you control an eighty pound boulder thrown into a ditch at another person. That high velocity splat from a boulder that big could have put my wife's eyes out. That rock could have crushed her little hands. Now he is coming for me. I am like a great white shark.

"Marilyn comes over to the fence and says, 'Come on Johnny. We can come back and work on this later. Let's go to the Light Show.'

"I feel nothing. I hear nothing. I have no idea Marilyn is even there.

"I am in great white mode, Brother. Partly this is because he has attacked when I wasn't looking at him. If he had screamed at me when I was looking at him, I could have maybe done something different. But when he lunges right over the fence and grabs me around the neck, I fall into the zone, the fight zone. This guy has assaulted my wife and now he is on me.

"He is in a fight. He doesn't know it, but I have glazed over here in the ditch with my head down. He has just bought a ticket and the show is starting. I am on automatic pilot.

"I am a five gallon bucket of gasoline and he has come up to me like a burning match. When he screams and grabs me, he brings the match and the gas together. He sparks an explosion. He created the situation. He brought the elements together. He touched it off. I nail his ass.

"I come up with everything that I have and plow my fist straight into his wide open screaming mouth. He is out, out cold sprawled on the ground knocked onto his side of the fence. He is out for a twenty count. I could climb over the fence and finish this job. I am making that move to climb that fence when an invisible hand reaches down and grabs my shoulder as if to say, "That will be enough, Johnny.'

"Kobalski comes to spitting teeth. He gets his cell phone out and calls the cops. He's spitting teeth while he is talking.

"The dispatcher is saying, 'Get away from the guy. Where is he at?'

"Right across the fence.'

"Leave. Go. Move.'

"Kobalski flees back up to his house up on the hill.

"I am just standing there like a deer looking into the head lights of a big old freight truck coming down the freeway. I'm not even there in my head."

"That's not good Johnny," I tell him across the table. "I've lost my appetite. A bad situation like that could ruin a man's life. What happened next?"

CHAPTER 25

JAIL

"Marilyn and I wait for the police. We haven't done anything wrong. That is what we think. This is America, the land of justice and freedom. The police are our friends. They'll sort this mess out real quick and see that we are innocent victims of this terrible bully, Frank Kobalski.

"The police arrive and go up the hill and talk to Frank first. Then they come down to our house to talk to us. We have meanwhile gone inside and are sitting in our front room.

"I know the older officer, Larry Smith. He asks, 'What happened, Johnny?' and we just start in on a conversation when the other officer, Morris Stonebreak, pops up and accuses, 'You're guilty. I can tell that you are guilty by the way that you're acting.'

"Say what?' I exclaim.

"He follows up his accusation with, 'Yeah. I can tell that you are guilty by the way that you are acting. You are just way too calm.'

"That doesn't set too well with me because I have been sitting right in this same living room in this same chair in the same way for twenty four years. No different than I am today. I take exception to what Stonebreak says and I inquire, 'Do I need an attorney?'

"Stonebreak snidely shoots back, 'I don't know. Why don't you come outside and we'll talk about it.'

"So, we go outside, and Stonebreak says, 'Is that the shovel that you beat Mr. Kobalski with leaning up against the plum tree over there?'

"I say, 'Are you putting words in my mouth?'

"He says, 'I'm arresting you.'

"And he arrests me standing right there by my front porch. Handcuffs me behind the back. Off they take me and book me in the Cheyenne County Jail. Strip me down and put me in one of their little striped yellow monkey suits. They take my socks. That is bad, real bad. I have neuropathy of the feet. The next thing that I know I am in the Cheyenne County Jail holding cell which is a very nasty little inconvenient place to be in, especially for someone that is a kind of basically an outdoor type. They might as well stuff me in a garbage can with a light bulb in it and put on the lid.

"Incarcerating somebody who lives in a little apartment on the thirtieth floor in New York City is not like incarcerating a local Oregonian who lives and works out in the woods and is used to a lot of space and expanse and has never been in trouble with the law and has never been confined to a small space.

"I am very uncomfortable and then I have my back problem and my hip problem. They have both been badly broken in logging accidents. If I am at home I can get by with the pain. I sit in a special chair and I sleep in a therapeutic bed. I sit, lie down, and move in particular ways to keep the pain bearable. But none of that is possible when I am confined to a space six building blocks wide and sixteen building blocks long, one chrome shitter, one chrome pay phone, nowhere to sit down, lights are on twenty four hours per day, with just three metal racks, one on each wall, one in the middle, three metal racks, each three bunks high starting six inches from the concrete floor. You can't sit on your bunks. They are too close together. There's just room to squeeze in. There are three racks with three bunks in each rack with one guy in each bunk, nine guys. The guy on top has got no shade. The top bunk is a double edged sword. The guy up there is in the light all day and all night every day and every night. There is not a bunk above you to give you a shadow from the light. You are in the sun.

It is like being in the desert twenty four seven. These lights are hot and bright. But the guys on top can actually sit down by sitting cross legged and leaning up against the wall. They can sit up upright. They have a place to sit. Nobody else has a place to sit except for the toilet. There's no hanging your legs over the bed. Guys locked in like this get real territorial, real violent, real quick.

"Sometimes I just sit on the shitter to have a place to sit. The majority of the guys in here are in here for drugs and parole violations and most of them are on prescriptions for that drug that they give people to come off of heroin, methadone. They just stare and fart, except when the chow comes. The guards only give us five minutes to eat. Then they start pounding on the cell door demanding our trays back. You gotta grab that chow tray and start shoveling grey globs and brown piles of disgusting stuff in your mouth fast if you want anything to eat.

"There is this one black guy in here, black as a magic marker, that I become friends with. He speaks English better than I do. He is not an African American. He is a British black guy. If I didn't see his face when he spoke, I wouldn't have known that he was black. If I had heard him speaking around the corner, I would have thought that he was a white guy. But anyway this guy is as black as a magic marker.

"I am having problems with my hip. I am having problems with my back. All of the sudden my feet are so cold that I start having a neuropathy attack. My feet are now starting to cramp up like a beetle's claw. It is a very painful foot cramp. Now the cramps are expanding up into my calf, into my lower thigh. I throw myself out onto the concrete floor, jack knife up, then straighten out, and flop around, smoothing the cramps out.

"When this cramp is gone, I have to get back into that bunk and lie flat on my back. I can roll either onto my right side or onto my left side but that is it. I am lying on solid steel. These are steel bunks. The little two inch pad under me is worn out. There might be an eighth of an inch between me and that steel bunk.

"Suddenly this black guy, OT is his name, a very nice guy with a heart the size of a watermelon, sticks his head in my bunk and says, 'You know Mr. Jones, they think this old grey haired man up on the top bunk is the grandpa in here, but I know who the old grandpa in here is, and it is you. You are a lot older than you look Mr. Jones. You shouldn't be in here. This isn't any place for you to be. I'll help you. I'll help you get back into that bunk when you throw yourself out onto the floor. I don't know what they are doing taking your socks. An old man like you needs his socks.'

"He is in the bunk above me. The next time that I spazz out, he gets up and comes down and helps me get back into my bunk. He covers up my feet to keep me from going into hypothermic shock. I am surprised that I don't go into one of those hypothermic attacks that I get. If it wasn't for OT, I would have one of those seizures that I have whatever they are.

"The colored guy is a God send. He helps me and he talks to me and there is another young guy in here that has some problems here in town, but he is a nice guy. I tell him and OT and everybody that is awake every story that I know in the three days that I am in here. I may sleep an hour in all of this time.

"Into this horror story pretty good, I am in so much pain that it starts affecting my eye sight. My eye sight is getting blurry. I am really in a bad way suffering with my hip pain and back pain. Diabetes is causing my legs to go numb and my blood circulation is getting really bad, causing me to be cold all of the time. I can no longer roll left or right. I just get in my bunk on my back and when I feel that I have to roll left or right I grit my teeth and pray to God that I won't have to move until the spasms start and fling me out onto the concrete floor.

"Then OT says, 'I'll get you some socks grandpa. I know how to get things in a joint like this. Give me some time and I'll get you some. There are extra socks in here and I know who has them and where they are.'

"He starts trading his food, the majority of his food for favors. Then he says, "Look what I have."

"He hands me a pair of socks. He helps me put the socks on my feet. I am so cramped up and in so much pain that I have to get up and get on the toilet. Then he puts those socks on my feet, gets me back in my bunk, and he gets me covered back up.

"He looks at me and says, "You are still shivering and shaking Grandpa. I'll get you some more socks. If you have the right stuff, the right chow, the right guy, I'll get you some more socks. There are more socks in here and I know where they are."

"Sure enough, he gets me another pair of socks. There are some guys in here that have more than one pair of socks because there are several people in here that have the cold feet thing. I don't have any idea where he gets me the extra socks, but I think that what he does is get my original socks back. He does something with one of the guards.

"OT is a real life saver.

"My bail is set at $380,000. I was arrested on second degree assault, but when I am indicted it is on first degree assault instead of second degree assault. The penalty for first degree assault is twenty years in prison, mandatory, every minute, every second, every day. It is a Measure 11 crime. Measure 11 is the Oregon Bully Protection Act.

"So I am out of jail, but I am looking at a full blown criminal trial for first degree assault which is the same as attempted murder. A conviction means twenty years in prison, end of life. The sentence is automatic. The convicted prisoner spends every second, every minute, every hour, every day in prison. No early out. No parole. For me, it is a life sentence.

"Shane, I voted for Measure 11. I remember when I voted on Measure 11. Measure 11 was presented to us as a situation where a rapist gets out of jail and rapes again. A killer gets out of jail and kills again. A kidnapper gets out of jail and kidnaps again. And so we wanted those violent criminals to serve their time with no early out. So we passed Measure 11. And like all things, there are two sides to it. And on the back side of Measure 11 is the Oregon Bully Protection Act. If you are an older person who is being bullied and accosted by a younger male bully who is big, you are in a very dangerous situation because if you protect yourself, you could end up getting charged with a Measure 11 assault charge. On the back of this Measure about murderers, rapist, and kidnappers are these assault one, two, and three sections. Never heard this when I voted on Measure 11.

"If you get jumped when you have something in your hand, you would be surprised what can be deemed as a lethal weapon. If you spit on a cop, that is a lethal assault because of AIDS. Your saliva is a deadly weapon. M&M's, the candy, can be a deadly weapon. The police, the DA, the judge can construe almost anything that you might have in your hand as a deadly weapon. An ink pen, deadly weapon. Pick anything that you might pick up or have on you, deadly weapon. Say that you are an older person and you are repairing a fence and this bully assaults you and you have a pair of fencing pliers in your hand when this assault happens and something occurs and if that guy gets hurt at all by that fencing tool and you cannot prove that you were in fear for your life, then you are going to prison for twenty years. No if, and, or buts about it. If you have left any mark on his face that can be deemed as maiming his appearance, a cut, a chipped tooth, you are going to prison.

"What you can learn from me in a very short time for a mere one hundred dollars will be the best money that you have ever spent in your entire life. Been there and done that. If you have a husband or wife who is having a conflict with a neighbor over any kind of dispute between your husband and another man between your wife and another man or anyone in any shape or form, I know something that you need to know right away to keep your life from spinning out of control into pure Hell. And I am willing to teach it too the World. I am calling this lesson 'Dispute Resolutions 101'.

"Yeah, Johnny, what is that?" I ask with genuine interest. Anything that a man learns from a horrendous situation like Johnny's, I figure should be valuable. I want to be healthy and happy which is just the opposite of his situation. If he knows how to avoid troubles like his, I want to know the secret.

He leans across the table, looks me in the eye, points his right index finger at me, and declares, "The first thing that I want you to do is to stop. You are heading in the wrong direction. Stop. Stop in your tracks. If the confrontation is in front of you, immediately do a 180 degree turn. Now when you get turned around, smile. Smile as big as you can smile. Bring this happiness from within you out. If you can whistle, whistle. If you can skip a jig, then skip a jig, because you have just made one of the best decisions of your entire ever loving life."

"Go take somebody that you care about out to a fabulous time. Live today especially in the now. Forget about the money. You have just saved so much money that it is unbelievable. Enjoy the moment of your success because you are the winner."

I laugh heartily. He cracks me up. He is speaking with all of the fervor of an evangelical preacher on the first night of a revival meeting. "That's good. That's really good," I agree.

"Buddy that's the truth from somebody that's been there. Put it in the back of your mind. The reason that a person needs to replay 'Disputes Resolution 101' in their mind is because you don't have a lot of time to think about things when it comes to that crucial moment. The decision that is going to get you in a big jam will happen in a split second. If you don't consider what you are going to do in that split second now before you get in it, the most very good guy in the world who thinks that he has got the best control of himself, will muck up. It is just the way of nature."

"Yes", I add. "It is like in martial arts training. You have to train for the situation before it happens. You have to get the right attitude."

"Oh, absolutely. Absolutely. You have to realize that this problem that you are heading into is going to take place in less than a second."

"Yeah, right."

"You are going to have to make a very quick decision in a situation where you are really not yourself, or in a position to be making a decision like that in a split second, because it could be the wrong one."

"You could be in the wrong frame of mind," I suggest.

"That's right. It's all down to that split second decision. That's why you have to have 'Dispute Resolutions 101'. I'm trying to assist that split second decision. I'm trying to stop that decision making process from coming to be. I don't want to put you in a position of having to respond in a split second without any preparation. That's why you want to make the call and sign up for 'Disputes Resolution 101' class. It's all down to how you act in the heat of the moment. And the fact of the matter is that nobody in this situation can dictate how he is going to act in the heat of the moment. He maybe thinks that he can, but reality is reality and he can't do it. Without some forethought into the situation, he cannot make the right decision. It happens too quickly."

"Wow! Yeah!" I'm witnessing like a lost soul jumping around in the pews at revival.

"Everybody has said, 'Oh, if I could just have that one second back. Just give me that one second back to do over. Just that one second to get me out of this Hell hole."

"That's right on the number, Brother," I proclaim.

"They are all praying for that one second to be returned to their lives," he continues. "Every one of those 41,500 prison inmates in the Oregon State Penitentiary are all praying to have that one second to do over again. That is where the weeds are cut from the mustard in 'Disputes Resolutions 101'. It's the split second and trying to avoid the confrontation and having to make a decision in a split second that is not going to be the right one."

"Damn! You're right. You're right. You have convinced me." I get out my pen and act like I'm ready to sign up.

"Everybody has to realize that," he states like a man who knows a great truth and just wants to share his knowledge for the good of the world.

Then he looks me square in the eyes and quietly adds, "And I can tell you that the prison cells in Oregon make the cells for the terrorists in Guantanamo Bay look like the Holiday Inn. You need to think about how you treat other people."

He leans back and smiles and raises both hands like he is surrendering and says, "Except I can't charge you the hundred dollars and give you this advice or really ever give you any advice because then I would be practicing law so I would be going back to jail again for giving out illegal legal advice. You gotta be careful in this country, but I am still going to tell you what has been on my mind."

"Think about this. There are men that live in New York City on the thirtieth floor, in an apartment that is four hundred square feet. That apartment has a bathroom that has a door to it. Other than that, it is a bedroom, kitchen, and living room, all of that in one room. In their state of mind, their situation, there is a lot of those guys capable of staying in those little units for months, for years. Those boys are preconditioned to human warehousing which is what prison is. Prison is a human warehouse thing. You have a spot, a slot, and in that slot you go. Prison is like looking at the old Post Office with all of the mail boxes. Modern city people are in one of those little boxes. Apartments and prisons are walls of mail boxes. That is the Oregon State Penitentiary, that is a New York City apartment complex, that is your little spot in the wall, and that is where you will be. People in this country have been conditioned to that warehouse of being deal. What is a high rise in New York City? That is a human warehouse. What is a prison? A prison is a human warehouse. You could exchange those things. You take a country boy from Oregon and you stick him in a little box like that with eight other guys that he has never seen in his life, he is going to come out of there like a deer that has just crossed the freeway under bright lights, Bud. I mean he is going to be spread out on all fours and his eyes are going to be that big around. And he won't know whether to shit, piss, or suck wind. It is a whole different thing."

I am stunned, stunned but amused by Johnny's revelations to me. I stutter, "Boy Johnny, this is a whole streak of bad luck......... I mean this was a pretty horrendous experience and it just goes on and on and on, one thing after another. I mean okay you are booked and you are going to go to jail for twenty years. Then the court case goes on for like eight months or something, and I heard that you were finally convicted of a misdemeanor and released."

"It was extended for over a year."

"What? You say that this went on for over a year? You had this whole thing hanging over your head for over a year? Man time flies. It doesn't seem like years have gone by. What have I been doing? Wow!"

"I had this whole thing hanging over my head for over a year, longer than a year. And the only memory that I have during this whole time, is that horrifying experience of being incarcerated in the Cheyenne County Jail holding cell and being tortured by those jailer bastards for days."

"Now I have a great amount of sympathy, but I also realize from my experience that a police officer can be his own worst enemy. He could easily be treated like an inmate, the way that he treated the inmate. You see what I mean?"

"What's that? I don't see what you mean."

"A police officer is his own worst enemy. Police create their own murderer. A cop killer doesn't accidentally murder that cop. A cop created that murderer in the first place, or the killer wouldn't have murdered that cop. There is something that that cop did to that guy that makes that guy want to murder that cop or any cop."

"Your experience with Stonebreak and the jailers makes you angry at police and government authorities generically?"

"Well it just kind of makes you realize, hey, I am a good, kind, caring, loving person; but when it comes to a cop, the way that I have been treated by cops, Omigod, it would be a real test of my will power if one of them was laid out on the side of the road to decide whether to stop and help him or to stop and piss on him."

I laugh surprised by the image of him standing by the road trying to decide what to do.

"Well, remember your lesson. You said it really great. The one about where you are going to counsel people about what to do when they are angry at their neighbor. But anyway, meanwhile you've got this eighteen months with this threat of death in this hell hole hanging over your head and the economy tanks. So your income is cut off and your bills are rising astronomically because you have lawyer's fees and everything."

"Yeah, I am financially distraught. I have sold my rental units which I owned free and clear before I got in a fight with my neighbor. I have sold my interest in my real estate that I owned free and clear. I have liquidated my 401 K's. I am right down to two dollars and a house that the guy I fought with is suing me for in a civil suit for damages for pain and suffering. And now the place that I bought to try and get away from the guy has gone into foreclosure too."

"You bought another place? So, you decided to just leave your home and move to a new place? You decided to take your own advice and turn away from this conflict and go somewhere else?"

"Absolutely."

"Rather than fight about the plugged up ditch. We just re-routed the ditch and moved. No excuse to even deal with the guy. I have been very nice to the guy since the fight. It is a very strange situation. The very first thing that people find hard to believe ----."

"So you go buy a ranch?"

"I buy a ranch far away, down in the South County, way out in the hills."

"What happens?"

"Well for one thing I have to do a lot of work on it to make it nice. Meanwhile, I am waiting for a land partition so that the title can pass over to me. I have put $120,000 cash down and given the title to my house to the seller to get this ranch free and clear and to get away from Willow Street."

"So you have bought this place and moved, and then you get completely bushwhacked on getting it."

"Yes, there is no question about that. The guy who sold it to me doesn't have a free and clear title to the property. Lord Jesus may it all work out."

"It is going to work out. We are going to work it out here, now. You know what Jesus said about neighbors, right?"

"Yes. Something like 'love thy neighbor as thyself' and 'do unto others as you would have them do unto you'."

"So we got a bad trend here, right? But you broke the trend. I just heard you break the trend with your counseling idea."

"You mean with the advice that I would give other people? Is that what you mean?"

"Yes, now you have to give that advice to Johnny."

"Right. I have already given it to another guy with amazing results."

"Huh? What are you talking about?"

"Brian, my partner, and I are sitting in our real estate office the other day having this same discussion that we are having, when Brian decided to call his friend Jim who lives over in Walpi.

"Jim was going to buy this ten acre parcel from this old man, but before he got it bought, the old man got the property subdivided into two lots. So, Jim, calls up his best friend, Bob, and says, 'Bob, why don't you buy this piece of property next to me outside of town. That way I'll know who the neighbor is and we like to hunt and fish together, so, we can have a wonderful life out there living next to each other.'

"Bob replies, 'Alright man. Let me check it out.'

"Bob buys the place. Bob helps Jim build a pole barn. Helps him put in an illegal septic system because Jim's wife doesn't want to walk clear back to the house to go to the bathroom every time that she needs to go to the bathroom when she is working on their horses.

"Bob and Jim are helping each other and life is good. They are living along side each other enjoying life.

"Then the old man who sold them the properties comes over one day to visit Bob. Bob has taken it upon himself to build a brand new really nice fence separating the two parcels because Jim has horses. While the old man is visiting, he is looking over at that fence and he says, 'I'm a little bit confused here Bob about that fence, unless it is a cross fence, but it is an awful nice cross fence.'

"Say what?' Bob asks.

"The old man replies, 'I was just wondering why you didn't put the fence on the property line way over there?'

"All of the sudden, this really neat piece of property that Bob thought was his, isn't. It is Jim's.

"Bob in his infinite wisdom gets really pissed off. He gets his backhoe, goes out in the field, throws a chain on the first fence post and drags the whole run of fence completely out with his backhoe. Next he starts digging a ditch where the fence used to be with the backhoe.

"He is doing all of this while Jim is at work. Jim's wife calls Jim and asks, 'Jim do you know what Bob is doing? Bob just tore out the pasture fence with a backhoe and he is digging a six foot deep ditch in the pasture, our pasture, the pasture with our horses in it, and the pasture with no fence now. One of our horses could fall in that ditch and break a leg.' Then she tells Jim, 'You need to get your ass home and get over there and get this straight with Bob. He is tearing up our property and he is endangering our horses.'

"It is at about this time that my partner Brian decides to check in with his buddy, Jim. He picks up the phone, dials Jim's number and when Jim answers, he says, 'Hi Jim. How's it going?'

"I'm headed home,' Jim replies.

"Headed home in the middle of the day? What's going on?' Brian asks.

"Oh, this damn buddy of mine just tore out the pasture fence. I'm going home and get my gun, get my 357 magnum, and I'm going to go over there and get this straight with him.'

"Brian begs, 'Jim don't do it. Tell you what, I have a friend name of Johnny sitting right here and he got in a little thing like this that got him put in jail. I am begging you not to confront Bob. Do not go to the gun cabinet. Throw the key away. Do not open the gun cabinet.'

"This is a half hour phone conversation. Brian and I are on one end of the phone and Jim is on the other end. Brian is standing up at his desk trying every way that he can to convince Jim not to get violent, but instead to talk to Bob like the friend that he is.

"He pleads, 'Jim please do not go to the gun cabinet.'

"Jim is heading in the house. He hangs up. As far as Brian and I know, he is heading for the gun cabinet and then for a show down over at Bob's place. Jim is going over there and get things straight.

"Guess what happens?"

I shrug. I don't have any idea. This could end bad, very bad.

Johnny continues.

"Jim starts to go to the gun cabinet and all of the sudden he is hearing Brian go, 'Jim, I am begging you do not do this. It is the wrong thing for you to do. This is big time trouble for you Bud. Do not go to the gun case.'

"Next thing Jim knows, he is heading out across his front porch, 357 mag in hand and headed for Bob's house. Before he steps off the porch, he hears those words of Brian's again, "Don't be stupid. Jail is really ugly Buddy."

"He decides to put the gun back in the gun cabinet and he calls the police.

"You will never believe what happens next."

I'm staring. I just shrug again.

"The police officer goes over to Bob's house. He talks to Bob about digging up the pasture, not just tearing the fence out because it wasn't on the property line but also about digging a big trench across the field. He tells him that tearing out the fence is one thing, but now there is a big ditch where the fence used to be.

"Standing right there on the porch, Bob punches the cop, knocks the cop out and then kicks and beats the snot out of the knocked out policeman right there on his front porch.

"Bob is in the Oregon State Penitentiary right now and will be there for some time. He assaulted a police officer.

"People need to know this. There is so much going on in life. You think that you've got things under control. You think you know how to handle the situation. Uhhhhh, yeah! But take it from somebody that has been there. You are wrong about that. Something could change and change that situation in a heartbeat.

"A lot of people don't think, 'What about the other guy?' Johnny announces.

The color is back in his cheeks. He is talking loud, waving his arms around. People in the other booths are looking at us.

"Yeah", I agree and then add, "This is strange, but I think that I'm starting to see a pattern here that might help us get what we want. What about other beings, besides humans such as plants and animals and whatever? Are you still hunting Johnny?"

The excitement and agitation drain out of him. He gets quiet again. He seems to be ashamed of something.

"Yes," he whispers apologetically, "but my luck just hasn't been good when it comes to killing."

"Let's hear about it," I push him. I'm on a roll. I'm starting to see connections.

CHAPTER 26

SHIAM

"Take for instance when my buddy, Luke Steele, and I decide that we will go buck hunting up Dog Creek. We get in my old pickup and go up the North River to Dog Creek. When we get there, we split up.

"I come in on the east side of Dog Creek. Luke comes in on the west side. Dog Creek is running north and south. So I am on the east side and he is on the west side and we are coming together in the middle of Dog Creek.

"And, boy oh boy, I get into some really good hunting on a bench up here. I can just feel that big old buck is here. I get real excited, and I have to take a crap. The minute I find me a buckskin log and get my pants down, the minute I set that rifle down, and do that thing. That great big buck, a great big four point, jumps up, just leaps and springs out into the open. Man, I just ----. I cannot get my ----. I am just done. He has me in a bad position and that is all there is to it. It is check mate.

"I think, 'Johnny you get excited and the minute you go to make the deal, the big buck gets away from you.'

"Anyway, I am still thinking about this a month later when Luke and I decide to go back in there to hunt again, but this time we are elk hunting.

"I say to Luke, 'We might get a chance to see that big old trophy buck again in here. We might get a chance to see if he made it through hunting season.'

"This time I go right up the main trail up Dog Creek and Luke breaks away up the left side. I go up the main creek. If you go up Dog Creek on the main creek, you come to a huge boulder in the creek, a boulder that is about three stories tall and about the size of a house. It is sitting right smack dab in the creek. Underneath the brush at the foot of this boulder is one creek, but over on the north side of the boulder, the back side of the boulder, five creeks come into the back side of that rock. One creek comes out the front side of the rock. Five creeks go into the back of the rock.

"I walk around the west side of the rock and I am walking across these little ridges. Each one of these little creeks is in a draw and there is a ridge between each one of them and I am walking over these little ridges just above the rock. I am walking up about ten feet and down into a little creek, up over, and back down into a little creek. I have the scope on my rifle dialed all the way up onto its highest magnification to see things far away. It rained hard last night and there is a heavy drip in the timber. You can hear that heavy drip and the fog has just started to set down into the tops of the trees, just down into where the limbs quit. When I started up into the timber, the fog was quite a ways above the tree tops. I come up over this ridge and down by a creek and look around. I am hunting to my left. I am scoping up into the open timber to my left under the fog all of the way up in the trees.

"I have the gun up and I am looking through the scope when suddenly I see a streak of brown, just a streak out in front of me, and I immediately swing onto what I saw streak. I have my scope magnification so high that it is like looking through a microscope. I can't figure out what I'm seeing because I am too close to whatever it is.

"I think to myself, 'Buck. It is that big buck that I had seen up here during hunting season.'

"Well I am sure right about that, but then I see black in there too. And I go, 'Buck, bear, big foot. Whoa!'

"All of the sudden, I am just panicked. I am so close. It is just twenty feet away. There is a little fifteen foot creek between me and it. I'm standing on about two feet of dirt right at the bottom of that little ridge, fifteen feet of water, a little flat on the other side probably eight feet wide, rock grotto behind that probably twelve feet tall. When I see black in my scope and that really scares me. The first thing that I do is start sucking and blowing air in panicked gulps and I fog up my scope.

"Omigod!'

"I am looking in this fogged up scope and I'm going, 'Buck, bear, big foot. Omigod. Monster bear with buck in face. Omigod!'

"My sucking and blowing is fogging up my scope. I'm just standing there gasping and I'm looking at my hand on the forearm of the gun and it is paper white. The hair on the back of my neck stands up on end and just shoves the brim of my hat right down on to the top of the scope. My whole world is reduced to this fogged over image of black and brown hair in the scope.

"I come to the conclusion that this is a monster black bear with that big buck in his jaws that I had seen last month. The bear has killed the buck in the creek while the buck was drinking water and that monster bear was then bedded down on the kill next to the creek. When I came up, he stood up with that buck in his face. He has eaten the hams and what he has is what is left of that buck in his face. He has chewed the back bone down like an icicle and he has the head, the front shoulders, the rib cage, everything but the hind quarters in his face. He is just wagging this trophy buck's head and rack left and right, right in front of me.

"I am standing there terrified, gasping. I am trying to back up, but this dirt that I am trying to back up on is wet and slippery. I take a step back, and I slide back into the creek. I take a step back, and I slide back into the creek. I cannot get backed up. I'm just standing there spinning wheels. Finally, I hit a rock or something in that mud that gives me a little grip and I'm able to pull myself back up on to that ridge out of the creek.

"Then things get very serious. The bear throws the buck down on the ground. He is standing erect looking at me, thirty feet away.

I've got a fogged up scope on him, right in the center of him, and the only thing that is crossing my mind is, 'Buddy, you got them hopped up 110 grain slugs in this 7 mm. Omigod. If you sizzle one of these 110 grain boat tail slugs through him going better than a mile a second and you don't hit bone, you are dead. He will leap that creek and kill you in a heartbeat. Omigod. You cannot get to your 180 grain slugs. You are standing here with these really light weight hopped up shells. These things throw a flame out of the barrel six feet long, eighteen inches wide, bright purple. Sound like a big old bull whip. Kerwhack!!'

"I'm thirty feet away from a monster bear with a slug that goes a mile a second, going, 'Holy Mackerrolly. You either hit bone and kill him or you are dead.'

"I am absolutely terrified.

"Shooting at him becomes something that isn't an option. I am not going to shoot at this big boy thirty feet away with what I have, not in these conditions.

"He is just looking at me, eye to eye, and all I can hear is the flare of this boy's nostrils. 'Brrrunhhh! Brrunhhh! Brrunhh!'

"I am going, 'Omigod! Omigod! Omigod!'

"To hear something like that breathing, to see something like that standing erect just thirty feet away from you and making that kind of noise is terrifying. I'm just watching and hearing that boy's nostrils going brrrunhhh, brrunhhh, brrunhhh.

"He's still standing up. I have seen a lot of bears, but I have not seen a lot of bears that stand up, upright. I've seen a lot of little bears, but no question, this is a mega, world record, monster bear, well beyond any world record that has ever been. I am absolutely looking at the mega world record black bear. No ifs, ands, or buts about it. The world record is like six hundred pounds. This boy is eight hundred and fifty, nine hundred pounds, hell, a thousand pounds of muscle, teeth, and claws. Every single tip of black hair on him is diamond chipped. The gleam in his eyes is like he has stars in them. The gleam in this guy's eyes is unforgettable. I have never seen a creature in my life that has that gleam in his eyes. It looks like he is looking right through me with some kind of beam. It is incredible, totally scary. He is immaculate. He is the biggest specimen of a boar black bear I have ever seen in my life and I know that he is a monster bear because when he moves, he moves just like Jell-O. Everything he does just looks like a floating mass inside a hide. I can tell right away that I have never seen anything like this in my ever loving life.

"There is a grotto just behind him that has a staircase up through the rock face up to the top of this grotto. It has some little fir trees in front of it, some sapling fir trees. He walks around in behind those saplings and he is peering at me from between two saplings. He is just standing there right across the creek. Suddenly he goes right up through that stair case to the top of that grotto and disappears over the ridge behind him.

"I am going, 'Omigod! He is gone.'

"I start walking up the ridge that I am on. Suddenly he appears again. I hadn't gone very far up the ridge, maybe sixty yards from that kill when he appears right on the ridge right across from me.

"He stands up and lets out the biggest roar that I have ever heard. He has those claws out. My God! The claws on the end of this guy's paws are just incredibly huge. They are six inches long. They are just incredible. He is up there and he is roaring at me and he is swinging those claws and the next thing that I know he charges me, roaring, running on two legs down the hill. He starts out on two legs roaring and screaming and running down the hill charging me for about thirty yards then he drops down on to all fours, cuts a little U turn and goes right back up to the top of the ridge.

"I am lying over behind a stump. I'm thinking, "Oh shit! Oh shit! He is going to attack me. He is going to come down through that draw, right up over to here. I better get prepared to defend my life. I'm going to have to shoot. I'm going to have to start shooting."

"When he gets up to the top of the little ridge, he stands up again. Does the roarrrr! And starts waving those claws.

"Boy! Then down the hill he starts running. To see a bear run down hill on his back legs is weird, really weird. I haven't seen one run on two feet before. I have seen little ones that just stand up to sniff you, but they don't actually walk around on two feet. This guy is incredible. He is walking around on two feet like I walk around on two feet. This guy can get around on two feet like a person. No problem at all. This guy can walk erect, no problem. He can go erect just as well as on all fours. I am seeing him do it.

"This time when he charges me, I am just within a whisker of touching one off because I think that I can get another round into my gun. I wouldn't even think this way if I didn't think that I could get another round in my gun.

"Luckily, I don't touch it off, and he goes right back up to the top of the ridge, stands up, roars at me, waves those claws around, and drops right over the back side of that ridge. Just gone. Gone just like that.

"I'm still lying behind that stump. I'm breathing a sigh of relief, ummphhh. I'm lying like a wet rag in behind the stump. What have I done to be so completely exhausted? Just the experience from where I met him to where I got up on this ridge is only five to ten minutes.

"The stare off when this first happens was a couple of minutes of sheer terror. I am over there shaking like a scared dog, trying to keep this gun on him.

"Then I almost shot him when he charged down the ridge at me. I barely have enough energy to get my ass up off from around this stump and to continue on. I am completely exhausted from sheer firkin terror.

"I've got to collect myself. I go, 'He's decided to go his own way. Shewww!'

"I'm looking at myself. I'm starting to get some color back. I am paper white. I am trying to get some color back into my skin, trying to get legs under me to where I can walk without shaking, and trying to get my breathing under control. I am absolutely terrified from this little event. No doubt about it. I have never experienced this kind of fear ever before in my life.

"I turn around and start hiking up the ridge. The fog suddenly decides to come down like an elevator to just twelve inches above the top of the bushes around me. I am looking at a salal brush patch that is two hundred yards wide, up the draw to my right a hundred yards, and up the draw to my left a hundred yards. I'm looking straight up this draw that is nothing but the biggest, thickest salal brush patch that I have ever seen and the salal bushes come right up to my chin.

"I am going, 'Omigod. How do I get through this?'

"As I study the top of this thicket of salal I see a little line going through it. I duck my head down under the salal and sure enough there is a trail underneath. Inside that salal is a bear trail that is about two feet wide and it is just as smooth as a baby's butt. It is as smooth a trail as I have ever seen in my life. To get places, I have to use this trail. My head is sticking above the top of the brush. I am scared. I start moving through the salal. This is safety off at all times. Before I go far the trail comes to a tree which has fallen across the trail.

"This windfall is six feet in diameter right in the middle of the trail. I have to get over this windfall that is lying in this salal patch, the biggest salal patch that I have ever seen in my life. I go over the windfall, safety off, barrel first. The trees in this salal patch are five foot, six foot in diameter. This patch is pretty open, but on my left and right are these big trees. I go around them safety off, barrel first. I am terrified but I don't know what else to do.

"This is what I am doing when it dawns on me, "Buddy, those diamond chips on that bear, this guy is just like Jaws on land. He is in this salal patch. He is in here with me. He is in this salal patch with me. I can feel him."

"I don't just have goose bumps. I am goose bumps. I am white as paste. I know that he is in the salal patch with me. I walk a ways. Then I have to duck into the salal patch to find the trail. Up on top of the bushes I can see a line, just an opening in the salal. I am getting pretty good at reading the trail from the top, but every once in a while I have to jump down into the bushes to check the trail. Then I discover that this trail has forks in it. I go up here and then all of the sudden the trail forks and goes off to the right, then suddenly it forks and goes off to the left. He has multiple trails underneath this salal.

"I am walking in this salal with my hunting rifle. The salal is up to my chin. My head is just above the salal, my head and neck sticking out. My visibility is one foot above the salal. At the top of my hat is the fog level. At my chin is the salal. This is the window that I have to work with.

"That boy could be anywhere in this salal and literally stand up right in front of me and I would never see his head. He is over eight and half feet tall. He is eight and a half feet to the eye balls, dead on, because I took my gun down when I backed up at the creek, and I looked the boy right in the eyes. I am standing on two and a half feet of dirt to the water's level. I'm six feet tall and standing on two and a half feet of dirt. He's right at the level of the water and I'm looking him right in the eyes. So, he is eight and a half feet tall to the eyeballs. This is one monster firkin bear. There is no doubt about it. I have stumbled into the monster, world record black bear.

"Then it crosses my mind that this could be Shiam, the Guardian Spirit black bear of the North Ochoco Indian dead, because we are hunting in the Dog Creek area. We are hunting right up to the funeral caves of the North Ochoco Indians where all of the regular Indians are buried, not the royalty, but the regular Indians are buried here.

"The Ochoco Indians say that Shiam, the black bear, leader of the animal people is the Guardian Spirit of the North Ochoco Indian dead who are buried in these funeral caves.

"I am now looking at a monster spirit bear, but he is very real. He is absolutely real. That spiritual thing just goes by real fast, because I am so scared. This is so real that the spiritual aspect of this deal does not reach much of the dawn of recollection at this point in time. Those realizations may filter through afterwards, if I live. I'm in a kind of chess game where the stakes are my life, my body, me. I gotta do everything just right, now, because I'm in here with him, with it.

"I am whooping for my buddy, Luke. I am whooping loud. I mean real loud. I can whoop loud enough to hurt somebody's ears. I have learned how to communicate in the woods. When you're scared and you are whooping for help, you can really lay one out there, and I am doing it. I am whooping for my friend to come and assist me, or at least to let him know of the situation.

"Finally I come to a place where the limbs and leaves kind of open up a little bit at the top of that big salal patch. There is a windfall there and I am exhausted. I sit down and relax. I'm regathering myself, regrouping a little bit, trying to catch my breath, getting back to a normal complexion, getting the goose bumps down off me, getting the hair laid back down on the back of my neck, getting back down to a normal person when all of the sudden I see something. I see a glimpse of something about a hundred and fifty yards off to my left in that little window below the fog and above the salal.

"I whip my scope on to that spot. This is so crazy. This bear for some reason is really comfortable standing upright on two legs. He is standing upright. When I whip my scope over there, it freaks me out, because I am looking at an upside down bear head, a really big one. What he has to do, he is standing up to see me, he has to bend down, and look at me through the window upside down. When I flash the scope on him, I am seeing a big, big bears head upside down in this fog window.

"Omigod, it is him!'

"I click the safety off and he stands up, steps backwards, and disappears. He had a drop off behind him, or something. He must have been up on a ridge looking at me. But he had to look at me upside down standing up which is pretty crazy.

"At this point in time, I am ready to start throwing lead at anything that moves. I am done. I am totally panicked. Somehow he knows. He doesn't hang around. Somehow he knows that I am going to start shooting and that is the last little look for me. He disappears.

"I whoop for my buddy, Luke, but Luke doesn't answer. Suddenly I get a really, really bad idea. I decide to go back to where the kill is because I am pretty sure that, that is that big four point buck that I had missed an opportunity to kill during hunting season.

"Yi, yi, yi! What am I thinking?'

"I go back down to the kill. I am sitting across the draw from where the kill is in the little grotto. I'm scoping down there about seventy five yards away from me. I can see the big buck lying there that the bear has walked away from.

"I decide that I am going to go over there and check out that buck. I am now returning to the scene of the monster bear's kill. What a dumb, dumb idea.

"I wade across the creek. It is only a few inches deep. I just wade right across. I get over there and I'm looking around. The grotto looks the same. Up at the top of the grotto, there are ornamental black huckleberry bushes. There is one great big black huckleberry bush up there. I am looking around thinking, 'Everything is pretty cool.'

"I bend my head down. I take the barrel of my gun and I touch one of the buck's tines and turn that rack a bit. That is all that I do, just touch the horns. The minute that the barrel touches that horn, I am white washed with ice water, just as if somebody has dumped a huge load of ice water right on top of my head. As fast as water can fall, I go ice cold from head to toe. Boom! My body knows before my brain knows. My body is going unnnhhunhh, unnnhhuhnn, unhhunhn. I am looking at my hands go paper white right in front of my eyes.

"I say to myself, 'Omigod, he's here! He has come back.'

"By my hair standing up, by the color of my skin, by my pulse, by my breath, I know. I hadn't done anything. All I had done was touch the barrel of my gun to this rack of horns. The moment that I did, my body went to ice from head to toe. As I watch, my hand that is on the rifle goes paper white. I know that he is here. I do not even raise my head up. I take a couple of steps back real slow and as I'm moving backwards real slow, I'm raising my head up real slow too.

"There he is at the top of the grotto, right behind the bigger ornamental huckleberry bush. He is standing up above that bush. He has both arms spread eagle. I am looking at a wing span that I cannot believe. I cannot believe how big this guy is when he has both of his arms out right and left and there are those six inch claws on the end of those arms. Are you kidding me? I am dead. He is going to leap right off of that grotto, right down on me. I put my head down. God walking on water. I tip toe backwards across that fifteen foot wide stream. When I get to the other side, my boots, swear to God, are not wet. I don't know how that happens. All that I know is I put my head down, tip toe backwards across that stream and just, boom, I'm on the other side of that stream. I can see that my boots are not wet, but that is not what I am worrying about.

"I look up just in time to see him drop out of sight behind that big ornamental huckleberry bush.

"I am back across the creek on that same two feet of dirt that I was slipping up and down on. There I am again, just spinning on that same dirt. I am terrified again, asking myself, 'What am I doing?' Telling myself, "You have to be the dumbest person on Earth to go back to a monster bear's kill like that."

"I sit down. I have a hard time getting a cigarette lit much less kept in my mouth. I am having a real bad time. Then I see my hunting partner, Luke, coming down the hill. At fifty yards, I start laughing at him because I can see that he is paper white and I know that he has met the exact same bear that I have seen.

"As he comes down the trail, we begin to laugh together, but I still want that trophy buck's head.

"Luke guards me with his big old gun while I go over to the kill and cut off and take that trophy buck's head that that monster bear has killed.

"I will never go back up Dog Creek. Luke will never go back up Dog Creek. We were both scared so bad that neither of us will ever go out anywhere in that area ever, ever, ever again. I have not even set foot on that side of the North Ochoco Highway since then, and I have no intentions of ever setting one foot on that side of the road ever again. Done."

"Johnny, did you say that that monster bear was a spirit bear?"

"I don't know. I am not sure of what an animal spirit even is. All that I know is that there was something beyond anything that I have ever known about that bear and he scared me real bad. I may be completely wrong about that bear. After all, he could have easily killed me, but he didn't. Maybe animals do have spirits like people. That whole spirit thing is too scary to think about."

CHAPTER 27

THE SNOW KLOO

"Fear, fear and doubt, Johnny those are terrible things. If we are going to get to joy and happiness, we are going to have to get beyond fear and doubt. Why don't we go for a walkabout in Eastern Oregon and camp out under the great American skies in the wide open spaces?"

"I am not going camping with you. You bet fear is a terrible thing and that is why I am not going walking about in no wilderness", Johnny states with sincere finality in his voice. "Fear from being lost in the woods is unbelievable. Just the fear when you realize that you are lost can kill you. You've got to fight the fear off, the fear, the actual raw panic. When you realize that you don't know where the Hell you are at, if you don't know where you are at, the problem that you have is: how do you get back to where you came from, if you don't know where the Hell you are at? You cannot let fear overtake you when you don't know where you are. You are not lost. You are just inconveniently in the wrong position to know exactly where you are. Don't panic. Don't ever think that you are lost when you are in this state of mind. You start out in this state of mind. You are always going to be in this state of mind. So, there is no such thing as lost. You always know where you are. You've just got to find out where you are at, where you are."

Johnny sagely adds, "My father told me, 'Son, relax, don't panic. You are never lost. Just go downhill. Follow the water downhill.' That was tremendous advice. I have been lost numerous times out there and the sheer panic from being lost is terrible. I was young when it happened to me the first time, but I had the wisdom of older people behind me. If I had been out there without the wisdom of my father, the sheer terror could have killed me. When you leave the beaten path and discover that you are lost, you have just walked into your own living Hell. Your fear surrounds you and if you don't have that confidence to know where you are at all times, you will die going round and round in circles. That is what happens to people who get lost. They die wandering around in circles lost. They die of terror and exposure very rapidly. No kidding."

"Well said. Well said, Johnny. That is why you and I have to go to the desert. We have to face our fears and quit wandering around in circles."

"Yeah. Well after the little event with the bear and after being lost, I have a lot of people that come up to me and go, 'well now Johnny, you're a homegrown Oregonian. I'll bet that you just love to go out in the woods and camp."

I tell them, "You are right about one thing. I am a homegrown Oregonian but there are a lot of things that you may not know about some home grown Oregonians and one of them is that the last place that I will ever be is camping in the woods at night."

As he speaks, he leans into me as if he is telling me a great secret, his eyes wide open, intense, staring.

His ludicrous statement takes me by surprise. I laugh nervously.

He ignores me and continues, breathing hard, white showing all around his pupils, "I know enough about the big woods to know that when the curtain is pulled and dark comes in the big woods, there is a world that becomes available that city people are not aware of and that is a very, very, very scary world, and that is nowhere that I want to be. I know better. I don't want to go through that fear terror panic thing. I don't want to put myself in the position to think, 'Oh, I'm out in the woods all by myself. I'm going to have a wonderful time."

"You are not all by yourself. Not even close."

"I'll tell you how I know that. In fact, I know that you know a lot of young guys that seriously want an adventure, want to go out in the big woods and look for some trouble. Well just send them Johnny's way cause I know the direction for some serious trouble. And if this lad that you send me will take me up on this offer, this offer comes with a bet. I'm going to take him to a special place in the woods and I'm going to propose to him that we make a $500 bet. That bet is this. I'll say to him, 'I'll bet five hundred bucks that if you come back at all, which the chances are that you probably will not, but if you do come back, I am betting that you come back with a different color of hair than you go in there with."

"That is how scary this place is Buddy. I'll tell you how I know that."

"We had been logging up in the Johnny Springs area. We'd clear cut six units and built five miles of logging road for the Northwood Lumber Company through steep canyon country in the great Northwest mountain wilderness. On a day off, Luke and I decide to go hunt one of those clear cut units.

"We drive up the new gravel road and pull up on to the logging landing which is a cleared, flat, rocked area about a hundred feet square sitting at the top of this ridge above the area which we had logged. If you were to step out on to the edge of this landing and trip, you are going rolling, tumbling, and bouncing a thousand feet straight down to the creek below. You probably won't be dead when you hit bottom, but you sure as Hell will hurt all over real bad. It is steep and a long ways down to the bottom of the canyon from where we are standing.

"We step out to the edge of the landing and start throwing rocks and chunks of wood over the edge down into the unit trying to spook something out. Way down over on the back side of the ridge on the far side of the canyon opposite from where we are standing, we hear something jump up and start coming towards us.

"I immediately say to Luke, 'Let's go get'em. There's something out there. Let's check it out, man.'

"I drop over the edge of the landing and race down the canyon wall to the creek below. The creek has a high clay bank on the other side. I leap over the creek and come to a deer trail. I am looking for a big bull elk's tracks on this trail.

"I say, 'There ain't even a buck track here. It's just does and yearlings. What do you think about that?'

"Hell, I am talking to myself. I think that Luke is right there too. Gone O. No Luke. I turn around. There is no Luke.

"All of a sudden, this thing comes right up on top of the ridge above me. I am at this point down in the creek and I have heard him come up on the ridge above me just a few hundred feet upstream from where I am standing. I know that he is up on the ridge because the crashing through the brush has gotten louder and closer. He has turned and started downstream on the top of the ridge towards me. I can't see anything through the rhododendron and chinquapin brush. The clear cut unit ends where I am standing, but I can hear him pull right up on to the top of the virgin forest area and start coming right down towards me. I am looking for backup from Luke. He is not there. I am spooked.

"The noise is absolutely terrifying. What in the Hell makes a noise coming through the brush like a five foot thick fir tree being fell through standing timber into a rhododendron patch? When those monstrous trees crash to the ground, they are loud. We are not talking swish, swish, swish. This noise that I am hearing is as loud a noise as I have ever heard in the woods without involving falling a tree or yarding a log through the brush on the end of a steel cable being pulled by a roaring diesel yarder. This thing is just booking it through twelve foot tall rhododendrons.

"I have been in those rhododendrons where he is. To get twenty or thirty feet with a hunting rifle would take me five minutes. That rhododendron in there is five inches through winding up ten to twelve feet tall and growing real close together. Luke and I both know this rhododendron patch. It is a nightmare rhododendron patch. You get in a rhododendron patch like that, you can die in a rhododendron patch like that. You can just get wore out because they are so close together. It is a duck, dive, weave, leg over this way, flip gun through there, sit gun here, slip between those. It is the God damnedest thing that you have ever gotten into in your life. I will guarantee you that you will go in there about thirty feet and you will go, 'You know what. It may take me another ten minutes just to go back the way that I just came, but this is not getting it at all.' You will turn around before you try to go through it. It is just too much of a nightmare. And when you get down in that rhododendron and that second growth timber, it is almost like you shut the lights off. It is so God damned dark down there that it is spooky.

"This guy is coming at me through these rhododendrons like he is taking a stroll through ferns.

"You can't find anything tougher than a rhododendron limb. That is the toughest wood in the world. But this puppy is moving on. Rhododendron doesn't slow this puppy down.

"There is something spooky to hearing a noise and never seeing anything. Noise like that stands the hair right up on you because you know it's not a bull elk. It's not a damned bear. They are both too smart. They wouldn't have come up on the ridge right up above me in the first place. Whatever is coming down that ridge at me shouldn't have come up on that ridge in the first place. That's not natural. We were up on the road looking down a steep clear cut face a thousand feet to the creek. Then it was another thousand feet up from the creek to the top of the opposite ridge and then another five hundred feet over that ridge on the opposite side of the creek to where this thing started out. This thing was on the other side of the ridge way away from us. It was on the backside of the opposite ridge, way down there. This thing could have just turned and gone quietly down that ridge. He had no reason that I want to understand to come over here but he did. He came right up towards us and now he is right up above me coming fast down the ridge towards me. He is big and loud and I am a thousand feet down at the bottom of a steep canyon alone.

"Then my mind flashes back to our old logging site night watchman for this job right here, Ray Owens. One morning we came to work and Ray didn't show up. The side rod says to me, 'Where's Ray?'

"I don't know', I answer. 'His rig is at his trailer.'

"The side rod says, 'He must have slept in or something. Johnny go get him.'

"Okay', I reply and off I go to get him.

"I go down to Ray's camp site and knock on his door.

"Who is it?' Ray calls.

"I say, 'It's Johnny.'

"I step in the camp trailer and look around, but I can't see anyone. I call out, 'Ray, where the Hell you at?'

"In here,' he says quietly in a shaky voice.

"He's back in the bedroom of that little camp trailer laying on his bed shaking with a Dirty Harry 44 magnum special pistol held out in front of him pointing that gun straight at me in two double fisted shaking hands.

"Startled, I try to say calmly, 'Ray, put the gun down.'

"God, I'm glad you come by Johnny. I'm so scared I can't even get out of this God damned trailer.'

"What?'

"He puts the gun down, gets up, and starts explaining, 'I was lying in here last night and ----.' He stutters and starts shaking again, then continues saying, 'You go out there and look. There's got to be some tracks out there. I think a giant Kloo-Kwallic come and saw me late last night. Something ran their hand across the top of this trailer house when they walked by it sometime after midnight and they rattled the door and the windows too. I thought that they were going to bust in. Whatever it was, it was big. I think that it was a monster Kloo-Kwallic.'

"We had shoved Ray out a pad for his trailer and covered it with loose rock. There are big tracks over two feet long coming down the cut bank behind the trailer and all around the trailer, but you can't tell what made those tracks. Something real big had walked by that trailer in the dark. No doubt about it. I can see big marks everywhere, but I just can't tell what made those marks. But I think Ray is right. It is some kind of big Kloo.

"Now, here I am back on this job site, and something real big is coming right at me.

"What in the Hell comes toward you in the wilderness when you chuck rocks into the bushes where it is? What makes a noise like a five foot through fir tree being fell out into brush? This is the kind of noise that boy is making now just wading though the timber towards me. And he is moving pretty fast too. What would have taken me five minutes, he is going through in seconds.

"Behind fear, I blow back up that mountain. I am spooked. Man, I come up through that clear cut in no time. When I take off, he turns away from the creek and stays on the opposite ridge in the timber. As I climb, I look back over my shoulder and I can see the wake of this thing plowing through the rhododendrons on the other side of the canyon going down stream, up on the ridge.

"I get up to the landing where Luke is sitting in my old Ford Station Wagon, driver door locked, all four doors locked. Got a little crack rolled down on the passenger side door window.

"I'm looking at him, 'Where the Hell you been Bud?' I shout.

"He's just non-nonchalantly sitting in there looking straight ahead, smoking a cigarette. I walk around the other side of the car where he is sitting. I am pissed. 'Jesus H. man, I thought that you were with me. I thought that you were right behind me. I'm down there. I'm all by myself. What the Hell is going on?'

"Still non-nonchalant, he rolls down his window another couple of inches, looks at me, it's just me alone, and says, 'Well, you know I been to Nam.'

"He just keeps sitting there calmly smoking that cigarette.

"I say, 'Jesus H., what the Hell does that mean? What does that have to do with anything?'

"That has plenty to do with everything', he replies. 'If you think that I have to go down there after that to tell you that that is trouble, you are wrong. Forget that. I can tell you that is trouble sitting right here. I don't have to go down there to tell you that that's trouble. I've been to Nam. I know what trouble feels like. That is trouble. Whatever that is. That is trouble Buddy. And I don't need to go down there to find that out. You want to go down there. Then have at it.'

"Well Jesus H., you could have said something Buddy. I guess I was just too gung ho. I was just over the bank and down there.'

"After this little revelation, Luke gets out and we climb up on the car hood and sit there listening to this thing continue on its way down into this wilderness area for about twenty minutes. We are hearing this thing down there for a couple of miles in the rhododendrons and second growth timber. There had been a big fire through there many years ago and the rhododendrons were just thicker than the hair on a dog's back and we can hear that thing wading through that rhododendron brush two miles away.

"I mean we are out in the big woods and it's pretty quiet, but we are hearing that guy miles away crashing through the woods on a compass heading. He is going somewhere straight ahead. That is unusual to hear something down in a canyon that far away running on a compass heading.

"Now who in the Hell would hear something like that, that far away in the woods, and go, 'I ought to go down there and find out what the Hell that is.' That would be a nut. We didn't go.

"Young studs say to me, 'Man, I would have been over there looking for hair.'

"I say, 'Well come on up. I'll show you the way. You can track him right on down if you want to Bud. Go right after the bugger whatever it is. But it is nothing that you would ever want to find. I can tell you that right now. What would you do with it when you found it? The killing would take place on the road before you even get anyplace over there. Done. Done and over with. I'll be glad to drive you up there and point you in the direction of some very serious trouble. It is there some God damned place and if you want to find it, if you want to spend the time and trouble to go find it, then you will find it."

CHAPTER 28

DEMETRIUS

"The fear of those incidents makes camping nothing that I would even consider. I would never stay a night in the dark in the big woods for love or money."

"C'mon Johnny. Lighten up. You're letting fear get the best of you. Don't take it personal. Everything isn't out to kill you. It's all spirit. Everything has a soul. It is all alive. It's all energy. Everything has a spirit. Everything, everyone matters. It is all sacred. Don't look at a bear or a deer as if you were looking at a puppet, a dead soulless piece of wood animated by unthinking, meaningless instincts. Think of them as another person, another guy, another gal. A bear isn't just a bear. A deer isn't just a deer. And they aren't out to hurt you."

He surprises me by agreeing, "Ain't that the truth? I've been giving that bear, Shiam, some very serious thought, and I have realized that what you just said is true. Bears aren't just bears and deer aren't just deer. Especially having met Demetrius, I know that you're right."

"Demetrius? Who's Demetrius?"

"Demetrius is a deer that I met on the property that I bought to get away from Willow Street. I told you about it, our place out in the South County hills. It has a little old cabin on it. The cabin was built in the early 1900's from rough sawn lumber and roofed with cedar shingles. It is a small house with a cozy front room with a wood stove. Off one side of the front room is an open kitchen which overlooks a small creek surrounded by alder and maple trees. Off the other side is a bathroom and a warm bedroom with an ancient cast iron bed. There are two more bedrooms upstairs. It is a friendly feeling place. It has never been painted. It has natural weathered wood siding. It is very organic looking. The most distinctive feature of the place is a big front porch surrounded by a flower garden. It is peaceful standing on that porch looking out over the little fields with fruit and nut trees growing here and there. Beyond the pasture, there are no neighbors to be seen in any direction, just the great Douglas fir forests of the Northwest.

"Johnny, how did you meet this deer and why did you name it? I thought that you killed deer. I didn't think that you met them and introduced yourself."

"This was strange alright. One day I am doing some remodeling on the cabin and working on the spring where we get water for the house and doing this and that. My wife and I are standing on the porch looking around and I say, 'Doesn't it seem like there would be quite a few deer around here?'

"As I'm saying this, a young little buck wanders around the corner of the house and starts nosing around the front porch. He is a friendly creature. He is checking out the flowers, the porch railing, the side walk, looking in the big front window, watching us. He is not frightened by us at all. Next thing we know he gets up on the porch and is wandering around the porch. The deer, my wife, and I visit together for a while as if he is a pet, an old friend. It is wonderful hanging around with this fellow, but after a while we decide to go in the house and make some popcorn and watch TV.

"It's a nice day. The weather is warm. When we go in the house, we leave the front door open. The next thing we know, that deer is creeping in the house like an old dog, checking everything out.

"We got to be good friends with this buck. He loved to go for walks up the old logging road with us and that cotton picking buck would sprint ahead of us on the trail and he would hide. When we would walk by where he was hiding, he would jump out and jump up and twist around and frolic, and then take off up the old logging trail and hide again. He likes playing this little hide and seek game with us.

"We had to give this game up though because he liked to friendly up with us a little bit too much. He would hide. Then when we would walk by, he would jump out and frolic around us like he does. He stands up on two legs and dances around, but then he started liking to dig us a little with those horns as he pranced around. To tell you the truth, that kind of hurts a little bit. That isn't fun. It was time for something new to do together.

"He likes to hang around on the porch. But then the craziest thing happened. One day he is sitting on the porch like a dog. This deer sets down just like a dog will sit down on the porch. He is anxious to get in the house too just like a dog. Well one day, my wife and I are sitting in the front room in our big old recliners watching TV. The deer comes in and sits down between us just like a dog and starts eating popcorn out of our popcorn bowl and watching TV with us. No kidding. My wife took his picture.

"From then on he likes to come in, sit down, eat popcorn, and watch TV with us. He sits on the floor like a dog and we give him his own popcorn bowl and he just sits like a dog and eats popcorn, and watches the show with us.

"Well, one day when I come home, I am coming up to the porch. The buck is standing outside the house beside the porch. He is looking me in the eye. I am looking back at him right in the eye. We are just standing there staring at each other and all of the sudden Demetrius just pops into my mind. I have no idea where that thought comes from. I have never heard that name before that I can recall. I don't have any idea where the word, Demetrius, comes from. Demetrius just pops into my mind as we stare at each other. It seems just as if this buck just introduced himself personally. So I name him Demetrius. That is how he gets his name. Demetrius, out of the blue, boom!

"Remembering standing there looking at Demetrius, reminds me of what happened out at that property in Carmel where I had that weird experience with that other buck that I killed, and of that other incident where I killed those other two bucks and then ended up killing my cat too. I didn't get it then when I did those things, but I get it now. Back then, out there getting ready to cut firewood, I thought that I was just interpreting the look on that other deer's face, but now after replaying that experience in my mind and talking to you, and after standing there looking in Demetrius's face, it dawns on me that possibly, because of the way that those words came to me when I was looking at that other forked horn buck, 'Hey, I just want to be your friend,' that I wasn't interpreting a look. Those words were more like first hand, coming right to me. It's just like that deer was speaking to me telepathically. The thoughts just flowed too much like a conversation back and forth between us. I was actually communicating with that deer mentally. That is what he had to be doing to hang around like that and get himself dead. This is a wakeup call for what happened at that terrible killing in Carmel.

"Unbelievable! I killed that guy after all of that that we went through together. Sickening! It was just there so blatant that not to figure out what was going on there was terrible. But if you've never had something like that happen and nobody has told you what is possible, how would you know? I've looked at many deer. I don't normally have things pop into my mind while looking at a deer. I should have been way more in tune to that than I was. I was just stupid. Stupid! That was one of the stupidest things that I have ever done. If there is anything that I've regretted in my life, that is one of the most regretful things that I have ever done. That is a haunting, haunting memory. That would be like me all of the sudden shooting you. No different. Really, no different.

"That fellow had done absolutely nothing to me. I didn't need the meat. That is also the only time that I have ever had that incident happen to me where I had like a good angel and a bad angel, one on each shoulder, and my head in the middle being torn apart. I heard those angels arguing back and forth. One is arguing into this ear. The other is talking into the other ear and I'm in the middle of this conversation. Things went horribly wrong because I had been used to killing. I was just in a very wrong head space and just did not put it together on that one and Demetrius and you have brought me back.

"As we're replaying these things, I just realized the great truth of an Ochoco Indian story. The one about when the Earth was young and man people and animal people spoke the same tongue and the great tragedy that has befallen us, and I know that the story is true. I am mortified that I did not put it together in time to save that fellows life and save me a lot of misery. I'll bet you anything that I could have walked right up to that forked horn and petted him, put my hand right on him. He was that kind of friendly. It is a haunting memory of killing a very unique creature in a unique situation. It was an awful thing that I did. It just takes my breath away. It just never dawned on me. That hurts me especially knowing the history of the Ochocos and being a teller of their history and knowing that when the world was young, man people and animal people spoke the same tongue. That is like going, you are what you are, and just not being able to figure out what I am. Crazy.

"Well I get it. And as a North Ochoco elder could only tell this story in the winter, seeing as this is December, I am right on cue to tell you about Mount Snow Forever. Do you want to hear the story?"

"Absolutely."

CHAPTER 29

FOREVER

He begins, "The snow never left Mount Snow Forever even when the sun was beaming down.

"That mountain was up there higher than Everest. It was one big mountain. The slopes of Snow Forever were lush and the animals lived there because there was all the feed and forage and beautiful spring water and everything that they needed and wanted. The animal and the man people lived there together in peace as brothers and sisters. Things were going along real well until one day an evil man was born into the family of the man people. This evil man decided that he needed to be eating the animal people and killing them for their hides for clothes. So that is what he starts doing and he convinces other man people to join him in slaughtering and eating the animal people.

"Shiam, the bear, was the leader of the animal people. He was confused about the evil man peoples actions. He had never seen this before. He had always gotten along with the man people. Now, all of the sudden there's these man people sniping off animal people, killing us for our flesh and hides.

"Shiam is concerned and he summons Eagle and tells Eagle to fly to the top of Mount Snow Forever where the animal people summon the Great Spirit to council and call the Great Spirit, Tamminus, to meet with them.

"When Eagle calls, Tamminus comes to council. He asks, 'Shiam, what makes you send Eagle to bring me to meet with you?'

"We have had a terrible thing happen to us,' replies Shiam. 'There is an evil ruler in the ranks of the man people and the man people are killing us for our flesh and our skins.'

"Tamminus asks, 'You're the leader of the animal people Shiam. What are you going to do about it?'

"Shiam is all flustered. 'I just don't know what to do. That is why I called you.'

"Tamminus says, 'Shiam your mind is empty. I'm going to put you to bed for two full moons. When you awaken, your mind will be full. When your mind is full, summon me back to council on the next full moon.'

"Sure enough, Shiam falls asleep, then awakens two moons later. He waits for the next full moon and summons Tamminus back to council. Tamminus comes and asks, 'Well Shiam, now that your mind is full from two full moons of sleep, what are you going to do?'

"Shiam says, 'We will have to flee this land. We will have to leave the slopes of Mount Snow Forever. We will have to go down to the lowlands and get away from the man people. We will leave the man people on the slopes of Snow Forever by themselves.'

"Crayfish who was among all of the animals who were listening cried out, 'How can I go? I am just a lowly crayfish.'

"Crayfish, I will help you,' Eagle offers. 'You pinch on to my talons and I will fly you to the down lands. We will all leave the slopes of Mount Snow Forever together. All of the animal people will leave together, Crayfish and all.'

"Tamminus says, 'Shiam, that is a wonderful idea. That is exactly what you should do, because what you don't know is that I am not happy with the man people for what they have done to the animal people. That is not what they were supposed to do. They make me very unhappy also. And now that you have decided to flee the land on the slopes of Mount Snow Forever, that will allow me to continue with what I have on my mind for the man people. When you leave these slopes, I will blow this mountain into evermore. There will be no more man people. You will be safe and you will be safe forever because I am going to destroy the man people. I am going to blow up the mountain and the man people together. So be it.'

"Shiam goes back to the animal people and the animal people make their exodus from Mount Snow Forever.

"And Tamminus, the Great Spirit, destroys Snow Forever and all of the man people with it, while the animal people are way down in the bottom lands safe from the eruption and the explosions.

"The animal people then have a good life. They have no more man people killing them. Many, many moons go by.

"Then Shiam sends Eagle to summon Tamminus back to council again on the full moon.

"Tamminus comes back and he asks, 'Shiam why would you summon me to council? Life is good. Food is good. You have no man people killing you. What else could there possibly be?'

"We are lonely,' Shiam replies. 'We miss the man people.'

"Even though the man people will kill you for your flesh and your skins, you miss the man people? Shiam, what is this about?' asks Tamminus.

"We are lonely. We want you to return the man people to the Earth. Even though they have done this evil to us, we forgive them. We are lonely. We miss them and we want you to return them to the face of the Earth.'

"Tamminus says, 'So be it, Shiam. I will return the man people to the Earth again, but no longer will you speak the same tongue and no longer will they be known as man people. From this day forth they will be known as humans and you and they will not speak the same tongue. So be it.'

"And that is the way it is today. That is what happened and that is the actual story as told by the Ochoco Indians. That is the true story. And that is my realization."

"I'm not clear on what your point is," I say.

Slightly exasperated he pulls it all down to, "I'm saying that I agree with you. We were all once one big happy family living in paradise. Then somebody got the idea that they were separate from everything else and that they could use others any way that they wanted for their own personal gratification without any consequences. But there are consequences when anybody acts with this us and them attitude. We are all connected on some cosmic level and what I do to you and to the waitress and to that dog out there in the parking lot matters, and not just to you and to them, but also to me. You are correct. We are all One somehow and there was a time and place when we knew that."

"If you've had this big realization, why are you so down?"

"I didn't mean to say that I've had a realization as in that I had one last week. I mean that I am having one right now. As we are talking I am seeing that all of these strange coincidences and stories seem to fit together with a message for me. I get it. I have to change my ways. We are all neighbors, all of us, people, bears, deer, squirrels, trees. We are all neighbors and we are all one Great Being and we all need to get along and help each other. It's all alive. It's all connected. What I think, how I feel, what I'm doing, it all matters. I am in charge of my own health, wealth, and happiness. I am in charge of the happiness and joy of everything around me. I am way more powerful than I thought."

"Fear is not even an issue. Getting to know who I am, what I am, and what is going on is the issue. Fear is another one of those non-issues, those hypnotic television news program issues, those weapons of mass deception paid for by advertisers issues. I have more important things to do. Fear doesn't have anything to do with me. Yea, though I walk through the valley of the shadow of death, I shall fear no evil."

"What happened Shane? How did we get here? How did we get to thinking like we have been thinking? Why can't we change? What is going on?"

"I don't know Johnny. Seems like we need to connect the dots and change our ways. You need to give Johnny some of that fine advice that you are giving out to other people. I'm going home and fix a vegetarian dinner for my Mom and Dad. Your company is always a most amazing pleasure, Brother."

I pay the bill and we get up and leave.

We saunter through the front door of Elmo's happy men. The cloud has lifted from over Johnny's head.

I hug him and say, "See you. Life's good. Stay cool," and start to walk away.

He shakes like you do to clear your head when you wake up and simply asks, "What was I thinking?" not expecting an answer. Still shaking his head with a puzzled smile, he walks off towards his Jeep.

CHAPTER 30

STATE OF GRACE

Two days later Johnny shows up at my house all smiles and says, "When I left you the other day, I had two dollars to my name. I was selling jewelry that I had worn out down at Diamond Donny's for gas money to get to work. I decide that I should make sure that I am not overdrawn at my bank. So, I go to the bank, walk up to the cashier and say, 'I got $2.06 in my checking account. I just want to make sure that I'm not overdrawn."

"The cashier looks at my check book, clicks some keys on a key board while watching a computer screen and says, 'Well actually you have $1,822.31 in your account.'

"I don't think so', I say.

"All of your checks are in. You haven't written a check in a month and a half. They are all in, and I will guarantee you that you have a balance of $1,822.31', she concludes."

As he is talking to me, Johnny pulls out his check book, opens it, and points to the last entries in the ledger.

"Here see my check book. Here is the $2.06 that I had as a balance when I went in the bank the other day. And here is the bank's balance of $1,822.31 that I just took off with after my discussion with the cashier."

"Wow! That is really good. That is epic." I exclaim.

Johnny continues, "I tell people about this and I think that they think that I'm trying to trick them. And here's the check that I started to write to the Court too. It's just incredible."

"Wait. What check to the Court? I mean, you go to the bank and there is $1,800 in your checking account? Then, what?"

"Well after I discover that I have $1,820 additional cash in my checking account from -----? Okay, somewhere in my life I made a mathematical mistake for $1,820. Lord Jesus, I'll take it, whatever it is. So anyway now I've got that $1,800. Then I go over to my office and I get my check too."

"Check?"

"Yes, my paycheck."

"But you haven't been getting any paychecks for months."

"No!! Right! I haven't. That $1,800 was just like it was beamed down from the gods. I was basically on the street."

"Yes!"

"Yes. So, the $1,800 gets me to the paycheck."

"But what's the paycheck for?"

"The paycheck is $11,440. That is my share of the real estate commission from selling the Kahlani Ridge Ranch. I put that $11,440 in the bank too."

"You haven't had a paycheck in a long, long time? Then you get $1,800 when you go to the bank. Then you go to your office and you get a paycheck for over $10,000?"

"Definitely. I had been waiting on that paycheck for a long time, but it wasn't a for sure deal. I was just right down to it. When I met with you at Elmo's, I was looking for anything just for gas money and I was worried about a last little check bouncing and hoping that maybe there might be an extra fifty bucks or anything that I might have overlooked in my checking account. I'm just down to playing it by the tank. Then I get the paycheck and I put it in the bank with the other $1,800. I go down to the Courthouse to pay my Court ordered restitution to Kobalski and the tab is double dead zero."

"How do you explain that?"

"The explanation is ----, I don't know." I think, "Well you dumb bugger, they took the restitution out of your bail money that you left there." But then I think, "Excuse me, bail comes in five and ten thousand dollar increments, not increments of $9,750, period." I immediately think, "That doesn't work. It doesn't fit, because there was no bail money left. The restitution bill is just conveniently a balance of zero. There was a debt of $9,750. I might have had $5,000 of bail money down there, but it would have been in the form of $5,000, or even $10,000, but I could not have ended up with a balance of zero."

"I didn't want to push the subject down at the Cheyenne County Courthouse though. How far do you want to dig with this Court gal? Do you want to argue, 'Hey, I didn't pay it!' Do you want to claim that you owe them money?"

"This is just cosmic. Can't be true. I am not going to argue, 'I really owe you money.' No. I am out of there."

"I questioned the gal twice. I did not do it a third time."

"She absolutely printed it right out, highlighted it, and said, 'Your balance is nothing. You owe us nothing."

"I didn't want to ask, is there anything left? I'm scared to ask if there may be money left down there, but I know that there isn't. I know that I had already doubled back and got everything that was there. I got it earlier and put it in my checking account just to keep going months ago."

"All of that money was just like beamed down from the gods, absolutely."

"What was the restitution for?"

"The restitution was for knocking out my neighbor's front teeth and to pay his medical bills, $9,750."

"You had to pay for his medical costs?'

"Yes."

"Well, what about your neighbor's civil suit against you for damages and mental suffering?"

"A civil suit is based on a two year time frame from the date of the incident. I went straight over to my attorney's office from the County Courthouse and I tell his secretary, Jeannie, 'Let's check and see if there has been a civil suit filed in Cheyenne County against me yet.'

"We are four days past the filing deadline.

"My neighbor's attorney had sent me a very nasty letter demanding a trust deed to my house and threatening a huge law suit if I didn't comply with his demand. I didn't have any money to pay my lawyer to even fight the civil law suit. So I hadn't done anything.

"Jeannie says, 'There has been no civil suit of any kind filed against you at this time.'

"I am amazed. And I know that the restitution money didn't come from my attorney, Harry David, either, because I show Jeannie the Court receipt and ask her to check the Court records balance from her computer. She does. She is elated that the balance is zero too. She is just as stunned as I am. She double grips that receipt and looks at it big eyed, Buddy.

"She just looks at it and goes, 'Merry Christmas. What can I say?'

"So it is very mysterious. But I am just not questioning it.

"Somebody who was at my trial that I've made money for in real estate or maybe an old friend of the family paid that restitution bill, but I don't know who it was. So I have been going around honestly and very sincerely wishing everyone a very Merry Christmas and a happy New Year. That money came from an unknown source. So I am acting like it came from everybody that I know that is a friend of mine."

"Right on! You make like it came from everyone that you know, so, every meeting that you have is with a dear friend who might be the one that paid your restitution bill?"

"Yes! I treat everyone like they're my Buddy. They are the one."

"That is good."

"I don't know what else to do. Thinking that it might have been them, I went over and saw Dick and Laverne, our old neighbors and from the bottom of my heart said, 'Hey man, life is good. Thank you so much. Merry Christmas, happy New Year.' They were thrilled to see me. We had a wonderful visit together, but they didn't say anything about the money. I just go around thanking everyone like that and having these wonderful visits."

"That is cosmic. That is a good one."

"That is what I finally did with being given those miraculous blessings because I don't know what else to do."

"No. That is too good. It is a magical world. That all is miraculous. It's really hard to believe that what you just told me really happened. I wouldn't even believe this story if I weren't standing her hearing it directly from the guy that it happened to. I just don't understand what is going on. I don't understand how we should be living. Let's go over to Gabriel's and see if he can help us understand what is happening to you, to us. Let's go ask him what the truth is."

CHAPTER 31

AN EXPLANATION

We get into the old beat up little pickup truck that was given to Johnny by his partner Brian during Johnny's trial to keep Johnny mobile. This pickup is not a pretty sight, but it has a four cylinder engine that runs cheap.

Gabriel meets us on his office door step with the front door open behind him and greets us as if we are in the middle of a conversation rather than having just arrived and gotten out of the pickup. He enigmatically says, "The truth is becoming known as we speak."

We are surprised by his greeting. We look at each other and raise our eyebrows. It is as if Gabriel has been listening to our conversation, or else he can read our minds, or else who knows what else that he might be doing. I have begun to notice that there is something supernatural about Gabriel. He does things and knows things that are hard to explain. We haven't even said hello. We didn't say anything about the truth to Gabriel, but I don't miss a beat, I ask, "What is the truth about what has been happening to Johnny and me?"

"The truth is," Gabriel says. "Everything else dances, dances around the truth."

"That is a beautiful image," I reply. "I am sure that it is profound, but for those of us here who are dying, what do we do with that?"

"I like that question," Gabriel smiles. "If the truth could be known, what would it matter? If the truth could be known in a world of maya, a world of illusion, a world of duality, what would it matter? Maybe the truth isn't what you are looking for."

"C'mon Gabriel, isn't the truth more valuable than a delusion or an opinion?" I dig in.

"The truth stops the show. The truth is beyond change, beyond even value. The truth is outside of the show and yet inside the show too. The truth dances and the show dances on the truth," he repeats.

This conversation seems to have taken a turn away from the subject that we came over to Gabriel's to understand. I want to know how to get miracles to happen in my life. I really only care about the truth in so far as it helps me get what I want. I am not interested in some abstract thought that doesn't mean a thing to me.

I argue, "I don't think that this information is of any use to us, who are in the show, of the show, by the show, and for the show."

"The truth brings healing," Gabriel offers.

Healing? Now that is useful information. We wanted to know about miracles such as mysterious cash showing up in checking accounts, but I am interested in healing. I'll go for a miraculous healing. I ask, "How does that work? I have a pain in my shoulder. How would knowing the truth make my shoulder feel better?"

He reaches down to where I'm standing and places his right hand on my left shoulder and says, "The truth is that you don't have a shoulder. So you don't have any pain."

I am surprised that anyone would seriously say something so obviously wrong. What planet is this guy from? I wonder if we are even speaking the same language. I just look back at him and say, "I don't know how that helps. I certainly seem to have a shoulder and I certainly seem to be in pain. What is the truth again?"

"The truth is that you are an extension of the consciousness of Divinity having an experience of a sore shoulder."

"Okay, well, this extension of Divinity doesn't want to have a sore shoulder any longer. How do I change that experience?"

"Step back out of the experience just for a moment. Step back out of the show for a moment. Can you imagine that?"

"I'm working on it. I'm having a hard time. I am struggling. Uhhh, the answer is no, I can't. I can't step out. I can't imagine outside of this, this world with my shoulder."

"The truth doesn't help with your pain. The truth helps you understand your experience of the pain. And when you understand the experience, you can change the experience."

I glance back at Johnny. He is standing there like a man who is standing in a puddle of water on a basement floor who has just reached over and tried to turn off a radio. When he touched that radio, all of the electricity in the wall surged into his arm and threw it across the basement floor with his body following behind it and smacked him and his arm against the wall hard. He is trying to figure out what just happened. I can see that he is confused. He is starring with a frazzled look at Gabriel. His mouth is open and his arms are straight down against his sides. There is a disheveled blank lost look about him. I am not going to let Gabriel do that to me. I am not going to let Gabriel's nonsense confuse me. I want answers, answers that I can understand. I look back at Gabriel.

I say, "Okay," and ask, "what is the truth in my experience of my shoulder pain?"

"The truth is that if you have a pain, there is also an opposite expression of vibrant health."

"You mean there is an experience of no pain, too?"

"Yes, that is what I mean."

"Okay. I choose to experience the no pain rather than to experience the pain. Does that just stop the pain?"

"It will. Not in the sense that you are thinking, but yes that is what can happen."

"How will it happen?"

"Your expression of will, your thoughts have at least two sides. Your thoughts are dualistic in nature. For you to have an idea of a day, first you experience a night and then you experience a day. Your perceptions are constantly changing much as day changes to night. A truth is an absolute. It is unchanging. Truth expresses a condition that is always the same. Otherwise it would be an expression of a conditional state and not be a truth. Your thoughts are constantly changing. They are not truth. They are your opinions which are relative to your own opinions and to the opinions of other at the same moment. Your thoughts along with the thoughts of others create a dance. If you are dancing with pain, you have painful thoughts. You may have started this painful dance carelessly. You may have done it thoughtlessly, but none the less you have done it and you can undo it by expressing the not pain, the joyful healthy shoulder. The truth is that you are neither sick nor healthy. You are choosing to express sickness or health. The solution to your pain experience problem is to be an expression of being that doesn't even know pain from the beginning. So, to solve your problem, you are not against pain. You do not choose to correct pain. You choose to be a healthy happy man who is having a wonderful time now. That is what you do and that is what you are."

"Hasn't happened. Isn't happening. Can't happen," I argue.

"It can happen," he counters, "but for it to happen you need to convince your self-esteem that it is not the center of all being. Men used to believe that the Earth was the center of all of creation and that everything revolved around them. Then this new concept came into vogue that says that man lives on a planet which revolves around a sun which is one of many suns in a galaxy and that there are an almost infinite number of galaxies. This theory knocks man off of center stage in his view of himself. Then man comes up with a new idea called evolution. In this theory all of life is evolving from lower to higher and higher forms and man is the peak of this evolutionary process. As the highest point of evolution, man is the highest point of creation. Man is important again. He is back on center stage in his mind. If modern men were to meet an angel or an alien who is super intelligent and super powerful, then they would be knocked off of the apex of evolution and their self-importance would be damaged again. Man's self-esteem would have to come up with a new reason for its all important central role in being. You are arguing with me because your self-esteem is telling you that I am insulting you. Your self-importance is struggling to come up with a story that justifies its survival on center stage. I am not insulting you, but I am threatening your false self-esteem. What I am saying is threatening your self-esteem because your self-importance is the illusion which is separating us. I am trying to re-unite us to stop the pain. You need to develop a new story and step into the new story.

"My shoulder still hurts. I am still here in shoulder hurting land and that is the truth."

"No. That isn't the truth. That is your experience."

"Okay, but what difference does that make to me?"

"An experience can be changed. The truth never changes."

"Oh brother! Okay. I want to change my experience. I don't even see how truth is relevant to me. I am experience. I am changing all of the time and I don't like the experience of pain in my shoulder. I want to change this experience. Altering this experience is what matters to me. How do I change this experience?"

"Breathing. Through breathing. You are breathing the experience."

"What? I'm breathing pain into my shoulder?"

"No. I don't mean that you are breathing pain into your shoulder. I mean that you can alter your experience of pain through your experience of breath. Breath is your master power switch. It is your connection between super consciousness and experience. No breath, no experience."

"Okay, so I can alter my experience by what, by being aware of each of my breaths, by breathing differently, by ----? What am I going to do with this awareness of breath to make this pain in my shoulder go away?"

"I am trying to bring your attention to how your experience is coming into being. How being is becoming from truth to being. Breath is your connection to becoming."

"Breath is my attachment to becoming?"

"It is not your attachment. It is the actual mechanism. If there is no breath, there is no experience."

"Are you saying that if I control my breathing, I control my experience?"

"Again, I am not explaining control. I am bringing your attention to breath."

"Okay. I am not sure what the difference is. If I am breathing my experience into being, what is breathing?"

"Stop right there. You are not breathing your experience into being. You are not controlling your breathing. You are being breathed into existence. Breath is your connection to Divinity, to the All, to Source. It is the point at which you drink being."

"What exactly does that mean, drink my being? What am I getting when I drink my being?"

"Let's practice watching the breath again and you can answer that question for yourself. All that is really happening here now is that you are breathing. Everything beyond that is conjecture. Let's bring your mind and body together. Take a deep breath. Feel the in breath wherever you feel it in your body, your nose, the back of your throat, your chest. Wherever you feel it, focus on that in breath. Now focus on the out breath. Continue focusing on the in breath and the out breath. If a thought arises, let it go. If you feel a pain, notice it and return back to breath. All that is happening is that you are here breathing. Everything else is conjecture. Take a deep breath. Where did you feel that?"

"In the back of my nose."

"Now take another breath and feel the out breath in the same place. That spot is the swinging door of the outer and the inner, of the you and the I. The inner is limitless and the outer is limitless. You and I are the same, are one, but we are not one. In the experience of the breath, we experience a swinging door. We experience the you and the I. We experience a swinging door and the limitless inner and outer worlds. We experience a great mystery. We are one, but there you are and here I am. Breath in. Breath out. Watch the breath in and out. Lava flowing to the sea doesn't need to know why it's flowing to the sea. You don't need to know. You just need to go. Breath in. Breath out."

"I can't. You said that I'm not breathing, that I'm being breathed, so, why should I even worry about all of this? There is nothing that I can do, is there? Let me phrase that differently. What can I do? You say that I am God. I am an extension of God. God is the 'I am' that is me. So, what is the 'I am' that is me here going to do? If that 'I am' is completely unlimited, creative to the nth degree, capable of anything, why is it even allowing itself to experience anxiety and pain? Why do I not heal my shoulder and win the lottery?"

"What is there to win that you haven't already won? If the 'I am' is to win the lottery, then everyone has to win the lottery. No one, no part of the 'I am' can be left behind."

"What does that mean? That is impossible. If I win the lottery, then everyone must win the lottery? We all win? We all go together? What do you mean? Let's look at this a different way. How about this? What can I do to make a difference? What can I do today that will make a difference? What can I do today that will make everyone and everything joyful and happy? What can I do right now to end pain and suffering and bring joy and healing into this world?"

"The most powerful thing that can be done is the expression of a vision. Everything that everyone does is an expression of their vision. No one can ever not create. Everyone is always creating. The most powerful thing that you can do to bring joy and happiness into this situation, is to express joy and happiness. You have to express that with confidence, without doubt, with a clear vision and a clear statement and speak it into being. Then see the miracles happening all around you all of the time."

"Without doubt? How can I overcome fear and doubt and lack and separation on a personal level much less on a global level?"

"You just need to get on track. You know what to do and if you get on track and stay on track then the next step is always made known to you. There are so many things that I am going to do to help you."

"Okay so how do I ----? We all know the bad secret. We are all familiar with bad things happening to us. We are all trying to do our best, but our best is still full of suffering. How do we get from suffering to joy and happiness, to not being lonely, to a life full of abundance and security? How do we get to the good secret from the bad secret? There are no humans that I know that aren't suffering and I am sure that the people that I know are probably suffering less than a lot of other people. So if we are suffering the least of all, and yet we are suffering, if everybody, well not everybody, but most people are suffering, how do we end suffering? How do we stop the bad secret cycle? How do I personally stop the bad secret and start the good one? I know of no one that isn't being crushed either physically, financially, emotionally, or spiritually, or in all four ways at the same time. How can we change this global dream, this attitude, this situation, this consciousness that we are experiencing? How do we change it to one of security and abundance and love and joy and happiness? Johnny and I just witnessed some miracles in Johnny's life. You seem to know about them. How can we get more miracles like those in our lives? You said not to worry about my bills that they were paid, but now my house has been foreclosed. It is gone. My pickup has been repossessed and it is gone. I am ignoring the other bills because you said not to worry about them because they are taken care of, but I can't really see that ignoring my bills is an effective way to handle them. They still seem to be there. There must be another alternative other than either being pushed by fear into giving away my life's substance in exchange for paid bills or just ignoring the bills and getting harassed all of the time. There must be a third way."

"Yes. There is a third way. It is called the positive way."

The positive way? That surprises me, catches my interest. I glance at Johnny. I can see by his eyes, by the way that he is leaning into the conversation, that Gabriel has his attention too.

I hesitate. Then I tentatively ask, "What is this positive way?"

"The positive way is being positive."

I look back at Johnny for support. He gives me an affirmative nod of the head, as if to say, "This could be useful."

I cautiously follow this third way, "Well give me an example of the positive way. I don't really understand what you are saying. Is the positive way what filled Johnny's checking account?"

"The positive way is when you be the way that you want it all to be."

"Well how do I be the way that I want it all to be? The world doesn't seem to be co-operating. My billfold isn't exactly overflowing with cash. The world seems to be being the way that I don't want it to be. How do I experience a life the way that I want it to be?"

"You are experiencing it the way that you want it to be."

I am insulted. That is the most obviously stupid thing that I have ever heard. I hop up on the step where Gabriel is standing, get in his face, and stab my right forefinger against his chest. All of the problems in the world are not my fault. He is not going to blame me for the world's troubles and get away with it. Not at least without a fight.

"No, I am not experiencing it the way that I want it to be," I shout in his face, glaring self-righteously at him. "I want it to be full of joy and happiness, abundance, security, and love. I do not want it to be full of poverty, sickness, loneliness, insecurity, abuse, and hatred. So, if you are telling me that I do want all of those bad experiences, then explain to me how I am wanting them? How is it that I want what I don't want?"

He doesn't move. Johnny doesn't move. The wind doesn't move.

Gabriel's expression hasn't changed, doesn't change, he casually says, "Say to yourself. I am going to do something amazing today. I am going to create a new world."

"That will break the bad dream?" I ask dropping my hand and sliding my eyes away from Gabriel and back to Johnny.

Johnny shrugs his shoulders, gives me a goofy look, and says, "I don't know."

Gabriel answers, "You don't break the bad dream. You create the good dream, the new dream."

I look back at Gabriel. I hesitate, then square my shoulders and ask, "Okay, again, how do we create the new dream? How do we do miracles?"

"Money is the thing that you need to work on. You have to work on not earning it. That way when you get it, when you receive it, you can't think that you were the cause of your getting it. Receive money like you receive your next breath. If you think that you are the cause then you will try to cause more of whatever you desire."

This is exasperating. Didn't he just try to blame all of my troubles and the world's troubles on me? Now he wants me to get money by not earning it. I listen to the traffic at the bottom of the hill below us. A truck is rumbling by. The noise annoys me. The constant low hum of traffic annoys me. I think that it has always irritated me. I have been ignoring it. I have been ignoring a lot of things. A lot of things annoy me. I am annoyed. Gabriel is annoying me.

I shoot back, "Aren't I the cause of all of the problems? Aren't I causing this by having good thoughts or bad thoughts?"

"No."

"Well doesn't it matter what I think? Or do or say or ------?"

"Yes, it does."

"How?"

"What you say or do is what you are and that matters to you in your experience."

"How is that different from having a positive or negative thought and that thought manifesting as an experience in my life? What is going on here? What is making things happen? How is this show being scripted, produced, and directed. I know what it means to do good or to be good, but I also know that doing that kind of good that I have been taught to do, doesn't make me feel good. I could do good by going to work and working real hard and making a lot of money or at least hoping to make a lot of money, but I don't feel good when I'm doing that because I don't want to be at that work place doing that work. I want to be somewhere else doing something else like what I would be doing on vacation for example. So if doing what I am told is good, is at odds with feeling good, how do I get doing good and feeling good all of the time together?"

I look at Johnny for backup. He nods in agreement.

I rush onward, "How do I overcome doubt and fear and place my absolute knowing in a vision of a time and place where my life and the lives of my friends and loved ones are taken care of by a power above and beyond anything that I can consider, beyond anything that I need to consider, and that, that power loves me and is taking care of absolutely every one of our needs and providing us with health, wealth, joy, happiness, love, and beauty? How do I know that? How do I experience that? How do I know for absolute certain that when I need cash that it will appear?"

"Envision that knowing with unshakeable faith," Gabriel states simply. "Imagine that world that you are envisioning. Walk around in it. Be at home in it. Feel its textures. See how it operates. Be how it operates. Start to experience its synchronicities. As you experience its synchronicities, faith begins to grow. When faith grows, courage grows. Then you can take another step. Then understanding grows, knowing grows, deeper faith grows, abilities grow. It is a process. You experience it as a journey, as a drama, as an unfolding. See miracles. Do miracles."

When he says this, I feel more confident, less under attack. I venture, "I think that I understand what you are saying. So, what is the next step?"

"The next step is always the same. Be impeccable."

"Be impeccable? What does it mean to be impeccable?

"It means to know without any doubt that we are great creative beings and that every word that we speak, every act that we do, creates who we are, what we are and where we are, and that if it is our desire to live in peace and joy and happiness and beauty, abundance, security and love, then that is what we must think, speak, and do with complete confidence and knowing, and that is what will be. If we see another or anything as separate from ourselves and unworthy of our love, devotion, respect, and friendship, then we have planted the seeds of fear and doubt and a drama of fear and doubt will proceed from that thought."

"That's a tall order. You are saying that every thought that we have creates our experience. There is no thought that isn't important, not even the smallest thought. There isn't any dimensionality to thought. There is no big or small. Every thought is huge and has the consequence of creating the entire universe and that if I maintain my thoughts in a particular form, then a particular universe, a particular experience will manifest. Is that what you are saying?"

"Yes."

"So the solution to all suffering and pain is right here right now?"

"Yes."

"Could you explain that a little more to me?"

"No. I think that you get it. Explain what you get to me. What does being impeccable mean to you?"

I think about the question for a moment, but I have an idea of what he is saying. It is as if I remembered something as he spoke. I offer, "Being impeccable means to act with integrity, to act with good intentions for everyone and everything, to be completely honest with no hidden motives or agendas with absolute certainty, courageousness and love and respect for myself and everyone else without any care or thought but that this is right, and that good, only good can come from this act, from these actions with this knowing, with this being, and that I have only wishes of the highest good will toward all of creation. That is being impeccable.

"I like that. Well said. So be impeccable. Act impeccably. The rest doesn't matter. It can all only be good. That is the truth. You are the miracle."

"Thank you, Gabriel. I was living in a sea of doubt and fear, but I understand what you have said. That gives me a path to follow. Thank you. Today is the first day of the best world ever. We are going to have fun. We are going to enjoy ourselves. It is going to be wonderful. It is wonderful. This is a grand and beautiful moment, right here, right now. Yes."

I look at Johnny. He hasn't moved. He is looking at us as if he is looking at a couple of madmen, but he is smiling.

PART THREE

~~~

"Beliefs control biology."

Bruce Lipton

BEYOND TAKING

CHAPTER 32

SURVIVAL OF THE MOST LOVING

"Gabriel, I am thinking that if we are going to live in a peaceful world full of abundance and joy, it is time to change the premise that the story of Earth is being played out on, the 'eat or be eaten' premise. Eat or be eaten doesn't seem like a very joyful and abundant life experience. However, eat or be eaten is our Earthly life experience. It is time that we change the whole basic idea. It is time to start a different story. Well, it wouldn't really be starting a different story because the story is already going, but it is giving the ongoing story a different twist? What do you say guys? Let's change the premise of our story. I am not saying that a new premise is better than the old premise. I'm just throwing out a new possibility. I believe that the basis of this whole system as we are currently envisioning it and living it, other than maybe for the plants, is a taking system. We have to take life to get and keep life. We have to take what we want, or at least what we need. This is a taking system here on Earth. If we don't take, something takes us. I am trying to imagine a system that isn't based on taking. Gabriel, could you give me an idea for a system based on something different? It couldn't be based on giving, because giving is just the opposite of taking, and in a giving system, the giver is just giving from a surplus that he has taken from somewhere else already. The alternative has to be completely different than giving or taking. We have to have a different way to sustain ourselves."

"Start with food," Gabriel suggests.

"Yes," I agree. "Food is a good place to start. Where are we going to get our life force, if we don't take it from another being, such as a plant or a cow? How do we exist if we are not taking?"

"Well Shane, why don't you start by not eating? You could start right now," he proposes.

"Whoa!" I step back off of the cement step which we are both standing on. Somehow I am always thinking that we are going one way, and Gabriel goes another unexpected, unwanted direction. I declare, "I don't think that I'm ready for that." I try a stall, "Can't we talk about this just a little?"

"We can talk about it forever," he says. "The question is, are we going to create a new world, a world not based on taking, a world not based on 'eat or be eaten', or not?"

"Yes," I agree, "we are."

"Okay then. Again, we go back to food and we start by rethinking where energy comes from and how we create and sustain our being."

"Yes. That makes sense," again I agree, "but I have a hard time giving up eating."

"You have a hard time giving up your body too," he responds and smiles.

"Yes. That whole 'letting go' thing I find disturbing. Can't we use the adding to theory versus the denying, stopping, letting go, giving up things alternative?"

"Well that is what we are doing. We are adding life force, creative power to your being."

I like that idea, and I say so. "That is powerful."

"Yes it is, and that is what you are. Start studying Breatharians and Immortalists."

"What is Breatharianism? Will you explain it to me?

"True Breatharians neither eat nor drink. They are becoming Immortalist. Immortalists are people who have lived in the same body for at least three hundred years. But the meaning of breatharian in common usage today includes all humans who don't eat food or eat very little, but who do drink water and maybe some tea."

"Is that possible? Where do they get their nourishment from? What sustains their lives, their bodies?"

"There are many different methods of sustaining your being. The two main types of Breatharians are the Sun eaters and those who have the ability to plug directly into the Divine matrix. Think of yourself as a battery operated vehicle that needs to periodically be recharged. You just need to learn where the plug-ins are and how to use the charger. There are techniques that someone who knows can teach you."

"Can't you just explain what to do to me? How exactly does it work? Can't you just tell me? I mean, can't you be a little more specific? I know that you have told me that we can live on something that you call manna and that this manna is an expression of Divine love, or something like that, but I don't understand what you are telling me. I'm not sure what you mean by love."

"Shane, how attached are you to your left leg? How much do you love your left leg? What does loving your left leg mean to you? What would you be willing to do to keep your left leg, to experience your left leg? What value does your left leg have to you? Would you eat your left leg? Would you abuse or belittle your left leg? Would you trade your left leg for a new car? All of existence is your left leg. When you see all of existence as your left leg, then you will understand what it means to love everything and everyone, and that is how God sees you and all of existence. It is all based on love. And love is not something abstract. Not only can you experience love, you can form it and eat it. Love is the abstraction that creates the action."

"Oh! I do kind of understand that. My problem is that I don't understand how to live on love, how to eat love. I am kind of stuck in the unpleasant situation of having to eat my left leg, to destroy parts of me to keep my existence going."

"Oh," as I say this, another piece of the puzzle falls into place. "This eat or be eaten way of living is an ugly situation. I'm like a cannibal who eats himself to get just a little more time. So each day he diminishes his possibilities by destroying a little more of himself. He thinks that he has to do this because there is nothing else to eat. He doesn't believe that he has any other option."

"Wow! That is an ugly image," Johnny says, "but I guess that is what an eat or be eaten world is all about."

"Yes it is," Gabriel agrees. "So now imagine a world where instead of destroying parts of yourself to exist, you create new ones that you have not even considered possible before and rather than your world shrinking constantly and your options becoming less and less until you die, think of a world where the possibilities become more and more and are unlimited and you never even consider death."

"Well that seems like a whole lot better option. I choose option number two," I loudly proclaim.

Johnny seconds my choice with a, "Me too!"

"Good. You guys won't need to eat anymore then. You are stepping into a much larger existence of unlimited potentialities, of greater opportunities, of incredible wonder and joy. You are entering a system of survival of the most loving."

"Survival of the most loving rather than survival of the fittest, I like that. That certainly changes the premise, changes everything. I like it. Let's do it," I say.

"How do we move into this new way of being?" Johnny asks.

CHAPTER 33

VEHICULAR CONSCIOUSNESS

"I have an idea," I announce. "I have been contemplating a different way of thinking of myself that may help in getting to this new way of being."

"Lately I have become aware that I am a self-conscious vehicular type of instrument like an automobile, a self-conscious automobile. I am not the driver of the automobile. I am the actual vehicle, but in this case, I am self-conscious, as probably all vehicles are. Otherwise they would fall apart, dissolve, lose their form and increase the entropy of the Universe."

"I am like a vessel that has a consciousness of itself, but there is a higher self that is driving the vehicle, and this is," I place my hand on my chest, "like an automobile and its driver. There is the vehicle and then there is the driver, and in this case, it is as if the automobile has become self conscious, but is not aware of the driver. The body, the vehicle, the ego, the personality doesn't know the over self or higher selves, the driver of the vehicle. That appears to be my situation right now. Most of the time I don't have a clue what is going on or what I'm doing. I'm just on automatic pilot flying around. I want to move from vehicular consciousness to driver consciousness, from vessel, from body awareness and self consciousness to overself awareness and consciousness. I want to understand the big picture, be conscious of what I'm doing, of what's going on."

"I just haven't in the past considered how things assemble and operate themselves whether it's quartz crystals, blue green algae, my kidneys and heart, a deer, Shane, a planet, or a solar system. Now that I am thinking about this though, I want to know the driver of this vehicle, this vehicle which is known as me, which I perceive as me. I know, when I contemplate breathing, that this vehicle is being controlled and operated from outside of my awareness. And my awareness, my body consciousness, my personality, me, the ego doesn't really understand very much about what is happening, but now that I know, that I don't know, and that I am not the big operator, I would like to be introduced to a higher operator. Gabriel, will you introduce us? Is the driver aware of me?"

He just stares at me. Johnny stares at me. I can't tell what they are thinking.

So, I try to explain myself, "I am not aware of the consciousness that is my pickup truck. There must be a consciousness that is holding my pickup together, allowing it to be, and giving it the capability to do what pickup trucks do, to carry me around, in not only a material sense, but in an energetic sense. I am speaking now in an energetic sense, not in a material sense. $E=mc2$. I am talking on the energy side, not on the mass side, not on the material side. On the energy side, there is some kind of consciousness there that is organizing itself as a pickup. In order for it to manifest itself as a pickup, there has to be an intelligence that takes on that shape and function and maintains that shape and carries on that function. But I the driver of the vehicle never speak to that consciousness, not at least consciously, and I just assume that the pickup will do what it does. I just assume that some guys at a factory somewhere made it and it will automatically hold its form and operate for awhile as a pickup is supposed to operate. Now I see that I am assuming a lot without giving it much thought. So whatever is driving the Shane body maybe just assumes that the Shane body just does this Shane body kind of activity just like a child who is playing with a doll. The same way that a child just moves the doll about, not thinking about whether or not the doll has a consciousness. This higher consciousness moves Shane around, just as I, Shane, just assume and expect my heart to beat and my lungs to breath and the pickup to go."

"What I am asking here is, is the higher consciousness that is moving me around aware that I, the vessel, have a consciousness, and that I am aware at a certain level, and can this higher consciousness speak to me?"

"That is what we have been doing, are doing," Gabriel quietly answers.

"Really? Is this higher self the ultimate operator, or does someone operate that level from an even higher level?"

"That is a difficult question to answer right now."

"What is explainable? What is the nature of this higher consciousness? Did it create this vehicle?"

"No. It is not the creator. It is also a created being."

"What does that mean? What is a created being? How are we created, for what purpose? How do we come into being?"

"Through thought."

"Okay. So where does thought come from?"

"Thought is the intent of Creator. Thought is the vehicle of self creation of the Self Created."

It is happening again. We are veering away from the safe guardian angel, higher self that I was imagining.

"I am getting frightened," I tell both of them. "This is like standing on quick sand. I'm starting to sink into the unimaginable, the unknowable, the unthinkable, the un-understandable."

"Yes. This is un-understandable," Gabriel agrees.

Johnny says, "It's like Shiam in my bear experience. It seemed as if there was more going on there than just a bear, but just the bear was enough to kill me. We are getting in over our heads, or at least over my head. How does the thought thing work?"

"Well, think about it," Gabriel answers. "In fact try it out. Take if for a drive. In other words, think something and see what happens. Actively become a creator. Consciously become a creator. You both already are creators. You have been doing that since you were created. You just haven't been doing it consciously. So, now consciously think something into being."

I enthusiastically jump in, "Okay. Now I am thinking a hundred million dollars into being."

"Well then Shazam! Poof! It is. You have it. That really isn't all that difficult. Think of something more abstract like world peace, universal love, healthy families, all of the beings of creation treating each other with respect and love and mutual support. No more pollution. And that is a small sample. You should certainly be able to move on to something even bigger."

"How about walking on water?" Johnny asks.

"You are still acting out of fear. You are still thinking like a vehicle, not like a driver."

"You're right. You're absolutely right," I agree. "This is going to take a great leap for us. This is going to take some thinking, some imagining. I intend to become a Breatharian. That is where this vehicle is going. I am going to transcend the limits of my current consciousness, be something completely different, a vessel with a different mind, a different consciousness."

"Okay! So be it! It is done. Now let us watch it unfold. You have spoken. So it is. It is in arstory," Gabriel happily declares, smiling enigmatically at me.

"I have to pull out the stops," I passionately plunge on. "I have to rearrange my thinking, my attitudes, my beliefs, and certainly my actions. I have to be careful. Got any thoughts on where we should take this creation?"

"No. It's your creation," Gabriel says. "What are your thoughts?"

"Wow! I have to be careful because I want to create happiness and joy, love and peace and abundance, wealth, health and harmony between all of creation, all species, all of creation including water, mountains, between plants and animals, and animals and animals, and between people and animals. I want to create understanding and co-operation and love between all of creation. I have to hold these thoughts and intentions and that is easy because that is being happy by being at peace and in harmony with all other beings in co-operative, supportive, mutually loving relationships. But, boy, that takes an adjustment in outlook, in attitude, and in my way, our way of acting. Got any thoughts on that or any support for what to do, or how to be?"

"Speak it. Conceptualize it, ritualize it, and speak it," Gabriel tells us. "You're doing it right now. You are empowering a great vision right now. Right now everything in creation is changing. It is aligning itself with your speaking."

"Every word that I speak is magic," I realize with wonder. "If I wish for there to be peace and happiness, abundance, health, youth, and vigor, then I have to speak that into every situation. I have to hold that thought. I have to hold that reference, that now, that moment. And all of creation comes into harmony with the words, the tune that I am singing. I am that powerful. I just have to focus and speak it in every situation, in every moment. Isn't that right, Gabriel?"

"Yes. You can't help but be creative. You are doing it all of the time. The question is whether you are going to speak joy, peace, and abundance; or whether you are going to speak fear, scarcity, and sickness. That is the only question for both of you. You are co-creators. What are you going to speak? The power of your speaking is without question. It is, because you are and that is how you were created. That is what you were created to do, to be. The only question is, what are you going to speak?"

"Yes, I see that now. I am going to enlarge my speaking, widen my horizons, focus my intentions. I am bringing great joy and happiness into the world."

CHAPTER 34

CREATION

Johnny shifts the conversation, "Gabriel, let's talk about God. How did this all get started?" He sweeps his right hand across everything that is in front of us. "What is the true creation story?"

"Well," Gabriel begins, "it is actually different than the creation stories that you are used to. It isn't that those stories aren't meaningful. It is just that they start the story from a point that is a long ways into the story, and the actual point of creation is actually now. Everything is created now, not in the past or in the future, but now. It is created now, and it is created with a past, and we are creating the past, you and I, all of creation are creating the past now, just as we are creating the future. We can change the past just as we can change our future. So, when you ask, 'how did this come to be, how was it created', that is a misunderstanding of what is happening in this creation, this moment."

He steps off the concrete platform which he has been standing on to get closer to Johnny and continues, "Think of a dream, of how when you enter a dream, the dream has a setting that is complete. There is a world in which you are acting. It has rivers and oceans, rocks and trees, and each of these things has a history, but in the split second before you entered the dream, they didn't exist. So you have created, we have created, a complete world with a history and setting. And in the dream that setting is fluid and flexible and that is a better explanation of the waking world than the one of it coming into being this way, and that it happened this way, and that this caused that. It's really way more fluid and dynamic than that. And to understand the past, you have to understand the now, the present, and understand that the present actually creates the past just as the present creates the future."

"Whoa, you are right," I jump in. "I really do have a misunderstanding of the past and of creation. I am imagining that there really is a past, and that something happened in that past, and that things are moving from the past through the present to the future. I am imagining that things which happened in the past affect the present and the future. I am a bit confused when you say that the present creates the past and that there really only is a now. Could you explain that a little more? Did I hear you correctly in that you said that I can actually change the past from the present in the same way that I am creating the future in the present?"

"Yes, that is what I said," he affirms. "You are misunderstanding the nature of time and creation. You are thinking of it as a continuum coming from somewhere and going somewhere, and you are at a point in between, but that isn't really the nature of time. There really is only now, a now that isn't actually either eternal or now. That is your experience. If you think about it, you will realize there can't be any beginning or any end. Those are really meaningless concepts even in your understanding. It is just the way that you experience things. So you give them a concrete, solid, real conceptual meaning to your vessel because that is the way that you are experiencing the situation. If you consider this through, you will realize that a final beginning and ending is an impossibility. Where is the beginning of infinite? Where is the end of infinite? There can be no beginning or end of infinite. By definition, there is no beginning or end to infinite, and yet within your framework, you cannot understand that. That is the absurdity of your understanding. Contemplating the beginning and the end of eternity shows you that you really must drop that way of thinking, that consciousness, and step to another level of understanding and being."

"Yes, I can see that," I affirm, "but I have a hard time imagining what a world beyond time and space is conceptually. I can easily intellectually recognize that I am in a situation that is beyond that concept. Somehow though I can't imagine or understand what you are telling me. This is bigger than my conceptualization of reality."

"Let me help you," Gabriel offers. "Take for example your Big Bang mythology. It is a wonderful story and would appear to explain everything, but it begs the question. What was before the Big Bang? The Big Bang would seem to be a big event and explain a lot, but the real question is: what was before the Big Bang?"

"Yes, okay, I'm not getting far with this. What was before the Big Bang? What is the answer?"

"What would you two fellows like to be before the Big Bang? That is the point. We are in that moment before the Big Bang. The now is before the Big Bang. We are creating the Big Bang now. The now is before the Big Bang."

"Whoa! That kind of twists logic, grinds logic -----, makes logic a big freight train that just ran off the track. I am really lost now Gabriel. Are you saying that I can create the past in the same way that I create the future, backwards, forwards, it's all the same?"

"Yes. I am saying that. It isn't like you are thinking. It's not like a time machine and you go back and change something. You are actually creating it right now. You are actually creating it and maintaining it right now. If you were wanting to change it, you would have to change the creation maintenance mode, but if you were in that mode, you wouldn't want to change it. It is all perfect as it is. But, yes, that is what I am saying."

"Wow! I am having a really hard time understanding the nature of the present. What is the nature of the present?"

"It is an eternal now."

"I am afraid that I cannot understand what an eternal now is."

"Yes, I know that. You need to meditate on the eternal now. Go into the eternal now. Realize that this is an eternal now. Conceptualize an eternal now. You have to work on that."

"Okay, I'll start right now."

"Remember that clever phrase by Janosh, 'We don't view things as they are. We view things as we are.'"

"Okay. I am in an eternal now. I am a created being in an eternal now. No wait! I am not even a created being. I am an eternal now. I am the eternal now. I am beyond creation. I am. I just am. I am and I do. I can't grasp this with my mind."

"No. That's right. You can't."

"Okay, so what ---. How ---. I can't even frame a question."

"Yes. That's right. You can't."

"This is the moment isn't it? This is the door to enlightenment isn't it?"

"Yes. This is the point. It is now."

"I see said the blind man as he fell from the cliff," Johnny says.

"I am in an eternal now. How exciting!! I am this. You are me and we are all together. We are together in the eternal now. What shall we do?"

"We are enjoying each other's friendship my beloved children."

"Yes. It is grand. Congratulations we are. I am just savoring this moment of realization, and that we are, that we are alive. You did it and we know it. Everything is possible. Nothing is possible. It all is. It all isn't. What shall I create?"

"I think that I will create a beautiful vessel and of course that vessel will encompass all of creation, because after all I am all of creation, this creation. I am that I am. I get to choose the nature of beauty. My old version was beautiful. It was wonderful, but it is time for a new vision, a new wonderful. I'll make a new one here in the eternal now."

"I am not going to change the past. I like it. It is good. It is wonderful. It is perfect. I am not going to change the future, but I am going to change the now."

"As I speak, I am envisioning it and changing it and making it now. It is a creation based on Divine love. It is Divine love made into flesh, materialized, manifested into the material realm to be experienced by the flesh."

"Beauty is determined by how much love is present. I am envisioning a landscape full of love, a landscape in which everything manifests itself in an awareness of love for each other element in the landscape. Water is an element there so that it might merge with all other existence in an ecstasy of joy. It rushes about with that expectancy of new lovers. The trees are whispering to all of existence. The mountains and the valleys are as grandfathers and grandmothers admiring new born children. All of existence goes about just as if they have just fallen in love, with that thrill, and expectancy, and joy and happiness."

"It is good. So be it. So be it. So be it. I have spoken it in the eternal now. So it is."

"I see it too, Shane," Johnny says. "I feel it too. That is powerful. That is good. It is wonderful."

As Johnny speaks, I am watching our vision and I see that something is wrong. I try to explain, "I see some darkness in this creation, as I look into the energy body of the vessel, this body, my body, I see the dark one in it."

"What am I to do?" I ask Gabriel. "I cannot fight with him. I must love him. I told him to go, but he refuses to go. Now of course I realize that trying to cast him out forcibly is the old way and that I shouldn't do that. What am I to do?"

"Go back in," Gabriel commands. "Talk to him as your friend in this new world of love. Remember, he is you. You are he. You are not looking at something that is not you. Would you wish to harm yourself? He is you. Remember that. Release him. Get to know yourself. Get to love yourself. Honor all beings even if you perceive that, that being is destroying you. It isn't. It can't. In this new understanding you cannot say, 'Get thee behind me Satan'. There is no Satan or behind me. There is only you. You cannot cast out parts of yourself. You must energize and fulfill and include all parts of you."

"Well I hurt. This body hurts. It seems as if I am just pruning a tree full of rot. It is as if I planted a bad seed and now I am trying to save this rotten plant by pruning it. This is Parker's life. We planted some bad seed and got a bad plant and now here I am pruning this bad plant, trying to make the best of a bad situation. Wouldn't it be best to plant a good seed in the beginning? We've got this body that we have gotten into this situation, so now we are trying to work with this body in this situation, but wouldn't it be better just to start over with a better seed, a better body? That is my question Gabriel. Shouldn't we just let this body, this ego, and this particular drama come to an end, and start all over as fast as possible, and start with a new, better model?"

"Well, yes and no. What you are saying is based upon a misunderstanding because you are not thinking in an eternal now. If you are in the eternal now, you will remember that the eternal past can be changed just as the eternal future can be changed. Your tree analogy breaks down when you understand the nature of time, that it is not linear as you are thinking it is. Everything is created and possible in the eternal now. Anything and everything can be changed in the blink of an eye, in less than the blink of an eye. Everything can be changed, everything, completely. Did you get that? Everything. Everything!"

"Nothing is as you think it is. Or rather everything is as you think it is," he says and then laughs as if someone has said something very clever and hilarious.

Johnny and I aren't laughing. We look at each other as if to say, "I don't get it."

Gabriel continues, "It is like that saying that you have been playing with. Things aren't as they are. They are as you are. So if you are something different, things are something different. Does that make sense?"

"Yes, it makes sense," I agree. "I just don't understand it. This eternal now thing is confusing me. I have seen how the past can be changed. The Christian Church says that we were created and then the scientists say, 'No. You have evolved'."

"All of the sudden history is completely different and that changes everything. Now with our new understanding, quantum physics understanding, everything is going to change again. I can grasp that. I can grasp that the past is flexible on the macro level, but I am looking at the past on a micro level, on me personally. That I could re-write my past in a meaningful way from the present, I just don't get that. I don't get that the past is present here in the now."

"Yes, that is a hard concept for the human mind at this time, at this point in the eternal now."

"Yes, it is," Johnny agrees. "So, how do we get from this understanding to an eternal now understanding?

"Boy Johnny, that is a good question. How do we make the leap from human consciousness to God consciousness? Well, let's go over the nature of the eternal now again."

"Okay," Johnny says.

"In the eternal now, everything is now, including the past and the present. You can go forward into the past as easily as you can go backwards into the future. It is eternally now. It isn't created or uncreated and it doesn't pass from here to there. That is not the real nature of the waking world. It is your experience as a point of awareness in the situation. That is what you are experiencing. You are experiencing streaming."

"What if I change my point of consciousness, my point of awareness?" I ask.

"Well, of course your experience will change," Gabriel confirms.

"Okay, let's do that," I offer. "Let's shift our point of consciousness. We can't shift it in a direction. Well, I guess that we could shift it in a direction. That would certainly give us perspective, but it's a frightening thought. It's kind of as if I shifted into the past, like a professor in a time machine, then I'm in the past, and not in the present. Then I don't know how to get from the past to the present. Rather than shift our point, let us say that we have to broaden our awareness. Does that make sense?

"Yes. It is going to be a bit different than your idea of broadening though. Your idea of broadening is just extending your awareness into a larger time frame. In other words, your awareness now includes say a few more years of the past and a few more years of the future. You are doing a linear expansion of time. Imagine seeing all of time complete from a beginning to an end. Now make a ninety degree turn and step completely out of that concept."

"Whoa! Unhhh. Unhhh. I am not sure where I would be. You are right. I was thinking of it in a time and matter sense. I have to think about this. I am having a hard time grasping what you just said."

"Are you getting this Johnny?"

"No way, man."

"Okay Gabriel," I'm back with a new thought, "how about this? Time can be the bad secret, can't it? If I believe in time, it can be a bad secret. It can be a good secret too because it is neutral, but for me, it is a bad secret. It has me. I actually believe in it. I actually believe that it is ruling the concept that is, that time has a meaning to me greater than I am. I know that that isn't true, but that doesn't stop me from believing that this is true. I just can't imagine a situation without the dimension of time. You say, 'There it all is, lying there in space. There is all of time. Now turn ninety degrees and leave time.' Then you ask, 'What is on the other side?' That is hard to imagine. I am having a hard time with that. In fact, I am afraid that it is going to take a leap into a different point of awareness. How would I shift my point of awareness to a point outside of time? I am going to need some help on that. But if I can shift to where I am outside of time then that will make healing my body, or changing things in time pretty easy."

"If you were outside of time, why would you even care what is inside of time?" Johnny asks. "I mean, I don't care about a particular dream once I wake up."

"Hmmm, I see your point Johnny. Time would be all right the way that it is if I could move in and out of it at will. I am concerned about time now because I am in it. I am being timecentric. I am a time nationalist. That is because I am viewing myself as being in time. If I were outside of time, I don't imagine that I would want to change it. I wouldn't identify with it. I wouldn't consider that this particular time is that important. It would be as if I were in a particular dream and suddenly woke up. I really wouldn't care very much about what was happening in the dream that I was in before I woke up. I can see that. There could be an infinite number of times."

I start imagining multitudes of times. When I am visually standing outside of this time, I see all of the other times, and I see an infinite amount of times out here, an infinite amount of possibilities and creations. I see them. They are all like in a bunch of lines. They are not really lines. They are more like galaxies. They are not lying side by side like a stack of lumber. There is a lot of space between them. Uhhhhh. Looking at this vision, I'm starting to get dizzy and confused. This gives me vertigo. I'm getting nauseous.

I come back to Gabriel and Johnny and say to them, "I see now that there isn't any one time. This realization changes my understanding as our understanding was changed in this time line when our belief changed from a belief that the Earth is the center of Creation, to one where the Sun is the center of our planetary system, and that this is a little planetary system on the outskirts of a galaxy, and that there are multiple galaxies spinning around in a very big chunk of space. Now I understand that this time line is just one time line amongst galaxies of time lines."

"That is a good start," Gabriel encourages. "Now take another step because that last step just begs the next question. What you realized is just a Big Bang of time lines. Go one more step now. Go another ninety degrees."

"My mind is seizing up with that image of galaxies of time. I need a little hint, a little push to get me beyond the galaxies of time vision. I am having visions of voyaging, as in Star Trekking between planetary time systems."

"You do that all of the time. It is called dreaming."

"Oh! Wow!"

CHAPTER 35

THINGS GONE BAD

"Beyond waking, beyond dreaming, where is that? What is that? I have to double back. I have to go back to our eternal now and start again. I am surprised to learn that not only is there an eternal now, but that there are an infinite number of eternal nows, galaxies of eternal nows spinning about in eternal spaces. However, I am not concerned about those other eternal nows. That is like being concerned about the atmosphere on Mars. I am on Earth. I am here and it is now. This is my concern. This is my point of awareness."

"And Gabriel, as I said at the start of our conversation, I am not happy with this point of awareness. It is full of suffering. I want to expand it, shift it, fill it with joy and happiness, peace, harmony, security, and an abundance of health and wealth eternally. How do I get from here to that happy point of awareness? I don't really care about those other times and places. I want a miracle today. I want to know how that cash got in Johnny's checking account."

Gabriel suggests. "If you cared about those other time lines, and knew where they were, you could just leave this one, if you don't like it, and go to one of those other places and times."

"That is an intriguing thought. Is that possible?" Johnny asks.

"Of course it is possible," Gabriel replies. "This is the eternal now. Everything is possible. Everything is probable. Everything is, has, and will happen. So it is absurd to say that you are suffering, and that you don't want to suffer. You are creators experiencing in an eternal now. So that means that you have chosen to be in a suffering situation. Right?"

"Gosh, I guess that is true, disturbing, but true," I respond. "I just don't know. This is difficult. Before I fly a rocket ship, maybe I should try riding a bicycle. Before I go jetting off to different time lines, I need to develop the ability to move around in this time line. I think that I've gotten ahead of myself. Let's come back to basics. Let's say that I have a back ache in this time and now and that my back ache is causing me to suffer. In the eternal now, how do I deal with my back ache?"

"Shane, you say the funniest things. I like the way that you framed that question. 'I have a back ache.' It is as if the back ache has you and you are powerless over the back ache. The back ache is something that is happening to you, a you. It is an event that is happening to you, a you, and that there is nothing that you can do about your back ache. Your back ache just came upon you as a surprise. It took you by surprise, and now you are forced to deal with a back ache, but you are not left with the understanding or the ability to do that. What an odd idea to have in the eternal now. How did you get yourself into this situation of believing that there is a yourself in this situation, to believing that you are surprised by pain in your back? That is almost more astounding than knowing that there are infinite galaxies of time. And in addition, you believe that you are helpless to do anything about the pain. The ability to believe that you are a being with a pain in your back is as astounding as believing that there was a time in history when humans believed that the Earth was flat. How do you believe that?"

"I am not sure. That is just what I believe. I believe that I am a body with a pain in the back."

"Wow! Congratulations! That is a real achievement."

"Well, if in the eternal now, if I am not a being with a pain in my back, what in the world am I? And why do I think that I am a being with a pain in my back?"

"You are me. I am you."

"Okay, who are we? What are we? Where are we? When are we?"

"We are everywhere, all of the time, everything. We are nowhere, never, and beyond all being."

"Well thank you for that, but I apologize, I guess that I asked that question in a larger sense than I meant it."

"None the less, that is the answer."

"Let's just keep this simple. Let's just focus on one thing. Let's just focus on back pain, pain in my back, pain in this individual being's back. How does this individual being in the eternal now experience a joyful, healthy, happy, strong, vibrant back?"

"You are just full of good questions aren't you?"

"I don't know. That is just what is bothering me. What is this eternal now and how does it matter? Is it a surf board that I can catch a ride on?"

"Indeed it is. It is that great long board in the sky with which you can catch that monster wave, the big one, and ride it all the way in to a shore in a tropical paradise."

"Okay, let's start paddling out. How do we do it? I am in an infinite now entering a finite place and time with a back pain. How do these two points of being relate to each other? Where's the connection?"

"That is obvious. The finite here and now exists within the infinite now."

"Of course, again, I guess that I didn't quite ask that correctly. How about this? How does one who is perceiving himself to be in the waking here and now, and who is not aware of the infinite now, become aware of the infinite now in a knowing sense that empowers him to act in such a way as to change the waking here and now, and get rid of a back pain?"

"For that understanding, the waking here and now isn't really important. You have to drop that understanding and go into the eternal now point of awareness."

"How does one shift to the eternal now point of view? I am running out of time. I am not in the eternal now."

"Yes, you are in the eternal now. That is the only place that you are, is in the eternal now. If you are, in the sense that you consider beingness, then you are in the eternal now."

"Oh, of course, I am in the eternal now, but the material world certainly has persistence of existence."

"Yes, it does. And if there is going to be balance in the waking world and less back pain for you, it is important that we discuss suffering, environmental destruction, cultural homogenization, emotional abuses, physical losses and deprivations, loneliness, ignorance, hatred, just plain mean hearted short sightedness, and greed."

"If we are going to experience more healthy vitality, joy, beauty, peace, abundance, security, and happiness, we need a solution to these unpleasant situations, and the solution is simple. We are the solution. The solution is in our hearts. It isn't outside of us."

"We are the Dreamers. We are the faces of God looking at the other faces of God. Smile. Smile and the World smiles back. Bring the dawn. Face the light."

"Humpty Dumpty had a great fall and all of the king's men couldn't put Humpty Dumpty back together again."

"What are you saying Gabriel?" Johnny asks. "What should our response be to things gone bad?"

"Things aren't bad. When we experience bad, we are being bad. Thousand dollar bills aren't either bad or good. They are just pieces of paper with ink on them. It is how people get thousand dollar bills and how people spend thousand dollar bills that is either good or bad. Actually the problem begins when people agree to believe in private property, in money, and when people separate different parts of being from other parts of being and agree to exchange themselves and others for these creations. That is where the whole idea of good and bad gets started."

I want to know, "What does this have to do with the actions of petro-chemical companies in the Caribbean and with oil spewing out of a hole in the ground and poisoning an entire eco-system? How are we responsible for that? What do we have to do with that? How are we being bad?"

"The answer is that we have everything to do with everything, and to the extent that we are aware, we are responsible. To be aware means to be awake, to be lucid, to know. If you are lucid, you are responsible because you have not changed the situation, if that is your wish. You guys are neither lucid nor awake at this moment at the level that you are able to change situations, but you can be."

"If you speak the words, 'In this moment, I choose to be lucid and awake', it may go through your hearts that maybe you do not want to be lucid and awake and maybe you do not want to change things. But do it anyway. Say after me, 'I take responsibility for that which is happening. I truly do want things to be different. I truly do want life to be based upon love and respect and beauty, harmony and wondrous joy. I choose to awaken'."

As we repeat these words after Gabriel, I know the answer. I am going to fall in love with a beautiful woman and we are going to flow our beings together in an ecstatic timeless moment of joyful creation. I am going to experience non-separation, the All. I have no idea what this means or how we are going to do it, but that is what is going to happen. Seems like fun. Sounds like a good idea.

I am daydreaming about all of this flowing together when I hear Gabriel loudly say, "Shane." He snaps me back into the here and now and tells me, "I want you to go to an associate of mine another Doctor of Well Being, Merlin Paul, who is a Master of the Journey. I want you to go over to his office now and have him examine your energy body, your chakras."

He hands me a business card with Merlin's address on it.

"I'll take you to your truck," Johnny offers.

"Alright, let's go," I say. "Thanks Gabriel. See you later. It was fun."

Johnny shakes Gabriel's hand, smiles shyly, and turns towards his pickup.

"It was a pleasure guys. You are great traveling companions. Bye," Gabriel says and turns to walk back to his office.

PART FOUR
Ω

"You were born for such a time as this."

James O'Dea

BEING THAT WHICH IS

CHAPTER 36

MERLIN

Soon I am standing alone on a quiet street knocking on the front door of a little white cottage built under the huge spreading arms of a grove of chestnut trees. A tall thin white man with flowing grey hair including a mustache and goatee greets me with a friendly smile. He is casually dressed in tan slacks and a blue cotton long sleeved shirt with the sleeves rolled up and with the collar open wide. He is wearing sandals on his feet

"Shall we talk, Shane?" he asks, as he shakes my hand. He has a firm grip that makes me realize that this guy is all muscle and bone. He smells like the wilderness, like the moon and the stars, like a joyful crystal clear mountain stream, like a desert wind, like ferns, moss, mushrooms, and giant redwoods, like snow capped peaks just one ridge beyond where you thought beyond ended.

"Doctor Rinpoche thinks that my chakras need examining", I inform him. "I have read and heard a lot about chakras but I am not really sure of exactly what a chakra is. Can you do that?"

"Indeed. I can do that and much more."

He leads me to a small room in the back of the house. In this room there is a table like a massage table and several chairs, a stereo, a book case full of books, and a book case filled with mysterious instruments. The room is decorated with plants, bird feathers, little rock carvings, and paintings of animals in the wild, wolves and bears, turkeys and deer. This all seems peaceful, calm. I relax.

Merlin takes a wooden top shaped ball about the size of my thumb which is tied to a string from among the mysterious instruments in one of the book cases. "Please stand by the work table," he says, pointing towards the massage table.

As I stand there, he holds the string and lets the top fall to about the level of my crotch. The top immediately starts pulling the entire string around in a clock wise direction. He repeats this procedure seven times between my crotch and the crown of my head, first in front of my body, then seven times in the back of my body. Sometimes the whole apparatus spins clock wise, sometimes it spins counter clockwise, sometimes it just goes back and forth, sometimes it flows in an egg shaped pattern, sometimes it makes big circles, and sometimes it doesn't hardly move.

Finally he stops, puts the top with the string down, and says, "I think that we should work on your heart chakra. There are several areas in your being where energy is not flowing smoothly and could use some adjusting, but your heart is especially calling for help. So, hop up on the table and lie down with your face up."

"Wait," I say, and ask, "can you explain what you just did and said means?"

He carefully considers me for a moment. Then he begins, "Besides your physical body, you have an energy body. Your energy body consists of billions of live intelligent threads of glowing energy which are connected to the unseen realms of creation where your primal essence, your jing springs from. These threads form the basis of your physical being, the basis of your body. As this energy, this information, whizzes through the space that is you, it meets and crosses other threads. In these nodes of meeting great things happen. The greatest of these nodes where great multitudes of threads are meeting, we call the chakras. The chakras begin below your tail bone and run up through your back past the crown of your head. There are seven or eight of these chakras depending on which nodes that you include in your count. Different schools of thought have different systems for naming and labeling these energy centers. There are other places all over your body where these threads intersect too. The liver, the gall bladder, the kidneys, and the thyroid are all other important intersections. Have you ever considered the consequences to you of having your thyroid removed? When an MD type of doctor decides that your thyroid is bad and removes it from your physical body, how does this loss, this empty space affect your energy body, affect who and what you are? What happens to that energy, that information, zipping through those threads in that area when that part of the circuitry is removed?"

"Imagine that there is a blueprint for your body, for your being. Imagine that this blueprint is alive and actionable like a circuit board. This explanation becomes a bit difficult to understand because the major part of this circuit board exists outside of your physical senses in an ethereal realm, so this blueprint is difficult for you to ascertain and to understand. This system is more like a blueprint that explains how you are meant to work, a blueprint that guides those beings who think about you and your being, a blueprint that influences their and your intentions; than a physical, electrical circuit board. This blueprint is knowable by you, but that requires training and sensitivity. So, for now, I am going to ask you to just listen and accept what I am saying. Later as you experience things, you can fit those experiences into what I have said and more understanding of what is happening will come to you. For now I just want you to know that over time parts of your energy body can become dysfunctional, that is, they do not operate in the way that you consciously wish that they would operate and affect the physical level of your being. You experience pain and unhappiness. Depending on your symptoms, a healing practitioner who is examining you might say that you have a bad heart chakra or a bad throat chakra, or he might say that a particular chakra is spinning in a negative direction, or he might say that a particular chakra is blocked, or he might say that a particular chakra has low energy. In the language of today with the understanding of today, it is difficult for the energy practitioner to communicate exactly what is happening to the person who is seeking the healing. As the person who is seeking the healing, you might experience bad circuits in the blueprint as low energy, or as gall stones, or as an abusive personal relationship, and these symptoms would be real on the physical plane. You do have gallstones, you or are in an abusive relationship, or you are depressed and lethargic. The healer looking at your chakras, at your meridians though would see an underlying problem in your energy body. If that energy problem is fixed, then the gall bladder spontaneously heals and the abusive relationship goes away or turns loving and you begin to feel energetic and happy. When one enters the energy realms, one enters a world of standing room only intelligences. The physical world, the world of the senses is only a small part of what is happening here now. We know this from our scientific instruments. Microscopes show us a whole world of tiny beings whom we are unaware of until we look in a microscope at a petri dish with a culture of bacteria growing in it. Then we become aware of billions of beings whom we are unaware of with our normal senses, but who have big effects on our physical lives. With a microscope we can see bacteria, viruses, yeasts, and parasites. Telescopes show us other realms. Other scientific instruments show us infrared worlds and other instruments enhance our hearing and make us aware of worlds of sound unknown to us otherwise. And these scientific instruments show us that these unseen worlds relate to and affect each other world in profound and complex ways."

"Chakras exist in a realm undetected by sight, sound, smell, taste, or touch. They are in a realm unseen by our scientific instruments also. Still they are there and the beings who can sense them and influence them are there too. The practitioner who works on people and animals' energy bodies learns to sense energy bodies and develops relationships with beings who influence these bodies. It is difficult to explain in the words of the currently commonly used ways to heal people what is done by the energy practitioner. When the energy worker says that you have a bad chakra and that he fixes it or even replaces it, that can be misleading. What he is saying is true from the position of the high tech beings who do this type of work, but what is more precise is that what those healing beings do is to establish a new intention within the bodies blueprint. There are all kinds of ways to explain these techniques and procedures, but what you and I are going to do today is establish a new intention in your blueprint in the area of your heart chakra."

"Merlin, I vaguely understand what you are saying, but can you give me some more concrete examples, some more explanations in everyday language of what you are saying that will help me to comprehend what you are telling me? How do chakras go bad?"

"There are internal and external reasons why chakras begin to function in ways that we find less than satisfying. Externally a person may threaten us in a way which harms our heart chakra. Then we find ourselves responding to this situation unconsciously in familiar emotional and mental ways which harm some of our other chakras and some of the other person's chakras. For instance, when we are 'threatened', we may go into an emotional mode of fear or anger and our thought which may go with this emotion is, 'they can't mess with me. I'll blow them away.' Then the chakras which are designed for more subtle pursuits of understanding and mediation, more subtle ways to use the information of what the other person really meant, ways which would bring harmonic resolution to the situation, are overridden. When this happens, we create a knife or spear of energy and project it into the other person's energy body in response to the shard which they jabbed into us. We think, 'Okay, see I'm right, you can't mess with me.' These thoughts go out as energy to control or force the other person to admit that we are right. They are shards of harmful energy which are embedded in the chakra of the other person. These shards can and do affect the other's chakras. Sending out this spear of energy also reduces the energy in our chakras. It may even be our intent to take out entire chakras in the other person and to render them meaningless, unable to connect to the universal web of information which the other person needs to survive and to be happy. Take for instance the professional football player, this is the way he has to think and act in order to succeed. This is also true for the modern corporate CEO. So when we look out at our normal modern world, everything may seem alright, but it only seems alright because we are not looking deep enough. Although this kind of behavior may be acceptable in the civilized world, it leads to damaged dysfunctional chakras which cause sickness and unhappiness in our lives. Internally, our chakras were damaged by the other person's assault on us. Then when we attacked the other person and damaged their chakras, we compounded the damage to our own chakras. When the other person responds to our threatening behavior, the situation spirals downward into sickness and unhappiness."

"Doing a recapitulation of our lives gives us back our original energy and dissolves the damage which is being done by the spears of energy. One recapitulates their life by going back through their entire life and going back through every relationship which they have had and remembering every situation where strong emotions were involved and releasing those emotions. That doesn't mean that if a person did something hurtful to you that you say that what they did is alright. You just see the situation for what it is and release the anger or hurt that you may carry or the longing and the remorse. This emotion, this memory is what is hurting you now. The person who inflicted the pain doesn't care. Your anger isn't hurting them. It is only hurting you. Let the anger or whatever the emotion is go. When this is done, you regain your original whole energy body, because each spear took a piece of that body away. Each spear that you were struck by and each spear that you threw damaged your once perfect and whole chakras."

"Another way that we damage our chakras internally is by not using them. When we don't use them we cut ourselves off from the sources of complex information that give us the enlightenment that should be ours and we replace that enlightenment with external dramas such as sports, political battles, economic struggles, and gossip."

"But still the real problem for most people today is the violent projectiles which we throw at other people. These projectiles are our words and thoughts. These words and thoughts have power and they affect others and they affect us. That is why good thoughts and prayers can heal. Another way of using the energy body that is a problem today in the external use of power is that people are unconsciously using energy cords which come from the area of our bellies to control others by grabbing ahold of them or by shooting emotional spears or arrows into them to persuade them that we are right. This is our ego ran amok. The more that we use these methods to influence others, the more addicted we become to these techniques and the less functional our chakras become."

"Acupuncture, herbs, chiropractic procedures, and massage are holistic ways to gradually clear out these accumulations and to reset us so that we return to the original settings and uses and power of the chakras."

I get it. I'm convinced. I say, "Okay. Let's do it." I take off my shoes and hop up onto the table. I peacefully lie down on my back.

He says, "Slow down your breathing until the in breath and the out breath flow together. As you start this way of breathing you are aware of where one breath ends and the next breath begins. So start on the out breath and slow your breathing down just a little bit on each breath. The flow of your breath is becoming smooth. There is no more coming or going. Now kind of vibrate the breath at the back of your throat like waves in the ocean, like snoring. Now you are opening a vibration. You can travel on that vibration into the dream world. I will begin adjusting the way that you are, and the way that you shall be, so that you may become more of what you wish to experience. I will begin at your feet and pass my hands over your entire body just a few inches above you. You may feel a tingling sensation or see things, but just relax and concentrate on your breathing."

Soft music is playing with water running through it. Sunlight lights the room softly through clean creamy white hemp curtains. I concentrate on my breathing and the vibrations in my head. I lose track of time, of Merlin. I'm seeing colors, deep sensual red, orange, and yellow colors. I'm seeing them so clearly that I think that Merlin is shining colored lights in my face. I crack an eye, against instructions, but Merlin is just standing with his hands poised above my belly. No lights, nothing, just standing there with his eyes closed, hands held out in front of him, palms facing downward towards me. Opening my eye even slightly breaks the spell and the lights and calm feelings which I was experiencing go away immediately. So, I close my eye and go back to breathing, drifting, determined not to open an eye again no matter what happens.

As I relax, a bright green light comes on. I lie in this green haze for some time. I am wondering where this light is coming from when I smell smoke, burnt electrical wiring smoke. It is that acrid awful odor that you smell when there is an electrical wire that is overloaded and the rubber on the wire starts to melt and burn. I am smelling that awful burning plastic stinking smoke smell.

I am thinking, "I should wake Shane up and get out of here. This house is catching on fire. I need to tell Merlin and get the hell out."

But I don't. I just keep lying there as the colors rise through green, blue, and purple. Suddenly I pop into a clear white light and wake up.

Merlin is standing at the top of my head with his left hand a few inches from the left side of my face and his right hand a few inches from the right side of my face.

When I open my eyes, he looks down and calmly and casually says, "That was bad. Did you smell that? I would swear that there was a pile of leaves burning in the corner of this room. Your heart chakra was so badly burnt that we had to cut it out, throw it away, and put in a new one. You're going to have problems in the heart chakra area for awhile. You are going to have to grow a new one. Sometimes chakras can't be repaired. Your heart chakra was burnt out and just flopping around, tattered, and blowing in the wind. Really, it was worse than useless. So now you have a new one, a baby heart chakra."

He starts to talk to me about love and love's divine nature. What he is saying is thrilling, excruciatingly beautiful, but I can't quite grasp the meaning of the words which he is speaking. I want to. I want to remember forever what he is saying but the wonderful words slip away like a dream that you want to remember but can't, slip away as he speaks. Gone, a sweet, sweet memory of what could have been, what should have been, of what is hoped will be, someday somewhere, for me and for everyone whom I have ever loved or will ever love.

In my heart, deep within Shane's being, I know that I am spinning positive in the heart chakra.

I am so excited. I jump up and start pumping Merlin's right hand with both of mine and hugging him and thanking him with tears of joy and revelation in my eyes.

I want to share my good fortune with someone. I decide to go see Lilith over at the Supplement Store. We have been hanging out together, going to dinner and visiting friends now for a couple of years. We share the same interests. I like her and respect her opinions. She is fun and funny, and cute and cool, great company. In the past I have even heard her mention Merlin Paul. I have heard her say how wonderful he is, but I didn't listen. I am becoming aware that a lot of people have tried to help me, to tell me things, but I wouldn't listen. I didn't listen. I don't listen. I have always been too busy listening to myself to listen to someone else.

.

CHAPTER 37

THE INVITATION

When I slip into the Supplement Store Lilith and her co-worker, Diana, are over in a corner with their backs to me stocking shelves with super foods in little brown glass bottles. They are talking intently and don't notice me. I can hear them. I stand there a few moments and listen. Lilith is saying, "I don't like Larry in that way?"

"What way?" Diana innocently prods.

"Well, you know, thaaat way."

"Oh, you mean that way?

"Yes, I mean that way."

"Well, tell me about that way."

"That way means that when you get around that person you just feel different."

"What's the difference between that way and ----?"

"That way means when that person walks in the room your heart pounds, you're excited to see them, you're happy, you feel good when they're around. Your toes curl. I had fun with Larry, but I don't have any desire to be with him in any other way."

"Besides that he really hurt my feelings. He knows that I like to be included when his old friends from Portland come to visit, that I like to help with the dinner, and the decorating. But he didn't invite me over when his old friends Bob and Carol came down. I just don't feel connected to him. I have been with a lot of men. I have been married. I have been in some real passionate affairs. I don't think that I have ever been in love though."

"My ex-husband and I have a child, but we agreed on nothing. We didn't do anything together. There was no connection. I never felt connected. When I think of all of the dating that I have done since I was seventeen years old, married twice, all of those boyfriends, I realize that I have never felt a connection. Sometimes I have felt a little bit of a connection, but that was over very fast."

"It is as if we were living in two separate fantasies and the two separate fantasies, the two separate dreams didn't connect and when the stress came it turned a light on and showed us that we were strangers living in two different worlds and that we weren't even living the same lives. We didn't have the same wants. We didn't have the same expectations. We didn't have the same goals. When we got up and went forward during the day we couldn't expect that what we did during the day would come to the same place that would make us both happy about what we had achieved during the day. We weren't connected in that sense."

"And when it was over I realized that there is a whole different type of connection too. There is a heart connection where you're just flat out crazy about someone. It is a romantic connection where it isn't explainable. You just know it by the feeling and it's not good for you or anything. It's not even about life. It's just flat out passionate insanity and we didn't have that connection for long either. No love. No real love."

"Love? What does love mean?" Diana asks wistfully. "What does that word mean?"

"It means everything," Lilith exclaims powerfully with firm conviction.

"It's like the guy is your best friend. They are interested in you. You are interested in them. Love grows. It is not that thing that happens when you are sixteen like when you go, 'Oh, Bill I am so in love with you'. Then the next day you forget Bill and it's Bob. 'Bob, I love you so much. Bill? Bill who?' No boundaries. Well it is that, but it's much more too. Bill and Bob know nothing about you. They don't know your favorite foods. They don't know anything about you. They are not interested in anything about you except maybe part of your body. But then as time goes on love is about you being interested in them and them being interested in you, and knowing things about each other, and having things in common. Being in love is about being comfortable and knowing that they care about you and you care about them. That is pretty important because it makes you feel complete and whole. It's amazing. You're not out there hanging on a limb. You're safe and secure. It is like, I feel good when he is around. I don't want to not see him. I am comfortable around him. It is always better to have him to hang out with. It is always better than being alone."

"I have always wanted to be in love, to be loved. Even as a little girl, I wanted to be in love, to have a husband, and to have a house with a white picket fence. I want to grow old together with my love, having our grand children come to visit our home and spend the night. That is all that I thought about from the time that I was a little girl."

"Then Kaboom! I experienced bad luck. Bad luck like Larry. He's not showing any interest in me. He's not inviting me into his life. He's not including me. He's not focusing on me. He's focusing on everything else."

"I can't believe that he doesn't notice that," Diana sympathizes with Lilith. "Oh well, you can't be mad at guys, they just don't get it. We should feel sorry for them."

I open the door and close it again with a little more authority. Lilith and Diana turn towards me. They both smile when they recognize me. Lilith starts walking towards me. I start getting excited. My heart starts pounding. My eyes aren't focusing. I feel nervous, hot, sweaty. She has such a powerful animal magnetism. She is walking towards me, but I feel as if I am being pulled into her, or at least I want to be pulled into her.

"Lilith, I just had this incredible experience over at Merlin Paul's. You are so right. I should have listened to you. I know that you told me about him and I just didn't understand. I feel so much better. Something has shifted, changed in me," I chatter away.

"You look good Shane, but I think that you always look good."

I am so pleased. She thinks that I look good? Surprised, I ask, "Really?"

"Yes, really," she replies.

She is standing very close, real close, and still smiling. I can feel her heat. I smell something wonderful. I can't quite place the memory but I know that it is something that I never should have forgotten, some place that I never should have left. I'm getting hotter. She really fills those jeans out very nicely down there and that frilly pink blouse is pushing out pretty good too. Oh my. She is? I wonder? I, she.

"There is this big Raw Food Event in Oakley this weekend," she seems to be whispering in my ear. "You know, Oakley is that spiritually cool little college town down south. Ben Bear, the rock star of the raw food world is also an Essene minister and he is going to marry Mark Monarch of the Raw Food Planet internet super food shopping site and Angela Dawn who is famous for a lot of things, but especially for blogging her green juice fast. The fast where she lost like a 150 pounds and became a beautiful fairy princess who is soon to be the wife of the wonderful Mark Monarch and the mother of beautiful curly haired blond children and living in the legendary Shangri-La of Villacabamba, Ecuador. One of our suppliers, Maca Mystery has given me two invites to the wedding. It is going to be a big show, lots of fun cool people. Want to go with me?"

"Yes", I almost shout, then catch myself and remember to look her in the eyes and not down there, and try to continue more casually, "I didn't have anything really important planned for this weekend. That sounds like fun. I would love to go with you. I have never done anything with you that I didn't enjoy. A Raw marriage? That's really clever. Sounds interesting. And Ben Bear, Mark Monarch, and Angela Dawn, and lots of interesting guests, and musicians, and, and, and ----."

I no longer can even remember why I came here. Do I need some supplements? I am lost. What did Johnny say to do when you're lost? Something like "flow downhill".

"Great. It's a long drive," she says. "Come over to my house at sunrise on Sunday so that we can get going early." She quickly hugs me as friends do and turns towards some new customers who have just walked through the door into the Store.

"See you on Sunday," I say.

"Only if you are lucky," she replies.

"I hope that I am," I respond sincerely hoping.

She stops, spins around, and almost laughing says, "That is such a good answer."

I leave while there is still hope.

CHAPTER 38

LILITH'S HOUSE

I rise in the dark, dress in blue jeans and a T-shirt, comb my long brown hair, drink a glass of high mountain spring water, put on sandals, and drive through the early morning darkness, through the lush countryside to Lilith's house on the hill.

Her home is a curious affair. There is more covered outside space than inside space, more palapa or pagoda than house. The walls and the inside floors are stone. The roof is a thick thatched grass of some type unknown to me. A large covered veranda takes up half of the house space. It has a blond wooden floor with natural wood grains of mahogany swirls that when you look down into them, you think of looking into the sky and watching the clouds drifting and shape shifting. This open area faces east, faces the rising sun. There are flowers everywhere.

When I walk up the wooden steps onto the south side of this porch, I see Lilith. She is dressed in a full length purple silk gown sitting on a cushion on the east edge of this wooden balcony. She is sitting in full lotus, hands on her knees, palms up, thumbs and index fingers touching, eyes wide open gazing at the area of purple sky where the sun is about to rise.

She turns to me and smiles. With her right hand she pats a cushion which lies to the right of her.

I take off my sandals and leave them on the steps. Then as I walk across the floor towards that cushion beside her, I grab another thick cushion. I then sit down cross legged high enough on the two cushions beside her to keep from breaking my knees.

She greets me, saying, "We are going to have the best time ever. Have you ever sun gazed?"

"No. Why would I? Won't you go blind if you look at the sun?" I ask.

Giggling she says, "We are going to have such fun." Then more seriously she adds, "The Sun is our friend, our Source. Think of going to a movie theater. You are sitting in a dark theater looking at a story on a screen in front of you. If you turn away from the screen and look at the back of the theater, you will be looking into a bright white light. The story is being projected on to the screen through that light. The light is the energy source. The Sun is our energy source. We can access that energy directly. We do access it directly, accidently every day; but when we access it directly, consciously, we really pump up our energy, our life force, our life potential. We wake up. Anthropologists accuse the ancient ones of being sun worshipers because what anthropologists do not understand they call religion. Well in this case anthropologist are sort of correct. What the ancient ones were doing was eating the Sun. They were having breakfast. They were breaking their fast, their time of being away from the light. They were re-charging their batteries. They were feasting on sunlight. And because the ancient ones knew that everything is alive, that everything has a spirit, and that everything is sacred; they were also worshipping. Everything that they did was worshipping. So, follow my lead."

She rises and walks down the steps and off from the porch and around to the east side of the house to a small area of bare dirt, no grass, no plants, clean bare dirt. She stands facing the Sun with her feet apart and with her hands down at her sides. The palms of her hands are open and turned towards the Sun. The sky on the eastern horizon is going from grey and purple to orange and yellow with a white light starting to peek over the distant mountains.

"Only stare into the Sun for ten seconds today," she warns me. "Each day you can stare into the Sun as it rises over the horizon or sets for another ten seconds, adding ten seconds more each day. But today, only look directly at it while you count to ten, just as it comes into view over the horizon. Then sit down and meditate until I am done gazing. I will stare at the Sun for some time because I have been doing this practice for a long time. Be at peace. When I am done gazing, I will bend down and touch Mother Earth, the bare dirt, with my right hand completing my grounding. Then we will give thanks and bless the day."

As a flat blinding sliver of the Sun pushes into view, an electrifying jolt hits me in my tail bone and starts to rise up my back. Inexplicably I actually feel heat on my open palms and on my face and tingling excitement in my body. I drink in joy through my eyes, joy that the Sun is rising, and joy that I am still here to be in another wonder filled day. It is great to be alive here now. What an experience!! Ten! I close my eyes. I can still see a flat Sun in a world of darkness. I touch the ground with my right hand and sit down cross legged, trying to clear my mind.

Where is my mind? It is not like my intestines. I know where my intestines are. Right here inside me. But my mind, where is it? Clearing my mind is like clearing the sky. Finally peace, joy, and happiness come for me.

After awhile, rustling silk brings me back to my body, to her body, to the dirt which I am sitting on, to the warm real woman standing to my left, standing facing east with her hands upraised palms facing up and back. I am very close, looking at her from behind just below her waist.

She speaks, "Father Sun and all things East of this circle thank you for being with us today. Welcome." She turns clockwise and faces South, "I look forward to journeying into your warm company today brothers and sisters of the South. Please welcome us with the same joy that we welcome you." She continues turning clockwise to the West as I follow, "All of Creation is precious and passing into darkness. Let us not miss a moment to share each other's precious beauty and love in this day which is given to us now." Continuing to turn, we face the North, "Spirits of the North, we are one. We are complete. Welcome." Looking upward, she says, "As above." Dropping her arms and looking downward, she finishes, "So below. Thank you Father Sky, Sister Moon, Mother Earth, Great Spirit. Welcome All. It is a good day. So be it. So be it. So be it. Aho."

She looks at me. Her eyes are sparkling, and I don't mean that metaphorically. There are stars shining in the black centers of each of her eyes. I am mesmerized. She says, "Let's go gather some of this wonderful chi," and starts walking towards the steps to the porch.

I follow her on to the veranda, shoeless, thoughtless, blissed out.

In the center of the wooden floor on the porch, she stops, turns to face me, and says, "Start shaking your body from head to toe, from arm to arm, from foot to foot." And she starts jiggling and giggling, shaking all over. "This is getting any stuck energy unstuck and moving, opening all of the meridians of our bodies, entering the movement of the Tao, relaxing, having fun."

"Breath deep," she commands me. "Chi is the vital energy that permeates the Universe. Gong means concentrated effort. Let's make a concentrated effort to concentrate some personal chi and resonate in harmony with the Universal chi. Let's do some qigong exercises. Just follow my lead. Relax. Breath deep. Breath all of the way down into your hips. Breath the world. You know the technique. On the in breath, breathe in everything in front of you, above you, behind you, whatever you are wanting to breathe in. Don't take shallow breaths of what is right in front of you as in the three feet that are in front of you. Breathe in to the outermost limits of your perception and then breathe out through your heart. Sweep it all in. Breathe it all out. Breath sweeps mind. Breathe in the Universe through your third eye. Breathe out through your heart chakra. Breathe in the Earth through your base chakra. Breathe out through your hear chakra. Keep breathing. Breathe in. Breathe out. Breathe in. Breathe out. Now I am reaching down and gathering a big ball of chi from the Earth down by my feet. Now I am slowly pulling this energy up into my body. Now I am pushing it over to you. Do you feel it? Try gathering some and pushing it into me."

I feel it when she pushes her open palms towards me. It feels as if the air compresses or like warm water pushes on me, through me, over me. I can feel the force, but it is gentle and flows through and around me. It doesn't push me over. It's pleasurable. I reach down to my feet and gather an armful from the Earth like I'm scooping up a beach ball and hugging it to my chest. I feel strong. Then I push it over into Lilith who is looking into my eyes and glowing. She responds by gathering the ball to her breasts and pulling it in.

Then she scoops up another ball and pushes it into me. Then I gather another ball and push it into her. We are slowly, rhythmically, powerfully pushing and pulling energy back and forth. What did she say about getting my Kundalini to rise? Something is definitely rising in me, on me as I watch her. When she bends over like that, I am visualizing some very personal empowerment here, now, where I push my personal chi deep in to her whole energy body.

Smiling she turns toward the Sun, moving into a stance like a martial arts warrior, breathes in deeply as she raises both open hands upwards in front of her towards the Sun. Holding her hands high, as if she is holding a big ball in the air, she steps back, breathing out, pulling the imaginary ball into her breasts. As she reaches her chest with the imaginary ball, she reverses her hands and flows them outwards away from her sides, as if she is spreading blessings to the Earth.

She explains, "Fire over water. Try it."

I feel so fruitful, so lush, so rich, so dynamic and creative. I pull the power from the Sun and rain it down on to the Earth spreading love, and life grows abundantly all around me as I flow up and down and out, as I repeat the move again and again.

Life is wonderful. I feel such love. Is it the Earth, the Sun, the fire, the water, the air, or is it Lilith? I could fly to Oakley without an airplane.

"Ready to go?" she asks.

I am ready for anything. I say, "Yes. Let me use your bathroom. Then I'll be ready."

I walk toward the back of the house, walking between a small office on the left, the kitchen on the right, and a bedroom on the left to the bathroom in the back on the right. Sitting on the closed top of the toilet is what looks to me like a fishing tackle box, but all of the drawers and compartments are full of little lidded dishes of paints, and tubes of colors and ointments, and brushes, and shoot, I have no idea what someone does with all of those things. You sure don't fish for fish with them or paint pictures.

Lilith puts a lot of effort into looking great, like she does. As my friend Jerry always says to me when he sees us together, "You're a lucky guy. That woman is real easy on the eyes."

I always agree.

I walk back out singing that Flatlanders' country song:

"My wildest dreams grow wilder every day.
There's nothing' I can do or say.
I only hope and pray I'll dream someday,
Just one dream wild enough to make you stay."

CHAPTER 39

THE WEDDING

As we drive south through the fertile green farmlands, Lilith asks, "Do you know what the greatest love story ever told is?"

I have no idea. I say, "No. Maybe 'Romeo and Juliet' or 'Desperate Housewives'."

"No, silly," She laughs. "The greatest love story is the story of the love between the Creator Spirit and its creation, the Created Being. The greatest love story is the story of how the Creator Spirit created a beautiful, beautiful Created Being that is loved unconditionally by the Creator Spirit, but the Created Being loves itself more than it loves the Creator Spirit. The Created Being rejects the Creator Spirit and goes out and creates its own creations. These creations love themselves more than they love their creator. In their self-love, they become separated, lonely, anxious creatures. The created beings create a world of life separate from the Creator Spirit. In this new world of the created creators, there is something wrong. It isn't a happy place. The created beings always want something that they can't have. Their world is never at peace, never happy. In this world there is always something to fear. Everyone is always afraid of being hurt, or left out, or of not getting what they need. Their creation is full of needs. When you live there you feel weak and alone and insecure. Everyone longs for something, but they don't know what. In separating themselves from the Creator Spirit's love, they forgot who they loved and how blessed they are. That is how the separation is accomplished. The creation ran away and forgot about who it ran away from. It has no memory. Well it has a memory but it is not a memory with enough information to remember how to get back to the loved one, to the Creator Spirit. This story is a terrible tragedy. There are moments when the created ones experience what it was like to be loved by the Creator. The orgasm is one of those moments. There are these flashes that make the created beings' long to return to the Creator Spirit, the loved one. And the Creator Spirit longs for the created beings to return, but the Creator Spirit cannot force the created beings to come back. This is the greatest love story because this is the story of how the created beings and the Creator Spirit are re-united. It is the story of how all of creation falls madly in love again with itself and the Creator Spirit, and of how the Creator Spirit joyously welcomes home his beloved creation. There is nothing but ecstatic joy everywhere all of the time in every thought when the creation and the Creator Spirit become One again."

As Lilith tells this story, I am feeling love for God for the first time in my life. I have always been afraid of God. Now I actually love God, me, Lilith, everything everywhere. I love God, us, as I have loved my lovers, and I know that God loves me. I just want to sit here and enjoy being in love with God and being loved by God. It is wonderful.

I experience this moment in which I love all of creation and I know that I have always loved all of creation. That is why I can't eat flesh and that is why I want to be a Breatharian. I love all of creation and I can't wish any of it harm, but I realize now that what I really love is the Creator. I forgot that I could see the Creator, but now I glimpse the Creator and I love the Creator. I love myself. I am love. I am loved and I am love. I am loved by the Force of Creation.

All that I want is to drift on this sea of love, this ocean of ecstasy. My heart is bursting with the love of God, my entire chest is bursting with joy. I am so glad to be home. I am so happy to be re-united with God. I want us to hug each other close and be re-emerged into each other, no male or female, just One.

I begin to silently pray, "God, how can we maintain our love now that we have found each other? How can we stay together?"

In my mind, I hear the answer, "Come to me now. Come to me completely."

"Alright," I answer with my mind. "I'm searching. I feel you with some point between my belly and my heart. I'm reaching out to you. How do I do this?"

"Reach not only with your feelings, but reach also with your creative sight. That is how you will remember me."

The emotions are getting so strong that I am beginning to get really upset. The longing is getting very powerful. I am sick with longing."

Silently in my mind I say, "I know that we love each other, but I can't see you clearly. I can't maintain our connection. Can you maintain it?"

And in my mind, I hear, "No. I maintain through you. You are the source."

"No," I strongly disagree with a powerful emotion. "You are the source. How can I be the source?"

"We are one. We are one even now when we are separated. You are the source of the separation. You hold the key to re-uniting us."

"I love you," I declare in a thought. "I want you. I want us to be together again. How can we be together?"

"Through Lilith."

"Through Lilith?" I ask without words, surprised, incredulous.

"Through feeling. Through feelings. Through Lilith," I hear without hearing with my ears.

When I get the image "Lilith", I remember that I am driving south on the freeway in a pickup truck talking to Lilith, that she is telling me a love story. I focus my attention on her sitting next to me.

She is concentrating on her story, saying, "That magical spot, that magical moment, that place of ultimate pleasure, that explosion of joy, that moment of ecstasy."

I have completely missed her story, her point. She must be talking about the orgasm, sex, men and women. I am trying to sort through what I remember about what she was saying and what the prayer voice said.

I say, "I don't understand. Why are there two different sexes? Why are there male and female energies and why are they separated from each other? I can understand what a male is and what a female is, but why, how are they separate?"

"We aren't, silly. You are. Weren't you listening to the story?" she asks. "You are separate and you are perceiving yourself as male and then you are merging yourself back into a female and then you are perceiving that as sexual energy as you are re-merging, re-emerging. Sexual energy is coming back into the Garden of Eden. Love is re-merging. Sex is re-entering the Garden. Love is coming back home. Love is ending the separation. An orgasm is the dissolving of the ego, dissolving the self back into the One, the All. That is why sex, the orgasm, and death are related. That is the relationship between sex and enlightenment too."

"So for me the vagina is the doorway through which I re-emerge into paradise, re-merge with paradise and lose my separation and self in the All? That is as close as I can get right now?" I ask.

"There are other ways, but that is the point of the story that I just told you," she replies.

"I don't want you to think that I am not a real macho guy, but I can't maintain sexual energy forever. I know that you are shocked, but there it is. Sex is like being on a drug that propels me into the orgasm state of being, but I can't stay on the drug forever. I can't maintain myself in a constant state of orgasm. Well maybe I can. I am certainly willing to try. At my current skill level though I am going to have to go with that famous saying of Baba Ram Dass's about drugs that the problem is that, 'you are always going to come down'. Got any ideas on how to maintain the sexual energy awareness by prolonging the orgasm and maintaining that awareness, that state of enlightenment, pleasure, being in paradise longer? Maybe that is what tantric yoga is about! Anything to say on any of this?"

"No. I wasn't offering you any doors to paradise. I appreciate your comments and I encourage your explorations and expansions of your perceptions and awareness. I am enjoying our inquiries. I believe that the more that we look, the more we will have those moments of seeing and then we will remember. Aren't you getting those flashes of something that is just right outside of your ability to recall?"

"Yes I am and I agree. I think that we should keep pushing for those flashes, those insights."

She laughs and says, "Keep your eyes on the road. There is the turnoff."

She is right. I almost miss our exit. The turnoff is quite a ways north of Oakley.

We leave the freeway on the west side and head south on old highway 99. We continue south a few more miles to where we turn right on Old Country Road. We wind through grass and oak covered foothills. Just where the oak savannah blends into the great Northwest fir forest, we turn left on a tree lined lane, go another few miles and turn right into the driveway of 7777 Buckhorn Drive.

There a bright cheerful young woman, who is dressed in an outrageously colorful forest costume, stands beside a big old country home. She waves to us and greets us with, "Hi! It's wonderful of you to come to the wedding of Mark and Angela. Just proceed along this driveway and go past the barn and park in the pasture around behind the barn beside the other cars."

She takes Lilith's invitations and waves us onward.

We drive by the big old red wooden barn and bump across the grass covered field where at least a hundred cars, pickups, and SUV's are already parked. Some of these cars have been here for days. We can see tents in the woods where people have been camped and partying for some time. This is quite the event. What a wedding!

We follow little signs deep into the forest to a little cottage with a big open shed. During most of the year this appears to be an herb growing operation but now it has been converted into a big open air restaurant. There are all kinds of raw vegan foods to sample: chips and salsas, lasagna, tacos, soups, salads and breads, cakes, cheesecakes, cookies and pies, and, of course, chocolate.

There are trays of raw cacao fudge and brownies. There are pitchers of chocolate almond mylks and smoothies. There are chocolate smoothies with maca, Siberian ginseng, blue green algae, and cordyceps. There are bowls of fruits of every shape, size, and description, fruits which have been chopped and diced and smothered with sweet creamy nut and date sauces. There are fruit juices and tropical punches. There are heavenly fruit super smoothies.

We dip chips made from a dehydrated mix of flax seeds, raw cashews, miso, and onions in salsas. We gorge ourselves on raw vegan lasagna and cheesecake and we drink big glasses of chocolate smoothies loaded with super powerful super foods.

We are over the Moon headed for the eleventh dimension.

We wander further into the woods passing energy workers' booths, reflexology and foot bath centers. We stop at a yurt offering full body massages. Only a fool would pass up a free massage and although we are feeling foolish, neither of us feels quite that foolish.

After our massages, we wander on passing a man giving out Zappers and an Immortalist teaching secret breathing techniques. When we come to a creek, a lovely little woodland stream running through this enchanted forest, the Maca Mystery people are there giving out shots of maca and little pieces of wood. When you rub these pieces of wood between your fingers, they emit a delightful aroma. The Maca Mystery people are delighted to see Lilith.

As we continue to wander, we realize that we are walking in a circle which encloses a flat space alongside the little creek and that people are gathering in this area. Something is about to happen. We follow the crowds gaze toward a rock bluff about two big men tall that overlooks this area where we are all gathered. Standing on a large flat rock jutting out of the bluff above our heads is Ben Bear.

He shouts, "Let the festivities begin. Bachelors go downstream. Bachelorettes go up stream. Later we will return here to the middle, to the center, and be re-united, to be re-membered."

With the rest of the guys, I follow Mark and Ben downstream to an area beside the creek with a low rock wall set into the hillside. A couple guys strip Mark down to his boxer shorts and hoist him up onto the flat top of the rock wall.

Ben presents the crowd with a big bowl of warm creamy chocolate. The crowd goes wild, cheering, pumping their fists in the air, yelling lewd wedding night suggestions involving creamy chocolate to Mark. Ben dips two fingers into the chocolate and paints some thrusting pyramidal mountains on Mark's naked chest. Then reloading his fingers with more chocolate, he adds a sun rising over the mountains and lots of little lines in front of the mountains, and says, "Mark, may all of your days be happy and the Sun ever shine on you and on your lover and on your companions and on all of your children's children's children's children's children."

Stepping back, he hands the bowl to Blaze and announces, "Okay, Blaze, it's your turn."

Blaze steps forward and paints a chocolate circle over Mark's left breast with a lightning bolt which plunges deep into the center of the circle and wishes, "May this be the best day ever. May our lives be full of love, lust, and good times, full of enlightenment, women, and children. Mark, may your bowl overflow with joy, beauty, and wonder, and spill over into all of ours. Love you dude. Life is good. You are better."

He hands the bowl to the guy next to him and steps back into the crowd. Each of us takes a turn at painting Mark and giving our blessings until he is completely covered in chocolate, a chocolate man, a man of energy, wonder, and blessings.

Ben hops up onto the stone wall, pulls out a big long thick cigar and proclaims, "This is a genuine Cuban cigar. You are looking at illegal pleasure. Let's light this baby up and enjoy the fruits of manhood."

"Yes!" roars the crowd.

"Let's do it."

"Let's get high."

"Burn. Burn. Burn."

Ben snips an end from the cigar and lights it with a big torch, sucks in a big mouthful and blows a ring into the air that looks like the sacred and holy vagina."

Mark watches the smoke and dreams, "I'm getting married, united in love", and walks away upstream.

Ben hops down and passes the cigar into the mob. A friend with some bottles of wine hands him one. He opens it, takes a long drink, and passes it into the rowdy assembly. Then he opens a couple more, taking a big swig from each bottle as he opens it, and then passing the newly opened bottle into the wild throng.

We are getting high. We are happy. It is a good day.

Meanwhile, Lilith walks north along the creek with her friend, Abbey a twenty seven year old woman from Maca Mystery. Abbey is wearing blue jeans, hiking boots, and a white silky long sleeved blouse. Her long brown hair flows around her sun tanned smiling face. She is telling Lilith, "I have a wonderful new boyfriend, Ricky. He is so much fun. We climbed Aspen Butte last weekend and camped beside this crystal clear mountain lake. Then we got totally lost and had to hitchhike back to his pickup, but we got a ride with this cool guy who left his family at their camp site and took us all of the way back to our pickup. He gave us beer and a joint. We were so high and happy. It was great. I love Ricky. We have so much fun. He works for Flow Kayaks."

They arrive at a little opening in the woods with chairs set in a semi-circle and a few tables scattered here and there. Abbey and Lilith sit in the front row. As the other women come into the clearing talking, hugging and laughing, and seat themselves, Angela enters and sits down in a chair in the middle of the half circle.

A bride's maid comes forward out of the group of women carrying a gold box with pink ribbons and a fluffy pink bow. She smiles and as she hands the gift to Angela, she suggests, "Enjoy".

Angela returns her smile and gushes, "Oh, I like gifts."

She carefully takes the ribbon and bow from the box and sets them aside. She lifts the lid from the box and surprised exclaims, "Holy shit! What is this?"

She sets the box lid down, reaches into the box, and pulls out a soft rubber cylinder which is shaped somewhat like a large banana. One end looks very much like an extra large penis with accessories. The other end is a box with a bunch of buttons.

There is nervous, embarrassed laughter in the crowd.

"A dildo Angela," Abbey explains. "You shouldn't need that. Let me have it," she offers.

Everyone laughs.

Suddenly whistles blow in the woods and police come out of the woods from every direction. There are policemen everywhere. They are very aggressive. They are shouting, "You are all under arrest."

"Nobody move."

"Don't touch your purses."

"We know that there are illegal drugs being used here."

"This is an illegal gathering."

Lilith is thinking, "Oh no! I am going to jail."

She is imagining her picture on the front page of the local newspaper.

The police are right on them, right there in the crowd. There are three of them.

Suddenly this loud music starts thundering: KA BOOM BA BOOM BA BOOM!

The policemen start dancing, grab hold of their pants and rip them away and throw them back over their heads. Then they tear off their jackets and shirts as they bump and grind in the crowd.

The women go absolutely crazy. They are shouting, "Take it off! Take more off!"

Women jump up on the chairs and the tables bumping and grinding to the music along with the policemen.

One of the dancers straddles Angela who is still sitting in the chair in the midst of this pandemonium. The dancer is bending over Angela wiggling his naked ass at the crowd. He has nothing on except a little g-string cup over his genitals which has a whistle hanging from it. He thrusts his hips into Angela's face and yells, "Get ready for your wedding night. Blow the whistle!"

Angela obviously wishes that Abbey didn't only get the dildo, but that she also was blowing the whistle. But in good humor, she blows the whistle.

The naked policeman whirls towards the crowd and dances through the screaming women while the other two policemen do the same. The women cheer and whistle and try to grab them. The policemen dance and shake their naked asses back into the woods.

The bridesmaid shouts to the crowd, "Alright ladies, let's go show those men how to get things done."

And the women walk back towards the wedding site wildly talking about men and laughing.

Abbey and Lilith are sitting on the grass at the foot of the cliff talking animatedly about something when I enter, but when they see me, they stop, and Lilith says, "Hi Shane. This is Abbey, my new best friend."

I recognize Abbey from the Maca Mystery booth. She really does seem like a nice girl.

I sit down as close to Lilith as I can without actually sitting on her, and the ladies go back to talking, but it seems as if they have changed the subject.

Suddenly Mark and Ben appear on the flat rock above us. A large attractive woman with braided blond hair joins them. She is wearing a flowing green gown. She begins to sing with the power of an opera diva, but I can't understand the words. My lack of understanding is not because the words aren't in English. It is because she isn't saying words. It sounds as if the great Northwest forest is pouring out its feelings, its love on us. As she sings, Angela wearing a flowing white gown, sunlight sparkling golden on her hair, joins Mark and Ben on the rock above us.

When the haunting melody ends, Ben declares, "Dearly Beloved, we are gathered here that we may help these two droplets of water flow together into that great Ocean of love, that we might all merge in this moment into a stream that merges with all of the other streams of life and becomes a powerful river, a powerful force, a powerful source of fertility, beauty, pleasure, and life."

"Water retains the memory of every form that it touches and let us remember that our bodies are mostly made up of droplets of water. So let us touch only beauty, love, and abundance, and water that is clean, clear, and beautiful, water that brings life and fertility to barren places. We are here today helping these two mountain streams flow together with the hope that as they couple in the open air with the sun shining, they will saturate Mother Earth with love and joy, and their abundance will overflow into all of our lives."

"Earth is our essence. We are children of Mother Earth. Mother Earth is our mother. She really is the essence of who and what we are. We are Earthlings."

"Fire, the Sun, is our father. The Sun is where we get our energy. We are Earthling essence which has been filled with energy by Father Sun."

"Water is the cosmic energy, the cosmic stranger. Water comes out of the aether into the warmed Earth and impregnates her, makes her moist with the possibility of movement, of joy. The coupling of Earth, Water, and Sun births the possibility of life, of you, of me."

"When the mysterious breath of life, Air, is breathed into the warm moist Earth, I am born. You are born. There is life on Earth.'

"The breath of life is the breath of Divine passion. It is the breath of love. It is the union, the coupling of gods and goddesses. As these Forces meet and penetrate and absorb each other in an ecstatic dance of beauty, joy, lust, harmony, and Divine love. Life is given birth in orgasmic ecstasy and flows throughout creation."

"Imagine, imagine the possibilities. How many ways can Earth, Sun, Water, and Air couple, flow, and dance? How many ways are there to be? How should we be, being?"

"How many ways might we couple? How many ways might we flow into each other? How many stories may we birth? How much joy can we experience? How much joy can we have?"

"Imagine."

"This is our moment to be in this Universe. This is our moment to create. This is our moment to moisten and fertilize the seed of life and this is our moment to watch it grow."

"We are here touching each other. Our minds are flowing together. Our hopes and dreams are merging. We were awesome individually. We are much more collectively."

"Where we were a drop of water, we are now a river, a force of nature. We have power and we also have the ability to bring growth, beauty, prosperity, and happiness."

"What will the dream be?"

"We are the great river of life and we bring fertility. We bring our imaginations. We bring our will for happiness, our will to unite and flow together."

"Breathe deep, sparkle. The breath of life is the breath of being, the breath of Divine Spirit, the breath of the great Unknown."

"You have everything. You are everything."

"Breathe deep, breathe long, relax."

"It is done. It will be."

"So be it."

"Bride and groom, you may kiss. I declare you re-united."

Mark and Angela hug and kiss, then turn towards us and holding hands raise their arms high into the air saluting us, saluting the setting Sun, saluting the rising Moon, saluting a night, a life of joy and pleasure.

"Let's party!" shouts Ben and leads the way upstream to another meadow where there are mounds of heart shaped chocolates on silver trays on tables and a DJ who is set up and ready to rock.

We each eat a couple of the chocolates. They are so good. I can't stop myself. I just eat one after another. People around me are doing the same.

Then Bear announces, "Don't eat too many of the chocolates. They have more than twenty five super foods in them and they will make you very happy for a very long time. They are energizing, stimulating, spirit connecting and building, and nutritionally fulfilling. There are ingredients in this chocolate that nobody hardly ever gets. There are super foods that almost no one has ever even heard of. Not just maca and Siberian ginseng and Chinese red ginseng, but goji berries, queen bee royal jelly, coconut oil and honey, acai, dates and durian, vanilla beans, chaparral, yerbe mate, noni, hemp seeds, and sheelajit. It'll do your body and soul good, but go easy."

Too late.

The DJ looks like a six foot six Jesus. He's dark with long flowing black wavy hair and he is wearing a white cotton peasant shirt and trousers and a robe and sandals. He looks like in his day job he probably teaches yoga and meditation, shares his wisdom and heals the sick, but tonight he is surrounded by a full DJ set up with stacks of amplifiers and huge speakers and turn tables, microphones and all of those things that DJ's need to make the dancers diaphragms shake and the dance floor rumble.

The music starts pulsing. Lilith's body starts rhythmically, gracefully moving in all of those places that make a man's heart skip over into the lust zone. I follow her into the dance. Minutes flow into hours.

My arms and upper body are too exhausted to move any more, but my legs keep bouncing with the rhythm. A hundred people smile and dance and sweat sweet sweat around me. Some are whirling like dervishes, others step like Native Americans, others sway as if they are dancing with unseen lovers. Everybody is moving to the same rhythm, the same beat.

Finally Lilith says, "This is fun, but we have to go home. We have a long drive."

She is so right. Life is good. We are happy together. We have a connection. We leave hand in hand

CHAPTER 40

LOVE

The next day is Lilith's day off. I am on fire. I want her. Talk about a train on a track heading for the tunnel. There is nothing else on my mind.

I go over to her house. She is standing on the porch weaving some kind of little yellow flowers into a crown.

Breathlessly I rush up onto the porch.

She hugs me and places the crown on my head.

"Lilith, we should make love," I declare.

She says, "What! What?" She takes me by the hand, walks me back over to the steps where we sit down together and she asks, "Are you sure?"

"Yes. I am sure." I declare.

"I don't know. Do you think that it will ruin our friendship? I don't want to mess up our friendship. When you have sex with someone, that changes everything. You might not ever be friends again. I don't want that. I am worried. We have been friends for years. Then we do this, and it is over. We're not friends anymore. I have to think about this. I really want to be with you, but I don't know what to do. I don't know what to say. I need a drink. Let's go to lunch. Let's go to the Beacon of Light Café down by the river."

We go out to her little red ancient Volkswagen Bug. I trip getting in and nearly slam my hand in the door. I am chattering incoherently.

I can see her thinking, "What is going on with this guy?"

We start driving slowly through Garden Valley along the river towards the Beacon which is a cozy little vegetarian meeting place overlooking a broad calm stretch of the river.

Lilith isn't saying much. She is nervous, thinking.

I just have to tell her how I feel. As she drives, I announce, "I want to experience love. I want to be loved. I want to love. I want to live in a Universe of love.

"I want to know love in every one of its possible meanings.

"I want to lust after a lover with unbearable desire.

"I want to be in love with the pleasure of eating chocolate bliss balls.

"I want to be loved by my mother and father. I want to love my children. I want to live in a lovely place, in a lovely time with lovely neighbors. I want to be loved by God and to never know fear or lack.

"I want to be surprised every day by loveliness and wondrous beauty presenting themselves to me and to my loved ones for our pleasure.

"I want to love all of the animals that I meet and to love all of the plants that I see. I want to love the water that I drink and that I bath in. I want to love the air that I breathe. I want to love the Sun that gives me life. I want to love the Earth that I walk on.

"I want to know the love of all the animals, and the plants, and the water, and the air, and the Sun, and of all of the Earth.

"I want to know the thrill of love. I want to know the ecstasy of love. I want to know the joy of love. I want to know the wonder and the mystery of love. I want to know the beauty of love.

"I want to be the thrill of love, the mystery of love, the beauty of love, the wonder of love.

"I want to be love.

"I am going to fall in love with everyone and everything that I meet.

"There is no one or no thing that is not adorable, that is anything but adorable.

"I love myself.

"I love you.

"What do I mean by love? What does love mean? What do I mean when I say, 'I love you'?

"I mean that I absolutely adore you. You are splendiforously beautiful. You are the most desirable being of luminous light and joy to ever grace this realm. Nothing is more precious than to be with you. Nothing would be more wonderful for me than to give you pleasure or to receive pleasure from you. The pleasure that you are giving now is wonderful, but the possibilities that I am imagining are unbearably more wondrous even than this moment.

"I am imagining chocolate bliss balls melting in my mouth with bursts of ecstatic pleasure. I am imagining hugs from a mother and a father filled with kindness and concern and promises of comfort and caring forever and ever. I am imagining the passionate embrace of a lover whose every touch sends shivers of promises of unknown ecstasy surging through my body into secret feelings that have never even ever been imagined in the dry formulas of mathematicians, emotions that only can be found in the explosion of ecstasy, in the hot gush of orgasm.

"I crave the gentle touch of the tree, the loving look of the sweet doe, the passionate kiss of my lover. I wish to slide the delicious wonder of fresh sliced peaches smothered in whipped cream into my mouth. I wish to hold a basket full of puppies and pet their soft fur and enjoy the sparkle of their joy and love for life. I wish to come into my love in search of that place, that moment when everything becomes nothing but pure pleasure and joy, an explosion of rapture. The unknown is known. We become One again.

"That is what I want for all of Creation.

"That is my dream. That is my desire. That is my intention.

"That my love, is our destiny."

I look over at Lilith. She looks absolutely stunned, as if no one has ever said anything like this to her before, but that she has always been waiting to hear it. There are tears in her eyes, but she is smiling.

"Ditto," she says. "I'll make love to you, but first you have to get me drunk."

CHAPTER 41

TANTRIC YOGA

During lunch, I am less than brilliant and I manage to drop my fork, spill my water, and accidently trip the waiter. None of this seems to bother Lilith in the least. She acts like a woman who has just won the lottery.

After lunch we continue to drive down the river. We stop at the New Harvest organic food and spirits store. Together we enter the rustic country store. The entire rear wall is a cooler full of micro-brew beers. The middle of the store is stacked ceiling high with wine and beer making supplies and books. The front of the store is wooden case stacked on wooden case of bottles of organic wine. The wooden crates are stacked on their sides with the bottles facing us.

I don't know a thing about wine or beer.

Lilith tells Steve, the owner, "I don't know a thing about wine and beer."

He smiles and answers, "Neither do I. We are all learning. But for a lovely lady such as yourself and your charming and handsome companion, I would suggest a smooth and sunny, but with a hint of muskiness, Oak Creek merlot."

Lilith is smiling as if she just remembered something important, something which she has been trying to remember for quite some time, but couldn't quite bring it up to the surface.

"We'll take it," she agrees.

"It's yours," Steve says, handing her a sapphire blue bottle shaped like a tear drop and half hidden in a woven grass basket.

"That looks like some powerful magic," I tell Steve. I smile my gratitude and shake hands with him. He returns my smile and friendly handshake. I like him immediately.

"Indeed," he affirms.

We leave the New Harvest a happy couple.

We go to the Wolf Creek State Park and wander through the forest talking and taking pictures of waterfalls and ferns and mossy trees and strange mushrooms. We stand very close for a long time just looking and feeling each other's heat.

When darkness comes we go to Lilith's and sit on the porch in the hammock, drink the Oak Creek merlot and watch the full moon rise.

Lilith tosses back the last drink in her glass, the last drink in the blue sapphire bottle, sets the glass down, turns towards me, leans over, and passionately kisses me. Then leans down and starts unbuckling my pants.

I remember what it means to be one with another. We pass beyond cares. We soar beyond time and space into the perfect moment.

CHAPTER 42

THE ASCENSION

I'm still asleep in the morning when Lilith leaves for work. At lunch time I am already lonely. I decide to go down to the Supplement Store to see Lilith. I stop along the way and buy a pretty note card and write my feelings for Lilith on it.

When I enter the store, Diana is asking Lilith, "So, is Shane that guy?"

Lilith replies, "Maybe."

Diana prods her, "What does that mean? Is he or isn't he?"

"Yeah. Yes he is," she responds.

I walk over and say, "Hi."

They look up surprised. They both smile and Diana says, "Hi Shane. You're glowing today," and she walks away.

I give my note to Lilith. She reads:

LOVE IS

Love is the rope that binds.

Love is the potion that heals.

Love is the vulnerability that creates.

Love is the door that opens.

Love is the street that winds.

Love is the life that flows.

Love is the mountain that stands.

Love is the bird in the distance.

Love is the lion that is near.
Love is a mountain lake.
Love is a mirror.
Love is Lilith.
Lilith is love.
I love you.
Shane.

She hugs me and kisses me on the cheek. Clutching the note, she says, "Wait here. I have a gift for you too."

She walks through the store into the back room and returns carrying a yellow envelope. She tells me, "I want you to know that with you I feel like I have hit the jackpot. So I bought you a little something on the way in this morning."

I open the envelope. It is full of lottery tickets.

"Good luck," she smiles and turns back to her customers.

I leave smiling too.

That night we dine together at Alex's Greek Restaurant on veggie gyros.

In the morning I check the internet, we have the winning numbers. We have won the big one, the Mega-Riches Lottery.

I rush down to the store, dash in, and blurt out, "We won. We have the winning numbers. We won the lottery. We're gazillionaires."

She looks at me as if she is surprised at my surprise and asks, "Was there ever any doubt? Love is abundance. We are abundant."

I grab her hand. "C'mon. We have to go tell Gabriel. Let Diana run the store for awhile."

We dash out of the store giddy with love, with cash, with hope and excitement.

Gabriel is standing by his front door water pitcher in hand, watering pretty purple flowers in a long low planter box.

Waving excitedly, I shout, "Gabriel, Gabriel we won. We won the Mega-Riches Lottery. What shall we do?"

"It is time," he responds. "You should start the Life's Better Wellness Center and the War on Illness campaign."

"Wait a minute Gabriel. The War on Illness campaign? Aren't we supposed to not be against anything but instead to move towards what we want to be? There has been a War on Cancer and a War on Heart Disease and a War on Drugs and a War on Teenage Pregnancy, and now there is more cancer, heart disease, teenage pregnancy, and drug use than there was before the wars started. War doesn't work."

"Yes. This is different. You really aren't going to fight a war about anything. This is an attention getting ploy with which you can rebalance this Universe. When you tell people to do something, they automatically do the opposite. They rebel. If you tell someone that it would be better for them to eat more fruits and vegetables and less cooked meat and bread, they agree and then they go have a big juicy hamburger with French fries and a large soda pop. They know that you are correct. They just don't want to do it. They don't think that fruits and veggies taste as yummy as a burger, fries, and a soda. They are in charge of their own life and they believe that they know more about what makes them happy than you do. They believe that they already know what they need to know and they are already doing their best and they don't need some know-it-all jerk telling them how to live."

"By doing what I am suggesting, you wouldn't be telling people what to do to be well and happy. You would be having a War on Illness. Everybody is against getting sick. Who's going to take the other side? Who's going to argue for illness? Who's going to say, 'I'm for more disease. I want more sickness?' Anybody who is against a War on Illness must be an evil villain. This would be a war against evil villains. So obviously you would be a religious organization. This would be a religion. The leaders of the War on Illness would be ministers who are ministering to the sick and the needy which includes pretty much the whole darn human race. Ministering would morph the War on Illness into the Life's Better Wellness Centers and the war would be won."

"I hadn't thought of it that way. That sounds pretty good. I'm convinced," I acquiesce smiling and hug him.

Then I pause. I am absolutely thunderstruck. This doesn't work. None of this works. This contradicts everything which Gabriel has taught me.

"Wait a minute Gabriel. You said that to win the Great Universal Lottery, you have to lose the Mega-Riches Lottery. Now here I am standing here with the winning Mega-Riches ticket and in love. This would seem to be the exact opposite of letting go."

"Well, if being in love and winning the lottery bothers you that much, then give me that winning lottery ticket and I know that Lilith wants to go to Italy. So I'll cash in the ticket and take Lilith to Rome."

"No. That's alright Gabriel. I'll keep the money and go with Lilith myself."

"There you go. When will men and women be anything other than men and women? Remember the story of Jesus going into the desert and fasting after his baptism and of how he was tempted by all of the good things of the Earth and how he was tempted to test God's love? The further that you go along the Wheel of Life, the greater that the temptations are. You're still caught on the Wheel of Life, but don't worry. When you let go even in the least, you receive. This isn't as easy or as simple as it seems. Remember, I said that when you let go, everything is lost and I also said that everything is gained. I also told you to let it all go and to become the unimaginable. I said that you are to become the unimaginable who is imagining. I said that we should expect the unexpected, that we should expect the unexpectable. I didn't say to let it all go and suffer. What did you expect? Lose your expectations. Lose your expectations too. It is easier to let go of suffering than it is to let go of pleasure, and remember that when I say to let go, I am not saying what you are hearing. You have left your past unattended."

"Creation is always going to be more wondrous than you can even imagine. People expect their saints to be celibate, pious, poor, and all-suffering. God expects his saints to be having the best time ever in the best creation ever, because God and his saints are One."

"Imagine that you are standing in the last minute of your life for absolute certain and that you have released your hold on everything that has to do with this life. Imagine that the afterlife and this life are both visible to you, like when you are waking up from a dream and you can still see the dream but you are re-entering your waking life and are aware that you are in bed sleeping too. In that moment you understand life and death and how everything comes together. But then, imagine that you don't die. Imagine that that moment goes on for a hundred years. How precious, how beautiful, how amazing would everything be? What would be possible? What would happen? What would you do? You are in that moment. Let your expectations go too."

Lilith asks simply, "Where do we start?"

"Intend to do what you will do," Gabriel responds. "Visualize and focus. Learn to learn. Your creative expression of time is limited. There isn't any time. Time isn't limited. It is your creative expression of time that is limiting. See the difference? Your expression, your conceptualization of time is limiting you, but time itself isn't limited. It is unlimited. It is only your creative expression of time that is limiting you."

"That is a little bigger than I can grasp," I interrupt him. I am still trying to catch up. "What you are saying is that we are not really limited and our options today, other than the limits that we are conceptualizing, are huge? As we conceptualize larger limits, larger creations are possible?"

"Yes, of course," he continues, "and larger temptations and greater suffering and pleasure too."

"Wait. You are saying that the possibilities for today are unlimited. Right?" I am still trying to grasp what he is saying.

"Yes. They are unlimited," he confirms.

"What about all of our problems?" I want to know.

"What problems? You don't have any problems. You only have opportunities."

"Wow! That is powerful," Lilith gasps and steps back, eyes wide, mouth open.

Lilith and I are now standing side by side on the lawn in front of Gabriel's office facing him and as we talk, Gabriel is beginning to glow like a big light bulb. We can see his body inside the glowing sphere, but his body is starting to disappear from his feet upwards.

"Yes. Yes, that is powerful," Gabriel agrees. Every day can be Sunday. Live every day as if it is Sunday. That's alright."

Only his smiling face is now visible inside the golden sphere. "Everything is sacred. Live well. Die easy. I go now. All that was mine is now yours. Where you are, I am always with you. Just call my name and I will appear to you. Lift your hearts and your sight a little higher. As the moon is above the Earth, I am above you," he says and his face disappears into the golden light.

The golden ball rises shining into the heavens.

I stand there in the grass on the hillside on this sunny morning watching Gabriel ascend, gripping Lilith's right hand in my left hand and the winning lottery ticket in my right hand.

Amazing! Astounding!

Life is good.

CHAPTER 43

HORUS

Together Lilith and I, still holding hands, look to the south where the day has suddenly grown dark. Just a few minutes ago we watched Gabriel change from a man into a ball of glowing white light and ascend into a blue sky, into the heavens. Now a boiling mass of heavy, black clouds are sweeping towards us. They are whirling like a load of clothes in one of those big, ugly, industrial washing machines down at the Logger's Laundromat over on old highway 66.

The wind is making it hard to stand up. We cling to each other with our feet braced against the growing force. We are still standing in the parking lot for Gabriel's office, but now we are hunkered down beside Lilith's 60's Volkswagen bug, a little rounded metal hill.

I grab the door handle and push the car door open against the wind. I can just barely get the door open and shove Lilith in ahead of me and then jump in behind her as the wind slams the door closed.

"What is going on," Lilith shouts above the roar.

"I don't know," I shout back.

The Volkswagen is shuddering and shaking. Leaves, tree limbs, plastic bags, and pieces of roofs are blowing all around us. As I'm looking out the passenger door window, a carpenter's claw hammer drifts by at eye level just a few feet away from my face, floating through the air as if it's a leaf. As I follow the hammer with my eyes, it sails by a temperature gauge on a metal pole. I start to look at the gauge, but before I can read it, the pole gracefully bends over and the gauge twists away from us.

There isn't any traffic on the streets below us. There are only parked cars which begin to jump into the air like popping pop corn. They sail through the sky like graceful paper airplanes until they smash into the roofs of buildings more like spears than paper gliders.

This all happens so quickly and so strangely that we aren't even frightened. We just sit there in shock and watch, amazed.

Then as suddenly as it started, it stops.

We stare into each other's wide open eyes with our jaws dropped down, and then hug, glad to still be alive.

All around us is chaos. Smashed and shredded this's and that's everywhere.

Lilith turns back to me with startled eyes and gasps, "The Mega Riches Lottery ticket! Do you still have that winning Lottery ticket?"

I had completely forgotten about the winning ticket that I had been holding when the tornado struck. Shocked with the realization, I look at her and open my empty hands. "No. No, I don't. I must have dropped it when I grabbed you and opened the car door and pushed you in and jumped in behind you. It's gone. It blew away. Let's look for it," I say desperately and grab the door handle.

"Oh no, damn!" She forcefully exclaims with heart breaking disappointment pulling the corners of her just closed mouth down. Millions of dollars are gone, gone in a moment, gone just like that. Then she looks at me and places her right hand on my left arm and with relief in her voice says, "But we're alive. We're still alive. That's incredible. This is strange, really weird. I am going to the store and see how Diana is, see how the store is. That tornado hit downtown pretty hard."

"Okay," I agree, "but I'm staying here and looking for that ticket. I'll find it," I assure her.

I am trying not to show my panic and desperation. I just lost millions of dollars, but I'm still alive. Things could be worse, way worse. One or both of us could have been hurt, hurt really badly, even be dead. I don't know whether to dance around singing hallelujah, or to lie down on the pavement and bash my head against the rocks.

I get out and she drives away. I make a desperate search of the parking lot and the surrounding area, but I quickly realize that my search is hopeless. This place is total chaos. Everything is trashed. Everything is gone. That ticket could be in Canada by now and in a million pieces.

Nothing is as it was. I go into Gabriel's office and heavily sit down behind his desk.

I loudly proclaim my misery to the walls. "Gabriel, the winning Lottery ticket is gone. All of our money is lost, gone. I need money."

His response is immediate.

"The basis of happiness isn't money."

I jump up banging my knees on his desk and knocking the dragon chair over backwards. I was just whining. I am angry. I'm frustrated. I didn't really expect an answer. I am alone. I'm sure that I'm alone. But I clearly heard Gabriel's voice as if I were hearing him with my ears, but I'm sure that there was no sound and that nobody is here in this office except me and I just watched Gabriel disappear in a way that looked very permanent. I am backed against a wall and looking everywhere, staring into the air, scared. My eyes are darting around, looking in the corners and behind things. My hands are gripped tight, knuckles turning white.

I cautiously ask speaking to nothing, "What is it then?"

I clearly hear Gabriel's voice again say, "In fact money is the basis of suffering for humans. It allows you to separate yourselves from others and then you try to horde this separateness and manipulate it. You become lost in enhancing the self, lost in power and greed, and there is never enough power, never a big enough self to be safe, secure, and happy. Struggle and fear become the main motivations of your lives."

I have absolutely no doubt now that this is a disembodied Gabriel speaking to me in my head somehow. I am no longer frightened. I am just confused, trying to think of a rational explanation for what is happening.

As if he is in my head following my thoughts, Gabriel says, "You are looking at the inside of your mind."

Now, I know that it really is Gabriel. "Stop Gabriel", I shout at the air. "I don't want to get all esoteric, confused, and even more scared. I am glad to hear you and to be with you, but stick to money and being. I really do need some advice. Just explain to me a better way of understanding and being. Being is a pretty important concept here now because now a days without money I'm going to pretty well run out of being and I just lost the winning Mega Riches Lottery ticket and all of our money. I'm in deep trouble."

"That's what the creators of history would like you to believe."

Still backed against the wall and speaking to the air in front of me because I don't see anyone, I remind him, "Remember Gabriel, I'm in history. That's where I'm at right now. So it is hard for me to imagine an alternative." As I speak, I pick up the dragon chair and then sit down in it closing my eyes. "In fact, I can't imagine an alternative. It's outside of my imagination. So how would an alternative work?"

In the darkness behind my closed eyes I clearly hear him respond, "First of all, it wouldn't work. Work is a concept inside of the money/separation paradigm. There is no work on the outside of that paradigm. There is beingness and there is doing. Neither of which are work. They are enjoyable, mysterious. They are interesting. They are done because that is what you would most enjoy doing. To understand that saying that 'money is the root of all evil', you must understand that it is the concept of money that we are talking about, not the paper with green ink on it. As soon as you conceive of the idea of private property, of yours and mine, you have entered into the problem that we are calling the root of all evil."

"But I can't see what I can do about it and I can't conceive of an alternative for myself individually or as a culture or society."

"Look at the other animals. Look at nature. None of the rest of nature is using money."

"Good point. So, why?"

"I don't know why. It doesn't matter. There doesn't have to be a reason and even if there is a good reason, it doesn't matter anyway. It still is what it is and that's all that matters."

"What matters, Gabriel, is that I need some resources, some money, some moolah, some cash, some gold, some jewels, something to exchange for what I need. In this question of being versus doing, I'm not sure that I understand the meaning of being. I think that I can understand doing, but to me when you be, you do. I don't understand being. Would you help me with that?"

"Yes."

"I don't see how it is possible to separate being and doing. Is it even possible to be without doing? I need a definition of what you mean by being."

"Being means to exist knowing that existence is complete in itself and can be separate from doing and is not maintained by doing."

"Well then where does being come from and how is it maintained? If my car starts running poorly and I don't do something to fix it, pretty soon it will break down and won't be an operating car anymore. Another example of doing to be would be that if I don't feed my body, it won't exist after a while. It seems that doing by me is required to maintain my beingness and the more that I do, the more pleasant my beingness is."

"That certainly seems to be what is happening here from a human perspective, but that is a misunderstanding."

"Misunderstanding of what, how?"

"You are not going back far enough in your understanding. Where does your food come from? From whence does it arise? Where does your transportation come from? Where does it arrive from? How does it come into beingness?"

"Well at some point in the past I earned the money to pay for the car and I earned the money to pay for the food by doing something for someone."

"Are you absolutely sure that is what happened and what is happening?"

"I can't imagine any other explanation or possibility. Everything is the result of doing. I am the result of my parent's doing."

"Well, okay, who are your parents the result of doing and their parents? Where is the original doing that creates being?"

"I don't know. You have me backed into that corner again of how does beingness come into being. I can't answer that. I don't know."

"That's an important question for you to answer don't you think? Otherwise how do we even know what you are perceiving? Otherwise you can just do, do, do and make, make, make and just keep doing the same thing over and over and over, and have the same experiences over and over and over, and then die. But you've missed the point, haven't you?"

"I don't know. Is there a point? I thought that we weren't concerned with why. You have just described life. Life is doing these particular behaviors such as having a job, a family, and a community; and doing these things over and over and having these experiences again and again; then dying. Is there something more? You keep coming back to that question of from whence does beingness arise and that once that it has arisen and you are it, what do you do with your beingness? So, what are the steps? Let's create some wealth right here, right now. Let's create something out of nothingness, something such as a unit of material reality such as a bar of gold. How does one go about creating a unit of material reality out of nothingness? How does one bring one more inch of material reality into being? How does one add an inch to the world? How does beingness come into being? Is there any way for a human to create an emerald from nothing?"

"No. Not an ordinary human."

"How about an extra-ordinary human?"

"Since when have men and women been other than men and women?"

"Not often, but it is possible for a man or a woman to become something more than we have imagined, right?"

"Yes, it is possible."

"Then could there be a human who could manifest an emerald?"

"Yes."

"How does one manifest an emerald?"

"By seeing it."

I start visualizing an emerald. "I see one. How do I acquire it? How do I actually bring it into my possession, to where I can actually feel it and hold it in my hand?"

"You must journey to where it is and ask it to come with you."

"How do I do that? I have no idea how to journey, number one. Number two, How do I discover where it is?"

"It will help you. I will guide you. You should journey into the darkness when my Son is on the other side of the Earth and you will find the Eye of Horus."

I know that by "my Son", he means the Sun and that he is saying that this journey should be made at night in the darkness alone. I even know how to make the journey without any further explanation by Gabriel. I also know that what he is calling the Eye of Horus is a large emerald. I just know, as if I have always known. I just somehow remember like remembering how to ride a bicycle. But my rational mind can't catch up and can't agree.

"Will it be real?" I ask. "Will I be able to give it to another human and will they be able to feel it and see it?"

"Yes."

"How do I approach the Eye of Horus?"

"You do not approach it. It is approaching you."

"That pretty well stops me. I don't see how an inanimate object can approach an animate being."

"Of course you don't see that. That is the point of what we are doing. Let's focus on the basics of what we are doing. We are manifesting something into being which previously didn't exist in your beingness."

"I am confused on this Eye of Horus. It may have previously existed and maybe I am finding it."

"Yes, I can see how you could think that. How can we do this so that you will not be confused by that idea?"

"Well I guess that the circumstances would have to be such that I'm looking at a particular space, at a particular time and it is not there and then suddenly it is there. Wait! That is a tough one. A bird could have dropped it when it flew over, or Aliens could have hypnotized me into some time lost thing and taken it from their space ship and put it there and erased my memory of their act. Of course any explanation like this is so preposterous that it bends the nature of my understanding anyway because the synchronicity of a bird flying by and dropping a large green stone right at that moment is so preposterous that it would have profound meaning and consequences anyway, and of course adding Aliens to the mixture in a way that there is actual physical proof of their existence would be incredible too. I guess anything of that nature would by definition add an inch to reality. It is just that it would be an inch that I hadn't considered. I am considering adding an inch as: POOF! Not being one minute. Being the next minute. I mean, now that I am thinking about it, there could be a good explanation. It is just that I haven't imagined the explanation, and if I haven't imagined it, or if I haven't experienced it, then I don't understand it. So, I don't think it. Okay, so what do I do?"

"Well first of all remember that you do nothing. You be something. The act of being creates the doing. The doing is being done not just with your hands and feet and eyes and ears and mouth and touch and smell, but also by your thoughts. You are not just a body. You are an area of beingness, an area of reality, a space in time, a drama that is happening. You are a story that is unfolding and all of the elements of that story are coming into being and out of being."

"Oh, I must be very careful of my thoughts."

"Yes. You must be very careful if you want to have particular experiences. Otherwise others will control the experience. Those who are aware of what I am saying and who control their thoughts, manifest their story, their experience, and if you are passive and unconscious and unaware of the situation that is unfolding, then you expand the drama, the story, the flow of those conscious individual spots."

"That seems crazy. I mean there are things that are real and happening, and I can't just change them by injecting my thoughts into the situation. That would be delusions of grandeur on a pretty hallucinogenic level."

"Would it? Why don't you try it and see? There is nothing other than your fears and thoughts and the parameters of your beliefs stopping you from experimenting and experiencing something else. It is your belief that you have those limits. Those beliefs have been given to you from outside of yourself. That is part of the other story. What if you don't accept those limits and start living a different story? What will happen?"

"Well, uhhh, I'm sure that there is a name for that type of deluded behavior, but I suppose that there is no harm in trying it as long as I can maintain contact with the world beyond the new dilemma, the new understanding, the new paradigm."

He jars me with a sudden twist in our conversation. "What happens when the Eye appears?"

I try to follow his thinking. I answer, "That creates a real shift. It particularly creates a real shift if everyone can see it. If it is just a pooka, an imaginary emerald that only I can see, it's still a big deal, especially if there are some other people who can see it too, but still by definition it isn't real unless everyone can see it. If everyone can see it, then that pretty much changes everything. It could still be like the Crystal Skull. There are always going to be skeptics and doubt, but certainly there is going to be at least one person who is going to know, and that is the being who made it manifest, me."

"Well let's be clear on the fact that the correct way of saying this isn't that 'we made it manifest'. You don't make anything manifest. You are being manifested."

"So how is this happening? How is this different from the way that I said it?"

"You are crossing back and forth, in and out, all of the time, and you bring things with you, same as memories. Think of them as memories of the future."

"Memories of the future! Wow! Memories of the future? I can't quite grasp the meaning of that. Traveling through space and time with memories of the future. I touch down and these memories of the future organize the present?"

"That is one way of gleaning an understanding of how things come into being. Memories of the future, when you remember them, they are. Remembering the future is very easy. You think of it as storytelling. Now when you tell the story, remember that it has already happened and that it is true. By true, I mean in the same sense that you would tell it if you were telling a story that has happened to you in the past and you are remembering how it happened. Now, when you tell a story about something that is going to happen in the future, tell it with the same remembering that you do when you tell a story about something that happened in the past."

I start telling the story. "I saw the Eye of Horus quite clearly. It looked like a shining faceted emerald about the size of the palm of my hand. It was in a very dark place. Everything around the Eye was black, but the Eye itself was glowing green, like an emerald with a light shining under it or in it. It radiated life, light, and energy. Even the walls in that room, if those were walls and that was a room, were black. There had to be light in this place though because I could see the things which the emerald was lying amongst on a solid table that looked like a big block of black rock. All of the things which were on the table were black too, except for the emerald. I couldn't see the Eye very clearly though, because it was lying down amongst these solid heavy black things that appeared to be rectangular blocks of rock in this inky dark place. These objects had square sides and were of similar size to the Eye, except they were a little bigger. When I look there now though, the Eye is gone. There is an empty place on the table where it was. The light or life as we know it is gone. There is a feeling of dark, inorganic energy filling the place. It is completely different now."

"Yes, the Eye is journeying to you."

"I am trying to remember how it gets to me."

"Well, don't you remember going into the desert and fasting and meditating?"

"Yes. It is hard to remember the future though," I state with deep conviction.

"It is hard to remember the past," he replies.

"It is hard to remember the present," I say, and we laugh together.

"I first saw it in the desert. I saw the emerald Eye in the desert. Is the Eye of Horus a dark thing?"

"No. It is just the opposite. It is the bringer of light."

"I'm glad to hear that. I don't know anything about Horus and I was worried about him, it, her. I'd like to know more about Horus. How do I go about knowing more about him?"

"Ask it to introduce itself to you."

"I'm afraid of him. I don't want to talk to him. I seem to remember," I say hesitantly, "that he is some kind of ancient god who could destroy me by looking at me."

"Oh, you do know him then," Gabriel replies in mock surprise." I know that he is smiling in the darkness.

"I can't state that anything that I'm thinking that I know," I say. "It is just what I've heard. I don't know if there is any truth in it." I am stumbling around in the dark, trying to remember, trying to think.

"Well, what did we decide about fear?"

"That it's based on ignorance and attachment."

"Yes."

"Okay, I'm still afraid, but I'll do it," I tell him.

I feel foolish even doing this. I don't expect anything to happen, or maybe I'm hoping that nothing will happen, but I obediently speak the words into the void in front of me, "Horus I ask you to come to me and speak to me about yourself and about this object, the Eye of Horus."

Immediately, in the darkness a booming voice which is full of magisterial authority states, "I am that I am." It is a huge voice, a voice like I imagine the voice of God would be like. This is like suddenly meeting a huge lion in the African bush face to face, up close, and personal. When it roars, your heart, your guts shake. When Horus speaks, I shake. There is no doubt in that voice. It is the voice of knowing and of power. Then he asks simply but with words laden with hidden meanings, "What is it that you wish to know?"

I'm caught. I am face to face with a great being, a great force, greater than I have previously known, or at least more dangerous than I imagine that I have previously understood, and I have been in some very dangerous situations. This is no time for mistakes, no time for pretend bravery, no time for confusion, no time for wondering what is real and what isn't real. But this whole experience is so surreal. I don't know whether I'm going crazy or not, but it doesn't matter because I have to play it like it's happening because I know at the gut level that this is serious business. Something is here, right here, and this guy is powerful, super powerful, and serious, definitely serious. No doubt about it. When Horus shows up, I realize how little that I know and how physically small that I am. I am ashamed to say it, but all that I can think about is staying alive.

"Horus, who are you?" I ask timidly. "What are you? I'm just looking for a physical description."

"You want a physical description of the non-physical. You truly are a fool," he sneers.

"Well what am I hearing?"

"You are hearing your own voice."

"But it isn't saying what I'm willing it to say."

"True."

"How would you describe your presence to those who are not present here now?"

"I don't. Let them come into my presence if they wish to hear me."

"How would this be achieved if they don't even know who you are or how or why we should seek you?"

"Their ignorance does not concern me. It is a concern of yours. You have not answered that question for yourself. So why should you wish to involve others. You might be getting them involved in something in which they shouldn't be involved."

"Still I'm curious," I go on. "Do you have a physical presence in this realm?"

"I can."

"What form would that presence take? Would I recognize it?"

"No! You hardly can recognize yourself."

"Describe how you would appear to me."

"No, but I'll describe how I would feel to you. You would feel nervous, maybe anxious even, but intensely curious, fascinated, awed, and perhaps you might feel this familiarity about the person or the situation. You'd feel compelled to pay close attention. Things would be revealed. Clarity would start to dawn on your consciousness. That is how you would know that you were in my presence."

"How is it that you speak to me immediately when I talk to you?"

"You have no idea what is happening. If you are going to develop a relationship in which you are conscious of my being, then you must change your attitude and your self-centered understanding into a broader awareness of the cosmos."

"Alright, but I am frightened. How, where do we start?"

"You are doing it again. You are looking at the Universe through your feelings and your eyes. I want you to look through my feelings and my eyes. We are one. Leave your body and enter mine. You are actually entering my mind, my awareness, my consciousness."

Suddenly I am looking at Shane, a small human character who is standing on a flat black plain in black space. I am huge. I pull back and I can see the Earth and I pull back further and I can see all of space. Then I zoom back and I am looking at Shane again. It is as if he is standing on a large flat stage, an empty stage, a dark stage. There are edges all around the stage. It is a flat space, not a round Earth. Everywhere that I look is blackness. In the distance overhead a grid of neon looking lights sizzle, bright fluorescent reds, greens, and blues, with bright white balls here and there at the intersections of thousands of neon threads. I am looking down on Shane as if he is standing on the edge of a flat black Earth and I am huge and hovering out in space. The lower half of me is below the horizon, below the edge of the stage.

I am having a hard time maintaining this viewpoint. Ooops, I slip out of Horus. Now my awareness is neither in Horus nor in Shane. It is hovering between them. I can see them both.

A voice commands, "Concentrate. You are trying to enter my perceptual reality."

I can't. I don't. I am myself again. I am Shane again. But now I am really scared, confused, and disoriented. I want to negotiate for my life up front. I say, "I am concerned about myself. I am concerned about you in relation to me and what you are capable of doing to me and your nature. I apologize for my selfishness, but I am worried about whether you would destroy me and why you would or would not destroy me."

He answers slowly, as if he is speaking to a teen age street gang punk who has just declared himself as the King of the Earth. "Your concerns are vain strivings, mortal delusions, illusions, concerns. You misunderstand who you are and what you are and who I am and what I am and why we are doing this."

I know that I am in over my head, way over my head. I just reply with the only thought that I have, "I am afraid."

"Yes. You should be. I can instantly strip the shell from the great being that is you and then the I of you would be dead. How do you want to play this?"

"I don't want to die."

"That's too bad," he says almost wistfully. "I'm willing to honor your great separation story, but remember you can not fool me. I stand at the threshold. I am looking in at your great scheme from the great without. Here, you are bringing a force into being that is capable of destroying your entire world, or of altering it and turning it to the light of the Great Beyond. I am of course indifferent. It's your dream."

"I thought that it was our dream."

He pauses, then says, "Yes. I stand corrected."

I am not even sure what we are talking about. I try to get some traction in this slippery conversation. I ask, "Horus, do you have a history?"

"I am history," he states flatly.

Well that doesn't help me. I try another track, "No. I mean do humans have a memory of you? Is there a mythology or story around you?"

"Humans have many stories and mythologies and names around me. Humans are very fond of names, of words, of stories."

When he speaks, when he says humans, something is being insinuated, something that I don't much like. The something, the thought, the idea, the image slithers in the dark just outside of my sight, just outside of my grasp. This is like talking to a giant cobra which is raised above me, staring at me and slowly waving its great hooded head back and forth. Its cold black eyes are locked on my blinking blue eyes.

But still I go on. I'm curious. I can't stop. This guy really interests me. My curiosity about him is greater than my fear of death. "Can you give me a specific name for you in history?"

"No!" he booms, then adds more quietly, even suggestively, "but I can give you a specific power."

I hesitate, thinking. I don't like that power idea. Things seem to go strange when power is discussed. I stall, saying, "I'm thinking." But finally, I confess, "I'm afraid of that word."

"Well you should be Shane Parker because remember one of the attributes of power is the ability to erase you."

He says Shane Parker like a slap in the face, like a punch in the gut. I am insulted. I back up.

"Wait a minute," I blurt out. "I thought that I was an immortal soul."

"I wasn't speaking to you, immortal soul. I was speaking to Shane Parker."

He clearly is addressing me as two separate distinct individuals, and one of those individuals he holds in obvious contempt.

"You are saying that there is a difference?" I ask incredulously, thinking that me is me, that I'm me, period.

"Of course there is a difference," he states with absolute certainty.

"Oh boy. I don't think that I want to know the difference," I groan.

"Of course, you don't want to know the difference. When everyone is aware of your game, they won't want to play with you."

I have no idea what he is talking about, what he is referring to as my game, but I have to ask. "Can you make my game known to me?"

"Yes, of course. Remember the story of the Toltec smoking obsidian mirror? Are you sure that you want to look upon yourself and see yourself, Shane Parker?"

I kind of remember the story of the smoking mirror. When you look into its black reflective surface, you see your true self. You know yourself as you truly are. In the story, it is said that most people hold an idea of themselves that isn't real. They hold an image of a self that is the person that they want to be or at least of a person who they want others to think that they are. When they see what they truly are, it is unbearable. They are instantly destroyed in terrible torment by what they see. I don't think that I believe that old story, or that there even is an obsidian smoking mirror, but why take a chance? I don't believe what is happening is happening but that doesn't seem to matter. It still is happening.

As I'm thinking, I say, "No. Let me think about that."

He doesn't let me think. An ornate full length black mirror appears on the stage in front of me. I look into it and see myself standing there amongst swirling grey smoke. Scenes from my life appear and fade away. I am appalled.

"That is terrible," I exclaim. My guts are being torn out of my insides. The pain and nausea are awful, but mostly I am just trying to hold my guts in by hugging myself with my arms. I scream, "You are tearing me apart. I want this to stop and stop now. I am dying."

"You are never together. That is the problem," he says calmly, clinically.

"No! Stop! I don't want to see myself. I can't bear to look."

"Of course you can't. But look a little deeper. Look a little further. I am not going to kill you, yet. I am not going to destroy you, yet."

As he speaks, I look away from the mirror and regain my composure and a little courage. "Okay, I believe you," I say. I've got a little confidence back. I concede, "I'll look a little further. But first I want a concession on your part." I ask, "Can I stop anytime?"

"Yes. I grant you that wish," he replies.

I look back into the mirror. I see more highlights or rather lowlights of my life replaying before me in the mirror. "Why do I look the way that I look?" I ask. "Why do I do what I do? Why am I acting like I act?" From out here, I don't want to act like I am acting in there. I don't want to be like I am, but in there my sad life just goes on and on. I don't change. From out here everything is so obvious, but in there it is all so confusing. I can't do this. I don't want to do this any longer. That isn't me. I am not this. I have to stop this. Either I am getting out of here, out of there, or this has to get out of me.

"Do you feel that in your gut? Do you feel how you are pulling apart by even thinking those thoughts? It isn't me. I am not pulling you apart. You are pulling yourself apart."

"I feel sick. I feel like I'm disintegrating."

"You are just being dramatic. You are just looking in a mirror. You can't stand to look. What you are seeing is killing you, but it isn't literally killing you, yet. You can go further."

"I don't like it. I don't want to."

"Of course you don't."

"I am not going to look at that."

"Have courage. Try."

With Horus's encouragement, I look back into the mirror and again what I see is awful, heart breaking, agonizing. Again I ask, "Why did I do that? Why do I do that?"

"You know not," he answers simply. "You are separate. You see not but yourself, a small self, a frightened self, a hopeless self, a careless ignorant self, a selfish insensitive mean self, a lazy greedy self, a manipulative dying self, a disintegrating insecure self-loathing self. Do I need to go on?"

"No. I recognize myself without this. Why do I even go on? Why do I even exist?" I am overwhelmed by despair.

"Well I've been giving you the rather negative side of your human experience. Turn away from the mirror and look at creation and feel your experience of life."

I turn away from the mirror and gaze to the South. I am looking at a mountain wilderness covered by trees with a river winding through it. It is a sunny spring day and I can see flowers blooming in a nearby meadow with a herd of elk grazing in it. I can hear birds singing and people laughing in a camp site behind me. "It's beautiful. It's wonderful. I'm enjoying it," I say.

"Do you want to give that up?" He asks.

"No," I reply. Then with real conviction, I state, "No, I don't."

"Well there you go," he says, as if he has explained it all, and I agree with him.

"What are you going to do?" He asks. "I am here because you called me. I am not here to destroy you against your wishes. In fact, I cannot say why I am here. Why am I here? Say it."

"I am not happy with this world. I wish to change it. I am not happy with myself. I wish to change myself. The most important thing that I have to do is to change myself. I have called on you to change myself. I wish to experience life, but not as an agent of death, but rather as an angel of light. I need a force from beyond to guide me. I cannot work from within because the rules of this world blind me to the possibilities. When I only see what is within, then I must act with the understanding that is given. So I just repeat the same world. I am afraid, because the unknown is unknown. It could, you could destroy me. I already know that within the rules of this world, I am destroyed anyway. It is only a matter of time. I see my death in the mirror. When I look in the mirror and see what is happening, I am hopeless. But when I look at the beauty and the wonder of life and nature, I don't want to die. I am absolutely thrilled with existence."

"Well then it seems like you've got a problem."

"Are you saying that you don't have the same problem?"

"Yes. I am."

"Okay. I want to be like you."

"You can't be like me and be you because the you to whom I am speaking would be dead. It would just not the death that you are imagining, but it would be just as final."

"Okay. I don't want to be like you. Damn! I am wasting time."

"Yes. This is the most important conversation of your life, of your being. You are Aladdin speaking to the jinni. What is your wish? What are you going to do? Remember you called me forth to make a stack of gold bars, a green emerald, but now you see that you are caught in the terrible dilemma of existence, and the wonderful opportunity and emotional excitement that existence offers, and the reason that you came out of non-existence into existence, and you see that you have been being petty and blind and ugly. What is your wish? If you could have anything that you wanted, what would you wish for?"

"I am really caught in a dilemma here. What good does it do me to enhance this short term structure here called my personality, this transient object of pleasure?

"I don't know. What is your answer to the question?"

"You. You interest me. You appear to exist. You certainly have a powerful and dynamic personality. You are capable of producing and manipulating anything imaginable by me in this situation. Your major existence would seem to be outside of this existence. Am I assuming correctly?"

"Yes."

"May I ask for some advice on this? Would that be using up my wish?"

"Yes. You can ask for advice and let me be clear, I didn't limit you to three wishes or anything like that, like Aladdin. Don't think that we are in that kind of situation. What would you like to know? Or rather, what would you like to understand?"

"Death. Death is worrying me, the death of myself, the death of my loved ones, death period of anything. Death is worrying me."

"Well, death should certainly worry Shane, but I don't know why it would worry you.

"Well, because I think that I am Shane."

"Yes. There is that problem for you and Shane."

"A person can't make a good decision unless they know the circumstances of their situation. I mean, after all, where are we trying to get from, to. If we don't know where we are, how would we know where we are trying to get to?

"Yes. So, is that a question?"

"No. No, I am just thinking out loud. When I looked in the mirror, I saw my condition, or rather I saw the condition of Shane. As you keep reminding me, there are two of us here, and I of course only see Shane. Why my sudden concern about death? Not that I wasn't concerned about it from the moment that I met you. I am not really sure about the meaning of death right now, but I know that it's final and important to Shane whom I believe that I am. I'm Shane. I am worried. I'm no longer sure that I want to add an inch to the world, an inch to Shane."

CHAPTER 44
THE PRECIPICE

Suddenly a strong whirlwind engulfs me. Everything is grey as if I am standing in a thick fog in the late afternoon. I am trying to hold the hair out of my eyes with my left hand and shield my eyes with my right. As the fog clears, I see that I am standing on the edge of a mountain road which has become a cliff, a rock face dropping a thousand feet straight away to jagged rocks along a raging river down below. The road at my feet has collapsed and disappeared into the canyon below. My toes are one step away from eternity.

The road used to go another forty or fifty feet, then it turned and went out around a rocky point that juts out from the face of the cliff ahead of me. But now all that is left is what appears to be part of the old road drainage system that ran along the inside left curb of the road. A flat smooth cement curb about two feet wide runs to my left for about forty feet where it meets the jutting rock face. Below this curb about six feet is a big iron pipe, a utility pipe, about twelve inches in diameter carrying water or something, a heavy black utility company pipe.

When the gone road went around the rock point, workmen had blasted a hole through the jutting rock at road level. This hole connects the road which I am standing on with the road on the other side of the slide. From where I am standing, this hole appears to be a slot in the mountain about eighteen inches tall, twenty feet wide, and fifty feet long. A person could maybe get in it and crawl on his belly to the other side and then continue on up the road towards town.

I want to proceed on up the road and over the mountain to town very much. The cement looks solid. The rock bench that it is sitting on is actually carved right into the cliff. There are no cracks or anything in the cement or the cliff bench. This curb just runs out there to where it reaches the slot in the rock wall on the other side of this chasm at my feet which was created in the road when it collapsed. Where the cement curb and the slot meet, there is a wide spot.

I decide to walk across the curb and then crawl through the slot and then continue on up the road.

I hurry across the narrow cement path to the wide spot. This area is about five feet wide and twenty feet long. I get down on my belly and look in the slot. It looks shallow. From over here, it doesn't look quite high enough to crawl through. It looks like if I go in there, I might get stuck. It's further than I thought to the other side too. It's a long ways to crawl in that cramped, tiny space. And what if there is an earthquake? What would happen then? What if this mountain starts to slide away again? That would be a terrible way to die, a terrible place to die, stuck inside of that hole, alone. The surfaces in that hole are hard and cold and wet and slimy, and maybe there are spiders and scorpions and snakes in there. I don't want to get stuck in there. I'm afraid of getting stuck in there. I don't want to die in there. It would be awful to be jammed in there. I can feel this whole mountain pushing down on me, squeezing me, buried alive, no way out, screaming, fighting, struggling, but it wouldn't matter. No matter what I did, I'd be there forever. No way out. Dead.

Panic seizes me. I can't crawl in there. I just can't do it. I can't go ahead. I can't do it. I have to go back.

I turn around and face back the way that I came, and for the first time, I look down, down into the gorge, down, down the face of the cliff at my feet.

There is a blue pickup truck smashed in the rocks down below. Some unfortunate soul wasn't paying attention to where he was going and didn't see the disaster that he was approaching in time to avoid it. This is terrible. As I continue to stare into the rocks in the canyon below, I see the lifeless body of the truck driver crumpled in the trees and rocks above the pickup. The odd thing about the body is that the left foot is pointing in the wrong direction.

In my confusion I think, "Oh, that is not good." I don't want to end up like that.

I step back up against the cliff and grab on with both hands down at my sides behind me. My heart pounds. I don't want to get near that edge.

I slide down the wall with my back pressed hard against the rock and sit down. I get on my hands and knees and crawl over to the edge, not out to the edge, just near enough so that I can peer over. Whoa! That's a long ways down. I quickly stand up and back against the cliff. I can't go out there near that edge again ever.

I have to return over that two foot wide ledge the forty or fifty feet that I came across, but I can't. I can't get within a foot of that edge.

I'm glued against the rock in the corner between the hole in the mountain and the cement ledge. I can't move. I can't go forward. I can't go back.

I'll die out here if I don't go forward or back but I absolutely am panicked. I cannot go forward or back. I can't go through that little hole. I can't crawl through that hole. I can't die stuck in that culvert and I can't go near the edge and slip and fall off that cliff. It's so far down. I couldn't stand the fall. I choke back a scream. I just can't go out there.

The situation is hopeless. It's unbearable. I don't have any options. There is nothing that I can do. I know that I am being irrational but I don't care. I would rather die here against this rock than fall off of that ledge or be stuck in that hole.

My world narrows, to crawl across that ledge or to go through that little hole. Which one? Which way? Which way? Which one? One or the other. I have to do one or the other. Die out here. Die in there. Fall from the cliff or die slowly, agonizingly, of thirst, stuck in that culvert. Which direction to go?

I hate heights. I hate that feeling of being in a high building, a sky scraper with floor to ceiling clear glass windows. I hate going near the windows and looking down. I hate walking across a high bridge and looking over the railing. I hate standing near the edge of a cliff and looking down. When I look over I feel like I'm being pulled over to my death by some invisible force. I know that I am going to fall and die. I know that something really bad is about to happen. I feel like just by getting near the edge that I am going to lose my balance and plunge over into a horrifying screaming violent death.

I can't stand it. I back tighter against the rock. The drainage hole is down at my feet. I squat down. The idea of being stuck in a tight place is horrifying too. I can't wiggle my arms or legs. I can't scoot forward or back. I am completely stuck with all of that weight pushing down, pushing down, slowly pushing down harder, squishing, squashing me.

I'm out here with no food and no water. It is getting dark.

Which way to go? Which way to go? I can't think. I can't choose.

If I do nothing, I'll die here pinned against this ledge, cold, freezing, hungry, thirsty, alone against this hard rock, or I can crawl across that ledge and slip with my left hand and plunge over that cliff and fall into those jaggedy sharp boulders down there, or I can crawl into that tiny hole and be stuck in there and crushed by the mountain slowly, slowly.

I scoot back and sit down in the corner with my back against the rock as far as I can get from that outside ledge over the cliff. I bury my head in my knees and hug my legs up against my chest. I am going to die out here. There is just no way forward that I can bear to take. My options are unbearable.

Everywhere that I look, things are bad. I don't want to do them. I can't stand what is going on. I can't do anything? What can I do? None of the ways open to me are bearable. The more that I think about it, the worse my situation is. I am eaten up with anxiety and fear and confusion. I am depressed and hopeless.

What can I do? What can I do? Where can I go? How can I escape? How can I get to someplace safe? Where are my friends? Why am I not loved? How did I get here? Why am I all alone? Why doesn't someone help me?

I fall asleep with my back against the rock.

"Hey! Hey! What are you doing down there? Can I help you?"

It's a voice from above. I'm startled. I look up. I hadn't even considered looking up. Suddenly I realize that I hadn't considered a lot of things, a lot of options.

The voice cries out again, "Hey, can I help you?"

Continuing to look up, I see a man looking down at me. He is wearing a yellow hardhat.

I yell back, "Yes. I'm stuck down here. Can you get me up and out of here?"

"Sure. Just a moment. I'll drop a belt down to you."

With great relief what I realize is that I hadn't really explored my alternatives. I hadn't even looked up. When I look up at the mountain behind me, I see built into the rock a ladder with a rail down the side of it. A climbing safety belt comes sliding down the rail beside the ladder.

All that I have to do is put the belt around my waist and cinch it tight. It is already hooked to the safety rail which is bolted into the mountain. I am saved.

I climb up the ladder just as the workmen do when they are working on the road and the utilities which are buried in the road. The big man in the hardhat reaches down and pulls me up onto the plateau and helps me unbuckle the safety harness.

"What were you doing down there?" He asks curiously, with an edge of hostility as if I shouldn't have been down there.

I answer innocently, "I was walking up the road and I wanted to get from where the road caved off of the mountain to that other side of the slide where the road is still good. So I was just going to crawl through the slot in the cliff, but when I got out there, I just couldn't do it."

"You crawled out onto that ledge without thinking of the consequences and all of the time that you have been out there, you haven't looked around to see if there are any other ways in or out of that spot? And all of that time you were terrified of losing your life?" He seems puzzled, actually surprised by my answer.

"Yeah, that is about the size of it," I agree.

"That's ridiculous," he says warming up to me and to the subject. "Man, you are a lot better than that. You are not even aware of your potential. Not understanding your situation can be a real problem. Letting your troubles run away with you and not understanding who and what you are can be a real party pooper."

It is a good thing that this guy came along. I just wish that he would have showed up sooner. "Gosh, I never even thought of that," I realize. "I was just so terrified when I looked through that narrow slot in the mountain that I had to crawl through or when I thought about getting back on that ledge, that I couldn't go forward or back. I just couldn't do it. You're absolutely right. The possibilities are infinite and yet, I was dying of terror on that ledge. I hadn't even begun to consider the possibilities, all of the choices. Yup. I'm in a ridiculous situation."

"Yes siree. Unseen possibilities. Unseen potentialities. Lot of people are stuck and can't go back and can't go forward either. They should be looking for some unseen potentialities too," he adds.

"Yup. I know that I'm kind of stuck in ways other than being out there on that ledge," I agree again.

He smiles and sticks out a big hand, "My name's Joe, Joe Norman. I am the maintenance supervisor on this section of the water main for Northwood. You're lucky I decided to check on this bad section of line today."

I return his smile and friendly handshake. "My name's Shane, Shane Parker. I will always be very glad that you came along, Joe."

"Well you better get in and ride with me," he points at a big white utility company truck with big tool boxes on the bed and a hydraulic lifting crane in the back. "I'll take you back to town with me."

"Yeah, you're right. I've had enough of this walking around up here in the mountains."

"You cool now Shane? That is what is important," he states with authority.

"I don't know Joe. What exactly do you mean by cool? How does one be cool?"

"Cool is the art of flowing smoothly. No hang ups. No jaggedy slam bam walls. No bleeding cuts. No black emotional bruises for anyone or anything. Smooth is an awesome ride through mysterious beauty, full of love and abundance every day in every way. Smooth is sunshine, roses, a warm hug and a lovely kiss. Smooth is being powerfully secure in everlasting abundance surrounded by the most wonderful, interesting, beautiful, loving people, plants, animals, and beings of all sorts and natures in the most beautiful surroundings imaginable."

"I don't think that I'm quite there Joe, but I like it. Let's be cool. Let's be smooth. How are we going to do it?"

He laughs, punches me in the shoulder and pushes me towards the truck.

As we walk towards the truck, he asks, "Hey Shane, did you hear that they had to raise the drinking age in the South County to twenty five?"

I am surprised. "No, I didn't hear that. Why would they do something like that?"

"Had to do it to keep the high school kids from drinking at school."

"But ----. Oh!" I burst out laughing.

We jump in the truck and head for town.

He starts talking. "Shane, let me ask you something. Do you consider yourself to be a religious man?"

"Uhhh, well, yes, yes I do. I'm a good Christian. I think that I keep the Ten Commandments most of the time. I'd have to get a copy and check that out, but yes I consider myself a religious man."

He swerves and misses a big pot hole in the road.

"So what do you think of governments? You like the government?"

I chew my lower lip and ponder the question. I don't like to discuss politics or religion. Someone always seems to get riled up.

I cautiously answer, "I'm not particularly fond of the present situation, but I guess that I consider government a necessary evil. I'm pro-government in general."

"Say Shane, did you hear about when Eve was in the Garden of Eden talking to God and God asked Eve, how do you like it here?"

"No Joe, I haven't heard about that."

Yeah well, Eve answered God saying, "I really like it here God. It's beautiful. The weather is great, and that Serpent is really amusing, but I'm kind of lonely. The cows have bulls. The does have bucks. Couldn't you fix me up with something like that?"

God thought about it a moment and then said, "Well I could make you a man."

"A man? What is a man?" Eve asked.

"Well they're pretty simple creatures, you know. Not too smart. Low range of emotional responses. They are arrogant, bullying, swaggering things. They mostly just like to get drunk and kill stuff. You'd have to guide him and help him, but I would give him a special attachment to help you with that loneliness problem and you'd never be bored."

"That sounds great," Eve responded. But then she thought about it and said, "Wait a minute. What's the catch?"

"Well, there's just one catch," God responded. You'd have to let the man think that I made him first."

Eve thought for a moment and then answered, "I can live with that."

So God brightly agreed, "Good. Then it's done. Now let's just keep this our little secret, girl to girl."

That last line is so preposterous that I don't even hear it a first. I'm still back at God making woman first. Isn't that blasphemy or something? Oh well, it is funny. I'm grinning. Then the "girl to girl" secret hits me and I laugh out loud. I feel a little guilty, like laughing at a dirty joke, but that's funny. Joe looks over at me and winks and laughs too.

Then he asks, "Why's God gotta be a man, I mean male? Why does God have to be separate from us? Why do we believe that God is somewhere just waiting to judge us and punish us? Paternalism was born when the first man dreamed of a separate ruling God. Mono-theism leads to fences, private property, and judgment. A separate ruling God leads to a separate ruling man. Mono-theism leads naturally to fascism. Naturally you would have a separate ruling person under the separate ruling God, both separate and ruling over the people."

"God is not separate from us. We are not separate from God. We are part of God. God is in us. Everything is God. God is everything. God is bigger, more all-inclusive, more mysterious than we have been believing. God encompasses all sides of being, not just good or bad, but good and bad, not just this or that, but this and that. God is not separate from us and judging us, but rather God is in us, with us, and of us. We are all of One Mind and that Mind is God and that God is us. We are God and God is us. We are One. We are all One."

I'm stunned. I say, "Don't hold back Joe. What do you really think?"

He smiles and swerves around a rock which has rolled down the mountainside and onto the road.

I'm not sure where to go with this conversation. I just sit here in the pickup staring out the window as the mountain scene rolls by. Joe slows, downshifts, and concentrates on the road ahead as we climb a twisty section of the road which is taking us up through a high mountain pass. Two ravens sitting on a boulder on our right take flight and glide along beside us then cross in front of the pickup and disappear into the West, into the setting Sun.

Suddenly Joe says, "The answer is seventy-seven," as if someone has asked a question. Then he laughs as if that makes sense.

I laugh too. It reminds me of the mice in "The Hitch Hiker's Guide to the Galaxy". What did they say? The answer to everything is forty-two? It doesn't make any sense. It is absurd, but it is funny.

I say, "Go left instead of right."

He agrees, "Without a doubt," as if we have a choice to go left or right.

"You know Joe, on that God thing, I can't quite agree with you. I haven't been being too Godly lately. You seem to be a pretty clever fellow though. So seeing as how I seem to have gotten messed up and separated somehow, off on a different path from you, how can I be re-united, be One again?"

"We were never separate. We've always been One. You only separated in your mind. Then you acted as if you were separated and created a drama of me-ness, a drama of meanness. Then you started acting like a near sighted skunk wandering around aimlessly, getting all pissy over this and that, and squirting stink here and there."

"So, how do you think God would want us to think? What message do you think God has for us?"

God would say, "I want Me to think of Me as you and you as Me. Everything is sacred, including you."

"Everything is sacred. I've heard that before. And by the way, how could this infinite God of ours have an opinion?"

"When 'I am' is speaking to you, 'I am' is not speaking in an all-knowing form. I am communicating in a finite way."

"So wouldn't that make you separate from your infinite, all-knowing, all-being self?"

"I am not separate anymore than you're separate. I am constricted or restricted."

"So you are saying that we become me's by being constrictions of the We, or rather by constricting the We?"

"The reason that we are struggling here, Shane, to understand each other is one of dimensionality. Everything is everything. You are imagining a big chunk of something and that we break a handful of that something off and then there is a smaller separate piece of this something and that we do that a whole bunch of times and we get a bunch of small separate pieces which are separate from the big chunk. You think that way because your visualization of reality is bound by your conceptualization of time and space. Let's give you a greater understanding of being by expanding your understanding of time and space, giving you a bigger, broader understanding of the meaning of time and of the meaning of space. Let's talk about sacred space, guilty space, and profane space."

"Alright," I agree, "I've got some time. I have some understanding of the meaning of what sacred space and time is from Sunday school classes. A sacred place or object or time is a thing or time that is set aside for the holy purposes of Divinity. This is as opposed to something which is profane which is a thing or place which is used for the common everyday purposes of normal usage."

"We are speaking the same language, Brother," he hollers as if we are at a revival meeting. "What I am saying is that nothing is profane. Everything is sacred. If God is everywhere in all things, in all places, at all times, in all beings; then everything, all of the time is sacred. Everything exists for Divine purposes. That is why all space and time is sacred. It is profane space that appears to have been set aside and made ordinary. There is nothing ordinary. Everything is extra-ordinary. Everything is astounding. Everything is awesome. We have just un-wowed it as a way of coping with our situation."

"Well, I am sorry Joe, but I'm listening, and what I just heard you say is that we find ourselves in a profane situation because we have to make things ordinary in order to cope with our strange surroundings and then we are separate from the sacred."

"Yeah Shane, that is sad, but it is true."

"Where is the sacred?" I ask somberly in frustration.

As the city appears on the horizon, Joe answers enigmatically, "Some people are gone before they were even here, before they were even in our story. The sacred enlightens one's sense of guilt. We must link minds."

CHAPTER 45

AMNESIA

Entering town on Central Avenue, he changes the subject, and asks, "Where are you going Shane?"

"I left my pickup in the mall parking lot up ahead off of Main," I reply.

But before we get to the turn off to the mall, he parks in front of the water utility company offices and offers, "I need to go in and file my report on the water line. Then I'll drive you up to the mall."

I answer, "Thanks Joe, but I'll walk. It's only a couple of blocks and I'll be there before you even get done in the office. I'll just run over to my car and be on my way home. I really appreciate your saving my life and giving me a ride to town."

"Okay man, but I really wouldn't mind taking you."

We get out of the truck and meet on the sidewalk. We shake hands and I hug him with gratitude. I hadn't realized how big he is. Hugging him is like hugging a bear. I repeat sincerely, "I really am glad to be here and glad to be alive. Thanks Joe. And I am glad to know you."

"I'm glad to know you too Shane. Be more careful. When I see you again, you can buy me lunch. Say Shane, we recently buried a man that looked just like you. Was that you or your twin brother?"

I pause and then laugh. "I'm still here Joe."

"That's a good thing Shane. See you." He turns and walks smiling into the company offices.

I walk up Main a few blocks, turn right, and continue north to the mall parking lot, but it's not the mall parking lot. There is a big parking lot, but it's the parking area for a big box store. I'm confused. I must be looking at the back of a big store at the back of the mall from a different direction than the way that I remember, but this must be the parking lot that I'm thinking of because I recognize this as the place where I left my pickup. I am sure of that. I left it right over there, but I can't remember exactly which row that I parked in. As I walk around, I don't see any blue pickups. It's a big blue pickup truck. How can I misplace a truck? This is frustrating. I push my mind, but I just don't have a memory of where I parked. How could I forget something so simple? Where is that memory? Oh well, it's not that big of a lot, I'll just walk around some more. I'm bound to see it. I walk to the middle of the lot and start spiraling outward. My pickup isn't here. Has it been stolen? Oh, I hope that it hasn't been stolen, but it may have been. The thought of my pickup being stolen worries me. Or worse yet, am I losing my mind? Did I park here? Did I even come here? Panic is getting a grip on me. Should I call the police and report it stolen or is something wrong with me? I might just be confused. Before I do anything rash like call the police, I had better go back to Main and see if I turned the wrong way or something.

I walk back the way that I came, but now I'm on Barbur Boulevard not on Main Street. I'm sure that I came this way, but I must have gotten turned around while searching in the parking lot. I'm lost. I'm not sure where I am. How can this be? Well if I don't know where I am, that isn't really important because I know who I am and I can just get a taxi and tell the driver where I live and he'll take me home. I think that there is a hotel down Barbur a few blocks to my left. I'll just go down there and get a taxi and go home that way.

As I walk down Barbur Boulevard, I pass a barber shop with a darkened window that reflects like a mirror. I am looking at my reflection thinking that I need a haircut when I notice the bank of newspaper vending machines beneath my reflection. I start reading the headlines. An article about an accident at a local construction site which resulted in the death of Shane Parker catches my attention. There is a picture of a man who looks nothing like me, of course, at the top of the article. I didn't even know that there were two Shane Parkers. I start reading the story. The other Shane lived in my neighborhood. He went to school where I went to school. He worked in the same company as I do. How odd that I never met him.

I'm reading the news story and looking at my reflection in the window behind the news stand. Then I notice that the reflection in the window is neither the person in the picture in the news article, nor the person who I think that I am. It's the face of another person, but it's my face. I raise my hand and touch my face and the hand in the window comes up and touches its face. Still it isn't the face of who I think that I am. I am not me. The memories that I have don't match that face. They aren't my memories. They are someone else's memories. I must have read them somewhere, or saw them on TV, or something. What are my memories? Where are my memories? Where was I born? Where do I live? What do I do? What am I if I don't know where I was born, or where I live, or what I do?

A Shane Parker is dead, but what does that matter to me? What is my relationship to the dead Shane Parker? I am not that Shane Parker. I'm not sure who I am, but I am looking at my reflection in that window and that picture in the newspaper is not a picture of me.

What do I do if I don't know who I am, or worse yet what do I do if I think that I know who I am and I am not who I think that I am. Who am I? What am I? What am I to do? What makes a person a person? Where am I to go? What am I to eat? Where am I to sleep? Do I have any friends or family? Do I have a pet at home who needs to be fed? Do I have a mortgage and car payments? Am I nothing, a nobody who lives under a bridge somewhere?

I have an aching sense of loss. I know that I am a father with a job and a respected member of my community, but I can't remember my address. It'll come to me.

I rush down to the hotel still wanting a taxi, but there is no hotel where the hotel should be. There is a restaurant where I remember that the hotel was last week, the last time that I passed by here. I slump down onto a bus stop bench.

Who am I if I am not who I think that I am? What am I? Where should I go? Without memories, I am nothing. If I am no one, with no place to go, and nothing important to do, what should I do with myself? My sense of loss is tearing my heart out, making me nauseous. I am in a complete world full of things and places and people. I just can't recognize anything, any place, or anyone. And no one recognizes me. Nobody has a picture of me in my uniform or smiling proudly on graduation day. I know that I have a home, but nothing looks familiar. I can't find something that leads somewhere to something that I recognize. My memories don't fit. How can memories not fit? I can understand forgetting. I must be forgetting, but I'm not forgetting. I am remembering wrong. How is that possible? Where am I? Who am I really if I am not the Shane Parker who I think that I am? My sense of loss overwhelms me and I begin to weep.

A pretty young woman dressed in jeans and sandals with a flowery blouse and a bright blue vest sits down on the bus stop bench beside me. I am humiliated. I try to get a grip, but my disorientation and sense of loss is choking me to death.

She says, "This is the most wonderful place that I have ever been." Then she asks, "How do you think that we would see this place if we were Zulus?"

I raise my head, look her in the face, and ask uncomprehendingly, "Zulus?"

"Yes," she explains. "If we had been born Zulus in Africa and raised in a tribal world, we wouldn't have the same values and opinions. We would see things differently. We would be different people than we are now."

I say, "Are you asking me who would I be if I didn't know who I am?"

She pauses, looks me in the eyes, smiles a big smile, and inquires, "Who are you?"

I feel my left front pants pocket where I keep my billfold. I am looking for my driver's license or some other piece of identification to show her. The pocket is empty. I say, "I don't know. I seem to have woken up as someone else, but I don't know who or what. What do you think that I should do?"

"Well I don't see that it matters whether you're Chinese, Ethiopian, German, or American."

"It matters to me because I am nothing."

"You don't look like nothing." She reaches over and feels my arm. "You don't feel like nothing."

"I am something. I just don't know what. I don't have a role to play in this world."

"If you don't have a role, if you don't have a mother and a father, if you don't have a wife and children, if you don't have a job and a home, what are you? What am I talking to?"

"I don't know. Other than being frightened and confused, I still think that I am the same person that I thought that I was. I'm alive and sitting here talking to you." I reach out and touch her. "I can feel you. You can feel me. I'm hungry. I have just lost my sense of self. I don't have any opinion about myself that is correct or provable. I lost myself not because I let it go, but because I lost it. I lost everything that was me but still I'm here, wherever here is."

"As far as I know, there is no other here," she says. "There must be something wrong with your understanding." She looks across the street and makes a long sweeping gesture with her right hand. "Isn't this lovely?" she asks.

I look about. She is right. We are in a lush valley surrounded by forested hills. The street that we are sitting on is lined by interesting old brick buildings and across the street is a little park with a giant old fruit tree full of ripe fruit. There is a flock of birds in the tree feasting and chattering. Every once in a while a hundred or more birds spring into the air and flash about making the most striking patterns. As they turn in one direction their black silhouettes are etched against the blue sky. When they turn in the other direction, their fluorescent, psychedelic backs flow past the old bricks and the trees strobing like those glass balls in flashy dance clubs. These patterns dazzle me as the birds wheel one way then almost instantly another. And all of the time some of the birds in the tree are singing the most wonderful song that I have ever heard. There aren't many people about, but those that are walking by are smiling, talking, and obviously happy and prosperous. This would seem to be the best of all possible worlds. I reflect upon my condition. I am strong. I'm healthy. I'm well dressed. I reach in my right front pocket and it is full of money. I remember my reflection in the barbershop window. I am handsome and in the prime of my life. I am sitting on a bench in the sunshine on a lovely afternoon by a park with trees full of ripe fruit and lively singing birds. I am sharing all of this beauty with a pretty young woman whose attitude sparkles with the same vibrancy as the Sun.

She says, "I think that it is wonderful that the bus company has switched over to being fueled by hemp oil."

I'm startled. I state, "I didn't know that."

She explains, "Now that hemp has been legalized we don't need petro chemicals anymore and the wars are over too. You did notice that the wars are over didn't you? Where have you been?"

"I haven't been paying attention. I have my own problems. I've been thinking about those problems. I've just been in myself in my personal situations."

"I'm glad that you dropped your personal problems and woke up to the present and the beauty of all of this," she says and as she talks she includes everything around us with a sweeping gesture with her hands.

"Until this moment I hadn't really thought of things in the way that you are framing them," I realize.

"Thank you," she replies. "Where are you going?"

"I'm not really sure."

"Then you are in the best of all possible situations. You are a wise man. You can sit here and enjoy yourself or you can go anywhere and enjoy yourself even more."

"Well yes, I suppose that I am and that I can."

"Why don't you come with me and visit the ashram where I am living. I am sure that a visit would make you very happy and you would make us very happy. You seem to be an interesting man with a lot to share."

I have never thought of myself as a person with a lot to share. Sharing hasn't been the center of my thinking. I have been scheming about accumulating wealth and power, not sharing. The world that I was inhabiting yesterday was focused on taking. This woman is proposing that I visit a world based on sharing and caring. I am not sure what that means, but I am intrigued.

"Your offer is most kind. I think that I would enjoy that," I respond. "Normally I would refuse because I believe that I have important things to do, but today I'm afraid that I have nothing else to do. My schedule is completely open."

"Good. Then it's settled," she responds with finality.

We sit for a while quietly enjoying the Sun. As a bus approaches I look at the placard above the front window. It says South Coast. The girl gets up.

I say, "Forgive me but I don't know your name."

She offers, "Serena." And asks, "What's yours?"

"I don't know. What would you like to call me?"

She says, "How about Blaze?"

I say, "Okay, I guess that I'm not Shane anymore." I follow her onto the bus.

We pass out of the city and drive down through the most beautiful forested hills that I have ever seen. It's warmer than I remember Northwood as being. It's almost tropical. The trees are towering broad leafed beauties. It's a majestic forest filled with brightly colored birds. We pass through a few little one and two store villages at crossroads with people smiling and wandering around.

Finally we stop at a wide slowly moving river at the end of the road. We get off of the bus with the last couple of passengers and walk across a swinging foot bridge high over the river. Some of Serena's friends are waiting for us on the other side in a little white four wheel drive pickup truck. We get in the back of the truck which proceeds to wind up into the hills on gravel roads.

High on top of a ridge overlooking the ocean we come to a group of houses nestled in the trees. The pickup takes us to one of the houses which is an office where all of the activities of this community are organized. I am given a cabin not far away.

Then we go to the Chocolate Bliss Bar which is a French style side walk café but sitting by paths through the woods rather than by a street. We have our choice of several chocolate concoctions and desserts of various types. All of them are made from fresh raw ingredients right here at the bar. We have chocolate smoothies and raw lemon cakes and chocolate bon bons. There are monkeys and birds of paradise in the trees above us. Children are running around and a man brings a pony. The children take turns riding the pony through the woods around the houses. Mothers are going in and out of a building nearby which is some kind of store. They are getting produce, nuts and honey, bright colored clothes and hats and baskets. Everyone looks like Serena and everyone speaks English. We are not in some foreign land. We are less than an hour from Northwood towards the coast. But everything seems so different, so wonderful, so beautiful, and I've never seen monkeys or birds with multicolored tails before. They must be the peoples' pets but they sure make this a mysterious and interesting place. I guess that I have never looked at the world this way before.

Serena says, "Let's go to dinner with some of the family."

We go over to a nearby open pavilion with a beautiful hardwood floor with tables about two feet high. We sit on cushions on the floor as we eat. The food is buffet style. Everyone just takes a plate and walks down a table lined with dishes full of food and takes whatever they want. The dishes are all raw vegetable and fruit preparations and sauces. Other than my name and my opinions, nobody seems to care where I come from, what I do, or what my old responsibilities were. They ask whether I'm enjoying the food and what I think of the sunset and how the ride up from the river was. Mark the head gardener for the family asks if I enjoy gardening. I discover that all of the food that we are eating is grown down at the bottom of this hill by a creek.

Mark asks, "Would you like to visit the garden?"

I am very interested to see how all of this food can be grown around here. I answer, "Yes, very much."

The conversations are about what is around us now and what we are doing now. Sometimes people pose a riddle or tell a joke. Sometimes they sing a song or play a musical instrument. There are animals, birds, and children wandering here and there getting hugs and kisses and pets from the adults.

After dinner I go with Mark to the garden and then to evening worship services. In the worship services we do some exercises, meditate for a short while, then hold hands and dance around in a circle and sing for the rest of the evening. After that we go off to our cabins which are scattered throughout the woods along paths that we walk chatting with each other in the moonlight.

Days go by and I slowly come to realize that I'm not Shane anymore. I never really ever was Shane. I was just playing a role that I had taken on. But I'm not Blaze either. Blaze is just another role. I am deeper. I am down underneath all of those ideas and opinions and layers of behaviors.

The time has come to go to the desert, to leave all contact with civilization, with ideas, with gadgets, with roles and personalities. It is time to go back to nature. It is time to go back to the beginning.

It starts to rain. It pours for days. The creeks and the river swell and start to run over the roads.

Serena comes to my cabin after lunch and says, "If you are going to leave, you must leave now. We must cross three creeks to get to the river. You didn't notice them when we came in, but now they are two feet deep and rising. In another couple of hours the pickup won't be able to cross them and they may not go back down for six months. Mark has to get a computer out to town and you can go with him if you hurry. I run to where Mark is waiting with a couple other people. I jump in the back of the truck. He gives me a black plastic garbage bag to make a rain coat to protect me from the pouring rain. We race to the river.

The quiet coastal river is now roaring and it is only a few feet below the rain slick metal foot bridge. We can't hold on to the wire rail because we have to carry the computer equipment. I am staring into that muddy swirling river all of the way across the bridge frightened that I will fall in and be swept away, but we all make it safely. On the other side some friends of Marks are waiting and take us back to town.

In town I buy camping equipment and a bus ticket to a bus stop in the central desert.

CHAPTER 46

THE DESERT

When I reach the desert, I start walking east out across the barren landscape. I cross sage brush flats which go on for days. I climb over mountains of barren rocks. I trudge alongside vast dry alkali flats. In the end there are no roads, no electric lights in the distance, no sounds of cars. There is only quiet and brown hills and valleys running on to the horizon in every direction.

Always I am looking for water. Water means life out here. In the distance I see a line of trees following a gorge up a mountain to a crevice at the top. If there are trees, there has to be water. I start following the trees climbing up the canyon face at 7:30 in the morning. At 12:30 sweating and exhausted, I summit the gap in the mountain and look on the other side. I see paradise. I am in the middle of a vast dry desolate desert looking at a hundred acres of blooming wildflowers: white, yellow, blue, and red, and green, green everywhere. Butterflies, thousands of butterflies, of every color and size float amongst the flowers. I can hear a spring bubbling through the trees near me, but there are two more forests along the valley floor and I can see a creek running alongside those distant trees and through the meadow that covers the valley floor. There is no evidence that any humans have been in this valley for years. There are no footprints, no bent down grass from four wheelers, no burnt fire rings, no beer cans. I sit down and a dragonfly lands on my foot. Here the bugs aren't even afraid of being smashed. They don't know about humans. There aren't any mosquitoes. I walk out into the middle of the flowers and sit down. In front of me is a bright bouquet of yellow and white flowers. A half dozen monarch butterflies land on the flowers not more than two feet in front of me. Two of the monarchs flit away to be replaced by a couple of neon blue butterflies. Then a white butterfly joins the feasting. Meanwhile fluorescent bright green and red and yellow bees crawl in and out of the flowers along with beetles and strange multicolored flies.

I'm home. I pitch my tent in the middle of the valley beside some trees on the edge of a meadow alongside a little creek of crystal clear fresh water that bubbles directly out of the ground nearby. In the evening I lie on my back in the grass and watch as thousands of white butterflies gather and rise up into the sky like snow falling up and drift away into the night as the sky fills with stars. I sit and begin to meditate watching my breathing, calming the mind, losing the thoughts. Night turns to day. Day turns to night. Night changes to day. Day changes to night. The Sun and the Moon and the stars whirl about my sitting form. The very stones around me begin to come to life. They were always alive. I just hadn't noticed. The butterflies and the bees and the dragonflies and the animals, chipmunks, antelope, and deer begin to gather around me at a respectful distance. The wind blows the grasses on the hillsides in dancing iridescent waves that rush across the hill creating whirling patterns like currents flowing in a maelstrom in an Arcadian sea.

The Sun blesses me. Mother Earth whispers secrets in my ear. The Moon speaks of love. The Water Spirit sings to me in the little brook. I breathe in. I breathe out. I breathe in. I breathe out.

I see it all, but I plunge downward into my soul where I hear the small still voice say, "Greetings beloved one. Child of the Universe be still and open your heart to divine love. We may cross over now."

What I remember is joy.

I am here. I am everywhere. I am nowhere.

In the darkness I see the Light again. I am the Light. The Light is me. And I know, it is done. I understand. I am whole, complete. I am the Light. I radiate creation.

I am of benefit to all. I don't do it. It flows through me. I am a conduit of goodwill and blessings. That is all that I need to know. That is all that we need to know. When the soul is transfigured, the body follows, and the community follows the body.

I laugh joyously. It is all so hilarious.

I am divine love, a realization of God's perfection. I am an angel of light, perfect in mind and body, beautiful, strong and vital. I bless and benefit all that surrounds me forever. All that surrounds me is divine love, a realization of God's perfection, beautiful, strong and vital, blessing and benefiting all that surrounds it forever. There is no opposition. There is only a stream of blessings and benefits forever. Time dissolves. There are no endings or beginnings. Eternity is now.

I remember. We are the unimaginable which is imagining.

I stand up, pack my backpack, and walk towards Northwood. The Gates of Balance are open so that we may now leave the realm of death and life and enter blissful eternity whole and complete.

THE BEGINNING

In the beginning was the word

The word is now

Now is perfection

Behold God

Go on

All one

ABOUT THE AUTHOR

Blaze is passively practicing the art of letting go and being.

INDEX

www.ingramcontent.com/pod-product-compliance
Lightning Source LLC
Chambersburg PA
CBHW031053260626
47172CB00001B/48